Anybody Out There?

MARIAN KEYES

Anybody Out There?

wm WILLIAM MORROW *An Imprint of* HarperCollins*Publishers*

Grateful acknowledgment is made to reprint the lyrics from "Goldfinger," music by John Barry, lyrics by Leslie Bricusse and Anthony Newley, © 1964 United Artists Music Ltd., © renewed EMI UNART Catalog Inc. All rights controlled by EMI UNART Catalog Inc. (publishing) and Alfred Publishing Co., Inc. (print). All rights reserved. Used by permission.

HarperCollins books may be purchased for educational, business, or sales promotional use. For information please write: Special Markets Department, HarperCollins Publishers, 10 East 53rd Street, New York, NY 10022.

FIRST EDITION

Designed by Janet M. Evans

Printed on acid-free paper

Library of Congress Cataloging-in-Publication Data

Keyes, Marian.
   Anybody out there? / by Marian Keyes.—1st ed.
     p. cm.
   ISBN-13: 978-0-06-073130-4 (acid-free paper)
   ISBN-10: 0-06-073130-3 (acid-free paper)
    1. Amnesia—Fiction.   2. New York (N.Y.)—Fiction.   3. Ireland—Fiction.   I. Title.

PR6061.E88A84 2006
823'.914—dc22   2005054127

06 07 08 09 10   WBC/RRD   10 9 8 7 6 5 4 3 2 1

For Tony

$\mathcal{A}$cknowledgments

This book wouldn't have been written without the help of countless generous, helpful people. Sincere thanks to . . .

My extraordinary editor, Alison Callahan, and the fantastic team at William Morrow for their unconditional support, vision, and enthusiasm.

Emma Parry, my wonderful agent.

Caitriona Keyes and Anne Marie Scanlon for vital support, New York information, and, most of all, the Feathery Stroker™ rant.

Nicki Finkel, Kirsty Lewis, Nicole McElroy, Jamie Nedwick, Kim Pappas, Aimee Tusa, and especially Shoshana Gillis for letting me in on the wonderful world of cosmetics PR.

Gwen Hollingsworth, Danielle Koza, and Mags Ledwith.

Patrick Kilkelly and Alison Callahan for the Red Sox info.

Conor Ferguson and Keelin Shanley for their scuba-diving story and Malcolm Douglas and Kate Thompson for technical scuba information. Any mistakes are mine.

Nadine Morrison for information on labradoodles. (Yes, they're real.)

Jenny Boland, Ailish Connelly, Susan Dillon, Cáron Freeborn, Gai Griffin, Ljiljana Keyes, Mammy Keyes, Rita-Anne Keyes, Suzanne Power, and Louise Voss for reading the manuscript at various stages and providing invaluable feedback and encouragement.

Eibhín Butler, Siobhán Coogan, Stephanie Ponder, Suzanne Benson and Patricia Keating for handy anecdotes on everything from blind dates to labor pains.

Kate Osborne, who paid for "Jacqui Staniforth" to be a character in this book, at a fund-raising auction for the Medical Foundation for the Care of Victims of Torture.

Special thanks to Eileen Prendergast for many, many things, including accompanying me to the air-guitar championships.

If I've forgotten anyone, I'm (a) mortified and (b) truly sorry.

As always, thanks to my beloved Tony for everything. Above and beyond.

Prologue

There was no return address on the envelope, which was a little weird. Already I was slightly uneasy. Even more so when I saw my name and address...

The sensible woman would not open this. The sensible woman would throw it in the bin and walk away. But apart from a short period between the ages of twenty-nine and thirty, when had I ever been sensible?

So I opened it.

It was a card, a watercolor of a bowl of droopy-looking flowers. And flimsy enough that I could feel something inside. Money? I thought. A check? But I was just being sarcastic, even though there was no one there to hear me, and anyway, I was only saying it in my own head.

And indeed, there was something inside: a photograph... Why was I being sent this? I already had loads... Then I saw that I was wrong. It wasn't him at all. And suddenly I understood everything.

Part 1

1

Mum flung open the sitting-room door and announced, "Morning, Anna, time for your tablets."

She tried to march briskly, like nurses she'd seen on hospital dramas, but there was so much furniture in the room that instead she had to wrestle her way toward me.

When I'd arrived in Ireland eight weeks earlier, I couldn't climb the stairs, because of my dislocated kneecap, so my parents had moved a bed downstairs into the Good Front Room.

Make no mistake, this was a huge honor: under normal circumstances we were only let into this room at Christmastime. The rest of the year, all familial leisure activities—television watching, chocolate eating, bickering—took place in the cramped converted garage, which went by the grand title of Television Room.

But when my bed was installed in the GFR there was nowhere for the other fixtures—tasseled couches, tasseled armchairs—to go. The room now looked like a discount furniture store, where millions of couches are squashed in together, so that you almost have to clamber over them like boulders along the seafront.

"Right, missy." Mum consulted a sheet of paper, an hour-by-hour schedule of all my medication—antibiotics, anti-inflammatories, antidepressants, sleeping pills, high-impact vitamins, painkillers that induced a very pleasant floaty feeling, and a member of the Valium family, which she had ferried away to a secret location.

All the different packets and jars stood on a small, elaborately carved table—several china dogs of unparalleled hideousness had been shifted to make way for them and now sat on the floor looking reproachfully at me—and Mum began sorting through them, popping out capsules and shaking pills from bottles.

My bed had been thoughtfully placed in the window bay so that I could look out at passing life. Except that I couldn't: there was a net curtain in place that was as immovable as a metal wall. Not *physically* immovable, you understand, but socially immovable: in Dublin suburbia brazenly lifting your nets to have a good look at "passing life" is a social gaffe akin to painting the front of your house Schiaparelli pink.

Besides, there was no passing life. Except...actually, through the gauzy barrier, I'd begun to notice that most days an elderly woman stopped to let her dog wee at our gatepost—sometimes I thought the dog, a cute black-and-white terrier, didn't even want to wee, but it was looking as if the woman was insisting.

"Okay, missy." Mum had never called me "missy" before all of this. "Take these." She tipped a handful of pills into my mouth and passed me a glass of water. She was very kind really, even if I suspected she was just acting out a part.

"Dear Jesus," a voice said. It was my sister Helen, home from a night's work. She stood in the doorway of the sitting room, looked around at all the tassels, and asked, "How can you stand it?"

Helen is the youngest of the five of us and still lives in the parental home, even though she's twenty-nine. But why would she move out, she often asks, when she's got a rent-free gig, cable telly, and a built-in chauffeur (Dad). The food, of course, she admits, is a problem, but there are ways around everything.

"Hi, honey, you're home," Mum said. "How was work?"

After several career changes, Helen—and I'm not making this up, I wish I was—is a private investigator. Mind you, it sounds far more dangerous and exciting than it is; she mostly does white-collar crime and "domestics"—where she has to get proof of men having affairs. I would find it terribly depressing but she says it doesn't bother her because she's always known that men were total scumbags.

She spends a lot of time sitting in wet hedges with a long-range lens, trying to get photographic evidence of the adulterers leaving their love nest. She could stay in her nice, warm, dry car but then she tends to fall asleep and miss her mark.

"Mum, I'm very stressed," she said, "Any chance of a Valium?"

"No."

"My throat is killing me. War-crime sore. I'm going to bed."

Helen, on account of all the time she spends in damp hedges, gets a lot of sore throats.

"I'll bring you up some ice cream in a minute, pet," Mum said. "Tell me, I'm dying to know, did you get your mark?"

Mum loves Helen's job, nearly more than she loves mine, and that's saying a lot. (Apparently, I have the Best Job in the World™.) Occasionally, when Helen is very bored or scared, Mum even goes to work with her; the Case of the Missing Woman comes to mind. Helen had to go to the woman's apartment, looking for clues (air tickets to Rio, etc. As if...) and Mum went along because she loves seeing inside other people's houses. She says it's amazing how dirty people's homes are when they're not expecting visitors. This gives her great relief, making it easier to live in her own less-than-pristine crib. However, because her life had begun to resemble, however briefly, a crime drama, Mum got carried away and tried to break down the locked apartment door by running at it with her shoulder—even though, and I can't stress this enough, *Helen had a key*. And Mum *knew* she had it. It had been given to her by the missing woman's sister and all Mum got for her trouble was a badly mashed shoulder.

"It's not like on the telly," she complained afterward, kneading the top of her arm.

Then, earlier this year, someone tried to kill Helen. The general consensus was not so much shock that such a dreadful thing would happen as amazement that it hadn't come to pass much sooner. Of course, it wasn't really an attempt on her life. Someone threw a stone through the television-room window during an episode of *EastEnders*—probably just one of the local teenagers expressing his feelings of youthful alienation, but the next thing Mum was on the phone to everyone, saying that someone was trying to "put the frighteners" on Helen, that they "wanted her off the case." As "the case" was a small office fraud inquiry where an employer had Helen install a hidden camera to see if his employees were nicking printer cartridges, this seemed a little unlikely. But who was I to rain on their parade—and that's what I would have been doing: they're such drama queens they actually thought this was exciting. Except for Dad and only because he was the one who had to sweep up all the broken glass and sellotape a plastic bag over the hole until the glazier arrived, approximately six months later. (I suspect Mum and Helen live in a fantasy world where they think someone's going to come along and turn their lives into a massively successful TV series. In which they will, it goes without saying, play themselves.)

"Yes, I got him. Ding-dong! Right, I'm off to bed." Instead she stretched out on one of the many couches. "The man spotted me in the hedge, taking his picture."

Mum's hand went to her mouth, the way a person would on telly if they wanted to indicate anxiety.

"Nothing to worry about," Helen said. "We had a little chat. He asked for my phone number. Cack-head," she added with blistering scorn.

That's the thing about Helen: she's very beautiful. Men, even those she's spying on for their wives, fall for her. Despite me being three years older than her, she and I look extremely similar: we're short with long dark hair and almost identical faces. Mum sometimes confuses us with each other, especially when she's not wearing her glasses. But, unlike me, Helen's got some magic pull. She operates on an entirely unique frequency, which mesmerizes men; perhaps on the same principle of the whistle that only dogs can hear. When men meet the two of us, you can see their confusion. You can actually *see* them thinking, *They* look *the same, but this Helen has bewitched me like a drug, whereas that Anna is just so what . . .*

Not that it does the men in question any good. Helen boasts that she's never been in love and I believe her. She's unbothered by sentimentality and has contempt for everyone and everything.

Even Luke, Rachel's boyfriend—well, fiancé now. Luke is so dark and sexy and testosteroney that I dread being alone with him. I mean, he's a lovely person, really really lovely, but just, you know . . . all man. I both fancy him and am repelled by him, if that makes any sense, and everyone—even Mum; I'd say even *Dad*—is sexually attracted to him. Not Helen, though.

All of a sudden Mum seized my arm—luckily, my unbroken one—and hissed, in a voice throbbing with excitement, "Look! It's Jolly Girl, Angela Kilfeather. With her Jolly Girl girlfriend! She must be home visiting!"

Angela Kilfeather was the most exotic creature that ever came out of our road. Well, that's not really true, my family is far more dramatic, what with broken marriages and suicide attempts and drug addiction and Helen, but Mum uses Angela Kilfeather as the gold standard: bad and all as her daughers are, at least they're not lesbians who French-kiss their girlfriends beside suburban leylandii.

(Helen once worked with an Indian man who mistranslated *gays* as "Jolly Boys." It caught on so much that nearly everyone I knew—including all my gay friends—now referred to gay men as Jolly Boys. And always said in an Indian accent. The logical conclusion was that lesbians were "Jolly Girls," also said in an Indian accent.)

Mum placed one eye up against the gap between the wall and the net curtain. "I can't see, give me your binoculars," she ordered Helen, who produced them from her rucksack with alacrity—but only for her own personal use. A small but fierce struggle ensued. "She'll be GONE," Mum begged. "Let me see."

"Promise you'll give me a Valium and the gift of long vision is yours."

It was a dilemma for Mum but she did the right thing.

"You know I can't do that," she said primly. "I'm your mother and it would be irresponsible."

"Please yourself," Helen said, then gazed through the binoculars and murmured, "Good Christ, would you look at that!" Then: "Buh-loody *hell*! Ding-dong! What are they trying to do? A Jolly Girl tonsil*ecto*my?"

Then Mum had sprung off the couch and was trying to grab the binoculars from Helen and they wrestled like children, only stopping when they bumped against my hand, the one with the missing fingernails, and my shriek of pain restored them to decorum.

After she'd washed me, Mum took the bandages off my face, like she did every day, then bundled me up in a blanket. I sat in the matchbox of a back garden, watching the grass grow—the painkillers made me super-dopey and serene—and airing my cuts.

But the doctor had said that exposure to direct sunlight was strictly verboten, so even though there was scant chance of that in Ireland in April, I wore a stupid-looking wide-brimmed hat that Mum had worn to my sister Claire's wedding; luckily there was no one there to see me.

The sky was blue, the day was quite warm, and all was pleasant. I listened to Helen coughing intermittently in an upstairs bedroom and dreamily watched the pretty flowers sway to the left in the light breeze, then back to the right, then to the left again . . . There were late daffodils and tulips and other pinkish ones whose name I didn't know. Funny, I remembered floatily, we used to have a horrible garden, the worst on the whole road, perhaps in the whole of Blackrock. For years it was just a dumping ground for rusty bicycles (ours) and empty Johnnie Walker bottles (also ours) and that was because, unlike other, more decent, hard-working families, we had a gardener: Michael, a bad-tempered, gnarled old man who used to do nothing except make Mum stand in the freezing cold while he explained why he couldn't cut the grass ("The germs get in through the cut bits, then it just ups and dies on you"). Or why he couldn't trim the hedge ("The wall needs it for support, missus"). Instead of telling him to get lost, Mum used to buy him top-of-the-range biscuits, then Dad used to cut the grass in the middle of the night rather than confront him. But when Dad retired they finally had the perfect excuse to get rid of Michael. Not that he took it graciously. Amid much mutterings about amateurs who'd have the place destroyed within minutes, he left in high dudgeon and found employment with the O'Mahoneys, where he rained shame down on our entire family by telling Mrs. O'Mahoney that he'd once seen Mum drying lettuce with a dirty tea towel.

Never mind, he's gone and the flowers, courtesy of Dad, are far nicer now. My only complaint is that the caliber of biscuits in the house has dropped dramatically since Michael's departure. But you can't have things every way, and that realization set me off on an entirely different train of thought, and it was only when the salt water of my tears ran into my cuts and made them sting that I discovered I was crying.

I wanted to go back to New York. For the last few days I'd been thinking about it. Not just considering it, but gripped by a powerful compulsion and unable to understand why I hadn't gone before now. The problem was, though, that Mum and the rest of them would go mad when I told them. I could already hear their arguments—I must stay in Dublin, where my roots were, where I was loved, where they could "take care of me."

But my family's version of "caretaking" isn't like other, more normal families'. They think the solution to everything lies in chocolate.

At the thought of how long and loud they'd protest, I was grabbed by another panicky seizure: I *had* to return to New York. I had to get back to my job. I had to get back to my friends. And although there was no way I could tell anyone this, because they would have sent for the men in the white coats, I had to get back to Aidan.

I closed my eyes and started to drift, but suddenly, like a grinding of gears in my head, I was plunged into a memory of noise and pain and darkness. I snapped my eyes open: the flowers were still pretty, the grass was still green, but my heart was pounding and I was struggling for breath.

This had started over the past few days: the painkillers weren't working as nicely as they had in the beginning. They were wearing off faster and ragged little chinks were appearing in the blanket of mellowness they dropped on me and the horror would rush in, like water from a burst dam.

I struggled to my feet and went inside, where I watched *Home and Away* and had lunch (half a cheese scone, five satsuma segments, two Maltesers, eight pills), then Mum dressed my bandages again before my walk.

She loved this bit, busying about with her surgical scissors, briskly cutting lengths of cotton wool and white sticky tape, like the doctor had shown her. Nurse Walsh tending to the sick. Matron Walsh, even.

I closed my eyes. The touch of her fingertips on my face was soothing.

"The smaller ones on my forehead have started to itch; that's a good sign, isn't it?"

"Let's see." She moved my fringe aside to take a closer look. "These really are healing well," she said, like she knew what she was talking about. "I think we can probably leave the bandages off these. And maybe the one on your chin." (A perfect circle of flesh had been removed from the very center of my chin. It will come in handy when I want to do Kirk Douglas impersonations.) "But no scratching, missy! Of course, facial wounds are handled so well these days," she said knowledgeably, parroting what the doctor had told us. "These sutures are far better than stitches. It's only this one, really," she said, gently stroking antiseptic gel onto the deep, puckered gash that ran the length of my right cheek, then pausing to let me flinch with pain. This wound wasn't held together with sutures; instead it had dramatic Frankenstein-style stitches that looked like they'd been done with a darning needle. Of all the marks on the face this was the only one which wouldn't eventually disappear.

"But that's what plastic surgeons are for," I said, also parroting what the doctor had told us.

"That's right," Mum agreed. But her voice sounded faraway and strangled. Quickly I opened my eyes. She was hunched in on herself and muttered something that might have been, "Your poor little face."

"Mum, don't cry!"

"I'm not."

"Good."

"Anyway, I think I hear Margaret." Roughly, she rubbed her face with a tissue and went outside to laugh at Maggie's new car.

Maggie had arrived for our daily walk. Maggie, the second eldest of the five of us, was the maverick of the Walsh family, our dirty secret, our white sheep. The others (even Mum, in unguarded moments) called her a "lickarse," a word I wasn't comfortable with because it was so mean, but admittedly did the job well. Maggie had "rebelled" by living a quiet, well-ordered life with a quiet, well-ordered man called Garv, whom, for years, my family *hated*. They objected to his reliability, his decency, and most of all his jumpers. (Too similar to Dad's, was the consensus.) However, relations have softened in recent years, especially since the children came along: JJ is now three and Holly is five months.

I will admit to having entertained some jumper-based prejudice myself, of which I'm now ashamed, because about four years ago Garv helped me to change my life. I'd reached a nasty little crossroads (more details later) and Garv had been endlessly, unfathomably kind. He'd even got me a job in the actuarial firm where he worked—initially in the post room, then I got promoted to the front desk. *Then* he encouraged me to get a qualification, so I got a diploma in public relations. I know it's not as impressive as a master's degree in astrophysics and that it sounds more like a diploma in Watching Telly or Eating Sweets, but if I hadn't got it, I would never have ended up in my current job—the Most Fabulous Job in the World™. And I would never have met Aidan.

• • •

I hobbled to the front door. Maggie was unloading children from her new car, a wide-bodied people carrier that Mum was insisting looked like it had elephantiasis.

Dad was also out there, trying to provide a foil against Mum's contempt; he was demonstrating what a fine car it was by walking around it and kicking all four tires.

"Look at the quality on it," he declared, and kicked a tire again to underscore his point.

"Look at the little piggy eyes on it!"

"They're not eyes, Mum, they're lights," Maggie said, unbuckling something and emerging with baby Holly under her arm.

"Could you not have got a Porsche?" Mum asked.

"Too eighties."

"A Maserati?"

"Not fast enough."

Mum—I worried that she might have been suffering from boredom— had developed a sudden, late-in-life longing for a fast, sexy car. She watched *Top Gear* and she knew (a little) about Lamborghinis and Aston Martins.

Maggie's torso disappeared into the car again, and after more unbuckling, she emerged with three-year-old JJ under her other arm.

Maggie, like Claire (the sister older than her) and Rachel (the sister younger than her) was tall and strong. The three of them come from a gene pool identical to Mum's. Helen and I, a pair of shortarses, look astonishingly different from them and I don't know where we get it from. Dad isn't terribly small; it's just the meekness that makes him seem that way.

Maggie had embraced motherhood with a passion—not just the actual mothering, but the look. One of the best things about having children, she said, was not having the time to worry about what she looked like and she boasted that she had totally given up on shopping. The previous week she'd told me that at the start of every spring and autumn she goes to

Marks & Spencer and buys six identical skirts, two pairs of shoes—one high, one flat—and a selection of tops. "In and out in forty minutes," she said, gloating, totally missing the point. Other than her hair, which was shoulder length and a lovely chestnut color (artificial—clearly she hadn't given up completely), she looked more mumsy than Mum.

"Look at that hickey oul' skirt on her," Mum murmured. "People will think we're sisters."

"I heard that," Maggie called, "And I don't care."

"Your car looks like a rhino," was Mum's parting shot.

"A minute ago it was an elephant. Dad, can you open out the buggy, please."

Then JJ spotted me and became incoherent with delight. Maybe it was just the novelty value, but I was currently his favorite auntie. He squirmed out of Maggie's grip and rushed up the drive, like a cannonball. He was always flinging himself at me, and even though three days earlier he had accidentally head-butted my dislocated knee, which was just out of plaster, and the pain had made me vomit, I still forgave him.

I would have forgiven him anything: he was an absolute scream. Being around him definitely lifted my mood, but I tried not to show it too much because the rest of them might have worried about me getting too fond of him, and they had enough to worry about with me. They might even have started with the well-meaning platitudes—that I was young, that I would eventually have a child of my own, etc., etc., and I was pretty sure I wasn't ready to hear them.

I took JJ into the house to collect his "walk hat." When Mum had been searching out a wide-brimmed, sun-deflecting hat for me, she'd come across an entire cache of dreadful hats she'd worn to weddings over the years. It was almost as shocking as uncovering a mass grave. There were loads, each one more overblown than the next, and for some reason JJ had fallen in love with a flat, glazed straw hat with a cluster of cherries dangling from the brim. JJ insisted it was "a cowboy hat" but really, nothing could have been further from the truth. Already, at the age of three, he was displaying a pleasing strain of eccentricity—which must have been from some recessive gene because he definitely didn't get it from either of his parents.

When we were all ready, the cavalcade moved forward: me, leaning on Dad with my unbroken arm, Maggie pushing baby Holly in the buggy, and JJ, the marshal, leading the party.

Mum refused to join us on our daily constitutional, on the grounds that if she came there would be so many of us that "People would be looking." And indeed we did create quite a stir: between JJ and his hat and me and my injuries, the local youths felt like the circus had come to town.

As we neared the green—it wasn't far, it just felt that way because my knee was so sore that even JJ, a child of three, could go faster than me— one of the lads spotted us and alerted his four or five pals. An almost visible thrill passed through them and they abandoned whatever they'd been doing with matches and newspaper and prepared to welcome us.

"Howya, Frankenstein," Alec called, when we were near enough to hear.

"Howya," I replied with dignity.

It had upset me the first time they'd said it. Especially when they'd offered me money to lift my bandages and show them my cuts. It was like being asked to lift my T-shirt and show them my knockers, only worse. At the time tears had flooded my eyes, and shocked at how cruel people could be, I turned around to go straight back home. Then I'd heard Maggie ask, "How much? How much to see the worst one?"

A brief consultation had ensued. "A euro."

"Give it to me," Maggie ordered. The eldest one—he said his name was Hedwig, but it couldn't really be—handed it over, looking at her nervously.

Maggie checked the coin was real by biting it, then she'd said to me, "Ten percent for me, the rest for you. Okay. Show them."

So I'd shown them—obviously not for the money but because I realized I had no reason to feel ashamed, what had happened to me could have happened to anyone. After that they always called me Frankenstein, but not—and I know this might sound strange—not in an unkind way.

Today they noticed that Mum had left off some of the bandages. "You're getting better." They sounded disappointed. "All the ones on your forehead are nearly gone. The only good one left is the one on your cheek. And you're walking faster than you used to, you're nearly as fast as JJ now."

For half an hour or so we sat on the bench taking the air. In the few weeks we'd been doing this daily walk, we'd been having un-Irishly dry weather, at least in the daytime. It was only in the evenings when Helen was sitting in hedges with her long-range lens that it seemed to rain.

The reverie was broken when Holly started screeching; according to Maggie, her nappy needed to be changed, so we all trooped back to the house, where Maggie tried, without success, to get Mum, then Dad, to change Holly. She didn't ask me; sometimes it's great having a broken arm.

While she was off dealing with baby wipes and nappy bags, JJ got a rust-colored lip liner from my (extremely large) makeup bag, held it to his face and, and said, "Like you."

"What's like me?"

"Like you," he repeated, touching some of my cuts, then pointing at his own face with the pencil.

Ah! He wanted me to draw scars on him.

"Only a few." I wasn't at all sure this was something that should be encouraged, so I colored in some halfhearted cuts on his forehead. "Look." I held a hand mirror in front of him and he liked the look of himself so much, he yelled, "More!"

"Just one more."

He kept checking himself in the mirror and demanding more and more injuries, then Maggie came back, and when I saw the look on her face, I was filled with fear. "Oh God, Maggie, I'm sorry. I got carried away."

But with a funny little jump, I realized she wasn't angry about JJ looking like a patchwork quilt—it was because she'd seen my makeup bag and got The Look, the one they all get, but I'd expected better from her.

It's been the oddest thing—despite all the horror and grief of the recent past, most days some member of my family would come and sit on my bed and ask to see the contents of my makeup bag. They were dazzled by my fantastic job and made no effort to hide their disbelief that I, of all people, had landed it.

Maggie walked toward my makeup bag like a sleepwalker. Her hand was outstretched. "Can I see?"

"Help yourself. And my wash bag is on the floor here. There's good stuff in there, too, if Mum and Helen haven't cleaned me out. Take anything you want."

As if in a trance, Maggie was removing lipstick after lipstick from the bag. I had about sixteen of them. Just because I can.

"Some of them haven't even been opened," she said. "How come Helen and Mum haven't stolen them?"

"Because they already have them. Just before . . . you know . . . everything, I'd sent a consignment of the new summer products. They already have most of these."

Two days after my arrival Helen and Mum had sat on my bed and systematically gone through my cosmetics, discarding almost everything. "Porn Star? Have it. Multiple Orgasm? Have it. Dirty Grrrl? Have it."

"They never told me about the new stuff," Maggie said sadly. "And I only live a mile away."

"Oh. Maybe it's because with your new practical look they think you wouldn't be interested in makeup. I'm sorry. When I go back to New York, I'll make sure to send things directly to you."

"Will you? Thanks." Then, a sharp look. "You're going back? When? Get a grip. You can't go anywhere. You need the security of your family—" But she was distracted by a lipstick. "Can I try this one? It's exactly my color."

She put it on, rubbed her lips against each other, admired herself in the hand mirror, then was cowed by sudden remorse. "I'm sorry, Anna. I've tried to avoid asking to see the lovely things, I mean, under the circumstances . . . And I'm disgusted with the others, they're like scavengers. But just look at me! I'm as bad as them."

"Don't be hard on yourself, Maggie. No one can help it. It's bigger than all of us."

"Is it? Okay. Thanks." She continued taking things out, opening them, trying them on the back of her hand, then closing them neatly. When she'd examined everything she sighed heavily. "I might as well see your wash bag now."

"Help yourself. There's a lovely vetivert shower gel." Then I thought for a second. "No, wait, I think Dad took it."

She sifted through the shower gels and exfoliators and body lotions, uncapping and sniffing and rubbing, and said, "You really *do* have the best job in the world."

My job

I work in New York City as a beauty PR. I am Assistant Senior Press Officer for Candy Grrrl, one of the hottest cosmetic brands on the planet. (You've probably heard of them; and if you haven't, it means someone, somewhere, isn't doing their job properly. I hope to Christ it isn't me.) I have access to a dizzying array of free products. I mean *literally* dizzying: shortly after I got the job my sister Rachel, who had lived in New York for years, came to my office one evening after everyone had gone home, to see if I'd been exaggerating. And when I unlocked the closet and showed her the shelves and shelves of neatly stacked Candy Grrrl face creams and pore minimizers and concealers and scented candles and shower gels and bases and highlighters and . . . she stared for a long, long time, then said, "I've got black spots in front of my eyes. I'm not joking, Anna, I think I might be about to faint." See—dizzying—and that was even before I told her to pick out some stuff for herself.

What makes it all exponentially fabulous is that it's not just Candy Grrrl stuff I get. The agency I work for, McArthur on the Park (founded and still owned by Ariella McArthur, she never sold out) represents thirteen other beauty brands, each more delicious than the previous, and about once a month we have a souk in the boardroom, where a full and frank exchange takes place. (Mind you, this is not official policy and never happens when Ariella is around.)

Besides free products, there are other perks. Because McArthur on the Park has the Perry K account, I get my hair cut and colored for free by Perry K. Obviously, not by Perry K himself, but one of his loyal minions. Perry K, the man, is usually on a private plane, being flown by a studio to North Korea or Vanuatu to cut some film star's hair on location.

(Free haircuts sound fabulous, but at the risk of seeming ungrateful, sometimes I can't help feeling it's a bit like high-class prostitutes being given regular, up-the-frock health checks. It seems caring, but it's only to ensure the girls do their job properly. Same with me, I've no choice about the haircuts. I *have* to have them and I get no input: whatever is on the catwalks is what I get given. Usually high-maintenance, feathery yokes which break my heart.

Anyway, after Rachel's visit, she got on the blower and told everyone at home about the goodies closet. A flurry of phone calls from Ireland followed. Was Rachel back on the drugs? Or was it true about all the free cosmetics I gave her? And if it was, could they have some? Immediately I parceled up an indecent amount of stuff and dispatched it to Ireland—I admit it, I was showing off, trying to prove what a success I was.

I am not just permitted to wear Candy Grrrl products, I am *obliged* to. We all have to take on the personality of the brands we represent. *Live it,* Ariella urged me when I got the job. Live it, Anna. You are a Candy Grrrl girl, 24/7, you are always on duty.

However, when you're sending products to other people, you're supposed to "sign them out"—every eyelash curler, every lip balm. But if you say they're going to the *Nebraska Star,* for example, and they're really going to your mammy in Dublin, people are unlikely to check: I am a trusted employee.

The strange thing is that normally I'm an honest person: if someone gives me too much change in a shop, I'll give it back, and I've never, in my life, done a runner from a restaurant. (Aren't there better ways to have fun?) But every time I liberate an eye cream for Rachel or a scented candle for my friend Jacqui or send a care package of the new spring colors to Dublin, I am stealing. And yet I don't have the slightest twinge of guilt. It's because the products are so beautiful, I feel that, like natural wonders, they transcend ownership. How could you fence off the Grand Canyon? Or the Barrier Reef? Some things are so wondrous, everyone is entitled to them.

People often ask me, their faces distorted with jealousy, "How do you get a job like yours?"

Well, I'll tell you.

How I got my job

After I got my diploma in PR, I got a job in the Dublin press office of a low-rent cosmetics company; it was crappy money, backbreaking work—mostly stuffing envelopes for mailshots—and as our bags were searched every evening when we left work, I didn't even have the compensation of free makeup. But I had some idea of how PR could be, the fun and creativity you could have in the right place, and I'd always had a hankering for New York...

I didn't want to go on my own, so all I had to do was convince my best friend, Jacqui, that she, too, had a hankering for New York. But I didn't give much for my chances. For years, Jacqui had been like me—entirely without a career plan. She'd spent most of her life working in the hotel trade, doing everything from bar work to hostessing, when somehow, through no fault of her own, she got a good job: she had become a VIP concierge at one of Dublin's five-star hotels. When showbiz types came to town, whatever they wanted, from Bono's phone number, to someone to take them shopping after hours, to a decoy double to shake off the press, it was her job to provide it. No one, especially Jacqui, could figure out how it had happened—she had no qualifications, all she had going for her was that she was chatty, practical, and unimpressed by eejits, even famous ones. (She says that most celebs are either midgets or gobshites or both.)

Her looks might have had something to do with her success; she often described herself as a blond daddy longlegs and, in all fairness, she was very *hingey*. She was so tall and thin that all her joints—knees, hips, elbows, shoulders—looked like they'd been loosened with a wrench, and when she walked, you could almost believe that some invisible puppet master was moving her by strings. Because of this, women weren't threatened by her. But thanks to her good humor, her dirty laugh, and her incredible stamina when it came to staying up late and partying, men were comfortable with her.

The visiting celebs often bought her expensive presents. The best bit, she said, was when she'd take them on a shopping trip; if they bought tons of stuff for themselves they'd feel guilted into buying something for her, too. Mostly teeny-tiny designer clothes, which she looked great in.

Like the professional she was, she never—well, rarely—got off with the male celebs in her charge (only if they'd just split up with their wives and were in need of "comfort"), but occasionally she got off with their friends. Usually they were horrible; she seemed to prefer them that way. I don't think I had ever liked any of her boyfriends.

The night I met her to make my pitch she showed up, her usual shiny, happy, hingey self, in a Versace coat, a Dior something, a Chloé something else, and my heart sank. Why would anyone leave a job like this? But it just goes to show.

Before I even mentioned New York, she confessed that she was sick of overpaid stars and their silly requests. Some Oscar-winning actor was currently in residence and making her life a misery by insisting that a squirrel was staring in the window at him and following his every move. Jacqui's gripe was not that it was mean-spirited to object to a squirrel looking at you, but that they were on the fifth floor—there *was* no squirrel. She'd had it with celebrity, she said. She wanted a complete change, to get back to basics, to work with the poor and the sick, in a leper colony if possible.

This was excellent, if surprising, news and the perfect time to take the U.S. work-permit applications from my bag; two months later, we were waving Ireland good-bye.

When we arrived in New York, we stayed with Rachel and Luke for the first few days, but this turned out to be not such a great idea: Jacqui broke out in a sweat every time she looked at Luke, so much that she nearly had to start taking rehydration salts.

Because Luke is so good-looking, people go a bit funny around him. They think that there has to be more to him than there is. But basically he's just an ordinary, decent bloke, who's got the life he wants, with the woman he wants. He has a gang of look-alike pals—although none are as physically devastating as him—collectively known as the Real Men. They think the last time anyone made a good record was 1975 (Led Zeppelin's *Physical Graffiti*) and that all music made since then has been unadulterated rubbish. Their idea of a big night out is the air-guitar-playing championship—there is such a thing, honestly—and although they are all gifted amateurs, one of them, Shake, showed real promise and actually got as far as the regional finals.

Jacqui and I set about looking for work, but unfortunately for Jacqui, none of the leper colonies were hiring. Within a week she'd got a job in a five-star Manhattan hotel, in an almost identical post to the one she'd left behind in Dublin.

In one of those strange twists, she met the squirrel man, who didn't remember her and spun her the same story about being spied on by a squirrel. Only this time they weren't on the fifth floor, they were on the twenty-seventh.

"I really wanted to do something different," she said to Rachel, Luke, and me when she came home after her first day. "I don't know how this happened."

Well, it was obvious: clearly she was more in thrall to that glittering, celebtastic world than she'd realized. But you couldn't say that to her.

Jacqui had no time for introspection: things were what they were. Which, as a life philosophy, has its merits—although I love Rachel very much, sometimes I feel I can't itch my chin without her finding a hidden meaning in it. But on the other hand, there's no point telling Jacqui if you're depressed because her response is invariably, "Oh no! What's happened?" And most of the time nothing *has* happened, you're just depressed. But if you try explaining that, she'd say, "But what have you got to be depressed about?" Then she'd say, "Let's go out and drink champagne. No point sitting around here moping!"

Jacqui is almost the only person I know who has never been on SSRIs or seen a therapist, she barely believes in PMS.

Anyway, just before Jacqui went into muscle spasm from mineral depletion from looking at Luke, we found a place of our own. A studio (i.e., one room) in a crumbling block on the Lower East Side. It was shockingly small and expensive and the shower was in the kitchenette, but at least we were in Manhattan. We weren't planning on spending much time at home—it was simply for sleeping in and having an address, a tiny foothold in the naked city. Luckily Jacqui and I got on very well, we could take such close proximity to each other, although sometimes Jacqui went out to bars and picked up men, just so she could have a good night's sleep in a normal apartment.

Right away I registered with several ritzy employment agencies, bearing a gorgeous, slightly embroidered résumé. I went for a couple of interviews but got no solid offers and I was just starting to worry when, one Tuesday morning, I got a call to hotfoot it to McArthur on the Park. Apparently the previous incumbent had had "to go to Arizona" (NYC speak for "going into rehab") in a big, fat hurry and they urgently needed a temp because they were preparing for a major pitch.

I knew about Ariella McArthur because she was—aren't they always?—a PR legend: fiftyish, big-haired, big-shouldered, controlling, impatient. She was rumored to sleep only four hours a night (but I later discovered she disseminated that rumor herself).

So I put on my suit and showed up, to discover that the office suites really were on Central Park (thirty-eighth floor, the view from Ariella's office is amazing, but as you're only ever invited into her inner sanctum to be bollocked, it's hard to savor it).

Everyone was running around hysterically, and no one really spoke to me, just shrieked orders to photocopy stuff, to organize food, to glue things to other things. Despite such shoddy treatment, I was dazzled by the brands McArthur represented and the top-end campaigns they'd run and I found myself thinking: *I'd give anything to work here.*

I must have glued the right things together, because they told me to come back the following day, the day of the actual pitch, when they were all even more twitchy.

At 3 P.M., Ariella and seven of her top people took up positions around the boardroom table. I was there, too, but only in case anyone needed anything urgently—water, coffee, their forehead mopped. I was under instruction not to speak. I could make eye contact if necessary, but not speak.

As we waited, I overheard Ariella say in a low urgent voice to Franklin, her second in command, "If I do not get this account I will kill."

For those who don't know the Candy Grrrl story—and because I've lived and breathed it for so long, I sometimes forget there are people who don't—Candy Grrrl originated with the makeup artist Candace Biggly. She began mixing her own products when she couldn't buy the exact colors and textures she wanted, and turned out to be so good at it that the models she was making up got all excited. Word began to filter down from The Most Fabulous On High that Candace Biggly's stuff was something special; the buzz had begun.

Then came the name. Countless people, including my own mother, have told me how "Candy Grrrl" was Kate Moss's pet name for Candace. I'm sorry if this disappoints you, but it's not true. Candace and her husband, George (a creep), paid an expensive advertising agency to come up with it (also, the growling-girl logo), but the Kate story has entered popular folklore and what's the harm in letting it stay there.

Stealthily, the Candy Grrrl name began to appear in beauty pages. Then a small store opened on the Lower East Side, and women who had never been below Forty-fourth Street in their *life* made pilgrimages all the way downtown. Another store opened, this time in L.A., followed by one in London and two in Tokyo, then the inevitable happened: Candy Grrrl was bought by the Devereaux Corporation for an undisclosed eight-figure sum ($11.5 million, actually. I found it in some papers in the office last summer. I wasn't looking, I just stumbled across it. Honestly). Suddenly CG went mainstream and exploded onto counters in Saks, Bloomingdale's, Nordstrom—all the big department stores. However, Candace and George weren't "comfortable" with the in-house public-relations service Devereaux was providing, so they invited some of New York's biggest agencies to pitch for the business.

"They're late," Franklin said, fingering a little mother-of-pearl pillbox. Earlier I'd seen him not so discreetly pop half a Xanax; I reckoned he was considering taking the second half.

Then, with a surprising lack of fanfare, in came Candace, looking nothing like a Candace—brown unstyled hair, black leggings, and strangely, not a scrap of makeup. George, on the other hand, could be considered good-looking and charismatic—*he* certainly thought so.

Ariella began a gracious welcome, but George cut right across her, demanding "ideas."

"If you got the Candy Grrrl account, what would *you* do?" He pointed a finger at Franklin.

Franklin stammered something about celebrity endorsement, but before he'd finished, George had moved on to the next person. "And what would you do?"

He worked his way around the table and got the usual cookie-cutter PR ideas: celebrity endorsement; feature coverage; flying all the major beauty editors somewhere fabulous—possibly Mars.

When he got to me, Ariella desperately tried to tell him that I was a nothing, a nobody, just one step up from a robot, but George insisted. "She works for you, right? What's your name? Anna? Tell me your ideas."

Ariella was in the horrors. More so when I said, "I saw these great alarm clocks in a store in SoHo at the weekend."

This was a pitch for a multimillion-dollar account and I was talking about weekend shopping trips. Ariella actually put a hand to her throat like a Victorian lady planning to swoon.

"They're a mirror image of a regular alarm clock," I said. "All the numbers are back to front and the hands go in the wrong direction; they actually turn backward. So if you want to see the right time, you've got to look at the clock in the mirror. I was thinking it would be perfect to promote your Time-Reversal Day Cream. We could do a shout line like 'Look in the mirror: You're reversing time.' Depending on costings we could even do an on-counter giveaway." (Note to the girl who wants to get ahead: never say "cost"; always say "costings." I've no idea why, but if you say "cost" you will not be taken seriously. However, liberal use of the word *costings* allies you with the big boys.)

"Wow," George said. He sat back and looked around the table. "Wow. That is great! The most original thing I've heard here today. Simple but . . . very wow! Very Candy Grrrl." He and Candace exchanged a look.

The high-tension mood around the table shifted. Some people relaxed but some others got even more tense. (I say "some others" but I mean Lauryn.) The thing is, though, I hadn't planned to have a great idea, it wasn't my fault, it just happened. The only thing I will say in my favor is that I'd stopped at Saks on the way home the night before, picked up a CG brochure, and learned about their products.

"Perhaps you might even consider changing the name to Time-Reversal *Morning* Cream," I suggested. But a tiny fierce head shake from Ariella stopped me. I'd said enough. I was getting overconfident.

Lauryn tinkled. "Well, isn't that the thing! I saw those alarm clocks, too. I—"

"Shut up, Lauryn." Ariella cut Lauryn off with terrifying finality, and that was that.

It was my finest hour. Ariella got the account and I got the job.

4

Dinner chez Walsh was from the local Indian takeaway and I did well: half an onion bhaji, one prawn, one chunk of chicken, two okra fingers (and they're quite big), approximately thirty-five grains of rice, followed by nine pills and two Rolos.

Mealtimes had become silent battles where Mum and Dad forced cheer into their voices, suggesting another forkful of rice, another chocolate, another vitamin-E capsule (excellent for preventing scarring, apparently). I did my best—I felt empty but never hungry—but whatever I ate, it wasn't enough for them.

Exhausted by the madras-based tussle, I retreated to my room. Something was rising to the surface: I needed to talk to Aidan.

I spoke to him in my head a lot, but now I wanted more: I had to hear his voice. Why hadn't this happened before now? Because I'd been injured and in shock? Or too subdued by the knockout painkillers?

I checked on Mum, Dad, and Helen, who were deeply ensconced in the kind of TV detective drama they're hoping will be made out of their lives. They waved me in and began elaborate shifting along the couch to make room, but I said, "No, I'm fine, I'm just going to—"

"Grand! Good girl."

I could have said anything—"I'm just going to set the house on fire," "I'm just going round to Kilfeathers to have a three-in-a-bed romp with Angela and her girlfriend"—and I'd have got the same response. They were in a profoundly unreachable state, similar to a trance, and would remain that way for the next hour or so. I closed the door firmly, lifted the phone from the hall, and took it into my room.

• • •

I stared at the little piece of machinery: phones have always seemed magical to me, the way they pull off the unlikeliest, most geographically distant connections. I know there are perfectly good explanations of how it all works, but I've never stopped being amazed at the wondrousness of people on opposite sides of oceans being able to talk to each other.

My heart was banging hard in my chest and I was hopeful—excited, in fact. So where should I try him? Not at work because someone else might pick up. His cell phone was the best idea. I didn't know what had happened to it, it might have been disconnected, but when I hit the number I'd called a thousand times, there was a click and then I heard his voice. Not his real voice, just his message, but it was enough to stop me breathing.

"Hi, this is Aidan. I can't take your call right now, but leave a message and I'll get back to you as soon as I can."

"Aidan," I heard my voice say. I sounded quavery. "It's me. Are you okay? Will you really get back to me as soon as you can? Please do." What else? "I love you, baby, I hope you know that."

I disconnected, feeling shaky, dizzy, elated; I'd heard his voice. But within seconds I'd crashed. Leaving messages on his cell phone wasn't enough.

I could try e-mailing him. But that wouldn't be enough either. I had to go back to New York and try to find him. There was a chance he mightn't be there but I had to give it a go because there was one thing I was certain of: he wasn't here.

Quietly I replaced the phone in the hall. If they found out what I'd been up to, there was no way in the whole wide world they'd let me leave.

5

How I met Aidan

The August before last, Candy Grrrl was preparing to launch a new skin-care line called Future Face (and the eye cream was called Future Eye, the lip cream Future Lip, and you get the picture...). Constantly on the quest for new and innovative ways to love-bomb beauty editors, I had a middle-of-the-night, lightbulb-over-the-head moment and thought I would buy each editor a "future" to tie in with the "future" theme of the launch. The obvious "future" to buy would be a personalized horoscope, but that had already been done for See Yourself in Ten Years' Time, our time-defying serum, and had ended in tears when the assistant beauty editor of *Britta* got told that she'd lose her job and her pet dog would run away within the month. (Funnily enough, although the dog stayed put, the job bit actually did come true; she had a total career change and now works as a hostess at the Four Seasons.)

Instead, I decided to buy some of those investment things, called "futures." I hadn't the first clue about them except what I'd heard about people pulling down millions of dollars working on Wall Street. But I couldn't get an appointment with a Wall Street futures analyst, even if I'd been prepared to pay a thousand dollars for every second of his time. I tried several and got stonewalled over and over. By then I was sorry I'd ever started, but I'd made the mistake of boasting about it to Lauryn, who'd liked the idea, so I was forced to work my way through less and less famous banks until finally I found a stockbroker in a midtown bank who agreed to see me and only then because I'd sent Nita, his assistant, tons of free stuff, with a promise of more if she could get me in.

So along I went, taking the rare opportunity to strip myself of as many kooky accoutrements as possible. Let me explain: all McArthur publicists have to take on the personality of the brand they represent. For example, the girls who worked for EarthSource were all a bit Hessian-ey and rough-woven, while the Bergdorf Baby team were Carolyn Bessette Kennedy clones, so etiolated, creamy-haired, and refined they were like another species. As Candy Grrrl's profile was a little wild and wacky, a little kooky, I had to dress accordingly, but I was so over it, so quickly. Kookiness is a young woman's game and I was thirty-one and burned out on matching pink with orange.

Thrilled to have the chance to dress soberly, I gloriously denuded my hair of all stupid barrettes and accessories and I was wearing a navy skirt suit (admittedly dotted with silver stars but it was the most conservative thing I had) and clopping along the eighteenth floor looking for Mr. Roger Coaster's office, passing neatly dressed, efficient-looking people, and wishing I could wear severe tailored suits to work, when I rounded a corner and several things happened at once.

There was a man and we bumped into each other with such force that my bag tumbled from my grasp, sending all kinds of embarrassing things skittering across the floor (including the fake glasses I'd brought to look intelligent and my coin purse that says *Change comes from within*).

Quickly we bent down to retrieve stuff, simultaneously reached for the glasses, and bumped our heads with a medium-to-loud crack. We both exclaimed "Sorry!"; he made an attempt to rub my bruised forehead and in the process spilled scalding coffee on the back of my hand. Naturally I couldn't shriek in agony because I was in a public place. The best I could do was shake my hand vigorously to make the pain go away, and while I was doing that and marveling that the coffee hadn't done more damage, we realized that the front of my white shirt looked like a Jackson Pollock painting. "You know what?" the man said. "With a little work, we could get a real routine going here."

We straightened up, and despite the fact that he'd burned my hand and ruined my shirt, I liked the look of him.

"May I?" He indicated my burned hand but didn't touch it because sexual-harassment lawsuits are so rife in New York that often a man won't get into an elevator with a lone woman, just in case he gets landed with a witness-free accusation of trying to see up her skirt.

"Please." I thrust my hand at him. Apart from the red scald marks, it was a hand to be proud of. I'd rarely seen it looking better. I'd been moisturizing regularly with Candy Grrrl's Hands Up, our superhydrating hand cream, my acrylic nails had been filled and were painted in Candy Wrapper (silver), and I'd just been de-gorilla'd, an event that always makes me feel joyous and skippy and carefree. I have quite hairy arms and—and God knows, this is not easy to talk about—but some of my arm hairs kind of... well... extend to the backs of my hands. The naked truth of the matter is that unchecked, they resemble hobbit feet.

In New York, waxing is as necessary to survival as breathing and you are only really acceptable in polite company if you're almost entirely bald. You can have head hair, eyelashes, and two sliverettes of eyebrows, but that's *it*. Everything else must go. Even your nasal hairs, which I hadn't yet been able to face. I would have to, though—if I was planning on having a successful career in beauty.

"I am so sorry," the man said.

"A mere flesh wound," I said. "Don't apologize, it was no one's fault. Just a terrible, terrible, *terrible* accident. Forget it."

"But you're burned. Will you ever play the violin again?"

Then I noticed his forehead: it looked like an egg was trying to push out through his skin.

"Oh God, you've a lump."

"I do?"

He shifted the light brown hair that fell across his forehead. His right eyebrow was split in two by a tiny, silvery thread of a scar. I noticed it, because so is mine.

Tenderly he rubbed the lump.

"Ouch," I said, wincing on his behalf. "One of the finest brains of our time."

"On the verge of breakthrough research. Lost forever." He pronounced "forever" as "forevah" like he was from Boston. Then he looked at my temporary ID badge. "You're a visitor here? ["visitah"]. Would you like me to show you the bathroom?"

"I'm fine."

"What about your shirt?"

"I'll pretend it's a fashion statement. Really, I'm fine."

"You are? You promise?"

I promised, he asked if I was sure, I promised again, I asked if he was okay, he said he was, then he went off with what remained of his coffee and I felt a little deflated as I carried on my way and found Mr. Coaster's office.

I tried to get Nita to explain to Mr. Coaster why I was splattered with coffee but she had zero interest. "Did you bring the stuff? The base in—"

"—Cookie Dough," we said together. There was a waiting list a month long for the base in Cookie Dough.

"Yes, it's in there. Lots of other stuff, too."

She began tearing the Candy Grrrl box apart. I stood there. A while later she looked up and saw that I was still standing there. "Yeah, go on in," she said irritably, waving her hand in the direction of a closed door.

I knocked and took myself and my dirty shirt into Mr. Coaster's office.

Mr. Coaster was a short, big-swinging-dick superflirt. As soon as I introduced myself, he gave me an overly twinkly grin and said, "Hey! Is that an accent I hear?"

"Mmm." I gave the photo of him—and who I can only presume were his wife and two children—a hard stare.

"British? Irish?"

"Irish." I gave the photo another meaningful eye flick and he shifted it slightly so that I could no longer see it.

"Now, Mr. Coaster, about these futures."

" 'Now, Misthur Coasther, about dese fewchurs.' I love it! Keep talking!"

"Ha-ha-ha." I laughed politely, while thinking *Fuckhead.*

It was a little while before I managed to get him to take me seriously and then it was only a matter of seconds before I discovered that "futures" were more of a conceptual thing, that I couldn't just waltz out the door with a handful of gorgeous futures, take them back to the office, wrap them in handwoven boxes from Kate's Paperie, and have them messengered over to ten of the city's most powerful beauty editors.

I'd have to come up with some other bright idea, but I wasn't as disappointed as I should have been because I was thinking about the guy I'd bumped into. There had been *something.* And not just the synchronicity of our his 'n' hers scars. But when I walked out of this building today the chances were that I would never see him again. Not unless I did something about it. If you don't ask, you don't get. (And even then it doesn't always work.)

First I'd have to find him, and this bank was a big place. And if I did manage to locate him, then what should I do? Stick my finger in his coffee and suck it suggestively? Immediately I ruled this out. (A) the heat of the coffee might melt the glue on my acrylic nail, causing it to fall off and swim around in the cup like a shark's fin and (b) It was a revolting thing to do anyway.

Mr. Coaster was explaining expansively and I was nodding and smiling, but I was far away inside my head, riveted by indecision.

Then, like a switch had been flicked, I fixed on a plan of action. I was suddenly certain: I was going to be up-front and honest, and I decided to enlist the help of Mr. Coaster. Yes, unprofessional. Yes, inappropriate. But what was to be lost?

"Mr. Coaster, sir," I interrupted politely. "On my way in here, I bumped into a gentleman, which resulted in him spilling his coffee. I'd like the opportunity to apologize before I leave. I didn't get his name but I can describe him." I spoke quickly. "He's tall, at least I think he is, although I'm so short everyone looks tall to me. Even you."

Shite.

Mr. Coaster's expression went instantly very stony. But I pressed on, I had to. How to describe my mystery man? "He's kind of pale, but not in a bad way, not like he's sick. His hair is light brown now, but you can tell he was blond as a baby. And his eyes, I think they might be green..."

Coaster's stony face remained stony. He could have given those statues on Easter Island a run for their money. He cut in on me. "'Fraid I can't help." And with lightning speed, I found myself outside his office, with the door shut firmly behind me.

Nita was studying herself in a compact; she looked like she'd tried on every single product simultaneously, like a little girl who'd gone berserk in her mother's makeup drawer.

"Nita, can you help me."

"Anna, I am totally in *love* with this gloss—"

"I'm looking for a man."

"Welcome to New York City." She didn't even look up from the mirror. "Eight-minute dating. Like speed dating, but slower. You get eight minutes instead of three. It's totally great, I got four matches last time."

"Not just any man. He works here. He's quite tall and...and..." There was no other way round this, I had to say it. "And, um, beautiful. He has a tiny scar on his eyebrow and he sounds like he might be from Boston."

Suddenly I had her interest. She jerked her head up. "Totally giving Denis Leary? But, like, younger?"

"Yesss!"

"Aidan Maddox. In IT, further along this floor. Make a left, then another, two rights, then you'll see his pod."

"Thank you. Just one other thing. Is he married?"

"Aidan Maddox? Oh my God. No, he's not married." She gave a little chuckle that said, *And he's never likely to be either.*

I found him and stood by his cubicle, looking at his back, willing him to turn around. "Hey," I said affably.

He swiveled around very quickly, like he was frightened. "Oh," he said. "Hey. It's you. How's your hand?"

I extended it for him to have a look. "I called my lawyer, the writ is on its way. Hey, would you like to go for a drink sometime?"

He looked like he'd been hit by a train. "You're asking me out for a drink?"

"Yes," I said firmly. "Yes, I am."

After a pause, he said, sounding perplexed, "But what if I said no?"

"What's the worst that can happen? You've already scalded me with boiling coffee."

He looked at me with an expression curiously akin to despair and the silence stretched too long. My confidence burst with a bang and suddenly I was desperate to leave.

"Do you have a card?" he asked.

"Sure!" I knew a rejection when I heard one.

I fumbled in my wallet and passed over a neon-pink rectangle with CANDY GRRRL in red wet-look type, followed in smaller writing by *Anna Walsh, public-relations superstar*. In the top right-hand corner was the famous growling-girl logo—an illustration of a winking girl, her teeth bared in a "grrr."

We both looked at it. Suddenly I saw it through his eyes.

"Cute," he said. Once again he sounded confused.

"Yes, it really gives the impression of gravitas," I said. "Well, er, sayonara."

I'd never before in my life said "sayonara."

"Yeah, okay, sayonara," he replied. Still sounding baffled.

And off I went.

So, you win some, you lose some, and plenty more where he came from. Anyway, I tended to like Italian and Jewish men; dark and short was more my thing.

But that night I woke up at 3:15 A.M., thinking about this Aidan. I'd really thought we'd connected.

But I'd had other intense, and ultimately meaningless, encounters in New York. Like the time the man on the subway had started talking to me about the book I was reading. (Paulo Coelho, which I *so* did not get.)

We had a great chat all the way to Riverdale; I told him all kinds of things about myself, like my teenage preoccupation with mysticism, which I was now mortified by, and he told me about his nighttime cleaning job and the two women in his life whom he was unable to choose between.

And there was the girl I'd met at Shakespeare in the Park—we'd both been stood up, so we talked to each other while we waited and she told me everything about her two Burmese cats, who she said had helped her depression so much that she'd reduced her dose of Cipramil from forty milligrams right down to ten.

It's a New York thing: you meet, tell each other absolutely everything about yourself, you *genuinely* connect, then you never see each other again. It's very nice. Usually.

But I didn't want my encounter with this Aidan to be a one-off and for the following few days I was a little expectant in every ringing-phone and incoming-e-mail situation, but nada.

6

Helen was clattering away at the ancient Amstrad, which lived in the hall, on top of the hostess trolley, and if you wanted to sit down to send an e-mail, you had to open the trolley doors and sit on a low stool, with your knees in the hot shelves.

"Who are you e-mailing?" I called.

She stuck her head around the door, winced at the sight of the tassels, and said, "No one, I'm writing a thing, you know, a telly script. About a detective."

I was speechless. Helen claimed—proudly—to be practically illiterate.

"I might as well," she said. "I've plenty of material. It's actually very good, I'll print it off for you."

The ancient printer screeched and squeaked for about ten minutes, then Helen proudly ripped off a single page and gave it to me. Still speechless, I read it.

Lucky Star
By and about Helen Walsh

Scene One: small proud Dublin detective agency. Two women, one young, beautiful (me). Other old (Mum). Young woman, feet on desk. Old woman, feet not on desk because of arthritis in knees. Slow day. Quiet. Bored. Clock ticking. Car parks outside. Man comes in. Good-looking. Big feet.

Me: What can I do you for?

Man: I'm looking for a woman.

Me: This isn't a knocking shop.

Man: No, I mean, I'm looking for my girlfriend. She's gone missing.

Me: Have you spoken to the boys in blue?

Man: Yes, but they won't do anything until she's been gone twenty-four hours. Anyway, they just think we've had a row.

Me (whipping feet off desk, narrowing eyes, leaning forward): And have you?

Man (morto): Yes.

Me: About what? Another man? Someone she works with?

Man (still morto): Yes.

Me: She working late a lot recently? Spending too much time with her colleague?

Man: Yes.

Me: It's not looking good for you, but it's your dime. We can try and find her. Give all the details to the old woman over there.

"Excellent, isn't it?" Helen said. "Especially the line about the knocking shop? And about it being his dime. Hard-boiled, isn't it?"

"Yes, very good."

"I'll do more tomorrow, maybe we could even act it out. Right, I better get ready for work."

At about 10 P.M. she reappeared at my door; she was dressed for surveillance work. (Dark, close-fitting clothes that are meant to be waterproof but aren't.)

"You need fresh air," she said.

"I got fresh air earlier." No way was I going to sit in a wet hedge for eleven hours while she tried to catch photos of unfaithful men leaving their girlfriends' apartments.

"But I want you to come with me."

Even though it would have been hard for Helen and me to be more different, we were close: maybe it was because we were the two youngest. Whatever the reason, Helen treated me like an extension of herself, the part that got up to bring her glasses of water in the middle of the night. I was her playmate/toy/slave/best friend, and needless to say, everything I owned was automatically hers.

"I can't come," I said. "I'm injured."

"Boo hoo," she said. "Boo bloody hoo."

It wasn't that she was trying to be cruel, it's just that my family doesn't believe in oversentimentality. They think it makes you more upset. Brusque chivvying, making no allowances—that's their modus operandi.

Mum appeared and Helen turned to her in complaint. "She won't come with me. It'll have to be you."

"I can't," Mum said. Dramatically she flicked her eyes in my direction, like I was mentally ill—and blind. "I'd better stick around here."

"Oh, *ding*-dong," Helen griped. "I'm off to spend the whole night sitting in a wet hedge and none of you care."

"Of course we care." Mum produced something from a pocket and gave it to Helen. "Vitamin-C sucky sweets; it might stop you getting those sore throats."

"No." Helen squirmed away and this confirmed something I'd suspected—she actually enjoyed the sore throats, they were an excuse to stay in bed, eat ice cream, and be horrible to people.

"Take the vitamin C. "

"No."

"Take the vitamin C."

"No."

"TAKE THE FECKING VITAMIN C!"

"Christ, don't have a cow. All right, then. But it won't work."

After she'd slammed out of the house, Mum got her sheet of paper and administered my final dose of pills for the day.

"Good night," she said. "Sleep tight." Anxiously, she said, "I don't like leaving you stuck down here on your own, with the rest of us all upstairs."

"It's okay, Mum. I mean, with my busted knee, it's easier for me to be downstairs."

"I blame myself," she burst out, with sudden emotion.

She did? Now, how did she figure that one?

"If only we lived in a bungalow! Then we could all be together. We looked at one, you know, your father and I, before you were all born. A bungalow. But it was too far from his work. And it smelled a bit funny. But now I regret it!"

This was twice in the one day I'd seen Mum upset. Normally, she was as tough as the steaks she used to make until we begged her to stop.

"Mum, I'm fine, don't blame yourself, don't feel guilty."

"I'm a mother, it's my job to feel guilty." In another burst of anxiety, she asked, "You're not having nightmares?"

"No nightmares, Mum, I don't dream about anything." It must be the pills.

She frowned. "That's not right," she said. "You should be having nightmares."

"I'll try," I promised.

"Good girl." She kissed me on the forehead and turned off the light.

"You were always a good girl," she called affectionately from the doorway. "A bit odd at times, but good."

Actually, I'm not really that odd at all—well, no more than anyone is; I'm just not like the rest of them.

All four of my sisters are noisy and volatile and—they'd be the first to admit it—they love a good row. Or a bad row. Any kind of row, really— they've always seen bickering as a perfectly legitimate means of communication. I spent my life watching them like a mouse watches a cat, curled up small and quiet, like a tiny, fringey-skirted sand mite, hoping that if they didn't realize I was there, they couldn't start a fight with me.

My eldest three sisters—Claire, Maggie, and Rachel—were like Mum: tall, fabulous women with cast-iron opinions. They seemed like a different race from me and I made sure never to get into disagreements with them, because any puny thing I said got dashed on the rocks of their robust, shouty certainty.

Claire, the firstborn, recently turned forty. Despite this, she remains a strong-willed, upbeat type who "really knows how to enjoy herself." (Euphemism for "unbridled party animal.") Back in the distant past, her life had a little hiccup, when her husband, patronizing James, left her on the same day she gave birth to their first child. This meant that she had the stuffing knocked out of her—for oh, close on half an hour—then she got over it. She met another bloke, Adam, and she had the good sense to make sure he was younger than her and easy to scare into submission. Mind you, she also had the good sense to make sure he was a dark, handsome hunk with lovely, broad shoulders and—according to Helen (don't ask)—a fine, big mickey. As well as Kate, the "abandoned child," Adam and Claire have two other children and they live in London.

Second sister: Maggie, the lickarse. Three years younger than Claire, Maggie distinguishes herself by refusing to be deliberately obstructive. But—and it's a big but—she's well able to stand up for herself, and when she gets an idea into her head, she can be as stubborn as a mule. Maggie lives in Dublin, less than a mile from Mum and Dad. (See, lickarse.)

Then comes Rachel, a year younger than Maggie and the middle of the five of us. Even before Rachel began being accompanied everywhere by Luke, she used to cause a bit of a stir—she was sexy, fun, a bit wild, and her little hiccup was quite a big one, really. Probably the worst of the lot—at least, until mine. Several years ago, while she'd first been living in New York, she'd developed a fondness for the devil's dandruff (cocaine). Things got very messy, and after a dramatic suicide attempt, she landed in an expensive Irish rehab.

Very expensive. Mum still goes on about how she and Dad could have gone on the Orient Express to Venice and stayed in a suite at the Cipriani for a month for the same money, then she always adds quickly, but not entirely convincingly, that you can't put a price on your children's happiness.

But it's fair to say that Rachel is also probably the Walsh family's biggest success story. A year or so after rehab, she went to college, got a degree in psychology, then an MA in addiction studies, and she now works in a rehab place in New York.

After the years she'd spent coked out of her head, it was very important for Rachel to be "real"; a laudable ambition. The only downside was that she could be a bit earnest. She often talked—approvingly—about people having "done work" on themselves. And when she was with her "recovery" friends, they sometimes joked about people who'd never been to therapy: "What? You mean, she still has the personality her parents gave her?" That was a joke, see. But if you scratch away at Rachel's earnestness, you don't have to try too hard before you've uncovered a version of the old person, who is lots of fun.

Next in line is me—I'm three and a half years younger than Rachel.

Then, bringing up the rear, is Helen and she's a law unto herself. People love her and fear her. She's a true original—fearless, undiplomatic, and willfully contrary. For example, when she set up her agency (Lucky Star Investigations) she could have had her office in a lovely suite on Dawson Street, with a concierge and a shared receptionist, but instead she situated herself in an estate of graffiti-covered flats, where all the shops had their shutters down permanently, and dodgy-looking youths in hoodies whizzed around on bikes, delivering screwed-up bits of white paper.

It's unspeakably bleak and depressing but Helen loves it.

Even though I don't understand her, Helen is like my twin, my dark twin. She's the shameless, courageous version of me. And even though she's always made fun of me (nothing personal, she does it to everyone), she's loyal to the point of fisticuffs.

In fact all my sisters are loyal to the point of fisticuffs—while it's okay for them to slag each other, they'd kill anyone else who tried it.

And yes, okay, they used to say that I was away with the fairies and "Earth calling, Anna" and that sort of thing, but to be fair, there were reasons: it was obvious I wasn't too keen on reality. Why would anyone be, I used to wonder, it never seemed that pleasant a place. Any opportunity for escape I was given, I took—reading, sleeping, falling in love, designing houses in my head, where I had my own bedroom and didn't have to share with Helen—and I was not the most practical person you could meet.

And then, of course, there were the fringey skirts.

It's mortifying to admit, but from my late teens onward I owned several long, hippie-type fringey skirts, some even with—oh God!—bits of mirrors on them. Why, *why*? I was young, I was foolish, but really. I know we all have our youthful fashion shame, the badly dressed skeletons in our closets, but my time in the fashion wilderness lasted the best part of a decade.

And I gave up going to the hairdressers when I was fifteen after they sent me out with a Cyndi Lauper. (The eighties, I can't blame them, they knew no better.) But the fringey mirrored skirts and messy hair were mere bagatelles compared to the shock waves of the compliment-slip story . . .

The compliment-slip story

If you haven't heard it already, and you probably have, because the world and his granny seems to know about it, here it is. After I left school, Dad swung me a job in a construction office—someone had owed him a favor and the consensus was that it must have been a pretty large favor.

But anyway, there I am, working away, doing my best, being nice to the builders who come in for petty cash, and one day Mr. Sheridan, the big boss, throws a check on the desk and says, "Send that to Bill Prescott, stick a compliment slip in the envelope."

In my defense, I was nineteen, I knew nothing of the language of administration, and luckily the check was intercepted before it went out in the post with my accompanying note: *Dear Mr. Prescott, although I have never met you, I believe you are a very nice man. All the builders speak highly of you.*

How was I to know that sending a compliment slip did not actually involve complimenting anyone? No one had told me and I wasn't psychic (although I wished I was). It was the kind of mistake any uninitiated person could make, but it became a watershed event: it took pride of place in the family folklore and crystallized everyone's opinion of me: I was the token flake.

They didn't mean it unkindly, of course, but it wasn't easy.

However, everything changed when I met Shane, my soul mate. (It was a long time ago, so long that it was permissible to say that sort of thing without getting sneered at.) Shane and I were delighted with each other because we thought exactly the same way. We were aware of the futures that awaited us—stuck in one place, shackled to dull, stressful jobs because we had to pay the mortgage on some horrible house—and we decided to try to live differently.

So we went traveling, which went down oh-so-badly. Maggie said about us, "They'd say that they were going up the road to buy a Kit Kat and the next time you'd hear from them, they'd be working in a tannery in Istanbul." (That never happened. I think she must be thinking of the time we went to buy a can of 7-Up and decided on a whim to skipper a boat around the Greek Islands.)

Walsh family mythology made it sound like Shane and I were a pair of work-shy layabouts, but working in a canning factory in Munich was backbreaking work. And running a bar in Greece meant long hours and—worse still—having to be nice to people, which, as everyone knows, is the toughest job in the world.

Whenever we came home to Ireland, it was all a bit "Ho, ho, ho, here they are, the pair of smelly hippies, coming on the scrounge, lock up your confectionery."

But it never really got to me—I had Shane and we were cocooned in our own little world and I expected it would stay that way forever.

Then Shane broke up with me.

Apart from the sadness, loneliness, woundedness, and humiliation that traditionally accompanies a broken heart, I felt betrayed: Shane had got his hair cut into something approaching respectability and had gone into business. Admittedly it was a groovy kind of business, something to do with digital music and CDs, but after he'd scorned the system for as long as I'd known him, the speed with which he'd embraced it left me reeling.

I was twenty-eight, with nothing but the fringey skirt I stood up in and suddenly all the years I'd spent moving from country to country seemed wasted. It was a horrible, horrible time and I ricocheted around like a lost soul, directionless and terrified, which was when Maggie's husband, Garv, took me under his wing. First he got me a steady job, and while I admit that opening the post in an actuarial firm isn't exactly scintillating, it was a start.

Then he convinced me to go to college and suddenly my life had taken off again, moving at speed in an entirely different direction. In a short space of time, I learned to drive, I got a car, I got my hair cut into a proper, medium-maintenance "style." In short, a little later in the day than most people, I got it together.

How Aidan and I met for the second time

A barrel-chested man slung a hamlike arm around my neck, swung a tiny plastic bag of white powder at my face, and said, "Hey, Morticia, want some coke?"

I extricated myself and said politely, "No, thank you."

"Aw, c'mon," he said, a little too loudly. "It's a party."

I looked for the door. This was dreadful. You'd think that if you took a ritzy loft overlooking the Hudson, added a professional sound system, a ton of drink, and a load of people, you'd have a great shindig on your hands.

But something wasn't working. And I blamed Kent, the guy throwing the party. He was a jocklike banker and the place was overrun with hordes of his Identi-Kit pals and the thing about these guys was they didn't need anything to boost their confidence, they were bad enough au naturel without adding cocaine to the mix.

Everyone looked florid and somehow desperate, as if the crucial thing was to be having a good time.

"I'm Drew Holmes." The man swung the bag of coke at me again. "Try it, it's great, you'll love it."

This was the third guy who'd offered me coke and it was kind of cute really, like they'd just discovered drugs.

"The eighties will never die," I said. "No, thank you. Really."

"Too wild for you, huh?"

"That's right, too wild."

I looked around for Jacqui. This was all her fault—she worked with Kent's brother. But all I saw were lots of shouty meatheads with saucer-like pupils, and trashy-looking girls, necking vodka straight from the bottle. I discovered afterward that Kent had put the word out that he wanted people to bring along the kind of girls who were six months away from rehab, who were in their final, promiscuous crash-and-burn.

But even before I'd known that, I'd known he was a creep.

"Tell me about yourself, Morticia." Drew Holmes was still at my side. "What do you do?"

I didn't even hide my sigh. Here we go again. This party was lousy with incessant bloody networkers, but—at their request, I might add—I'd already explained my job to two other guys and neither of them had listened to a word, they were just waiting for me to shut up so they could monologue about themselves and how great they were. Cocaine really kills the art of conversation.

"I test-drive orthopedic shoes."

"Well!" Deep breath before he launched into it. "I'm with blah bank, blah, blah...tons of money...I, me, myself, being fabulous, blah, pro-motion, blah, bonus, workhardplayhard, me, mine, belonging to me, my expensive apartment, my expensive car, my expensive vacations, my ex-pensive skis, me, me, me, me, MEEEEE..."

Just then a canapé—it was going very fast but I believe it was a miniburger—caught him on the side of the head, and while his eyes bulged with rage as he sought the perpetrator, I slipped away.

I decided I was leaving. Why had I come in the first place? Well, why does anyone go to the party of someone they didn't know? To meet men of course. And funnily enough, whatever the hell was going on with the planets, for the previous couple of weeks, I'd been *overrun* with men. I'd never experienced anything like it in my life.

Myself and Jacqui had gone to the eight-minute speed dating that Nita at Roger Coaster's office had told me about and I'd got three matches; a handsome, interesting architect; a red-haired baker from Queens who wasn't a looker but was very nice; and a young, cute bartender who said words like *dude* and *shibby*. Each had submitted a request for a date and I'd agreed to all three.

But before you start thinking that (a) I'm a three-timing slut (and it's actually four because I haven't told you yet about the blind date that my lovely Korean colleague, Teenie, had set up for me), or (b) that the whole thing was a recipe for disaster—that I was bound to be caught and end up with no one, let me explain the rules of Dating in New York City, especially the whole exclusive/nonexclusive end of things. What I was currently doing was Dating Nonexclusively—a perfectly acceptable state of affairs.

How it is in Ireland is, people just drift into relationships. You start by going for a couple of drinks, then on another night you might go to a film, then you run into each other at a party given by a mutual friend, and at some stage you start sleeping together—probably this night, in fact. It's all very casual and drifty and most of the initial propulsion depends on accidental meetings. But although no one ever says anything about exclusiveness or nonexclusiveness, *he's definitely your boyfriend.* So if you discovered the man you'd been sharing fireside nights and videos with for the last few months having a nice dinner with a woman who wasn't (a) you, or (b) a female relation of his, you'd be perfectly within your rights to pour a glass of wine over him, to tell the other woman that she's "welcome to him." It is also appropriate at this point to wiggle your little finger and say, "Hardly worth it, though, is it?"

But not in New York. You'd think, *There's one of the men I've been seeing nonexclusively having dinner with a woman he's also seeing nonexclusively. How civilized we all are.* No wine gets poured on anyone; in fact, you might even join them for a drink. Actually, no, scratch that, I don't really think you would. Maybe on paper, but not in reality, especially if you liked him.

However, it's an ill wind, and during this time of nonexclusivity, you can ride rings around yourself; you can sleep with a different man every night should you so wish and no one can call you a six-timing tramp.

Not that I'd touch any of the overgrown frat boys at this party, no matter how accommodating the system. I battled through the crowded room. Where the hell was Jacqui? Panic flickered as my path was blocked by another man with yet another jocko name, a short butch thing. In fact, now that I think about it, it might *actually* have been Butch. He pulled at my dress and said peevishly, "What's with all the clothes?"

I was wearing a black wraparound jersey dress and black knee boots, which seemed not unreasonable attire for a party.

Then he demanded, "What's with the Addams-family thing you've got going on?"

The strange thing was I had never before in my life been accused of looking like Morticia. Why, why, *why?* And I wished he'd let go of my dress. It was stretchy but not in the first flush of youth and I feared it could lose its bounce and never return to its correct configuration. "So, Goth girl, what do you do when you're not being a Goth girl?"

I was wondering whether to tell him I was an elephant voice coach or the inventor of the inverted comma, when a voice cut in on us and said, "Don't you know Anna Walsh?"

Butch said, "Say what?"

Say what, is right. I turned around. It was Him. The guy, the one who'd spilled coffee on me, the one I'd asked out for a drink and who'd blown me off. He was wearing a beenie and a wide-shouldered workingman's jacket and he'd brought the cold night in with him, refreshing the air.

"Yeah, Anna Walsh. She's a . . ." He looked at me and shrugged inquiringly. "A magician?"

"Magician's girl," I corrected. "I passed all my magician exams but the assistant's clothes are a lot cooler."

"Neat," Butch said, but I wasn't looking at him, I was looking at

Aidan Maddox, who had remembered my name, even though it was seven weeks since we'd met. He wasn't exactly how I remembered him. His tight hat made the bones of his face more pronounced, especially his cheekbones and the lean cut of his jawbone, and there was a twinkle in his eyes that hadn't been there the last time.

"She disappears," Aidan said. "But then—as if by magic—she reappears."

He'd taken my number but he hadn't called and now he was hitting me with some of the corniest lines I'd heard in a long while. I looked at him in cold inquiry: What was his game?

His face gave nothing away but I didn't stop looking at him. Nor he at me. What seemed like ages later someone asked, "Where do you go?"

"Hmm?" The someone was Butch. I was surprised to find him still there. "Go? When?"

"When you get magically disappeared? Hey, presto!" He winked brightly.

"Oh! I'm just out back, having a cigarette." I turned back to Aidan, and when his eyes met mine again, the shock of our connection made my skin flame.

"Neat," Butch said. "And when you get sawn in half, how does that work?"

"False legs," Aidan said, barely moving his lips. His eyes didn't leave my face.

I could actually feel poor Butch's smile trickle away. "You guys know each other?"

Aidan and I looked at Butch, then back at each other. Did we? "Yes."

Even if I hadn't known that something was happening with me and Aidan, the way Butch treated us was a sign: he backed off—and you could tell that ordinarily he was supercompetitive. "You kids have fun," he said, a little subdued.

Then Aidan and I were left on our own.

"Enjoying the party?" he asked.

"No," I said. "I hate it."

"Yeah." He scanned the room, at a different eye level from me. "What's not to hate?"

Just then, a short, dark man, the sort of man who'd been my type until I'd met Aidan, butted his way between us and asked, "Whereja get to, buddy? You just took off."

A look passed over Aidan's face: Were we ever going to be left alone? Then he smiled and said, "Anna, meet my best buddy, Leon. Leon works with Kent, the birthday boy. And this is Leon's wife, Dana."

Dana was about a foot taller than Leon. She had long legs, a big chest, a fall of thick multitoned hair, and radiant, evenly tanned skin.

"Hey," she said.

"Hey," I replied.

Anxiously, Leon asked me, "It's a sucky party, right?"

"Um..."

"You're with the good guys," Aidan said. "Tell it like it is."

"Okay. It's supersucky."

"Jeez." Dana sighed and fanned her hand in front of her chest. "Let's mingle," she said to Leon. "Sooner we start, sooner we can leave. Excuse us."

"Bail just as soon as you can't stand it," Leon told Aidan, then we were alone again.

Was it the two giggling men running off to the bathroom like a pair of schoolgirls with their little plastic baggie or the poor six-months-away-from-rehab girls scooping out the creamed chicken from the choux pastry horns and smearing their fronts with it that made Aidan ask, "Anna, can we get out of here?"

Can we get out of here? I looked at him, annoyed at his presumption. All that spur-of-the-moment, let's-do-the-relationship-right-here stuff is fine when you're nineteen, but I was thirty-one years old. I didn't just "get out of here" with strange men.

I said, "Let me just tell Jacqui I'm leaving."

I found her in the kitchen, showing a cluster of rapt people how to make a proper Manhattan, and told her I was off. But before I could leave, I had to retrieve my coat from beneath a grunting couple having sex in Kent's bedroom. All I could see of the woman was her legs and shoes, one of them with gum stuck to the sole.

"Which coat is it?" Aidan asked. "This one? 'Scuse us, buddy. Just need to get this—"

He tugged and the coat moved an inch, then another, then with a final yank, it slithered free and we were out the door. On a high from our escape, we couldn't wait for the elevator, so, fueled with more energy than we'd normally have, we belted down several flights of stairs and ran right out into the street.

It was early October, the days were still bright but the nights were chilly. Aidan helped me on with my coat, a midnight-blue velvet duster, painted with a silvery cityscape.

"I like your look." Aidan stood back to check me out properly. "Yeah."

I liked his, too. With the hat and the jacket and the big boots, it was very Workingman Chic. Not that I was going to tell him. And good thing Jacqui wasn't there to hear Aidan because remarking on my clothes was classic Feathery Stroker acting-out. (Details on Feathery Strokers to follow.)

"Just a point I'd like to clear up," I said, a little snippily. "I didn't 'disappear.' I went *away*. Because you didn't want to go for a drink with me, remember?"

"I did want to. I wanted you from the very moment you head-butted me. I just wasn't sure I could have you."

"Excuse me, *you* head-butted me. What sort of not sure?"

"Every sort."

Two blocks away we found a small weird underground bar, with red walls and a pool table. Dry ice curled around our knees—the barkeep explained they were trying to re-create the glory days before the smoking ban—and at Aidan's request, I told him all about my life as a magician's girl.

"We're called Marvelous Marvo and Gizelda. Gizelda is my stage name and we're *huge* in the Midwest. I sew all my own costumes, six hundred sequins per outfit, and I do them all by hand. I go into a meditative state when I'm doing it. Marvo is actually my dad and his real name is Frank. Now tell me about you."

"No, you tell me."

I thought about it for a while. "Okay. You're the son of a deposed East European despot who stole millions from his people." I smiled, a little cruelly. "The money is hidden and the two of you are looking for it." He looked progressively more anxious as his identity worsened. Then I took pity and redeemed him. "But the reason you want to find the money is to return it to your impoverished people."

"Thank you," he said. "Anything else?"

"You've a good relationship with your first wife, an Italian tennis player. And porn star," I added. "In fact, you were an excellent tennis player yourself, you could have gone professional, until RSI put paid to it."

"Speaking of which, how's your burned hand?"

"Good. And I'm happy to see you've recovered from the coma I put you in. Any side effects?"

"Evidently not. Judging from how this Saturday night has turned out, I seem to be smah-tah than evah."

That Boston accent again. I found it devastatingly sexy.

"Say it again."

"What?"

"Smarter."

"Smah-tah?"

"Yes."

He shrugged, willing to please. "Smah-tah."

A rush of physical desire, similar to but worse than hunger, overtook me.

I'd want to keep an eye on that.

"Game of pool?" I suggested.

"You play?"

"I play."

Double entendre central and a meaningful eye meet that depth-charged something down low in me.

After twenty minutes of potting balls into swingy pockets that reminded me of testicles, I beat Aidan.

"You're good," he said.

"You let me win." I poked him in the stomach with my pool cue. "Don't do it again."

He opened his mouth to protest and I pushed the cue a bit farther. Nice hard stomach muscles. We held a look for several seconds, then, in silence, returned our cues to the rack.

When the bar closed at 4 A.M., Aidan offered to walk me home, but it was too far. By about forty blocks.

"We're not in Kansas anymore, Toto," I said.

"Okay, we'll get a cab. I'll drop you off."

In the backseat, listening to the driver yelling in Russian on his cell phone, Aidan and I didn't speak. I took a quick look at him, the lights and angular shadows of the city moving across his face, making it impossible to see his expression. I wondered what would happen next. One thing I knew: after the last knock-back, no way would I be offering business cards or convivial nights out.

We pulled up at my crumbling stoop. "I live here."

Privacy would have been nice for our awkward "what happens now?" conversation, but we had to sit in the cab because if we got out without having paid, the cabdriver might have shot us.

"Look . . . I guess you're seeing other guys," Aidan said.

"I guess I am."

"Can you put me on your roster?"

I thought about it. "I could do that."

I didn't ask if he was seeing other women; it was none of my business (that's what you had to say anyway). Besides, something in the way Leon and Dana had behaved with me—pleasant but not terribly interested, like they'd been introduced to a lot of girls by Aidan over the years—made me sure he was.

"Can I have your number?" he asked.

"I already gave you my number," I said, and got out of the cab.

If he wanted to see me that badly, he'd find me.

I woke up in the narrow bed in the sofa-filled front room and spent several dopey minutes trying to look out of the window. Here came the elderly woman and her dog; I watched sleepily. Then less sleepily. I half sat up: I wasn't imagining it. That poor dog did not want to do its business but the woman was insistent. The dog kept trying to get up and leave but the woman wouldn't let her. "Here!" I couldn't hear it, but I could see her say it. Odd.

Then in came Mum and I partook of a hearty breakfast—half a slice of toast, eleven grapes, eight pills, and a record-breaking sixty Rice Krispies—because I needed to convince her how well I was getting. While she was washing me—a miserable business with toweling cloths and a bowl of scummy lukewarm water—I went for it.

"Mum, I've decided to go back to New York."

"Don't be shagging well ridiculous." She continued rinsing me.

"My scars are healing, my knee can take weight, all the bruises are gone."

It was strange, really; I'd had myriad injuries, but none had been serious. Although my face had been black-and-blue, none of the bones had been broken. I could have been crushed like an eggshell and spent the rest of my life looking like a Cubist painting (as Helen had put it). I knew I'd been lucky.

"And look how fast my fingernails are growing." I wiggled my hand at her; I'd lost two fingernails and the pain had been—I'm not joking—indescribable, far worse than my broken arm. Even the morphine-based painkillers couldn't entirely negate it; the pain was always there, just slightly further away, and I used to wake in the nighttime with my fingers throbbing so much they felt swollen to the size of pumpkins. Now they barely hurt.

"You've a broken arm, missy. Broken in three places."

"But they were clean breaks and it doesn't hurt anymore. I'd say it's nearly better."

"Oh, you're a bone surgeon now, are you?"

"No, I'm a beauty PR and they won't keep my job open forever." I let that thought settle with her, then I whispered darkly, *"No more free makeup."*

But not even that worked. "You're going nowhere, missy."

However, I'd picked my time well: that very afternoon I had my weekly hospital checkup, and if the professionals said I was getting better, Mum wouldn't have a leg to stand on.

After lots of hanging around, an X-ray was taken of my arm. As I'd thought, it was healing fast and well; the sling could be removed immediately and the plaster could come off in a couple of weeks.

Then onto the skin specialist, who said I was doing so well that the stitches could be taken out of my cheek. Even *I* hadn't expected that. It hurt more than I'd thought it would and an angry, red, puckered line ran from the corner of my eye to the corner of my mouth, but now that my face was no longer being held together by navy-blue thread, I looked far, far more normal.

"What about plastic surgery?" Mum asked.

"Eventually," he said. "But not for a while. It's always hard to tell how well these things will heal."

Then on to Dr. Chowdhury to have my internal organs poked and prodded. According to him, all the bruising and swelling had subsided and he said, like he'd said on the other visits, how unbelieveably fortunate I'd been not to have ruptured anything.

"She's talking about going back to New York," Mum burst out. "Tell her she's not well enough to travel."

"But she was well enough to travel home," Dr. Chowdhury said, with undeniable truth.

Mum stared at him, and even though she didn't say it, not even under her breath, her "Fuck you, fuckhead" hung in the air.

Mum and I drove home in grim silence. At least Mum did, my silence was happy and—I couldn't help it—a little smug.

"What about your gammy knee?" Mum said, suddenly animated: all was not lost. "How can you go to New York if you can't climb a step?"

"I'll make you a deal," I said. "If I can walk to the top of the stairs on it, I'm well enough to go back."

She agreed because she thought I hadn't a hope of doing it. But she had no idea how determined I was to leave. I would do it. And I did do it—even though it took over ten minutes and left me covered in sweat and a little puky from the pain.

But what Mum was missing was that even if I hadn't been able to get past the first step, I was leaving anyway. I needed to get back and I was starting to get panicky.

"See?" I gasped, sitting down on the landing. "I'm all better. Arm, face, innards, knee—better!"

"Anna," she said, and I didn't like her tone, it was so somber. "There's more wrong with you than just physical injuries."

I processed that. "Mum, I know. But I have to go back. I *have* to. I'm not saying I'll stay there forever. I might arrive back home very quickly, but I've no choice. I must go back."

Something in my voice convinced her because she seemed to deflate. "It's the modern way, I suppose," she said. "Getting closure." Sadly, she went on, "In my day there was nothing at all wrong with unfinished business. You just left a place and never went back and no one thought there was anything wrong with that. And if you went a bit funny in the head and had nightmares and woke the whole house, running around in the middle of the night screeching your head off, the parish priest would be brought in to pray over you. Not that it ever helped, but no one minded, that's just the way it was."

"Rachel will be in New York to help me," I reassured her.

"And maybe you'd think about going for some of that counseling stuff."

"Counseling?" I wondered if I was hearing right. Mum totally disapproved of any kind of psychotherapy. Nothing would convince her that therapists employed confidentiality. Although she had no proof, she insisted they regaled people at dinner parties with their clients' secrets.

"Yes, counseling. Rachel might be able to recommend someone for you."

"Mmm," I said musingly, as if I was considering it, but I wasn't. Talking about what had happened wouldn't change a single thing.

"Come on, we'd better tell your father what's happening. He might cry, but ignore him."

Poor Dad. In a houseful of strong women, his opinion counted for nothing. We found him watching golf on telly.

"We've a bit of news. Anna's going back to New York for a while," Mum said.

He looked up, startled and upset. "Why?"

"To get closure."

"What's that?"

"I don't really know," Mum admitted. "But apparently her life won't be worth living without it."

"Isn't it a bit soon to be leaving? What about the broken arm? And the gammy knee?"

"All on the mend. And the sooner she gets this fecking closure, the sooner she'll be back to us," Mum said.

Then it was time to tell Helen and she was quite distraught. "War crime!" She declared. "Don't go."

"I have to."

"But I thought we could go into business together, you and me. We could be private investigators. Think of the laugh we'd have."

Think of the laugh *she'd* have, snuggled up in her nice warm dry bed while I loitered in damp shrubbery doing her job for her.

"I'm more use to you as a beauty PR," I said, and she seemed to buy that.

So they sent for Rachel to bring me back.

10

While I waited to see if Aidan Maddox would find my number and ring me, I got on with my life. I had my hands full of speed-dating dates.

However, Harris, the interesting architect, turned out to be a little too interesting when he suggested that, for our first date, we have a pedicure together. Nearly everyone shrieked that it was adorable, that it was original, and that he obviously wanted me to have a good time. But I had my misgivings. As for Jacqui, who had no time for that Feathery Strokery sort of nonsense, she nearly went through the roof.

She threatened to walk past the salon and shame me; luckily she was working that evening, and when the time came and I was sitting beside Harris, the two of us like a king and queen, raised above the salon on matching thronelike padded seats, up to our ankles in little pools of soapy water, I've never been so glad.

Two women bowed before us, tending to our feet. All I could see were the tops of their heads, and I was too ashamed to carry on a relaxed conversation in their abject, silent presence. Harris, however, seemed perfectly comfortable, asking away about my job, telling me all about his. Then he produced a cocktail shaker and two glasses, poured me a drink, and raised his glass. Christ, a toast! "To the Mets winning," I said quickly.

"To toe sucking," he said.

Oh no. Oh, dear me, no.

So he had a foot thing. Which was fine. Fine. Not for me to judge. Just don't include me in it.

Not that he planned to. As soon as we'd finished and paid, he said to me, quite nicely, "We didn't click. Have a good life." Then briskly he strode away on his freshly buffed feet.

Bloodied but unbowed, I prepared for my date the following evening with Greg, the baker from Queens. Although it was October and far from warm, he'd suggested a picnic in the park. I had to hand it to them, these New York guys had really raised their dating game.

We were meeting straight after work because Greg went to bed very early on account of having to get up in the middle of the night to make bread. Also, after seven-thirty, it would be too dark to actually see each other and what we were eating. As I marched along to the park, I insisted that I felt hopeful. So this was a little unusual, but so what? Where was my sense of adventure?

At the park, I saw Greg waiting with a rug over one arm, a wicker picnic basket on the other, and—with a thrill of horror—some sort of fool panama hat on his head.

It's a terrible thing to say but he was a lot fatter than I remembered from the speed dating. That night we'd been sitting down with a table between us and I only really saw his face and chest, which had been bulky but not noticeably tubby. But, seeing him at full height, he was...he was... diamond-shaped. His shoulders were normal size, but he really sort of *exploded* around the waist area. His stomach was massive—and although it kills me to say it because I hate when men say it about women—he had a ginormous arse. An arse you could play handball against. But curiously his legs weren't too bad and sloped down to a pair of neat little ankles.

He spread out the rug on the grass, then tapped his basket and said, "Anna, I promise you a feast of the senses."

Already I was afraid.

Reclining on the rug, Greg opened his basket, took out a loaf, then closed the basket quickly, but not before I'd seen that all that was in it was loads of bread.

"This is my sourdough," he said. "Made to my own recipe."

He tore a bit off, in a real bon vivant's way, and approached. I could see the way this was going: he was planning a seduction via bread—once I'd tried his creations, I'd go all swoony and fall in love with him. I was dealing with a man who'd seen *Chocolat* once too often.

"Close your eyes and open your mouth." Oh, cripes, he was going to feed me! God, how excruciating, how *9 1/2 Weeks*.

But he didn't even let me eat the damn thing. He rubbed it around inside my mouth and said, "Feel the roughness of the crust on your tongue." He moved it back and forth and I nodded yes, I was feeling the roughness.

"Take your time," he urged. "Savor it."

Oh God, this was a public place, I hoped no one was looking at us. I opened my eyes and shut them again quickly: a woman walking her dog was in fits. Her hands were on her knees, she was laughing so much.

When Greg felt my tongue had been sufficiently cut to ribbons by the rough crust, he exclaimed, "Now taste! Taste the salt of the dough, the sourness of the yeast. You getting it?" I nodded yes, yes, saltiness, sourness. Anything to speed this up.

"Taste anything else?" Greg asked.

I couldn't say I did.

"A sweetness?" he prompted. I nodded obediently. Yes, a sweetness. Make this be over.

"A citrus sweetness?" he said.

"Yes," I mumbled. "Lemon?"

"Lime." He sounded disappointed. "But close enough."

Next up was an aged-cheddar-and-red-onion focaccia, which I had to smell for about half an hour before I was permitted to eat any. Followed by a French yoke—perhaps a brioche—where I had to admire its many airholes, which apparently gave it its delicious lightness.

The pièce de résistance was a chocolate bread, which he made me crumble, so that little nuggets of chocolate went all over my skirt and, despite the cold evening, managed to melt.

Over the course of ninety long, chilly minutes, Greg made me lick bread, smell bread, watch bread, and caress bread. The only thing he didn't make me do was listen to it.

And there was nothing else to eat: no coleslaw, no chicken legs, no turkey slices.

"We live in carb-phobic times," Jacqui later remarked. "Does he know anything?"

Bloodied but, at this stage, quite bowed, I was in no mood when, the following day, the cute bartender rang me at work and said, "Got a great idea for our date."

I listened in silence.

"I'm part of a project where we build houses for some poor folks in Pennsylvania—they provide the materials, we provide the labor."

A pause for me to praise him. I didn't. So, sounding a little confused, he continued: "Going down this weekend. Be great if you'd come along. We could really get to know each other and . . . you know . . . do some good for our fellowman."

Altruism: the latest fashion. I knew all about these projects. Basically a group of young New York pissheads descend on a poor rural community in Pennsylvania and insist on building some misfortunate bastards a house. The city folk have the time of their lives, running around, playing with power tools, and staying up all night, drinking beer round a campfire, then effing back to New York and their lovely level-floored apartments, leaving the poor rural community with a leaky, lopsided house, in which all furniture sits on a slope, and if something has wheels, it rolls across the floor until it bangs into the wall.

"You gotta give something back" is the mantra of these guys. But what they really mean is "Ladies, see what a wonderful human being I am." And sadly, many women fall for the ruse and sleep with them at the drop of a nail gun.

Weariness washed over me.

"Thank you for asking," I said. "But I don't think so. Nice to meet you, Nash—"

"Nush."

"—sorry, Nush. But I just don't think it's for me."

"Whatever. Got plenty of other chicks."

"I don't doubt it. I wish you well."

I slammed the phone down and turned to Teenie at the next desk. "You know what? I've had it with New York men. They're fucking lunatics! No wonder they have to go to speed dating, even in a city where women are crawling the walls with desperation for a date."

Teenie pursed her silver lips into a sympathetic moue. (She never wore normal-colored lipstick; unlike me, kookiness came naturally to her, she was kooky to the bone. Despite this we were great pals, she was my favorite of all the McArthur staff.)

"Whoever heard of going on a date and building a house? A fucking *house*—"

The phone rang, interrupting my rant; I took a deep raggedy breath and said, "Candy Grrrl publicity, Anna Walsh speaking."

"Hey, Anna Walsh, it's Aidan Maddox speaking."

"Oh, right."

"What have I done?"

"Are you calling to ask me out?"

"Yes."

"Bad timing. I've just sworn off New York men."

"Oh, that's okay. I'm from Boston. So what's going on?"

"I've had the weirdest week, with the weirdest dates. I don't think I can take another one."

"Date? Or weird date?"

I thought about it. "Weird date."

"O-kay. How about we go for one drink? Is that unweird enough?"

"Depends. Where are we having it? A beauty salon? A freezing park? The surface of the moon?"

"I was thinking more of a bar."

"Okay. One drink."

"And if, by the end of the drink, it's not working out for you, just say you've got to go because there's a leak in your apartment and the plumber is coming. How does that sound?"

"Okay. Just one drink. And what will your get-out clause be?" I asked.

"I don't need one."

"You could say you've got to get back to the office to finish stuff for a breakfast meeting the next day."

"'That's very thoughtful of you," he said. "But I don't think so."

11

Mum fought her way over to my bed.

"I just spoke to Rachel. She'll be here on Saturday morning." Two days away. "And the two of you'll be flying back to New York on Monday. If you're still sure that's what you want."

"It is. Is Luke coming over with her?"

"No. And thank God for that," Mum added heartily, lying down beside me.

"I thought you liked him."

"I do like him. Especially since he's agreed to marry her."

"I think it might have been since she agreed to marry him."

Rachel and Luke had been living together for so long that even Mum had given up hoping that Rachel would "stop making a show of us all." Then, just over two months ago, to everyone's great surprise, they announced their engagement. Initially, the news plunged Mum into despair because she concluded the only reason they were getting married after all this time was because Rachel was pregnant. But Rachel wasn't pregnant; they were getting married simply because they wanted to and I'm very glad they went public when they did, because if they had waited even a few days longer, they'd have felt that out of deference to me and my circumstances, they couldn't. But the date was set, the hotel was even booked—it was owned by a "recovery" friend of Rachel's who was giving them a good deal. Mum had been horrified when she'd heard: "A drug addict! It'll be just like the Chelsea Hotel"—and if Rachel and Luke backed out now, they knew I'd feel even worse.

"So if you like Luke, what's the problem?"

"I just wonder..."

"What?"

"I wonder does he wear underpants?"

"Jesus," I said faintly.

"And if I stand too close to him, I feel like I want to...to...I feel like I want to *bite* him."

She was staring at the ceiling, locked in some Luke-centric reverie, when Dad stuck his head round the door and said to Mum, "Phone."

She gave a little jump, then heaved herself off the bed, and when she returned, she was clearly troubled.

"That was Claire."

"How is she?"

"She's coming from London on Saturday afternoon, that's how she is."

"Is it a problem?"

"She's coming because she wants to see Rachel in person to beg her not to get married to Luke."

"Ah." Just like she'd begged me not to marry Aidan.

Maybe she'd had a nerve doing such a thing, but as it had happened, I'd definitely had my doubts. I'd known Aidan was a risk—although, funnily enough, not in the way it turned out.

Should I have listened to Claire? In the last few weeks spent sitting in the garden watching the flowers, letting my tears leak into my wounds,

I'd thought about it a lot. I mean, look at me now, just look at the state of me.

I kept asking myself if it was better to have loved and lost. But what a stupid, pointless question because it's not like I was given any choice.

"I'm not having Claire shag up this wedding on me," Mum said.

"It's not her fault." After her own union had gone so disastrously wrong, Claire began to deride marriage as "a load of bollocks." She went on about women being treated like serfs and that the "giving away" bit reduced us to nothing but chattel, being passed from the control of one man to another.

"I want this wedding to go ahead," Mum said.

"You'll have to get a stupid-looking hat. Yet another one."

"A stupid-looking hat is the least of my worries."

When Rachel arrived on Saturday morning, the first thing Mum said to her was, "Look radiant, for the love of God. Claire is coming to tell you not to get married."

"She isn't?" Rachel was amused. "I don't believe it. She did that to you, too, Anna, didn't she?" Then, realizing she'd put her foot in it, she jerked as if someone had just rammed a poker up her bum. Quickly she changed the subject. "How radiant do you want me to look?"

Mum and Helen surveyed Rachel doubtfully. Rachel's look was the low-key sleek New York downtime one: cashmere hoody, canvas cutoffs, and superlightweight trainers, the kind that fold in eight and fit in a matchbox.

"Do something with your hair," Helen suggested, and obediently Rachel unclasped a clip on top of her head and a load of heavy dark hair tumbled down her back.

"Why, Miss Walsh, you're beautiful," Mum said sourly. "Comb it! Comb it! And smile a lot."

The thing was, Rachel was already radiant. She usually was. She had an air about her, a sort of throbbing stillness, with the faintest suggestion of a secret dirty streak.

Then Mum clocked the Ring. How had she not noticed until now? "And wave that yoke around every chance you get."

"'Kay."

"Right, let's see it."

Rachel eased the sapphire ring off, and after a scrabble between Helen and Mum, Mum got it. "By Janey," she said fiercely, clenching her hand into a fist and punching the air. "I've waited a long time for this day."

Then she examined the ring in great detail, holding it up to the light and squinting, like she was a gem expert. "How much was it?"

"Never you mind."

"Go on, tell us." Helen joined in.

"No."

"It's meant to be a month's salary," Mum said. "At *least*. Anything less and he's taking you for a fool. Right! Time for us all to make our wish. Let Anna go first."

Mum gave me the ring and Rachel said, "You know the rules: turn it three times toward your heart. You can't wish for a man or money, but you can wish for a rich mother-in-law." Again, as she realized what she'd said, she went poker-up-the-bum frozen.

"It's okay," I said. "It's okay. We can't go on tiptoeing round it."

"Really?"

I nodded.

"You sure?"

I nodded again.

"Okay, let's see your makeup bag."

For a while, squashed between Rachel, Helen, and Mum, all of us strewn with cosmetics, everything seemed normal.

Then we pretended to be Claire.

"Marriage is just a form of ownership," Mum said, doing Claire's soapbox voice.

"She can't help it," Rachel said. "Her abandonment and humiliation traumatized her."

"Shut up," Helen said. "You're ruining the fun. Chattels! That's all we are, chattels!"

Even I joined in. "I thought getting married was all about wearing a lovely dress and being the center of attention."

"I hadn't thought through *any* of the gender-political implications," we all (even Rachel) chorused.

We laughed and laughed, and even though I was aware that at any moment I might descend into uncontrollable weeping, I managed to keep laughing.

When we'd finished making fun of Claire, Rachel said, "What'll we talk about now?"

Mum suddenly said, "I've been having funny dreams lately."

"About what?"

"That I'm one of those girls who's marvelous at kung fu. I can do one of those kicks where you twirl around in a circle and take the heads off of twenty fellas while you're doing it."

"Good for you." It was nice to have a mother who had fashionable dreams.

"I was wondering if I might take up Tae Bo or one of them yokes. Maybe myself and Helen could do lessons."

"What are you wearing in the dreams?" Rachel asked. "Special kung fu pajamas and stuff?"

"No." Mum sounded surprised. "Just my ordinary skirt and jumper."

"Ahhh." Rachel held up a finger in an attitude of wisdom. "That makes a lot of sense. You feel you're guardian of the family and we need protection."

"No, I just like being able to kick lots of men in one go."

"Clearly you're under almost intolerable stress. With everything that's happened with Anna, it's understandable."

"It's nothing to do with Anna! It's because I want to be a superhero, Charlie's Angel, Lara Croft self-defense woman." Mum sounded close to tears.

Rachel smiled very, very kindly—the sort of kindly smile that gets people killed—then went off upstairs for a snooze. Mum, Helen, and I lay in silence on my bed.

"You know what?" Mum broke the quiet. "There are times when I think I preferred her when she was on the drugs."

13

For our one-drink date, Aidan and I went to Lana's Place, a quiet, up-market bar, with concealed lighting and muted, sophisticated tones.

"This okay?" Aidan asked as we sat down. "Not too weird?"

"So far," I said. "Unless it's one of those places where the bar staff tap-dance at nine o'clock every night."

"Jesus." He clutched his head. "I never thought to check."

When the waitress took our order, she asked, "Should I open a tab?"

"No," I said. "I might have to leave in a hurry."

"If you turn out to be a weirdo," I said after she'd gone.

"I won't be. I'm not."

I didn't really think he would be. He was different from the speed-dating guys. But it doesn't do to be too trusting.

"We have matching scahs," he said.

"Hmm?"

"Scahs. On our right eyebrows. One each. Isn't that kind of...special?"

He was smiling: I wasn't to take this too seriously.

"How'd you get yours?" he asked.

"Playing on the stairs in my mother's high heels."

"Age what? Six? Eight?"

"Twenty-seven. No. Five and a half. I was doing a big Hollywood-musical-style thing, and I fell down the stairs and at the bottom hit my forehead on the corner of the convection heater."

"Convection heater?"

"Must be an Irish thing. Metal yoke. I needed three stitches. How did you get yours?"

"Day I was born. Accident with a midwife and a pair of scissors. I also got three stitches. Now tell me what you do when you're not being a magician's assistant."

"You want the real me?"

"If that's okay. And if you could speak quickly, I'd appreciate it. Just in case you decide to leave."

So I told him all about my life. About Jacqui, Rachel, Luke, the Real Men, Shake's air-guitar prowess, Nell, my upstairs neighbor, Nell's strange friend. I told him about work, how I loved my products, and how Lauryn had stolen my promo idea for the orange-and-arnica night cream and passed it off as her own.

"I hate her already," he said. "Is your wine okay?"

"Fine."

"Just that you're drinking it kind of slowly."

"Not as slowly as you're drinking that beer of yours."

Three times the waitress asked, "You guys okay for drinks?" and three times she was sent away with a flea in her ear.

After I'd brought Aidan up to speed on my life, he told me about his. About his upbringing in Boston, how he and Leon had lived next door to each other, and how unusual it was in their neighborhood for a Jewish boy and an Irish-American boy to be best friends. He told me about his younger brother, Kevin, and how competitive they'd been as kids. "Only two years between us, everything was a battle." He told me about his job, his roomie, Marty, and his lifelong love of the Boston Red Sox, and at some stage in the story, I finished my glass of wine.

"Just hang on while I finish my beer," he said, and with admirable restraint, he made the last inch last a full hour. Finally he couldn't avoid being done and he looked regretfully at his empty glass. "Okay, that's the one drink you signed up for. How's the plumbing in your apartment?"

I thought about it for a moment. "Perfect."

Well?" Jacqui asked, when I got in. "Nut job?"

"No. Normal."

"Vrizzzon?"

I thought about it. "Yes." There certainly had been a frisson.

"Snog?"

"Kind of."

"Tongues?"

"No." He had kissed me on the mouth. Just a brief impression of heat and firmness and then he was gone, leaving me wanting more.

"Like him?"

"Yes."

"Oh, really?" Suddenly interested. "In that case, I'd better take a look at him."

I set my jaw and held her look. "He is not a Feathery Stroker."

"I'll be the judge of that."

Jacqui's Feathery Stroker test is a horribly cruel assessment that she brings to bear on all men. It originated with some man she slept with years ago. All night long he'd run his hands up and down her body in the lightest, feathery way, up her back, along her thighs, across her stomach, and before they had sex he asked her gently if she was sure. Lots of women would have loved this: he was gentle, attentive, and respectful.

But for Jacqui it was the greatest turnoff of her life. She would have much preferred it if he'd flung her across a hard table, torn her clothes, and taken her without her explicit permission. "He kept stroking me," she said afterward, wincing with revulsion. "In this awful feathery way, like he'd read a book about how to give women what they want. Bloody Feathery Stroker, I wanted to rip my skin off."

And so the phrase came about. It suggested an effeminate quality that instantly stripped a man of all sex appeal. It was a damning way to be categorized and far better, in Jacqui's opinion, to be a drunken wife beater in a dirty vest than a Feathery Stroker.

Her criteria were wide and merciless—and distressingly random. There was no definitive list but here are some examples. Men who didn't eat red meat were Feathery Strokers. Men who used postshave balm instead of slapping stinging aftershave onto their tender skin were Feathery Strokers. Men who noticed your shoes and handbags were Feathery Strokers. (Or Jolly Boys.) Men who said pornography was exploitation of women were Feathery Strokers. (Or liars.) Men who said pornography was exploitation of men as much as women were off the scale. All straight men from San Francisco were Feathery Strokers. All academics with beards were Feathery Strokers. Men who stayed friends with their ex-girlfriends were Feathery Strokers. Especially if they called their ex-girlfriend their "ex-partner." Men who did Pilates were Feathery Strokers. Men who said, "I have to take care of myself right now" were *screaming* Feathery Strokers. (Even I'd go along with that.)

The Feathery Stroker rules had complex variations and subsections: men who gave up their seat on the subway were Feathery Strokers—*if* they smiled at you. But if they grunted "Seat," in a macho, no-eye-contact way, they were in the clear.

Meanwhile, new categories and subsections were being added all the time. She'd once decided that a man—who up until that point had been perfectly acceptable—was a Feathery Stroker for saying the word *groceries*. And some of her decrees seemed downright unreasonable—men who helped you look for lost things were Feathery Strokers, whereas no one but extreme Feathery Stroker purists could deny that it was a handy quality for a man to have.

(Funnily enough, even though Jacqui fancied Luke something ferocious, I suspected *he* was a Feathery Stroker. He didn't look like one; he looked like a tough, hard man. But beneath his leather trousers and set jaw he was kind and thoughtful—sensitive, even. And sensitivity is the FS's defining quality, his core characteristic.)

It was only when I realized how anxious I was that Jacqui might dismiss Aidan as a Feathery Stroker that I saw how much I liked him. It wasn't that Jacqui's opinions affected me, it just makes things a bit awkward if your friend despises your boyfriend. Not that Aidan was my boyfriend...

My last proper boyfriend, Sam, had been a great laugh, but one terrible night he'd got tarred with the Feathery Stroker brush for eating low-fat strawberry-cheesecake yogurt, and although it had nothing to do with me and him breaking up—we hadn't been built to last—it made life a little bumpy.

I'd never seen a Feathery Stroker being decategorized: once a Feathery Stroker, always a Feathery Stroker. Jacqui was like the Roman emperor in *Gladiator,* the thumb went up or the thumb went down, the fate of a man was decided in an instant and there was no going back.

I abhor the Feathery Stroker test, but who am I to judge because I have a "thing" about nuzzlers. Men who nuzzle. Men who badger you in a hands-free way with their face and head, nudging their head into your neck, polishing their forehead against yours, before finally kissing you—sometimes with accompanying croony noises. I don't like it at all. At all.

"So when are you seeing this possible Feathery Stroker again?" Jacqui asked.

"I said I'd give him a call when I was in the mood," I said airily.

However, he rang me two days later, said his nerves couldn't take the waiting for me to ring, and would I meet him for dinner that evening. Certainly not, I replied, he was a stalker and I had a life. Mind you, I could do the following night if he wanted...

Four nights after that dinner, we went to a jazz thing, but it wasn't too bad, the musicians took breaks after every second song—or so it seemed—so there were plenty of opportunities to talk. Then around a week later, we went to some fondue yoke.

In the meantime I went on the date with Teenie's friend (to the Cirque de Soleil, a terrible night, a circus is a circus, gussying it up with a French name changes nothing), and in theory I was open to all offers, but the only man I saw was Aidan. Nonexclusively, of course.

He always asked after everyone—Jacqui's job, Shake's air-guitar practice et al.—because even though he'd never met them, he knew so much about their lives. "It's like *The Young and the Restless,* or something," he said.

We never strayed into serious territory. I had questions—like why he hadn't rung me when I'd first given him my card or why he'd said he'd wanted me but didn't think he could have me. But I didn't ask them because I didn't want to know. Or rather, I didn't want to know Yet.

On around our fourth or fifth date, he took a breath. "Don't be scared but Leon and Dana want to meet you, like, properly. What do you think?"

I thought I'd rather remove my kidneys with a blunt spoon.

"We'll see," I said. "Funnily enough, Jacqui wants to meet you, too."

He had a little think. "Okay."

"Really? You don't have to. I told her I wouldn't ask because it might scare you away."

"No, let's go for it. You make her sound great, but will *I* like her?"

"Probably not."

"What?"

"Because," I said. "You know when two people are meeting for the first time and the other person—me—really wants them to like each other and they say, 'You'll love each other'? Their expectations are too high, so they end up being disappointed and hate each other. The key here is to lower expectations. So no, you won't like her at all."

• • •

he three of us will have dinner!" Jacqui declared.

We would not. What if she and Aidan didn't hit it off? Two to three hours making light conversation while forcing food down tense throats—aaarrrgh!

A quick postwork drink would do; nice and easy and, above all, short. I decided on Logan Hall, a big, rackety midtown bar, noisy enough to cover up any dips in conversations. It would be packed with wage slaves kicking back and letting off steam.

On the designated night, I arrived first and fought my way through many tantalizing conversations—

"...she is so fired..."

"...a bottle of Jack Daniel's in his sock, I swear it..."

"...under his desk, sucking him off..."

—and got a booth on the balcony. Jacqui was next to arrive, and eight minutes later, Aidan hadn't yet appeared.

"He's late." Jacqui sounded approving.

"There he is." He was downstairs, pushing his way through the throngs, looking a little lost. "We're here," I called.

He looked up, saw me, smiled like he really meant it, and mouthed, "Hey."

"Christ, he's gorgeous." Jacqui sounded astonished, then recovered herself. "Which counts for nothing. You could have the best-looking man in the world but if he won't eat the bar nuts because he's got a Feathery Stroker fear of germs, it's curtains."

"He'll eat the nuts," I said shortly, then stopped because here he was.

He kissed me, slid in beside me, and nodded hello to Jacqui.

"Can I get you guys a drink?" A waitress was flinging down cocktail napkins, then placed a bowl of mixed nuts midtable.

"A saketini for me," I said.

"Make it two," said Jacqui.

"Sir?" The waitress looked at Aidan.

"I've no mind of my own," he said. "Better make it three."

I wondered what Jacqui would conclude from that. Were mixed drinks too girlie? Would it have been better if he'd had a beer?

"Have a nut." Jacqui offered him the bowl.

"Hey, thanks."

I smirked at Jacqui.

It was a great night. We all got on so well that we stayed for a second drink, then a third, then Aidan insisted on picking up the bill. Again, this worried me. Would a non–Feathery Stroker have insisted we split it three ways?

"Thank you," I said. "You didn't have to do that."

"Yes, thanks," Jacqui said, and I held my breath. If he said stuff about it being a pleasure to be out with two such lovely ladies, we were sunk. But he just said, "Welcome," and surely this would count in his favor in the final Feathery Stroker shakedown?

"Better go to the ladies' room," Jacqui said. "Before the great migration home."

"Good idea." I followed her and asked, "Well? Feathery Stroker?"

"*Him?*" she exclaimed. "Definitely not."

"Good." I was pleased—delighted even—that Aidan had passed with such flying non–Feathery Stroker colors.

With warm admiration, she added, "I bet he's a hard dog to keep on the porch," and my smile wobbled just a little.

14

On Saturday afternoon, a taxi drew up outside chez Walsh. The door opened and a high-heeled spindly sandal appeared, followed by a tanned leg (slightly orange and streaky around the ankle), a short frayed denim skirt, a straining T-shirt that said MY BOYFRIEND IS OUT OF TOWN, and a fall of vanilla-striped hair. Claire had arrived.

"She's forty," Helen said, in alarm. "She looks like a tramp. She was never that bad before."

"This is much more like it, better than that bloody Margaret," Mum said, heading to the front door and welcoming Claire by calling out at the taxi, "Mutton dressed as lamb! Good girl yourself."

Grinning, Claire swung up the drive, displaying six inches of thigh that was only slightly cellulity, and into Mum's embrace.

"I've never seen you looking so well," Mum declared. "Where did you get that T-shirt? Listen, would you have a word with Margaret; she's your younger sister and she looks older than me, she's bad for my image."

"The state of you," Helen said scornfully. "Dressed like trailer trash—at forty!"

"And you know what they say about forty?" Claire put her hand on Helen's shoulder.

"Your arse hits the floor?"

"Life begins!" Claire yelled right in to her face. "Life BEGINS at forty. And forty is the new thirty. And age is only a number. And you're only as young as the person you're feeling. Now fuck off!"

She pivoted on her narrow heel and, with a dazzling smile, gathered me into arms. "Anna, how are you feeling, love?"

Worn-out, actually. Claire had only been home a matter of seconds and already the shouting, the insults, and the abrupt changes of mood had plunged me right back into my childhood.

"You look loads better," she said, then began surveying the hall, looking for Rachel. "Where is she?"

"Hiding."

"I'm not FUCKING hiding. I'm FUCKING meditating." Rachel's voice came from somewhere above us. We all looked up. She was lying on her belly on the landing, her nose poking through the banister. "You could have saved yourself the journey because I'm definitely marrying him and how do you reconcile your feminist principles with a skirt that short?"

"I'm not dressing for men, I'm dressing for me."

"Yeah." Mum sneered.

Eventually Rachel snapped out of the childish state we all seemed to have reverted to (especially Mum) and became all wise and serene again and agreed to give Claire her ear. Me, Helen, and Mum asked if we could be in on it, but Rachel said she'd prefer if we weren't and Helen lowered her eyes and said, "Obviously, we respect that." Then the minute the pair of them closeted themselves in a bedroom, the three of us raced up the stairs (well, they raced and I hobbled) and listened at the door, but apart from the occasional raised voice, "Chattels!," "Objects!," and Rachel doing her superirritating, "I understand" murmur, it quickly got boring.

Claire, having failed in her attempt to talk Rachel out of getting married, departed in high dudgeon on Sunday evening. (After first clearing out my makeup bag of the last few remaining lipsticks. As she said, she had not only her own needs to consider but those of her eleven- and five-year-old daughters, who needed to impress their peers.)

That night, Dad came to talk to me—as best he could. "Ready for the oul' journey tomorrow?"

"Ready, Dad."

"Well, um...good luck when you get back and keep up the oul' walking," he said stoutly. "It helps the oul' knee."

The number of times he said "oul" was an indication of how mortified he was: the "oul" index was at an all-time high. Dad would lie down and die for me and all his family, but he would not, *could* not, talk about emotions.

"Maybe when you get back, take up an oul' hobby," he suggested. "Keeps the oul' mind off things. Golf maybe. And that'd be good for the oul' knee, too, of course."

"Thanks, Dad, I'll think about it."

"Mind you, it needn't be golf," he amended. "It could be any oul' thing. Lady things. And we might be over at some stage to help with Rachel's oul' wedding to that hairy molly."

At the airport Mum studied the departure board, looked from me to Rachel, then exclaimed, "Isn't it a bloody shame that both of you live in New York." She put her hands on her hips and thrust her bosom at us. She'd persuaded Claire to give her her "My Boyfriend Is Out of Town" T-shirt and kept trying to draw attention to it. "Would one of you ever move somewhere else so we'd have a free place to stay. I've always liked the sound of Sydney."

"Or Miami," Dad said, then he and Mum bumped hips and sang, "Welcome to Miami!"

"Say your good-byes," Rachel said coldly.

"Ah right, of course." They looked a little red-faced, then took a deep breath and launched into a flurry of kindness and concern. "Anna, you'll be okay, pet." "You'll get over it." "Just give it time." "Come home anytime you want." "Rachel, make sure you look after her."

Even Helen said, "I wish you weren't going. Try not to go too mental."

"Write to me," I said. "Keep me posted with your screenplay and send me funny e-mails about your job."

"Okay."

But the really peculiar thing was that despite all their well-wishing and hand squeezing and encouragement, no one so much as mentioned Aidan.

15

After Jacqui had decreed that Aidan would be a hard dog to keep on the porch, she told him, "You pass. We like you. You can come out with us whenever you like."

"Er, thank you."

"In fact, tomorrow night it's Nell's strange friend's birthday. The Outhouse on Mulberry Street. Come along."

"Um, okay." He looked at me. "Okay?"

"Okay."

The love-in between Jacqui and Aidan continued the following night, when, in the heaving bar, Jacqui indicated an Adonis leaning against a wall. "Look, your man's gorgeous. On his own. Think he's waiting for someone?"

"Ask him," Aidan suggested.

"I can't just go over and ask him."

"Want me to go?"

Her eyes nearly fell out of her head. She clutched him. "Would you?"

"Sure." We watched Aidan shoulder through the crowd, say something to the Adonis, saw the Adonis say something back, then twist his head to have a look at the little knot of us. Further chat ensued, then Aidan turned to come back . . . followed by Adonis.

"Sweet Jesus," Jacqui hissed. "He's coming over."

Sadly, Adonis turned out to be called Burt and up close he had a peculiar immobile kind of face and no interest in Jacqui, but as a result, Jacqui thought Aidan was the cat's pajamas.

Great stuff. Everyone getting on well. However, because Aidan had come out with my friends twice, I was obliged to meet Leon and Dana and I was not looking forward to being judged and found wanting. But—

unlike the last time I'd met them—they didn't treat me like a cardboard-cutout woman, and we had an unexpectedly (unexpected on my part, anyway) nice time.

Then, a few days later, the Real Men had a Halloween party, where they (the Real Men) dressed up as themselves. I was standing around wondering whether Aidan was going to show when someone appeared in front of me, wearing a sheet over his head and going, "Wooooooh!"

"Right back at you," I said.

Then the person lifted the sheet and exclaimed, "Hey, Anna, it's me!"

It was Aidan; we shrieked with surprise and delight. (Not that it was that surprising to see each other, but anyway.) I launched myself at him and he grabbed me, his arms around my back, our legs tangled together, and a jolt of want leaped from me. He felt it, too, because his eyes changed, instantly becoming serious. We held the gaze for a timeless moment, then Nell's strange friend stuck a pitchfork in Aidan's arse and broke the spell.

At this stage I'd seen Aidan about seven or eight times and not once had he tried to jump me. Every date we'd gone on, we'd had just one kiss. It had improved from quick and firm to slower and more tender, but one kiss was as good as it got.

Had I wanted more? Yes. Was I curious about his restraint? Yes. But I kept it all under control and something had held me back from getting Jacqui in a headlock every time I came home from an unjumped-on night out and tearfully agonizing: What's his problem? Doesn't he fancy me? Is he gay? Christian? One of those True Love Waits gobshites? Feathery Stroker in disguise?

Aidan rang the day after the Halloween party and said, "Last night was fun."

"Glad you enjoyed it. Listen, on Saturday night, Shake's in the local heat of the air-guitar championship. We're all going along to laugh. Like to come?"

A pause. "Anna, can we...talk?"

Oh Christ.

"Don't get me wrong. I really like Jacqui and Rachel and Luke and Shake and Leon and Dana and Nell and Nell's strange friend. But I'd like to see you, just the two of us?"

"When?"

"Soon as possible? Tonight?"

A funny feeling started fluttering in the pit of my stomach.

It increased when Aidan said, "There's a nice little Italian on West Eighty-fifth."

There was more than a nice little Italian on West Eighty-fifth. Aidan lived on West Eighty-Fifth.

"Eight o'clock?" he suggested.

"Okay."

We got through our food superspeedily; an hour and a half after we'd arrived, we were at the coffee and kicking-out stage. How had that happened?

Because our minds weren't on our food, that's how. I was very, very nervous—although I shouldn't have been. Shortly after we'd come to New York, me and Jacqui had done a class in seduction techniques. "We're out of our depth in this city," Jacqui had said. "New York women are very experienced. If you and me can't pole-dance we'll never get blokes."

I had only gone along for the laugh. My feeling was that if a man refused to sleep with me because I wouldn't be his private dancer, he could so forget it. However, the class had been more interesting than I'd expected and I'd picked up a couple of handy hints on how to undress. (When you take your bra off, you should wave it above your head like you're trying to lasso a runaway steer, and after you slide out of your knickers, you must touch your toes and waggle your bum right in meladdo's face.)

So, in theory, I could pull one or two sexual tricks out of the box. And yet when Aidan twirled my hair around one of his fingers and said, "Come back to my place. See who won *The Apprentice* before you embark on your long journey downtown," all the little hairs on the back of my neck stood to attention and I thought that I might varmint.

When he let us into his apartment, I stood in the hall, listening. "Where's Marty tonight?"

"Out."

"Out? How out?"

A hesitation. "Very out."

"Hmm." I pushed open a door and walked into a bedroom. I took in the neat crisp bed linen, the candles dotted about, the meadow-fresh smell. "This yours?"

"Um, yes." He followed me in.

"And it always looks this good?"

Pause. "No."

I flicked my eyes at him and we laughed nervously. Then his expression changed to something far more intense and my stomach plunged. I moved around his room, picking things up and putting them down.

The candles on his nightstand were Candy Grrrl ones. "Oh, Aidan, I could have got you these for free."

"Anna?" he said softly. He was right beside me, I hadn't heard him approach. I looked up.

"Fuck the candles," he said.

He slid his hand along my neck, under my hairline, sending electric shivers down my back, brought his face to mine, and kissed me. Tentatively at first, then suddenly we really went for it and I was overwhelmed by his nearness, the roughness of his hair, the heat of his body through the thin cotton of his shirt. I moved my thumb along the leanness of his jawline, my fingers down the line of his spine, my palm against the jut of his hip bone.

His shirt buttons had opened and there was his stomach, flat, muscled, a line of dark hair, leading downward . . . I watched my hand pop the button on his jeans. It was a reflex action, anyone would have done it.

Then we froze; now what?

My hand was shaking slightly. I looked up at him. He was watching me, his expression beseeching, and slowly I found myself lowering the zip, the details of his erection visible against the straining denim.

Lean flank, tiny bottom, a line of muscles along the back of his thighs, he was even more delicious than I'd imagined. Leaning over me, his shoulders flexing, he unwrapped me like I was a present. "Anna, you're so beautiful," he said over and over. "You're so beautiful."

His erection felt like silk, soft and hard between my thighs, and he kissed me everywhere from my eyelids to the backs of my knees.

All my training went by the board. I'd really meant to twirl my bra above my head but in the heat of the moment I forgot. I'd other stuff on my mind: I rarely come with men the first time I'm with them, but the things he was doing to me, the slow manipulation of his penis against me, inside me, the heat and the need and the pleasure building, swelling me...

We picked up speed and I wanted more.

"Faster," I begged. "Aidan, I think I'm going to..." He was moving faster and faster into me, and I was still building, building, moving toward the top, then after a second of pure nothingness, I exploded, exquisite pleasure radiating outward and inward, afterwaves throbbing through me.

Then he was coming, his fingers tangled in my hair, his eyes closed, his face a picture of anguish, saying my name. "Anna, Anna, Anna."

For a long time afterward, neither of us spoke. Slick with sweat and knocked out by pleasure, we were flattened against the sheets. I was having little conversations with myself in my head: *That was amazing. That was incredible.* But I said nothing; anything would sound like a cliché.

"Anna?"

"Mmm?"

He rolled over on top of me and said, "That was one of the best things that has ever happened to me."

But it wasn't just good sex. I felt like I knew him. I felt like he loved me. We went to sleep spooned together, his arm tight around my stomach, my hand resting on his hip.

• • •

I awoke to the sound of a cup clattering beside my ear. "Coffee," he said. "Time to get up."

I pulled myself out of my blissful slumber and tried to sit up.

"You're already dressed," I said, surprised.

"Yeah." He wouldn't meet my eye. He sat on the foot of the bed, pulling on his socks, his face bent downward, his back to me, and suddenly I was wide-awake.

I'd been here before and I knew the rules: keep it light, don't push him, let him do his elastic-band thing.

Well, fuck that. I deserved better.

I sipped my coffee and said, "You haven't forgotten tomorrow night? Shake's air-guitar stuff? You still coming?"

Without turning to look at me, he mumbled into his knees, "I won't be around this weekend."

I forgot to breathe. I felt like I'd been slapped. Looked like I should have done the toe-touching, bum-waggling thing after all.

"Gotta go to Boston," he went on. "Stuff to sort out."

"Whatever."

"Whatever?" He turned around. He looked surprised.

"Yes, Aidan, whatever. You sleep with me, you go weird on me, and now, all of a sudden, you're not around this weekend. *Whatever.*"

His face drained of color. "Anna, yeah, look. I guess there's no right time for this." Something bad was coming. The end of me and Aidan. Just when I'd really started to like him. Bums.

"What?" I asked sharply.

"But how would you feel about, you know, you and me, being exclusive?"

"Being *exclusive?*"

Being exclusive was nearly like getting engaged.

"Yeah, just you and me. I don't know if you're still seeing other guys..."

I shrugged. Neither did I. And there was a much more important question: "You still seeing other girls?"

A pause. "That's why I need to go to Boston."

On the flight from Dublin to New York, my injuries caused a few nudges, but nothing like the stir they'd caused on the outward journey. Especially as Rachel, my fierce protector, challenged and psychoanalyzed any other passenger who stared too hard at me.

"Why are you so fascinated with mutilation?" she asked angrily of one person who kept turning around in his seat to look at me. "What are you afraid of?"

"Stop it," I said to her. "He's only seven."

Once we'd landed and got our luggage and gone outside, I had a bit of a freaker about getting into a taxi. I was literally trembling with fear, but Rachel said, "This is New York City, you'll need to use cabs all the time. You're going to have to get back on the horse at some stage. Why not do it now while I'm here to take care of you?"

I had no choice: I either got in the cab or got the plane back to Ireland. With knees that felt watery with dread, I got in.

On the drive Rachel talked about things—stuff that had nothing to do with anything, but was diverting all the same. Celebrities who'd lost weight. Gained weight. Hit their hairdresser. It kept me calm.

Then we crossed the bridge into Manhattan. I was almost surprised to find that it was still there, still going on with its business, still being Manhattan, regardless of what had happened to me.

Then we were in my neighborhood, the so-called Mid-Village.

(Between the charm of the West Village and the edginess of the East Village, Mid-Village was a realtor's term to try to give character to a place
that didn't really have much. But with Manhattan rents being what they
were, me and Aidan were unimaginably grateful to live there.)

And then we were outside our apartment building and the shock of
seeing it still standing there made my stomach lurch so much I was afraid
I'd puke.

Even with Rachel carrying my luggage, climbing up the three flights
of stairs on my bad knee was a bit of a challenge, but as soon as I put my
key in the lock—and Rachel insisted that it was I who opened the door
and not her—I sensed someone else in the apartment and I almost jack-
knifed with relief: he was still here. *Oh, thank God.* Only to discover that
the person was Jacqui. Thoughtfully, she'd come along so I wouldn't be
upset by arriving at an empty place, but my disappointment was so acute
that I had to check every room, just in case.

Not that there were many rooms to check. There was the living room
with a cramped kitchen annex carved out of it, a half bath (i.e., a shower
and no bath), and at the back our gloomy bedroom with its sliver of glass
looking into the stairwell (funds hadn't stretched to a proper window).
But we'd made it cozy: a lovely big bed with a carved headboard, a couch
wide enough for us to lie on side by side, and vital accessories like scented
candles and a wide-screen TV.

I hobbled from room to room, I even looked behind the shower curtain,
but he wasn't there. At least the photos of him were still on the walls; some
"thoughtful" soul hadn't taken it upon themselves to get rid of them.

Rachel and Jacqui pretended nothing strange was happening, then
Jacqui smiled and I stared at her in shock. "What happened to
your . . . teeth?"

"Present from Lionel 9." Some rap star. "He decided at four in the
morning to get his teeth gold-plated. I found a dentist willing to do it.
Lionel was so grateful he gave me the gift of two gold incisors. I hate
them," she said. "I look like a bling Dracula. But I can't get them removed
until he's left town."

Rachel clapped her hands together in a parody of good humor and declared, "Food! It's important to eat. What'll we have?"

"Pizza?" Jacqui asked me.

"I don't mind. I'm not the one with gold-plated teeth." I gave her the Andretti's leaflet. "Will you order?"

"Better if you do," Rachel said.

I looked at her bleakly.

"Sorry," she said awkwardly. "But it is."

"When I order they never bring the salad."

"If that's how it has to be..."

So I rang Andretti's, and as I predicted, they forgot the salad.

"I told you," I said with weary triumph.

But neither of them rose to the challenge, and as soon as we'd finished eating, Jacqui produced a twelve-inch-high heap of envelopes. "Your mail."

I took the bundle, put it in the closet, and closed the door tight. I'd look at it sometime.

"Er...don't you want to open it?"

"Not right now."

A tricky silence.

"I've just got here," I said defensively. "Give me a chance."

It was strange to see the two of them united against me. It's not that they didn't like each other—not exactly—but Rachel's motto was "The unexamined life isn't worth living," while Jacqui's was "We're not here for a long time, we're here for a good time."

They had never bitched to me about each other, but if they were to, Rachel would say that Jacqui was too shallow and Jacqui would say that Rachel needed to lighten up.

The crux of their differences was Luke: if pressed, Jacqui would admit that she thought Luke was wasted on Rachel, with her fondness for early nights.

However, Rachel once let slip that the only vice she had left was sex, which instantly made me imagine her and Luke up to all sorts of kinky stuff. But that's not something you want to think too much about, not about anyone.

After further silence, I said, "So! Jacqui, what's happening with you? Are you over Buzz yet?"

Buzz was Jacqui's ex-boyfriend. He had a year-round tan and tons of confidence and money. He was also incredibly cruel—he used to leave Jacqui sitting by herself for hours in bars and restaurants, then he'd tell her she'd got the time or the venue wrong.

He would argue that pink was green just for the hell of it, tried to make Jacqui have a threesome with a prostitute, and drove a red Porsche—so pitifully naff—and made the guy at the garage clean the tires with a toothbrush.

Jacqui used to keep saying what a bastard he was and that she'd had it with him; no, she'd *really* had it with him this time; but she always gave him one more chance. Then he'd broken up with her on New Year's Eve and she'd been devastated.

Jacqui never got a chance to answer me. As if I hadn't spoken, Rachel said, "There are lots of messages on your machine. We thought you might like someone here when you're listening to them."

"Why not?" I said. "Hit it."

There were thirty-seven messages. All kinds of people had come out of the woodwork.

"Anna, Anna, Anna..."

"Who is *that*?"

"...It's Amber. I just heard..."

"Amber Penrose? It's forever since I've heard from her. Delete!"

"But won't you listen to her message?" asked Jacqui, who was manning the machine.

"No need. I could write the script. Look, I'll remember everyone who rang," I said. "I'll get back to them. Delete! Next!"

"Anna," someone whispered. "I've just heard and I can't bel—"

"Yeah, yeah, yeah. Delete!"

Rachel muttered something. I caught the word *denial*. "At least write down their names."

"I don't have a pen."

"Here." She passed me a pen and a notebook that had magically materialized on her person, and obediently I wrote down the names of everyone who had called, and the trade-off was that I didn't have to listen to their full commiserations.

Then Jacqui and Rachel made me switch on my computer and retrieve all my e-mails: there were eighty-three. I scanned the senders' addresses; I was only interested in getting an e-mail from one person and it wasn't there.

"Read them."

"No need. I'll get round to them. Now look: I'm sorry, girls, I need my sleep, I've got work in the morning."

"What!" Rachel yelped. "Don't be so insane. There's no *way* you're well enough either physically or emotionally to return to work. You're in total denial about what's happened to you. You need serious help. I mean serious!"

She went on and on and I just nodded and said calmly, "I'm sorry you feel that way." Like I'd seen her do to people who were pissed off with her. After a while, she abruptly stopped ranting, looked at me through eyes narrowed with suspicion, and said, "What's your game?"

"Rachel," I said, "thank you for all your kindness, but the only way this will be okay is if I carry on like normal."

"Don't go to work."

"I have to."

"Don't go to work."

"I've already told them to expect me."

A face-off ensued. Rachel was very strong-willed, but at that moment, so was I. I sensed her start to buckle, so I seized my advantage. "Luke will be wondering where you are."

I began edging them toward the exit, but I swear to God, I thought they'd never leave. At the door, Rachel insisted on delivering a speech.

She even cleared her throat. "Anna, I can't know exactly the hell you're going through, but when I admitted I was an addict, I felt like my life was over. How I got through it was, I decided, I won't think about forever, I won't even think about next week, I'll just think about getting through today. Break it down into small pieces and you might find that you can do for one day something that, if you thought about having to do it for the rest of your life, would kill you."

"Thank you, yes, lovely." *Get out.*

"I put that toy-dog thing in your bed," Jacqui said. "To keep you company."

"Dogly? Thank you."

As soon as I was sure they were really gone and wouldn't be leaping back in the door to check on me, I did what I'd been dying to do for hours—I rang Aidan's cell phone. It went straight to voice mail, but even so, it was such a relief to hear his voice that my stomach turned to water.

"Aidan," I said. "Baby, I'm back in New York. Back in our apartment, so you know where to find me. I hope you're okay. I love you."

Then I wrote him an e-mail.

To: Aidan_maddox@yahoo.com
From: Magiciansgirl1@yahoo.com
Subject: I'm back

Dear Aidan,
It feels funny writing to you like this. I don't think I've ever writ-ten you a proper letter before. Hundreds and hundreds of little e-mails, yes, to say who was bringing dinner home and what time would we meet and that sort of thing, but never like this.

I'm back in our apartment but maybe you already know that. Rachel and Jacqui came over—Jacqui got a present of two gold teeth from a client—and we had pizzas from Andretti's. They forgot the salad, like always, but gave us an extra Dr Pepper.

Please be okay, please don't be frightened, please come and
see me or get in touch somehow, I love you.
Anna

I read back over what I'd written. Was it light enough? I didn't want
him to know how worried I was, because whatever he was going through
was bound to be difficult enough without me adding to it.

Decisively I hit send with my index finger and a red-hot shock
shot from my regrowing nail up my arm. Christ, I'd have to go easy on
the grand-gesture-style typing with the two fingers with banjaxed nails.
The pain was enough to make me queasy and momentarily it distracted
me from the sudden wave of feeling that enveloped me. Something like
rage or sadness at not being able to protect Aidan, but it was so fleeting it
was gone before I could grasp it.

In the bedroom, tucked into Aidan's side of the bed, was Dogly, the
toy dog he'd had since he was a baby. He had long swingy ears, syrupy
eyes, and an eager, adoring expression, and his caramel-colored fur was
so thick it was more like a sheep's fleece. Not in the first flush of youth—
Aidan was thirty-five, after all—but not bad for his age. "He had some
work done," Aidan said once. "Eyes lifted, collagen injection to plump
out his tail, a little liposuction on his ears."

"Well, Dogly," I said. "This is a bit of a disaster."

It was time for my last batch of pills of the day and for once I was
grateful for the mood-altering stuff—the antidepressants, painkillers,
and sleeping tablets. Coming back to New York was harder than I had
expected and I needed all the help I could get.

But even filled with enough mellowing stuff to knock out an elephant,
I didn't want to get into bed. Then, like an electric shock, I noticed his
gray sweatshirt on our bedroom chair, as if he'd just pulled it off and
flung it there. Cautiously, I picked it up and sniffed it and enough of his
smell still lingered to make me dizzy. I buried my face in it and the intensity of his presence and absence made me choke.

It didn't have the special lovely smell of his neck, or of his groin, where everything was stronger, sweeter, and more feral, but it was enough to get me into bed. I closed my eyes and the pills pulled me into an undertow of sleep, but in that halfway state which precedes unconsciousness, one of those horrible ragged chinks opened up and I caught a glimpse of the enormity of what had happened. I was back in New York, he wasn't here, and I was alone.

I slept heavily and dreamlessly, probably thanks to the pills. I rose through layers of consciousness, pausing at each one until I was ready to move on—like a scuba-diving ascent: preventing the emotional bends of a sudden shocking burst through the surface of sleep—so that I was quite peaceful by the time I opened my eyes. He wasn't with me and I understood that.

The first thing I did was switch on the computer, checking my e-mail, hoping for a reply from him. The indicator said there were five messages and I stopped breathing, my heart pounding with desperate hope. The first was an offer for tickets to a Justin Timberlake concert. Then one from Leon saying he'd heard I was back and to call him, one from Claire saying she was thinking of me, one offering to enhance my penis size, and, finally, a blocked virus. But from Aidan, nada.

Disconsolate, I trooped off to shower and was shocked to find that I could barely wet my body, never mind my hair. Have you ever tried to have a shower without getting one arm wet? For the past eight or nine weeks everything had been done for me, so much so that I hadn't noticed how incapacitated I was. I had another of those nasty chinks of clarity: I was way out of my depth here, on every level.

I reached for my shower gel and a memory hit me like a blow; it was No Rough Stuff, the new Candy Grrrl exfoliator. That last day, all those weeks ago, I'd been test-driving it. I'd given myself a good scrub with the lime- and pepper-scented grains, and when I got out of the shower, I'd asked Aidan, "Do I smell nice?" Obediently he'd sniffed me. "Great. Although you smelled even nicer ten minutes ago."

"But ten minutes ago I only smelled like me."

"Exactly."

I had to hold tight on to the sink until the feeling passed, clenching with my one good hand until my knuckles went as bone white as the enamel.

Time to get dressed. My already low heart dipped a little lower and Dogly watched sympathetically. It was the fecking kookiness, hanger after hanger of it, plus rack after rack of colorful shoes and bags—and, worst of all, the hats. I was facing into my thirty-third birthday, far too old for this. What I needed was a promotion, because the farther up the feeding scale you went, the more you were allowed to wear suits.

To: Aidan_maddox@yahoo.com
From: Magiciansgirl1@yahoo.com
Subject: Kooky girl goes back to work

Today's outfit—black suede boots, pink fishnets, black crepe-de-chine vintage dress with white polka dots, pink three-quarter-length coat (also vintage), and butterfly bag. Silly hat, I hear you ask—oh, but of course: a black beret at an angle. All in all, a little subdued, but I should get away with it today.

I would really like to hear from you.
Your girl, Anna

He always got a kick out of my work uniform. The irony was that he tried to subvert his conservative suits with funky ties and socks—Warhol prints, pink roses, cartoon superheros—and I was desperate to be somber and tailored.

While I was online, I had an idea: I'd read his horoscope to see if I could get any clue about how he was. Stars Online for Scorpio said:

> **Usually you're philosophical about change, but recently even you have been overwhelmed by events. Many of the month's dramas climax around Thursday's eclipsed Full Moon. Until then, investigate everything, but make no commitments.**

I was concerned about the "even you have been overwhelmed" stuff. I felt helpless, then angry. I wished it had said something comforting, so I went back a couple of pages and clicked on Today's Stars.

> **The sun's shining down on that part of your chart related to pure self-indulgence. You'll feel like baring your hedonistic streak today. So long as it's legal and doesn't hurt anyone else in the process, feel free to have fun!**

I didn't like that either. I didn't want him baring his hedonistic streak with anyone other than me. I clicked on Hot Scopes!

> **Resist the temptation to resuscitate dying plans, relation- ships, or passions. You're beginning a new cycle and over the coming weeks you'll learn about all manner of exciting offers!**

Ah, here! I didn't want him learning about all manner of exciting of- fers if I wasn't one of them. I made myself disconnect—there was a dan- ger that I could sit here all day until I found the horoscope that made me feel better—left another quick message on his cell, and finally left the apartment. Out on the street, I found I was shaking. I wasn't used to go- ing to work on my own; we always got the subway together—he got off at

Thirty-fourth Street, I carried on up to Fifty-ninth. And had New York always been this loud? All those cars beeping and people shouting and buses' brakes screeching, and this was only Twelfth Street. How noisy was it going to be uptown?

I began walking toward the subway, then stopped as I considered what it would be like down there. Steps up and down everywhere; my knee was aching, far worse than it had done in Dublin. I'd only taken half of my usual dose of painkillers because I didn't want to start nodding off in meetings and it was a shock to discover how much pain the painkillers had actually been killing.

But how else was I going to get to work? I shrank from getting into a cab. I'd coped with taking one from the airport because Rachel had been with me, but I was petrified at the thought of being in one alone.

Riveted by indecision, trapped whichever way I jumped, I considered my options. Go back to the apartment and spend the day there on my own? That was the least palatable.

After standing on the sidewalk and getting curious looks from passersby for an indeterminate time, I watched myself hail a cab and, in a dreamlike state, get in. Could I really be doing this? The fear was profound; saucer-eyed, I watched all the other cars, flinching and shrinking whenever any of them came too close, as if my scrutiny alone would prevent them from driving into me. Suddenly, with a bang to my chest that nearly stopped my heart, I saw Aidan. He was sitting on a bus that had paused at an intersection. It was only a sidelong view, but it was definitely him, his hair, his cheekbones, his nose. All the city noise retreated, leaving only a muzzy, staticky buzzing, and as I clawed for cash and reached for the door handle, the bus surged forward. In a panic, I twisted around and stared out the back window.

"Sir!" I said to the cabdriver, but we were moving also and already too far gone. It was too late to turn and the traffic going back downtown was stuck solid. I lost my nerve: I'd never catch him.

"Yeah?"

"Nothing."

I was trembling violently: the shock of seeing him. It didn't make sense for him to be on that bus—he was going completely the wrong way, if he was going to work.

It couldn't have been him. It must have been someone who looked like him. Really like him. But what if it *was* him? What if this had been my one chance to see him?

The security guards couldn't believe I was back. No employee of McArthur on the Park had ever taken such a long time off work before—like *never,* not for holidays, not for "going to Arizona" because most people who "went to Arizona" didn't come back to work. Weren't *let* back.

"Hey, Morty, Irish Anna's back."

"She is? Irish Anna, we thought they'd sacked your ass. And whatcha *do* to your face?"

They delicately high-fived my bandaged right hand, and I joined the throngs of people streaming to the banks of elevators. I squashed into the crammed metal box, everyone holding their coffee and avoiding one another's eyes.

On the thirty-eighth floor, the elevator doors opened with a silent swish. I struggled to the front and popped out like a pinball. The cream carpet was thick and soft, the very air smelled expensive, and an unseen voice said, "Welcome back, Anna." I nearly jumped out of my skin. It was Lauryn Pike, my manager, and she looked like she'd been standing there all night, waiting. Tentatively she extended her hand, like she was thinking of touching me compassionately, then thought better of it. I was glad. I didn't want anyone touching me, I didn't want to be comforted.

"You look great!" she said. "Really rested. Your hair has grown. So! Ready to go, yeah?"

I looked terrible, but if she acknowledged that, she might have to make allowances for me.

Right, about Lauryn. She was scrawny skinny, always cold, had very hairy arms and a nasty brown cardigan, nearly as hairy as her arms, which she wore in the office, always dragging and wrapping it about her undernourished body in an attempt to get warm. She burned with a manic intensity and had very poppy eyes, like a Latter-day Saint. (Or maybe she just had an overactive thyroid.) If I'd been a magazine beauty editor and I saw Lauryn coming to pitch me a Candy Grrrl piece, I'd hide under my desk until she'd gone.

Despite that, Lauryn got *loads* of coverage. Likewise with men: regardless of her bulgy-eyed boniness, and knobbly elbows and lumpy knees, she often got taken away for weekends to the islands by lookers. Figure that one. (As we say around here.)

I can't understand it because it's not as if it's easy to find men in New York, even for the un-poppy-eyed woman: it's comparable to ragged bands of women tramping wearily through a smoking, destroyed, post-apocalyptic cityscape, foraging for the smallest bits of usable stuff, like the people in *Mad Max* had to do.

And it's not as if Lauryn was such a great person. Her job mattered to her far too much, and if someone else succeeded, it was as if she'd failed. She threw an empty Snapple bottle at the wall when Lancôme's Superlash mascara got coverage in *Lucky* the same month it went head-to-head with Candy Grrrl's Flutter-by.

All of a sudden I was gripped by terrible fear that I wouldn't be able to handle being back at work, but I said, "I'm good to go, Lauryn."

"Good! Because we have, like, a *lot* happening right now."

"Just bring me up to speed."

"Sure. And you let me know, Anna, if you can't cope." She didn't mean this in a kind way. She meant for me to let her know if she needed to sack me. "And when will that . . . thing . . . on your face be better?" They hate physical imperfection round here. "And your arm? When will it be out of the cast?"

Then she noticed my bandaged fingers. "What's that all about?"

"Missing nails."

"Jesus H," she said. "I'm gonna throw up."

She sat down and breathed deeply but didn't throw up. In order to throw up, it's necessary to have something in your stomach and there was scant chance of that having happened.

"You gotta do something about them. Go see if you can get them fixed."

"Yes, but...okay."

A flash of silver caught my attention—it was Teenie! Wearing a silver boiler suit, tucked into orange, vinyl knee boots. Today her hair was blue. To match her glittery blue lips. "Anna!" she said. "You're back! Ooh, your hair is pretty. It's gotten so long." Together we discreetly sidled away from Lauryn and Teenie said quietly, "Sweetie, how're you doing?"

"Okay."

"You are?" She quirked a blue, glittery eyebrow at me.

I slid a glance at Lauryn; she was far away enough not to hear. "Okay, maybe not exactly, but, Teenie, the only way I'll get through this is if we pretend everything is the way it always was."

I couldn't have anyone's sympathy, sympathy meant that it had actually happened.

"Lunch?"

"Can't. Lauryn says I've got to get my nails fixed."

"What's up with them?"

"They're missing. But they're growing back as fast as they can."

"Eew."

"Yes, well," I said, going to my desk.

This was the longest I'd ever been away from my job and things felt familiar, yet very different. The temp—or temps—had rearranged my stuff, and someone had put my photo of Aidan in a drawer, which made me briefly but corrosively angry. I took it out and banged it down on the spot it always stood on. And they said *I* was in denial?

"Oh my gosh, Anna, you're back!" It was Brooke Edison. Brooke was twenty-two and loaded and lived with Mommy and Daddy in a triplex on the UES (Upper East Side). She took a car service to work every single day—not the subway, not even a cab, but an air-conditioned Lincoln Town Car with bottled water and a polite driver. Brooke didn't actually need to work, she was just filling in time until someone put a massive rock on her finger and moved her to Connecticut and bought her a station wagon and three perfect, highly gifted children.

She'd been hired as the Candy Grrrl junior, the person who did the heavy lifting, like stuffing envelopes with samples for the magazines. But she was always having to leave work early or come in late because she was attending charity benefits or having dinner with the chairman of the Guggenheim, or getting a ride in David Hart's helicopter to the Hamptons.

She was sweet, obliging, and quite intelligent, and did everything perfectly. When she *did* it. Which, like I say, wasn't that often. We picked up the slack a lot.

Ariella kept her on the staff because she knew *everyone*—people were always being her godmother or her dad's best friend or her old piano teacher.

She did her private-girls'-school-in-Europe walk over to my desk, swinging her thick, glossy, naturally beautiful hair, which glowed with privileged rich person's health. Her skin was fantastic and she never wore makeup, which would have been a sacking offense for me and Teenie, but not for her. Same with her clothes: Brooke wasn't even remotely kooky and no one said a thing. Today she wore wide-cut pants in greige cashmere and a dinky little fawn sweater, also in cashmere. I didn't think she knew that there were other fabrics and a rumor persisted that she'd never bought anything from Zara *in her life*. She shopped at the three Bs— Bergdorf, Barneys, and Bendel, the golden triangle—and get this: sometimes her *dad* bought her clothes. He took his "baby girl" on weekend sprees and said, "Make your father happy, let me buy you this vintage bag/embroidered Japanese coat/Gina sandals."

This is not conjecture, this is actual reportage of a real event, because one Saturday Franklin was in Barneys spending money on his hot young (penniless) boy, Henk, in the hope that he wouldn't leave him. Next thing Franklin spots Brooke and Old Man Edison (who is richer than God) looking at Chloé bags. At first Franklin thought the old guy was Brooke's boyfriend, and when he heard the desk clerk say, "Hey there, Mr. Edison," he nearly puked. He said it was pedo stuff, nearly like incest. I don't think he really meant it, Franklin is simply phenomenally mean-spirited. He hates everyone, except Henk, and sometimes I think he hates him, too. (Henk is Franklin's trophy wife—a skinny, sly-eyed boy, with jeans hanging indecently superlow, displaying a narrow, sinewy abdomen. His hair is highlighted cream, silver, and honey and he gets it cut in a mad, sticky-up do at Frédéric Fekkai. He doesn't have a job, probably because his hair care takes up so much of his time. Franklin bankrolls all of this primping, but occasionally Henk stays away nights and goes downtown to play with his rentboy chums. I really like Henk, he's very, very funny, but if he was my boyfriend, I'd be on sixteen Xanax a day.)

In addition to the nonstop cashmere, Brooke always wore at least five different items from Tiffany. Mind you, everyone wore stuff from Tiffany. You had to. I think you'd be asked to leave New York if you didn't.

She extended her hand (with short, neat, clear-glossed nails), didn't even flicker as she scanned my scar, and said with genuine-sounding sincerity, "Anna, I am so sorry about what happened."

"Thank you."

Then she left; she didn't labor it—an awkward situation, handled just right. Brooke always got everything just right. She was the most appropriate-aware person I had ever met. She also knew exactly what to wear in every eventuality and it was already in her wardrobe. In triplicate. She inhabited a world with strong rules and she had the money to obey them. I often wondered what it must be like to be her.

Brooke had an Identi-Kit chum, Bonnie Bacall, who "worked" on

Freddie & Frannie, another in-house brand. They were BFFs (best friends forever) and both girls were actually very sweet, and if sometimes they were hurtful or cruel, it wasn't because they meant to be. Not like Lauryn.

"Okay, people," Lauryn called. "Now that Anna has finished her conversations, could you all possibly spare me a few moments of your time for a Candy Grrrl briefing." (Said sarcastically.)

All day long, everyone was looking at me—but never directly. When I met girls from other brands in the corridors or the washrooms, they gave me slanting, sidelong glances, and as soon as I left I knew they were whispering about me. Like it was all my fault. Or contagious. I tried defusing things by smiling at them, but then they looked away quickly, a little horrified.

Luckily, because this was New York, no one really gave a shite. For a short while I'd be an object of curiosity, then they'd lose interest.

Midmorning, Franklin took me into Ariella's inner sanctum so I could thank her for keeping my job open. One entire wall was filled with photos of her with famous people.

In her "trademark" powder-blue power suit, she acknowledged my gratitude by nodding slowly, her eyes half closed. There was nothing more disconcerting than Ariella in her Capo di Tutti Capi mode.

"Maybe sometime you can do something for me." Either she had a permanent sore throat or she deliberately put on a hoarse Don Corleone–style mumble. "I need a favor, I can count on you?"

I work very hard for you, I wanted to say. *Before all this happened, I got more coverage than any of your other publicists and I intend that that will be the case again. You didn't pay me for one second while I was away and it's not like I took off on a whim.*

"Of course, Ariella."

"And get a haircut."

She nodded at Franklin in his immaculate suit: the signal to take me away.

Out in the hallway, Franklin circled a manicured thumb between his eyebrows, where his frown lines would be, if they weren't being Botoxed into submission every six weeks. "Jesus, God," he sighed. "Is it just me or does she seem a little . . . *psychotic* to you?"

"No more than usual. But I might not be the best judge right now."

He did his sympathetic face. "I know, baby cakes. So how ya doing?"

"Okay." There was no point in saying any more. He had zero interest in anyone else's problems. But he was totally up-front about it, which meant I didn't mind. "How've *you* been? How's Henk?"

"Bleeding me dry and breaking my heart. Got a joke for you. What's the difference between your dick and your bonus?"

"Henk will blow your bonus?"

"Got it."

"You get a bonus?"

"Er . . ." He patted me on the shoulder and pulled the shutters down on his face. "You'll be okay, kiddo."

I'd have to be.

Just because Franklin was hilariously funny and willing to talk about his personal life didn't make him my friend. He was my boss. In fact, he was my boss's boss. (Lauryn reported to him.)

"And you heard Ariella. Get a haircut. Go see someone at Perry K."

Just what I needed: ridiculous high-maintenance hair when barely one of my hands was operational.

At lunchtime I tried to get my nails done, but when I took off the bandages and revealed them to the manicurist she went green and said they were far too short for acrylic ones to be fitted. When I returned with the bad news Lauryn behaved as if I was lying.

"The girl told me to come back in a month," I protested weakly. "I'll get them done then."

"What-ev-er. Eye Eye Captain—I want your thoughts on the campaign by weekend."

When Lauryn said she wanted "my thoughts," she actually meant that she wanted a fully realized campaign, complete with press releases, spreadsheets, budgeting, and a signed contract from Scarlett Johansson saying she was so thrilled to be the new face of Candy Grrrl that she'd do it for free.

"I'll see what I can do." I dashed to my desk and started speed-reading through the Eye Eye Captain data.

It wasn't until late afternoon that I checked my e-mails. Unlike my home e-mail, my work stuff had been opened and answered. I scrolled back through them, doing a crash course in catch-up. A lot were from beauty editors asking for products which the greedy cows would probably never give coverage to, or from people I'd been putting campaigns together with, or from George (Mr. Candy Grrrl) with fool ideas of his own. Then my heart nearly jumped out of my mouth: this was what I'd been waiting for. In bold black type—meaning it was new and unread— was an e-mail from Aidan.

To: AnnaW@CandyGrrrl.com
From: Aidan_maddox@yahoo.com
Subject: Tonight

Just tried to call, but you're on the line. Wanted to catch you before I left. See you tonight. Nothing to report, just wanted to tell you that I love you and will love you forever and ever, no matter what happens.

A xxxxxxxx

I read it again. What did it mean? He was coming to see me tonight? Then I noticed the date: the sixteenth of February, and today was the twentieth of April. This wasn't new; all the adrenaline racing through my poor hopeful body pulled up in a big halt and went home in disgust. I was a dope and I could only blame the drugs. This must have arrived after I'd left to meet him that evening nine weeks ago. And because it was obviously personal, the temp hadn't opened it and had left it for me to read.

The first time I met the Maddoxes

What are you doing for Thanksgiving?" Aidan had asked.

"Dunno." Hadn't given it much thought.

"Want to come to Boston and spend it with my family?"

"Um, okay, thanks. If you're sure."

A low-key response, but I knew that this was a big deal. Not as big as I'd realized, though. When I told people at work, they freaked.

"How long have you guys been exclusive?"

"Since Friday."

"*Last* Friday? You mean the Friday that was five days ago? But this is *way* too soon."

In the unwritten New York dating rules, I was jumping the gun by at least seven weeks. It was forbidden—indeed, up until now, it had been thought technically *impossible*—to move directly from a declaration of exclusivity to meeting his family. It was most unorthodox. Highly irregular. No good would come of it, they all prophesied, shaking their heads despondently.

"It's still four weeks away," I protested.

"Three and a half."

I didn't need their doom and gloom. I had my own worries: Aidan had told me about Janie.

It should have been the subject of a late-night confessional, but circumstances dictated that it was a morning bean spilling—the morning after we'd first slept together and he'd gone weird on me. It had made me late for work but I didn't care. I had to know.

Here's the gist: Aidan and Janie had gone out with each other for about a hundred and sixty-eight years. They'd been brought up a couple of miles from each other in Boston and had been an item for a long, long time, right since high school. They went away to different colleges and the relationship ceased by mutual consent, but when they arrived back in Boston three years later, everything kicked off again. All through their twenties they were a loved-up couple and they became part of each other's family, Janie joining the Maddoxes on their summer vacations in Cape Cod and Aidan going along with the Janies to their place in Bar Harbor. Over the years, Aidan and Janie broke up a few times and tried dating other people, but they always returned to each other.

Time passed and they moved into apartments—but not together—and the marriage hints from their families were starting to get a little heavy when, about eighteen months before I met him, Aidan's firm transferred him to "the city." (Everyone says "the city" when they mean New York, which seems hard to understand because Boston isn't exactly a hamlet with three houses and a pub.)

It was a bit of a shock all around but Aidan and Janie kept reminding each other that New York was a mere hour's flight away, they'd see each other every weekend, and in the meantime, Aidan would look for another job back in Boston and Janie would apply for jobs in NYC. So off Aidan goes, promising to be true.

"You can guess what happened," he said.

Actually, I was still trying to figure it out. That first night when he'd asked me to put him on my roster, he'd given the impression that he was available—albeit in a nonexclusive way—but had I been conned into muscling in on someone else's man?

"You've barely paid off the taxi into Manhattan when you've got your lad out and you're trawling the bars, looking for takers?"

He laughed a little sadly. "Not exactly. But, yes, I slept with other women."

In his defense he refused to blame the many temptations of NYC, the exquisite-looking, brazen ladies who'd done classes, learning how to twirl their bras over their heads like they were lassoing a runaway steer.

"No one to blame but me," he said miserably. "I wanted to flagellate myself with shame. That old Catholic guilt, it gets you every time. Don't laugh, but I did something I hadn't done for the longest time: I went to confession."

"Oh. Are you, like . . . a practicing Catholic?"

He shook his head. "A recovering Catholic. But I felt so shitty I would've tried anything."

I didn't know what to say.

"Janie deserved so much better from me," he said. "She's a great human being, a very good person. She sees the positive in every situation without being, like, a Pollyanna chump."

Oh God. I was going head-to-head with a living saint.

"That first day we met, when I spilled coffee on you, I'd just made a fresh resolution—yet another one—that I was going to be totally faithful to Janie. I really meant it."

So that was why he'd been so odd when I'd asked him out. He hadn't said, "Thanks but no thanks." Or "Hey, I'm flattered, but . . ." Instead he'd given off waves of despair.

"So what happened?" I asked angrily. "Am I another of your guilty slips? Another trip to the confession box on the cards?"

"No. No, no, no, not at all! About a month later when I was in Boston, Janie said we should take some time out."

"Oh?"

"Yeah. And although she didn't say it straight out, she hinted that she knew about the other women."

"Oh?" Again.

"Yeah, she knows me very well. She said we'd been messing around for too long, it was make-or-break time. A final attempt to see if we were right for each other, you know? See other people, get stuff out of our systems, then see where it left me and her."

"And?"

"I'd shredded your card. I was so scared I was going to call you that I made myself destroy it the day you gave it to me. But I couldn't stop thinking about you. I remembered your name and where you worked, but I thought it was too late to call.

"You know, I nearly didn't go to that party that night, and when I saw you there, talking to that meathead, *that* made me believe in God. Seeing you, it was like . . . like getting hit with a baseball bat . . ." He looked like he was going to puke. "I don't want to scare you, Anna, but I've never felt this way about anyone else, ever."

I said nothing. I felt so guilty. But I couldn't help also feeling . . . a little . . . flattered.

"I wanted to talk to Janie before I talked to you. I didn't know if you'd want to, like, be interested in being exclusive—I hate that stupid word—but either way it's totally over for me and Janie. But I feel bad that you know before she does."

Tell me about it.

And shallow girl that I was, I wanted to know what Janie looked like. I had to clamp my lips together extremely tightly to stop myself asking, but it didn't work and little sounds escaped. *Mwahdoz zhee mlook mlike.*

"Wha—oh! What does she look like?" His face went suddenly blank. "Um, you know, nice, she's got"—he made a rotating gesture with his hand—"hair, curly hair." He paused. "Well, she used to. Maybe lately it's been straight."

Okay, he hadn't a clue what she looked like. He'd been with her for so long that he didn't look at her properly anymore. Nevertheless, a powerful intuition was warning me that I should not underestimate this woman and the strength of Aidan's attachment. They'd shared fifteen years of history, and like a boomerang, he kept returning to her.

He went to Boston, and all weekend, I felt mildly queasy; contradictory thoughts chased one another in a never-ending circle. At the air-guitar competition, Shake accused me of not paying attention when he'd been on, and he was right: I'd been staring into space wondering how

Janie was taking it—I hated myself for being responsible for someone else's unhappiness. And how much did I like Aidan? Enough to let him end a fifteen-year relationship for my sake? What if I was only messing him around? Or what if he changed his mind and got back with Janie? That terrified me; I really liked him. Really, really liked him.

And what would happen if he couldn't keep his mickey to himself? What if he wasn't just unfaithful to Janie, but habitually frisky? I'd better not start thinking that I'd be the one to cure him; instead I should start running in the opposite direction at high speed. Then I was back to wondering how Janie was feeling...

She took it pretty good." Aidan showed up on my doorstep on the Sunday evening.

"Really?" I asked hopefully.

"She kind of hinted...you know...that maybe she might have met someone else, too."

This was balm—for half a second. You know how thick men can be; no doubt Janie had done what she could to save face, but right at that moment she was probably running a hot bath and getting the cutthroat razor out of the bathroom closet.

As the plane touched down in Logan, full of Thanksgiving returnees, I asked Aidan, "Tell me again, how many girls other than Janie have you brought home for Thanksgiving?"

He thought for ages, counting stuff out on his fingers and whispering numbers under his breath, and eventually said, "None!"

It had become a familiar routine over the previous four weeks, but now that I had actually arrived in Boston I felt sick. "Aidan, it's no joke. I shouldn't have come. Everyone will hate me for not being Janie. The streets will be lined by angry Bostonians stoning the car and your mother will spit in my soup."

"It'll be fine." He squeezed my fingers. "They'll love you. You'll see."

His mom, Dianne, picked us up at the airport and instead of pelting me with gravel and shrieking "HOMEWRECKER!" she gave me a hug and said, "Welcome to Boston."

She was lovely—a bit scatty, driving erratically and blathering away. Finally we fetched up in some suburb that wasn't a million miles different from the one I came from, in terms of demographics, cars in the drive, nosy neighbors staring like hostile village idiots, etc., etc.

The house, too, seemed familiar: with horrible swirly carpets, awful soft furnishings, and crammed with sports trophies, nasty paintings, and gawk-making china ornaments, I felt right at home.

I dropped my bag on the hall floor and almost the first thing I saw was a photo on the wall of a younger-looking Aidan with his two arms around a girl, hugging the back of her body to the front of his. Right away I knew it was Janie. So how did she look? Oh, you know, all smiley and happy, how do people usually look in photos? Those on display in curlicued, silvery frames anyway. I felt a little shaky even before I'd absorbed that she was beautiful: dark, long corkscrew curls (their beauty not even marred by a Staten Island topknot and a green scrunchy) and perfect teeth in a wide smile.

But clearly it had been taken a long time ago, judging by the scrunchy and how bright-eyed and innocent Aidan looked—maybe she'd aged badly.

Someone shouted, "Dad, they're here," and a door opened and a young man appeared: dark, built, very smiley, *extremely* cute. "Hi, I'm Kevin, the younger brother."

"And I'm Anna—"

"Oh yeah, we know *all* about you." He dazzled me with a smile. "Wow. Any more like you at home?"

"Yes." I considered Helen. "But you'd probably be terrified of her."

He didn't realize I wasn't joking and he laughed, a proper belly laugh. "You're a riot. This is going to be fun."

Next to appear was Mr. Maddox, a lanky bloke with a vague, wavery voice. He shook hands with me but said little. I didn't take it personally: Aidan had warned me that when he did talk, it was usually about the Democratic Party.

Kevin insisted on carrying my bag to my bedroom, a room that could have been twinned with the spare room in my parents' house. They could have done a cultural exchange and put a sign saying so outside each door; ferocious curtains, a matching ferocious quilt, and a wardrobe crammed with someone else's old clothes and about half an inch of space and two hangers for mine. Lucky I was only staying one night. (Taking no chances, Aidan and I had decided not to overdo things on the first visit.)

Then I saw it. On the dressing table: another picture of Aidan and Janie. A "motion" shot; they were turned toward each other and it had been taken half a second before they kissed. This time there was no scrunchy—her hair was held back from her face by Aidan's hand.

Again I felt queasy, and after eyeballing it for a few minutes, I laid it facedown. No way was I going to sleep in this room watched over by a prekissing photo of Aidan and Janie. A light knock on the door made me jump guiltily and Dianne breezed in with an armload of stuff. "Fresh towels!" Instantly she noticed the toppled picture. "Damn! Oh, Anna! It's stood there for years, so long I don't even see it anymore. That was so tactless of me."

She picked it up, left the room with it, and returned empty-handed.

"Sorry about that," she said. "Truly."

This was no Mrs. Danvers situation. She seemed sincerely sorry to have upset me.

"Whenever you're ready for dinner, come on down."

The dinner was the whole Thanksgiving nine yards: a massive turkey and millions of spuds and vegetables and wine and champagne and crystal glasses and candles. The atmosphere was very friendly, I was almost a hundred percent sure that Mrs. Maddox hadn't spat in my soup, everyone was chatting away, and even Old Man Maddox made a joke, and although it was about the Democratic Pah-dy and I didn't understand it, I laughed obediently.

There was just one thing: not *every* one of the many photos on the dining-room walls was of Aidan and Janie, but there were enough to keep giving me little shocks. Over the years Janie's hair had got shorter. Good. Men like woman with long hair. And she'd plumped out a little but she still looked very cheery and pleasant, the kind of woman that other women like.

In the middle of swallowing a mouthful of turkey, I spotted yet another picture that I'd missed earlier and once again my gullet shut down briefly. I took a swig of wine to assist things along and Old Man Maddox asked, "Janie, dear, can you pass the roast potatoes."

Who?

I looked from side to side, but as the dish of spuds was in front of me and Old Man Maddox was looking my way, I concluded that it must be me he was talking to. Obediently I shunted the bowl along and Kevin gave me a comforting wink and Aidan and Dianne looked horrified and mouthed, "Sorry."

But two seconds later, Dianne said, "Oh, Aidan, we met Janie's dad at the hahd-ware stoh, he says to tell you he finally finished the shed and to come by to see it. How long ago was it that you guys stah-ted on it...?"

Then Old Man Maddox piped up. "You might like to know what he was doing at the hahd-ware store?" he asked Aidan. He'd suddenly gone all bright-eyed and amused—it must have been the drink. "Buying paint, that's what. White paint, by the way. For their place in Bah Hah-ba. He gave it one summer like you asked him to, but we still can't figure what came over you two guys, painting the place pink."

Flushed with amusement, he looked from Aidan to me, then panic flickered behind his eyes. *She's not Janie.*

After dinner, Aidan and I sat in the den; things were a little tense.
"I don't belong here, I shouldn't have come."

"No, you should! Really, you should. It'll get easier. I'm so sorry about my dad, he's a bit . . . he doesn't mean it—he's in a world of his own half the time."

We sat in silence.

"What are you thinking?" he asked.

"About the carpet." It had some funny spiral pattern. "If you stare at it long enough, you feel like your eyes are on springs. It's like they're zooming out of my head, then bouncing back in."

"I feel more like the floor is lifting up toward me, then falling down again."

We sat in companionable silence, watching the carpet do its thing, and suddenly we were friends again.

"It'll be okay," Aidan said. "Just give it time. Please."

"Okay," I said. "My parents used to treat Shane like family, too."

"They loved him?"

"Well . . . no . . . actually they hated him. But they still treated him like family."

The following day we went to the mall because there's only so much sitting around your new boyfriend's parents' house, living in fear of hearing further reminiscences about his ex-girlfriend, you can do. I kept stumbling over conversations like "Remember that holiday on Cape Cod. All of us in the RV? Remember Janie did something or other?"

But once we were in the mall I cheered up because when I'm away from home, even shops that are normally beneath me suddenly become exciting. I visited CVS, Express, and a whole load of other crappy places, Aidan bought me a souvenir of Boston—a snow dome—then said, "Guess we'd better go back."

So we got in the cah and had just left the pahking lot, when it happened. Even before Aidan made a funny, involuntary noise, I'd noticed the jaw-clenching tension suddenly emanating from him.

I looked out of the window, my eyes scudding from side to side, desperate to see what he'd seen. A woman was walking toward us. But we were moving quite fast, we'd already passed her, and my intuition was yelling, *Look around, look around, quickly.*

I whipped my head over my shoulder. The woman was walking away from us, wearing jeans and looking (I couldn't help but notice) quite broad in the butt. Of course, I should have been proud that Aidan was the kind of guy who didn't discriminate against girls with big bums, but I had other things on my mind. She was quite tall and her hair was straight and dark and hung to her shoulders. Her bag was nice, I'd seen them in Zara. In fact I'd nearly bought one myself but I already had another that was very similar. I kept watching until she disappeared into the lot.

I turned back and settled myself firmly against the seat. "That was Janie, wasn't it?" If he lied to me at that moment, there would be no future for us.

He nodded, a little grimly. "Yes, that was Janie."

"A bit of a coincidence."

"Yep."

Back at the Maddoxes, having a cup of coffee before leaving for the airport, I noticed several fat photo albums in the bookcase and I suddenly imagined them whooshing out from their shelves, their pages flying open and the photos taking flight, filling up the room like a flock of birds. Hundreds of them, flying past me, getting tangled in my hair as they documented countless Aidan and Janie events: Aidan and Janie at their prom; Aidan and Janie at their high-school graduation; Aidan and Janie at Aidan's thirtieth-birthday dinner; Aidan and Janie at the surprise pah-dy Aidan threw for Janie's promotion; Aidan and Janie at their high-school reunion; Aidan and Janie winning a bowling trophy; Aidan and Janie on holiday in Jamaica, cooking clams together in Cape Cod, at the farewell shindig before Aidan went to New York, painting the house in Bah Hah-ba pink . . .

• • •

We were very quiet on the flight home. The visit had been a terrible mistake, a risk worth taking but that hadn't worked out. Aidan was a great guy in lots of ways but he had too much baggage and too much unfinished business. He belonged in Boston with Janie, and I admitted to myself that, no matter what, he would always return to her and she would always take him back. They had too much history, too much in common.

He was gray green with tension and in the cab from the airport he held my hand so tight he hurt my fingers. He was trying to figure out a way to tell me it was over, but there was no need, I knew exactly what was going on.

The cab dropped me at my apartment and I kissed Aidan on the cheek and said, "Take care of yourself."

As I clambered out of the cab he called after me, "Anna?"

"Yes?"

"Anna, will you marry me?"

I stared at him for a long, long moment, then said, "Get a grip on yourself," and slammed the car door.

20

To: Aidan_maddox@yahoo.com
From: Magiciansgirl1 @yahoo.com
Subject: You're going to love this!

Coming in to work this morning (second day back) I met Tabitha from Bergdorf Baby and she checked out my scar and said, Hey, that look is beyond! Then she got it that it was a real scar and she literally recoiled in horror. Her head pulled back so far her skull was practically resting between her shoulder blades. She went straight to the bathroom. I think she might have varminted.

I hope you're okay, I love you.

Your girl, Anna

To: Aidan_maddox@yahoo.com
From: Magiciansgirl1@yahoo.com
Subject: You're going to love this too!

People at work think I've been to Arizona. On my way back from lunch with Teenie, I met an EarthSource girl in the elevator and she said that she hadn't seen me in a while, and I said, No, I've been out of town.

I thought everyone here at work knew what had happened but I suppose those EarthSource girls are space cadets. It must be the diet of mung beans. She asked how long I'd been gone and I said, About two months. Then she gives me a meaningful look and mouths something, and I had to lean closer to her rough-woven, sacking pinafore and say, I'm sorry, what was that? So she does it again and this time I got it and she was saying, One day at a time.

Er, right...

I hope you're okay, I'm thinking of you all the time, I love you.

Your girl, Anna

To: Aidan_maddox@yahoo.com
From: Magiciansgirl1@yahoo.com
Subject: Thursday's clothes

A yellow poplin Doris Day style shirtwaister, over black leggings patterned with blue spiky hearts, a denim jacket with the sleeves cut off, and my blue pumps, the ones you said were the pointiest shoes ever made, so pointy that the last six inches are invisible. No hat today—a little treat for myself.

I love you.

Your girl, Anna

I was writing him two or three e-mails a day, keeping the tone light and breezy. I didn't want to guilt him out by saying how desperate I was to hear from him. Better to just keep the lines of communication open so he'd contact me if he could. I was also checking his horoscope every day, trying to get some insight into how he might be feeling. Stars Online said:

> Don't allow others' need for closure to force you into hurried decisions. Since you're unlikely to know all your options until early May, they'll just have to wait.

I didn't really like that, so I went to Hot Scopes!

> Career-minded Scorps could be looking at an overseas business trip. Could be, you meet a desirable stranger who speaks a different language. Whatever or whoever it turns out to be, you'll be pleased that the world is a small place!

I didn't like that *at all*. It made me cry. Quickly I clicked on Today's stars.

> Try to make plans and you'll only encounter frustration. Be a free spirit and by mid-May you'll be so confident that you'll wonder why you ever worried.

That was better. No desirable strangers. I shoved my feet into my pointy blue pumps and picked up my keys, but at the door of the apartment

I stopped, then went back to the phone. I just wanted to ring his cell phone. Again. The pleasure of hearing his voice, even if it was just his phone message, was like a mouthful of chocolate when you're craving sugar.

The best in landlubberly eye care! I stared at my screen and took a swig of coffee. No, the coffee didn't help—the line was still atrocious. I deleted it and faced my blank monitor, willing inspiration to strike. I was trying to write a press release for Eye Eye Captain, our new eye treatments, and was attempting a play on mutiny, salt water, piracy, rum, and other ship-based stuff. But it so wasn't working. I'd seen Aidan again on the way to work this morning. This time he was walking along Fifth Avenue in a jacket that I didn't recognize. He'd found time to buy new clothes but not to call me? Once again, the taxi was moving too fast, so I didn't get the driver to stop. But now I desperately wished that I had and the regret was interfering with my concentration. Or maybe it was the painkillers. *Something* was filling my head with cotton wool.

I typed *Eye, Eye, Captain,* then had absolutely nothing further to say. God, I really needed to get it together. It wasn't as if I was in the lowly position of junior account assistant (that was Brooke now). I was assistant senior account manager and I had responsibilities.

How I got promoted

The summer I joined Candy Grrrl, our Lip-plumping Iced Sorbet Übergloss sold out across the world and there were fights at makeup counters. Well, there weren't really. What actually happened was that at Nordstrom in Seattle there was a little tussle between two sisters over the last Candy Grrrl gloss in the Pacific Northwest. However, it was settled quite amicably—I believe the terms were that the one who got the gloss would babysit the other one's kids that night. But some smart girl (me) managed to spin the incident into an (almost) news story. I issued a press release with a big, bold header, CANDY GRRRL BITCH FIGHT, and the gods must have been smiling on me because the *New York Post* and *Daily News* picked it up. Then the regionals, then there was a small segment on CNN. See, it was August, nothing else was happening. But by then enough buzz had been generated so that there really *were* scuffles at Candy Grrrl counters. At the Manhattan Bloomingdale's concession one woman shoulder-shoved another and the shoved woman said, "Hey! Watch it! It's not even your color!"

Then Jay Leno made a joke (not very funny, but who cares) about people pulling guns on one another at Candy Grrrl counters, and the net effect of all the publicity was that I got promoted. Wendell, the person I replaced at Candy Grrrl, got moved sideways to Visage, our po-faced French brand, and she happily surrendered her pink trilbies and novelty shoes for pencil skirts and fiercely waisted jackets.

I typed *Eye, Eye, Captain* one more time. I was actually scared. This was my third day back at work and I still hadn't produced so much as a decent press release. I realized I had hoped that the short, sharp shock of returning to work would snap me back into normality, but it hadn't happened. I felt like I was in a dream, trying to run, with legs of lead. My head wouldn't think, my body was in pain, everything felt like the world had tilted off its axis.

Forty minutes later, my screen said:

TAKE IT ON BOARD, ME HEARTIES!
You can sail the high seas but Eye Eye Captain is the most effective,
most advanced one-stop eye treatment you'll find.
Dark circles?—All washed up!
Morning puffiness?—Throw it overboard!
Fine lines and wrinkles?—Make 'em walk the plank!
The parrot on your shoulder?—Sorry, that's your problem.

Teenie looked over my shoulder at my screen. "Yo ho *ho*," she said, with sympathy.

"You'd want to see my other attempts."

"It's your first week back, you're out of practice."

"And on heavy medication."

"It'll get easier. Want me to have a go?"

Teenie did her best to help me, but Teenie had her own troubles: she was responsible for the diffusion ranges, Candy for a Baby and Candy Man. Mind you, with only twelve products in the children's line and ten in the men's, she had nothing like the same responsibility as me. (Fifty-eight products, in innumerable colorways, and counting. We seemed to launch something new every other week.)

Lauryn ran in and shrieked, "Is that press release ready?"

"Just coming," I said while Teenie muttered in my ear, "First the fat gets metabolized. Then the lean tissue; eventually the muscle goes, and finally the organs. At this point the body is actually digesting itself. Would that dumb woman ever eat something?" Teenie was studying medicine in night school and liked sharing her knowledge.

I printed out my crappy press release and went to Lauryn's desk, ready to play the humiliation game.

The responsibility for Candy Grrrl's publicity was shared out between me and Lauryn like this: *I* did all the work and came up with all the ideas. While *she* made my life a misery, was paid 50 percent more than me, and got all the credit.

I had a second-tier duty: badgering beauty editors, taking them out to lunch, telling them how lovely Candy Grrrl products were, and persuading them to give us a four-line sound bite and a photo on their Beauty News page. This was a massively important part of my job, so much so that my performance was targeted; the inches of magazine coverage I generated were measured, then compared with how much would have had to be spent in advertising to get the same space.

My target this year was 12 percent higher than the previous year's, but I'd lost two months' worth of badgering while I'd been in Ireland. It was going to be hard to make it up. Would Ariella or Candace and George Biggly make allowances? Probably not. Looked at objectively, why should they?

I gave Lauryn my Eye Eye Captain press release. A one-second glance was all it took.

"This is shit." She threw it back at me.

That was fine. I always had to present her with at least two attempts; she would trash my first offering, then trash the second, then she usually accepted the first.

Unpleasant perhaps, but it was nice to know where I stood.

I didn't leave work until about seven-thirty, and when I got home there was an e-mail from my mother—something which had never happened before.

To: Magiciansgirl1@yahoo.com
From: Thewalshes1@eircom.net
Subject: The woman and her dog

Dear Anna,
I hope you are keeping well. Just remember you can come home whenever you want and we will mind you. I am writing in connection with the woman and the dog who was "doing his business" at our front gate.

Oh, cripes, what can of worms had I opened?

I will admit that we all thought you were imagining things, as a result of the tablets you are on. But I am not afraid to "step up" to the "plate" (what does that <u>mean</u>? Is it a barbecuing term?) and say I was wrong. Myself and Helen have watched her over the last few mornings and it has become clear to us that she is indeed urging her dog to "pee" at our front gate and I just wanted to keep you "in the loop" as they say. As yet we haven't identified her. As you know she is an old woman and all old women look the same to me. As you also know your sister Helen has high-powered binoculars, which your father paid for. But she will not give me a "go" of them, she says I have to pay her the going rate for her time. I do not think this is one bit fair. If you are talking to her, will you tell her I said that. Also if she tells you any "scoop" on the woman's identity be sure to let me know.

Your loving mother,

Mum

22

Less than a week after he first asked me to marry him, Aidan did it again, this time with a ring, made by a jeweler I'd once said I liked. In white gold with a delicate band and seven diamonds in a star setting, it was a very nice ring and I was very freaked out.

"Snap out of it," I said to him. "Take it down a notch or two. We had one bad weekend, you're overreacting."

I hurried home to Jacqui and related what had happened.

"A ring?" she exclaimed. "You're getting married!"

"I'm not getting married."

"Why not?"

"Why should I?"

"Duh...because he asked you?" Testily, she said, "It was a joke. Sort of. So why won't you marry the guy?"

Incoherently, I spluttered, "Reason (a) I barely know him and I've spent so much of my life being impulsive, I've used it all up. Reason (b) Aidan has too much baggage and I don't want a fixer-upper. Reason (c) As you yourself, Jacqui Staniforth, said—and I bet you're right—he's probably a hard dog to keep on the porch. What if he's unfaithful to me?"

"Actually, it's none of the above," Jacqui said. "It's reason (d) Because you're a late starter. Which means," she said loudly, "that while every other single woman of our age would be *delighted* to marry anyone, even a three-eyed dwarf who has to shave his nose, you're still naive enough to think you shouldn't go round marrying the first man who asks you. Yes, you barely know him! Yes, he's got baggage! Yes, he might have trouble keeping his lad in his pants! But basically, Anna Walsh, you haven't a fucking CLUE how lucky you are!"

I waited for her to finish shouting.

"Sorry," she said, her color high, her breathing louder than usual. "Got a little...overexcited there. I'm really sorry, Anna. Just because he has only two eyes and is of average height and nose-hairiness for his age, is no reason to marry a man. Not at all."

"Thank you."

"But you do love him," she accused. "And he loves you. I know it's been quick, but it's serious."

The next time he produced the ring I said, "*Please* stop."

"I can't help it."

"Why do you want to marry me?"

He sighed. "I can list the reasons but it still won't convey anything like enough: you smell good, you're brave, you like Dogly, you're funny, you're smart, you're really, really cute-looking, I like the way you say 'curly-wurly,' I like how your head works, how we can be talking about FedExing my Mom's birthday gift to Boston and you suddenly say, 'It's impossible for someone to look sexy while licking a stamp'..." He spread his hands in a gesture of helplessness. "But it's much, much more than that. Like much, much, much, much more than that."

"What's the difference between how you feel about me and how you felt about Janie?"

"I'm not dissing Janie, because she's a great person, but there's no comparison..." He snapped his fingers. "Okay, got it! Have you ever had, like, a really bad toothache? One of those screaming ones where it's like electricity crackling up into your head and ears, it's so bad you can nearly see it? Yeah? Okay, convert that same intensity into love and that's how I feel about you."

"And Janie?"

"Janie? Janie is like when you bump your head on a low ceiling. Bad but not unbearable. Am I making any sense?"

"Strangely, yes."

Obviously, I'd known the first time we'd met that there had been *something,* some connection. Then, accidentally bumping into each other seven weeks later looked like a "sign" that we were meant to be together, but I didn't want to live my life by "signs," I wanted to live them by facts.

Fact 1. I couldn't deny that he'd severely disrupted my peace of mind; despite my insisting that we barely knew each other, privately I felt that we knew each other extremely well. In a good way.

Fact 2. It was different from the way I'd felt about any man in a long, long time. I suspected—feared even—that I was badly in love with him.

Fact 3. I valued loyalty and in many ways Aidan was extremely loyal: he embraced Jacqui, Rachel, even Luke and the Real Men, calling them "man" just to fit in. He celebrated my work victories and he'd hated Lauryn long before he met her.

Fact 4. I wasn't going to get sidetracked by the physical side of things, because you can fancy anyone. But, as it happened—and it's really neither here nor there—we couldn't keep our hands off each other.

On paper so many of the boxes were ticked. The problem was Janie. I couldn't forgive Aidan for dumping her.

But when I took my woes to Jacqui, she said, "He dumped her for you!"

"It still feels wrong. And he was with her for a thousand years, he only knows me five minutes."

"Listen," she said earnestly. "Really listen to me. You often hear of people who go out with someone for years and years, then they break up and two days later they're getting married to someone else. We've seen it, haven't we? Remember Faith and Hal? She broke it off with him after eleven years and immediately—so it seemed—he married that Swedish girl and everyone said, 'There goes the rebound kid,' but they're still together and they've three children and they seem happy. When people move that fast, everyone says, 'I'll give it a month,' but often they're wrong, often it works. And I've a feeling that's what's going on here. You don't have to be with a person for a hundred years before you're sure. Sometimes it happens in an instant. You've heard the saying: 'When you know, you know.'"

I nodded. Yes, I'd heard it.

"So do you know?"

"No."

She sighed heavily and muttered, "Christ."

In all the time I was with Janie," Aidan said, "I never asked her to marry me. And she never asked me either."

"I don't care," I said. "I'm freaked out enough, having such an intense relationship with you so quickly, but all this marriage stuff is really doing my head in."

"What are you so scared of?"

"Oh, you know, all the obvious reasons: I'll never be able to sleep with anyone else ever again, I don't want to be part of a smug couple who finish each other's sentences, etc., etc."

But my real fear was that it mightn't work out, that he might run off with someone else—or more likely, go back to Janie—and I'd be absolutely destroyed. When you love someone as much as I suspected I loved Aidan, there was so much further to fall.

"I'm afraid that it might all go horribly wrong," I admitted. "That we'd end up hating each other and losing our trust in love and hope and all the good things. I couldn't bear it. Then I'd become an over-made-up lush with big hair who drinks martinis for breakfast and tries to sleep with the pool boy."

"Anna, it won't go wrong, I promise. This is good stuff, you and me, as good as it gets. You know that."

Sometimes I did. Which meant that—like the urge I got on the top of a tall building, to just jump off—my biggest fear of all was that I might say yes.

"Okay, if you won't marry me will you come on vacation with me?"

"I don't know," I said. "I'll have to ask Jacqui."

"Kill or cure" was Jacqui's conclusion. "It could be a total disaster, trapped in a foreign country with nothing to say to each other. I'd say, go for it."

I said I'd go so long as he didn't once ask me to marry him. "Done," he said.

I went to Ireland for Christmas, and when I got back, Aidan and I went to Mexico for six days.

After the cold and drear of a New York winter, the white sands and blue skies were so dazzling, it almost hurt to look at them. But the best bit of all was having Aidan on tap twenty-four hours a day. It was sex, sex, and more sex. First thing in the morning, last thing at night, at all points in between . . .

To make sure we got out of bed once in a while, we checked out the dusty local town and decided to do a beginners' scuba-diving course, which was run by two expat Californian stoners. It was dirt cheap, and with the benefit of hindsight, maybe we should have been concerned. Also by the waiver form we had to sign, stating that in the event of death, mutilation, shark attacks, post-traumatic stress disorder, stubbed toes, broken nails, lost prosthetics, and whatever else, they were in no way, shape, or form responsible.

But we didn't give a damn, we were having a great time, crouched in the tiny practice pool with nine other beginners, making Os with our thumb and index fingers and sniggering and nudging, like we were back at school.

On day three, we were taken out for our first dive in the sea, and although we were only twelve feet beneath the waves, we were transported to another world. A world of peace, where all you can hear is the sound of your own breathing and everything moves with slow grace. Swimming through blue water, it was like being suspended in blue light. The water was as clear as glass and sun rays filtered all the way to the bottom, to highlight the white sand on the ocean floor.

Aidan and I were mesmerized. Holding hands, we slowly flapped past delicate coral and fish in every imaginable colorway: yellow with black spots, orange with white stripes, and funny, transparent ones with no color at all. Shoals of them in formation, moving silently past us, heading for somewhere else.

Aidan pointed and I followed his finger. Sharks. Three of them, hanging around at the edge of the reef, looking mean and moody, like they were wearing leather jackets. Reef sharks aren't dangerous. Usually. All the same, my heart beat a little faster.

Then, just for a laugh, we took out our mouthpieces and used each other's spare "octopus" air tube, becoming one unit, the way "lovairs" in films set in the 1930s link arms and drink champagne from each other's glass (and they're always those shallow champagne glasses with the ridiculously wide rims, so that the champagne spills everywhere and you're barely able to drink any yourself, never mind your loved one, but what harm).

"Wow, that was amazing," Aidan raved afterward. "It was exactly like *Finding Nemo*. And you know what else it means, Anna? It means you and I have something in common. We have A Shared Interest."

I thought this was his cue to ask me to marry him again but I gave him a look and he said, "What?" and I said, "Nothing."

The last day was the big banana, the grand finale. They were taking all of us to deeper waters, which involved decompressing on our ascent. That meant hanging around for two minutes every fifteen feet while our air yoke resomethinged. We'd been practicing in shallower waters, but this time it would be for real.

But on the boat taking us out, events turned pear-shaped: Aidan had developed a cold, and although he was pretending he was in the full of his health, the instructor noticed and nixed Aidan's dive.

"You won't be able to equalize the pressure in your ears. Sorry, man, you can't go."

Aidan was so disappointed that I decided I wouldn't go either. "I'd rather go back to the cabana and have sex with you. We haven't done it in over an hour."

"How about you go for your dive and *then* come back to the cabana and have sex with me? You can have both. Go on, Anna, you've been so excited about this dive and you can tell me all about it when you get back."

Because Aidan wasn't coming, I had to get another "buddy"—even though I hate the word *buddy*. Except when it's used as an insult. (Example: "What's it to you, buddy?")

I got buddied with a man who'd been reading *Codependent No More* on the beach. He'd come on holiday on his own and had been buddied with the instructor for every other dive.

Final instructions were called to us before we jumped off the side of the boat, then we splashed down into that silent other world. Mr. Codependent wouldn't hold my hand, but that was fine because I didn't want to hold his either. Swimming along, we'd been near the ocean floor for several minutes—it's hard to keep track of time down there—when I realized that on my last two inhales, no air had come out of my tube. I took another suck just to make sure, and no, nothing was happening. It was like the surprise I get when a can of hair spray is used up; it's something that I think is never going to happen. I press and press on the nozzle thinking, *It* can't *be empty,* then realize it is and that I'd better stop unless I want the fecker to explode.

My indicator said I still had twenty-five minutes of air left but nothing was coming out; my tube must be blocked. So I tried my octupus arm—my spare tube—and felt the first tickle of fear when nothing came out of that either.

I stopped Mr. Codependent and signaled *No air.* (A slicing action at the neck that the Mafia use when they talk about "taking care" of people.) It was only when I went to grab his octopus and take a lovely mouthful of oxygen that I noticed there wasn't one! No extra air tube! The gobshite! Even in my shock, I knew what had happened: he'd detached it in order to demonstrate his lack of codependence. In his head he'd probably been saying proudly, *I walk alone; I depend on no one and no one depends on me.*

Well, that was just tough because, seeing as he'd abandoned his spare tube somewhere, he'd have to give me a go of his own mouthpiece. I pointed and signaled *Give it to me,* but as he went to take it out of his mouth, he panicked. Even through his mask, I could see it. It was like when Bilbo Baggins had to hand the Ring over to Master Frodo. He knew it had to be done, but when it came to actually doing it, he couldn't.

Codependent was too scared to leave himself without air for even a few seconds. One hand guarding his air tube, he jabbed toward the surface with the other: Go up. To my horror, he started swimming away from me, still protecting his air supply.

The others had gone on ahead, I could see them disappearing into the distance. There was no one to help me. *This isn't happening, please God, let this not be happening.*

I was forty-five feet beneath the surface and I had no air. I felt the full weight of all that water pressing down on me. Up until now, it had been entirely weightless, but all of a sudden it might kill me.

The terror was so bad I felt like I was dreaming. *Surface,* I thought.

I've got to get to the surface. I stared upward. It looked a very long way away.

Diving upward, my legs kicking, my lungs bursting, I raced up, up, up, breaking all the rules, thinking, *I'm going to die and it's all my own fault for going on a cut-price scuba course.*

Every fifteen feet I was supposed to hang around decompressing for two minutes; never mind two minutes, I didn't have two *seconds*.

I kicked past a surprised shoal of clown fish, praying to break the surface. My blood roared in my ears and images flitted into my head. Then I realized what was happening—my life was flashing before my eyes. *Fuck,* I thought, *I'm definitely going to die.*

My life didn't flash sequentially, but highlit unexpected stuff, things I hadn't thought about for years—or ever. My mother had given birth to me and I thought, *What a nice thing that was to do. What a generous act.* Next person to appear in my head was Shane: I'd stayed with that bloke for far too long.

Why did I have to die? Well, why not? There were six billion people in the world and I was as insignificant as everyone else. They were dying all the time, why shouldn't I?

Mind you, it was a shame because if I got another shot at my inconsequential little life, I'd...

Just when I thought my head was going to burst, I broke the blue line that separates the two worlds. The noise and the glare hit me, a wave slapped me in the ear, and I was tearing the mask off my face, gulping in glorious oxygen, amazed not to be dead.

The next thing I remember, I was lying on the deck of the boat, still heaving desperately for air, and Aidan was bending over me. His expression was a mixture of horror and relief. I made a monumental effort and managed to speak. "Okay," I gasped. "I'll marry you."

23

In the darkness, I woke with a bump, my heart beating fast and hard. The light was switched on before I knew I had done it and I was superalert and awake. I was on the couch. I'd nodded off there in my work clothes because I'd kept postponing the moment when I had to go to bed alone.

Something had woken me. What had I heard? The sound of a key in the door? Or had the front door actually opened and closed? All I knew was I wasn't alone. You can tell when someone else is in your space; it feels different.

It had to be Aidan. He'd come back. And although I was excited, I was also a bit freaked. Out of the corner of my eye, over by the window, I saw something move, something fast and shadowy. I whipped my head around but there was nothing there.

I stood up. There was nobody in the living room, nobody in the kitchenette, so I'd better check the bedroom. As I pushed open the door, I was sweating. I reached for the light switch, almost paralyzed with terror that a hand might grab mine in the dark. What was that tall narrow shape over by the closet? Then I hit the switch and the room flooded with light and the dark, ominous shape revealed itself as our bookshelf.

Hearing my own gaspy breathing, I turned on the bathroom light and pulled back the wave-patterned shower curtain with a violent swish. No one there either.

So what had woken me?

I realized I could smell him. The tiny space was filled with him. The panic was back and my eyes scudded around looking for—what? I was afraid to look in the mirror, in case I saw someone else looking at me. It was then that I saw that his wash bag had slipped off the crowded shelf on to the tiles. Things had tumbled out and a bottle of something had broken. I crouched down; it wasn't Aidan I could smell, it was just his aftershave.

Okay. So how had the wash bag fallen? These apartments were old and rickety; someone slamming their front door could generate enough shock waves to nudge an overhanging wash bag off a ledge onto the floor in someone else's apartment. No mystery there.

I went to get a brush to clean up the broken glass, but in the kitchenette another smell awaited me, something sweet and powdery and oppressive. Nervously I sniffed the air. It was some sort of fresh flower. I recognized the scent, I just couldn't... and then I got it. It was lilies, a smell I hate—so heavy and musty, like death.

I looked around fearfully. Where was it coming from? There were no fresh flowers in the apartment. But the smell was undeniable. I wasn't imagining it. It was real, the air was thick and cloying.

After I'd tidied the broken bottle away, I was afraid to go back to sleep, so I switched on the TV. After a trawl through all the lunatics on the cable channels, I found *Knight Rider,* an episode I hadn't already seen. Eventually I drifted back into a half sleep, where I dreamed I was awake and Aidan opened the door and walked in.

"Aidan, you came back! I knew you would."

"I can't stay long, baby," he said. "But I've something important to tell you."

"I know. So tell me, I can take it."

"Pay the rent, it's overdue."

"That's it?"

"That's it."

"But I thought..."

"The bill is in the closet with all the other mail. I'm sorry; I know you don't want to open any of it, but just find that one. Don't lose our apartment. Be a hero, baby."

"Anna, where are you?" It was Rachel.

"Work."

"It's ten past eight on a Friday night! It's your first week back, you should be building up slowly."

"I know, but I've so much to do and it's taking me forever to do it."

Spending half the previous night watching *Knight Rider*, instead of being asleep, hadn't helped. I'd been wiped all day—exhausted and slow-witted. Lauryn was piling stuff on me, Franklin was on at me to get my hair cut, and to add to my woes, a small, determined gang of EarthSource girls thought I was an alcoholic.

One of them—Koo? Aroon? Some silly earthy name, anyway—came right up to my desk on Friday morning and invited me to a lunchtime meeting—that's AA meeting, by the way—with some of the other "McArthur recovery babes."

My heart sank to the soles of my glittery, wedge-heeled sneakers. The weariness! "Thank you," I managed. "That's very nice of you . . ." I wanted to say her name, but wasn't sure what it was, so had to make do with a mumbly, all-purpose "ooo" sound. "But I'm not an alcoholic."

"Still in denial?" A sad shake of her middle-parted, lank-haired head. "Surrender to win, Anna, surrender to win."

"Okay." It was just easier to agree.

"It works if you work it, so work it, you're worth it. If you want to drink it's your business, but if you wanna stop, it's ours."

"Thank you. You're lovely." *Now please piss off before Lauryn comes over.*

Rachel said, "Some of the Real Men are calling round to play Scrabble.

It might be an easy way for you to start meeting people again. Could you face it?"

Could I? I didn't want to be alone. Mind you, I didn't really want to be with anyone else either. Paradox as that was, it made sense: I simply wanted to be with Aidan.

In the four days I'd been back in New York, I'd never had so many invitations in my life. Everyone had been fantastic, but, as yet, the only people I'd been up for were Jacqui and Rachel (who came as a job lot with Luke). There were loads of people I still had to get back to: Leon and Dana; Ornesto, our Jolly Boy upstairs neighbor; Aidan's mother. Anyway, all in good time . . .

I switched off my PC and jumped in a cab on Fifty-eighth Street—it was getting slightly easier to be in them. En route I called Jacqui and invited her along.

"Scrabble with the Real Men? I'd rather set myself on fire, but thanks for asking."

Apart from Luke, Jacqui had no time for the Real Men.

Luke let me in. Although his rocker-type hair was a lot shorter now than when he'd first met Rachel, he still wore his jeans just that smidgen too tight. My eyes were always drawn inexorably to his crotch. I had no control over it. It was a bit like the way everyone had started addressing all conversation to my scar instead of to me.

"Come on in," he invited my scar. "Rachel's just having a quick shower."

"Grand," I said, to his crotch.

Rachel and Luke's apartment was a rent-controlled place in the East Village. It was massive by New York standards, which meant you could stand in the middle of the living room and not be able to touch all four walls. They'd lived there for a long time, nearly five years, and it was very cozy and comfortable and full of stuff with meaning: patchwork quilts and cushions which had been embroidered by addicts Rachel had helped, shells

Luke had brought back from the the picnic celebrating Rachel's fourth clean-and-sober birthday—that sort of thing. Lamps cast pools of soft light, and the air smelled of the cut flowers in a bowl on the coffee table.

"Beer, wine, water?" Luke asked.

"Water," I told his crotch. I was afraid that if I started drinking I would never stop.

The buzzer went. "It's Joey," Luke said. Joey was his best friend. "You sure you'll be okay around him?"

I tried to tell Luke's face, I really did, but my eyes just slid down his chest and fastened onto his bulge. "No problem."

Seconds later, Joey strode in, closed the door behind him with some fancy foot rotation, grabbed a straight-backed chair, twirled it round, pulled it to him, and planted himself in it, facing into the chair back, all without splitting his jeans or squashing his goolies. Very gracefully done.

"Hey, Anna, sorry about your . . . you know . . . it's rough." He was one person who wouldn't be killing me with kindness. Suited me.

He gave my scar a long, brazen stare, then produced a packet of cigarettes and hit the box in some fashion, and a cigarette somersaulted upward and into his mouth. In a fluid arc, he scratched a match along the red-brick wall, and just as he was about to light the cigarette, Rachel's disembodied voice, from another room, said, "Joey, put it *out*."

He froze in surprise, the lit match in his hand, and mumbled through the cigarette in his mouth, "I didn't know she was home yet."

"Oh, I'm home all right. Out, Joey. *Now*."

"Fuck," he said, shaking the match out as it started burning his fingers. Slowly he returned the cigarette to its box, then sat—there's no other word for it—brooding.

But it was nothing to do with Rachel not letting him smoke. Joey was always like that.

His habitual humor was one of dissatisfaction with the world. Lots of people, after meeting him for the first time, would say, with sudden venom, "What the fuck was up with that Joey bloke?"

He could be actively and gratuitously obnoxious. Like, if someone got a radical new haircut and everyone else would be oohing and aahing, Joey would be more likely to say, "Sue. You'd get millions."

Other times he said nothing at all. Just sat in a group of people watching everyone with narrowed eyes, his mouth set in a grim line, while something—a muscle? a vein?—jumped in his jaw. As a result of this, a lot of women found him attractive. I always knew that they had crossed the line from thinking he was a grumpy fucker to fancying him when they said, "I've never noticed it before, but Joey looks a bit like Jon Bon Jovi, doesn't he?"

He had never, to my knowledge, had a long-term relationship, but he had slept with thousands of people, some of them related to me. My sister Helen, for example, as part of her "tag and release" program. She said he "wasn't bad in the scratcher," which was high praise indeed.

Rachel said he "has anger issues." Other people who didn't know about things like anger issues said, "That Joey chap would want to learn some manners."

A few minutes later saw the arrival of Gaz and Shake, the air-guitar champ. They did their best not to stare at my scar. This they achieved by looking at some point about eighteen inches above my head when they were talking to me. But they both meant well. Gaz, a beer-bellied, balding sweetie—not the brightest, but never mind—pulled me to his squashy tummy in a tight hug. "It's a bad scene, Anna, man."

"Yeah," Shake said, shaking back the shaggy head of hair of which he is justifiably proud and which gave him his name. "It sucks." Then he, too, embraced me while not actually looking at me.

I stood and endured it. It had to be done. Now that I was back, sooner or later I would meet everyone I knew and the first encounter would always be like this.

"Hey, you know, Anna, thanks, man, for that Candy Grrrl big hair mousse," Shake said. "It's the gear. Volumetastic."

"Oh, it worked, did it?" I'd given it to him a few months back. He'd been obsessed with making his hair as big as possible for the air-guitar finals.

"And that spray, man. We're talking rock hard."

"Well, good. Just tell me when you need more."

"'Preciate it."

Rachel emerged from the bathroom in a steamy cloud of lavender. She smiled sweetly at Joey as she passed; he glowered back at her. As the lads got stuck in to their Scrabble and beer, we curled on the couch in a softly lit corner and Rachel gave me a hand massage on my nongammy hand.

I was just starting to doze off when the buzzer went again. To my surprise it was Jacqui. She burst into the apartment, full of shine and sparkle and chat: she'd had her gold-plated teeth restored to normality, someone had given her a Louis Vuitton something, and she was on her way to a private view.

"Hi." She waved at the Real Men at the table. "I can't stay long. But as the private view is only two blocks down I thought I'd drop in and say hi. See how the Scrabble is going."

"How honored are we?" Joey drawled. He was doing something with a matchstick in his teeth.

Jacqui rolled her eyes. "Joey, you brighten every room you leave."

She came over to me and Rachel. "Why is he always so horrible?"

"He doesn't like himself very much," Rachel said.

"Don't fucking blame him," said Jacqui.

"And he turns that dislike outward," Rachel continued.

"I don't get it. Why can't he just be normal? Well, fuck it, I'm off. I'm sorry I came. Have a good night," she called over to the table. "Everyone except Joey."

She left and the Scrabble kicked off again, but about half an hour later, I was seized by a strange panic: suddenly I couldn't be with these people any longer.

"I think I'll be off now," I said, trying to keep the urgency from my voice.

Luke and Rachel watched me anxiously. "I'll come down and put you in a cab," Rachel said.

"No, you're not dressed, I'll do it," Luke said.

"No, please, I'm fine." I looked longingly at the door. If I didn't leave soon, I'd burst.

"If you're sure."

"I'm sure."

"What are you doing tomorrow?" Rachel asked.

"Going shopping with Jacqui in the afternoon." I raced through the words.

"Want to go to a movie in the evening?"

"Yeah," Luke enthused. "There's a digitally remastered version of *North by Northwest* showing in the Angelika."

"Fine, yes, fine," I said, my breath constricted. "See you tomorrow, then."

"'Night."

"'Night."

And then the door was being opened and I was free. My pulse rate slowed down, my breathing became easier. I stood on the sidewalk and felt the panic abate. Then it built back up again as I thought: *God, how bad is it that I can't even be with my own sister? And now I have to go back to my empty apartment.*

What a pisser: I couldn't be with people and I didn't want to be alone. Suddenly my perspective whooshed and I was far out in space, watching the world. I could see millions and millions of people, all slotted into their lives; then I could see me—I'd lost my place in the universe. It had closed up and there was nowhere for me to be.

I was more lost than I had known it was possible for any human being to be.

And then I was back on the sidewalk again. What was I to do?

I started walking. I hobbled a wandering, circuitous route, but eventually I reached my building, because there was no place else for me to go. At the bottom of the steps, as I wasted a few more seconds hunting in my bag for my keys, someone yelled, "Baby cakes. Wait up."

It was Ornesto, our upstairs neighbor, coming down the street in a bright red pimpy suit. *Shite.*

He caught me up and said accusingly, "I've been calling you. I have left you, like, eight trillion messages."

"I know, Ornesto, I'm sorry, I'm just a little weird—"

"Whoa! Would you look at that face! Whoo-ee, baby cakes, that is *bad*." He practically ran his nose along my scar, like he was hoovering up a line of coke, then pulled me to him in a painful embrace. Luckily Ornesto was very self-obsessed and it didn't take long for his attention to snap back to him.

"I'm home for a New York minute, then I'm going right back out to look for"—he paused to yell—"HOT MEN. Come and talk to me while I get changed into my party frock."

"Okay."

In Ornesto's Thai-themed apartment, right beside a gold Buddha, there was a photo stuck to the wall with a kitchen knife. It was of a man's face and the knife went right through his open laughing mouth.

Ornesto noticed me looking. "Ohmigod, you totally missed it all. His name is Bradley. I thought it was the real thing, but you would not believe what that man did to me."

Ornesto had very bad luck with men. They were always cheating on him or stealing his expensive heavy-bottomed saucepans or going back to their wives. What had happened this time?

"He beat me up."

"He did?"

"Can't you see my black eye?"

He displayed it proudly. All I could see was slight purplish bruising beside his eyebrow, but he was so pleased with it that I sucked in my breath sympathetically. "That's terrible."

"But the good news is that I've started taking singing lessons! My therapist says I need a creative outlet." Ornesto—unexpectedly, perhaps—was a veterinary nurse. "My voice coach says I have a real gift. Says he never saw anyone get the breathing right so fast!"

"Lovely," I said vaguely. No point acting too interested: Ornesto was a great man for new passions. He'd have had a row with his teacher and completely turned against the singing by next week.

I looked around; I could smell something . . . Then I noticed it on his table. A big bunch of flowers. Lilies.

"You have lilies?" I said.

"Yeah, trying to be good to myself, you know? So many guys in line to treat me bad. Only one I can depend on is me, myself, and I."

"When did you get them?"

He thought about it. "Right about yesterday. Something wrong?"

"No." But I was wondering if it had been Ornesto's lilies I had smelled last night. The smell could have come through the air vent into my kitchen. Was that what had happened? Had it been nothing at all to do with Aidan?

I used to dream of a white wedding.

The kind of dream where you jerk awake in the middle of the night, drenched in sweat, your heart pounding. A dream in the worst nightmare kind of way.

I could see it all. The months of bickering with my mother over broccoli. On the day itself, trying to fight a path through my sisters—all of them my bridesmaids—to get space in a mirror to put my makeup on, and having to talk Helen out of wearing my dress. Then Dad walking me up the aisle muttering, "I feel a right gom in this waistcoat."

But there's nothing like a near-death experience to bring things into focus.

After I'd recovered from my scuba-diving ascent—I had to spend a short time in a decompression thing, then a much longer time accepting Codependent's abject apologies; clearly the whole incident had set him back terribly, I'd never met anyone so needy—I rang my mother to thank her for giving birth to me and she said, "What choice had I? You were in there, how else were you going to get out?"

Then I told her I was getting married.

"Sure you are."

"No, Mum, I really am. Wait, I'm going to put him on the line."

I handed Aidan the phone and he looked terrified. "What do I say?"

"Tell her you want to marry me."

"Okay. Hello, Mrs. Walsh. Can I marry your daughter?" He listened for a moment then gave me back the phone. "She wants to talk to you."

"Well, Mum?"

"What's wrong with him?"

"Nothing."

"Nothing obvious, you mean. Has he a job?"

"Yes."

"A chemical dependency?"

"No."

"Cripes, this is a break from tradition. What's his name?"

"Aidan Maddox."

"Irish?"

"No, Irish-American. He's from Boston."

"Like JFK?"

"Like JFK," I agreed. Her lot loved JFK, he was up there with the pope.

"Well, look what happened to him."

Petulantly I said to Aidan, "My mother won't let me marry you in case you get your head blown off in an open-top car in a Dallas motorcade."

"Hold your horses," Mum said. "I never said that. But this is very sudden. And your history of . . . ah . . . impulsive carry-on is a long one. And how come you never mentioned him at Christmas?"

"I did. I said I had a boyfriend who kept asking to marry me, but Helen was doing her impersonation of Stephen Hawking eating a cone and no one was listening to me. As usual. Look, ring Rachel. She's met him. She'll vouch for him."

A pause. A sneaky pause. "Has Luke met him?"

"Yes."

"I'll ask Luke about him."

"Do that."

Any excuse to speak to Luke.

"Are we really getting married?" I asked Aidan.

"Sure."

"Then let's do it soon," I said. "Three months' time. Start of April?"

"Okay."

In the New York dating rules, after a relationship "goes exclusive," the next step is to get engaged. This is meant to happen after three months. Basically, the minute the period of exclusivity starts, the women set a stopwatch for ninety days, and as soon as it *brrrrings*, they shout, "Right! Time's up! Where's my ring?"

But Aidan and I broke all records. A two-month period between going exclusive and getting engaged and three months between getting engaged and getting married. And I wasn't even pregnant.

But after my brush with death beneath the waves, I was full of vim and vigor and there seemed no point in waiting for anything. My urgent need to do everything *right now* passed after a couple of weeks, but at the time I was going round seizing the day left, right, and center.

"Where will we do it?" Aidan asked. "New York? Dublin? Boston?"

"None of the above," I said. "Let's go to County Clare. West coast of Ireland," I explained. "We went there for our holidays every summer. My dad's from there. It's lovely."

"Okay. Is there a hotel? Give them a call."

So I rang the local hotel in Knockavoy and my stomach flipped alarmingly when they said they could fit us in. I hung up the phone and backed away.

"Christ," I said to Aidan. "I've just booked our wedding. I might have to varmint."

Then everything happened very fast. I decided to leave the menu to Mum because of the great broccoli wars of Claire's wedding. (A bitter standoff that lasted almost a week with Mum saying that broccoli was "pretentious" and nothing more than "jumped-up cauliflower" and Claire shrieking that if she couldn't have her favorite vegetable at her wedding, when *could* she have it?) The way I saw it, the food at weddings is always revolting, so why argue over whether your guests should have disgusting broccoli or inedible cauliflower? "Work away, Mum," I said magnanimously. "The catering is your area." But minefields lay in the most innocent-looking of landscapes—I made the mistake of suggesting that we should have a vegetarian option and that set her off: she didn't believe in vegetarianism. She insisted it was a whim and that people were only doing it to be deliberately awkward.

"Grand, grand, whatever," I said. "They can eat the bread rolls."

I was far, far more worried about the bridesmaid issue. I really felt I couldn't cope with all four of my sisters arguing over color and style and shoes. But in a fantastic stroke of luck, Helen refused to be one because of the superstition that if you're a bridesmaid more than twice, you'll never be a bride. "Not that I'm planning anything," she said, "but I want to keep my options open."

Once Mum heard that, she forbade Rachel from being a bridesmaid because that would put the kibosh on her ever marrying Luke, then after a big summit, it was decreed that I would have *no* bridesmaids but that Claire's three children would be flower girls. Even Luka, her son.

Then there was the dress. I had a vision in my head of what I wanted—a bias-cut satin sheath—but couldn't find it anywhere. In the end it was designed and made by a contact of Dana's, a woman who ordinarily made curtains.

"I can see the headlines now," Aidan said. " 'New York Bride in non–Vera Wang dress shocker.' "

And, of course, there was the invitation list.

"Okay with you if I invite Janie?" Aidan asked.

It was a tricky one. Naturally I didn't want her there if her heart was broken and if, at the "Does anyone object?" bit, she was going to jump to her feet and screech, "IT SHOULDA BEEN ME!"

But it would be nice if we could meet and be civilized.

"Sure. You've got to invite her."

So he did, but we got a nice letter back, thanking us for the invitation but saying that, as the wedding was in Ireland, she wouldn't be able to attend.

I didn't know whether I felt relieved or not. Anyway, she wasn't coming and that was that.

But it wasn't.

Because when I went on to our wedding-list Web site, I saw that someone called Janie Sorensen had bought us a present. For a minute I thought, *Who on earth is Janie Sorensen?* Then I thought, *It's Janie! Aidan's Janie.* What had she bought us? I clicked like mad to get the details, and when I saw, I felt like I'd been punched in the stomach. Janie had bought us a set of kitchen knives. Really sharp, pointy, dangerous ones. Fair enough, we'd put them on our list, but why couldn't she have got us a cashmere throw or a couple of fluffy cushions, which were also on the list? I sat staring at the screen. Was this a warning? Or was I reading too much into it?

Later I tentatively put it to Aidan and he laughed and said, "That's typical of her sense of humor."

"So it was deliberate?"

"Oh yeah, probably. But nothing to be scared of."

There was more to come.

Less than a couple of weeks later, on a Friday night, I was at Aidan's place, looking through take-out menus and calling out dinner suggestions to him. He was pulling off his tie and, at the same time, opening his mail, when something in one of the envelopes shocked him. I felt it across the room.

"What?" I asked, staring at the card in his hand.

He paused, looked up, and said, "Janie's getting married."

"What?"

"Janie's getting married. Two months after us."

I was carefully watching his reaction. He was smiling like billy-oh and he said, "This is great. Just great." He seemed genuinely happy.

"Who's she marrying?"

He shrugged. "Someone called Howard Wicks. Never heard of the guy."

"Are we invited?"

"No. They're doing it in Fiji. Just close family. She always said that if she got married she'd do it in Fiji." He read through the letter again and said, "I'm really happy for her."

"Do they have a present list?" I asked.

"I don't know," he said, "but if they do we could send her a garrote or something? Maybe a nice big machete?"

Despite delegating as much as we could, organizing the wedding was three horribly stressful months. Everyone said it was our own fault, that we hadn't given ourselves enough time, but I suspected that if we'd given ourselves a year the stress would have expanded to fill the available time, so that we'd have had a horribly stressful year instead of just three months.

But it was all worth it.

On a bright, blustery blue day, on a church on a hill, Aidan and I got married. The daffodils were out, throngs of shocking yellow, bobbing in the brisk breeze. Spring-green fields were all around us and the foamy sea sparkled in the distance.

In the photos taken outside the church, men in shiny shoes and women in pastel frocks are smiling. We all look beautiful and very, very happy.

I checked Aidan's horoscopes. Hot Scopes! said:

> **Oh, boy, you are HOT today. Smokin'. Solar activity in Scorpio means this is the right day to get that new romantic relationship off the ground.**

Hot Scopes! was the worst site. It always said something to upset me. I shouldn't do this, I really shouldn't. I knew it was all crap but I couldn't stop myself. I was desperate for some sort of indication of how things were for him. Stars Online said:

> **Yes, it's hard for you to rein in your natural urge to leap before you look—in affairs of the heart especially. But showing self-restraint is the only way forward if you want a happy ending.**

That was more like it. And what had Today's Stars to say for itself?

> *Keeping a firm grip on reality is vital for you over the next seven days.*

To: Aidan_maddox@yahoo.com
From: Magiciansgirl1 @yahoo.com
Subject: Monday's clothes

A red satin embroidered cheongsam (that's Chinese dress to you), over cutoff jeans and red patent sneakers. My hair is in an updo held with chopsticks, in a cunning ruse to avoid wearing a hat. It is now 6 days since I've worn one, I'm having a quiet little rebellion. I wonder how long it will take for someone to notice, and believe me, they *will* notice.

I'd really like to hear from you, I love you.

Your girl, Anna

When I walked into the office, Franklin did a quick sweep over me, resting slightly longer on my hair. He knew something was missing, but was too agitated to decide. That's because it was time for the MMM (Monday Morning Meeting); an hour and a half in hell would be preferable.

In preparation, Franklin corralled his "girls"—the people working on Candy Grrrl, Bergdorf Baby, Bare, Kitty Loves Katie, EarthSource, Visage, and Warpo (a brand that was even more edgy than Candy Grrrl—you'd want to see what they had to wear; I lived in dread of being moved to their team).

"Good job," Franklin said to Tabitha. Bergdorf Baby's new night serum had got a great write-up and—much more important—photo in Sunday's *New York Times*.

To me and Lauryn: "We gotta get things back on track, ladies."

"Yeah, but—" Lauryn started.

"I know all the reasons," Franklin said. "All I'm saying is, you've got to catch up. Big-time."

Lauryn gave me a hard sideways look; she had plans for me. She was going to try assigning all my time to her feature ideas, while I needed to start generating captions and photos on beauty pages and getting my targets back on track. Which of us would win?

We streamed into the boardroom. We were all there, all fourteen brands. Some women were clutching newspapers and magazines. They were the lucky ones, the ones who had managed to get coverage.

I even had one or two pages myself. Not in the newspapers, obviously. While I'd been away, it looked like nobody had bothered to keep the badgering of newspaper beauty editors up-to-date—I didn't know what those temps had actually *done*.

But because of the glossies' long lead time, some of the schmoozing I'd done months ago had borne fruit—like putting bulbs down in September and flowers appearing months later, the following spring.

Along the wall, people jostled for space, trying to become invisible; you could almost smell the fear. Even I felt anxious, which was unexpected. After what had happened I'd have thought that a public bollocking at work wouldn't touch me. But clearly it was a Pavlovian response; something about standing in this room on a Monday morning tripped my fear switch.

Monday mornings were horrible. I knew they were horrible for everyone, everywhere, but they were extra horrible for us because so much of our success or failure depended on what had appeared in the weekend newspaper supplements. It was so *obvious*.

Sometimes, if they'd been let down by a beauty editor and hadn't got the coverage they'd expected, girls threw up before the meeting.

As we took our places, Ariella ignored us. She was sitting at the head of the long table, flicking through the glossy pages of a magazine. Then I saw what it was—we all saw at the same time: this month's *Femme*. Shit. It wasn't on the newsstands yet. She'd got an early copy and none of us knew what was in it.

But she was going to tell us. "Ladies! Come in, come closer. See what I'm seeing. I'm seeing Clarins. I'm seeing Clinique. I'm seeing Lancôme. I'm even seeing fucking Revlon. But I'm not seeing..."

Who was it? It could have been any of us. But who *should* it have been?

"...Visage!"

Poor Wendell. We all lowered our eyes, ashamed but oh so glad it wasn't us.

"Wanna talk to me about that, Wendell?" Ariella asked. "About the most expensive campaign we ever did? Where exactly did we fly those leechy beauty gals to? Couldja just remind me?"

"Tahiti." You could barely hear Wendell's voice.

"Tahiti? Ta*hit*i! Even *I* haven't been to fucking Tahiti. And they couldn't give us a lousy four-by-two? Whatcha do to her, Wendell? Throw up on her? Sleep with her boyfriend?"

"She was all set to give us a quarter page, but Tokyo Babe just brought out their new eye cream and her editor overrode her because they advertise so heavily."

"Don't give me excuses. Bottom line: if someone else gets coverage, you have failed. You are a failure. You have failed, Wendell, not just because you didn't work hard enough but because you couldn't get them to like you enough. You're not a likable-enough person. Have you gained weight?"

"No, I—"

"Well, SOMETHING'S wrong!"

Horrible but true. So much of the PR game depended on personal relationships. If a beauty editor liked you, you had a better chance of your brand fighting its way to the top of the pile. But there was precious little anyone could do if a major brand threatened to pull a twenty-thousand-dollar ad if you didn't give them nice coverage.

After the main event—the humiliation of Wendell—we moved on to Any Other Business. This was where Ariella pitted brand against brand. If one had done well, it was an opportunity to point out the failings of another. She also enjoyed pitting Franklin against Mary Jane, the coordinator of the other seven brands.

Then it was all over for another week.

As everyone trooped back out, several people murmured, "That wasn't too horrible. She was okay today."

And the great thing about the MMM was that once it was over, the week could only get better.

To: Aidan_maddox@yahoo.com
From: Magiciansgirl1@yahoo.com
Subject: On the mend

Got the plaster off my arm today. It doesn't look like my arm anymore, it's a puny, shrunken little thing and *so* <u>hairy</u>, nearly as hairy as Lauryn's arms. My knee is pretty good (and not hairy). Even my nails are growing. It's just my face now.

　　I love you.

Your girl, Anna

To: Aidan_maddox@yahoo.com
From: Magiciansgirl1@yahoo.com
Subject: My name is Anna

Today someone left an AA meetings list on my desk. Anony-mously, as it were.

　　I love you.

Your girl, Anna

To: Aidan_maddox@yahoo.com
From: Magiciansgirl1@yahoo.com
Subject: New hair!

I begged Sailor for a low-maintenance cut but he told me we have to suffer for our beauty and gave me a "directional" brushed-forward shaggy yoke. The only good thing is that it covers a lot of my scar. But when I try to blow-dry it myself, it'll be such a disaster I'll have to start wearing hats again. Obviously it was all a big conspiracy.

I love you.
Your girl, Anna

All week, I put in twelve or thirteen hours a day at work, and somehow enough time passed so that it got to be Friday evening. But no sooner had I let myself in and put down my keys than I saw, like a big guilt-making accusing thing, the flashing light on my answering machine. Bums. How bad was it? How many messages? I kept my feet planted where I stood and leaned the top half of my body over to look: three messages. I looked at Dogly's kindly face and said, "I bet they're all from Leon."

He had me badgered with messages. *Badgered.* I'd had a couple of near misses at work, when he'd withheld his number, but so far I'd manage to avoid talking to him. I'd have to ring him back soon; it was only a matter of time before he arrived in person at the apartment—or far more scary, set Dana on me. But I just couldn't bear to, not yet anyway.

Instead, I turned on the computer—and my heart lifted when I saw that there was a new e-mail. I held my breath and waited, frozen with hope. But it was from Mum! That made twice in one lifetime. What could be up?

To: Magiciansgirl1@yahoo.com
From: Thewalshes1@eircom.net
Subject: Mystery

As regards the woman and her dog, I am still keeping you "in the loop," as they say. There has been plenty of "action." This morning I "lay in wait." She normally comes at ten past nine, so I was ready for her. As soon as she appeared, I pretended to be putting out the bins which I thought was a good "ruse," even though bin day is Monday and it is your father's job anyway.

"Nice morning for it," I said, meaning, "Nice morning for making your dog do his wees at an innocent stranger's gate." Right away your woman pulls at the lead and says, "Hurry up, Zoe." Now we have a clue. What a name for a dog! Then something terrible happened, the woman gave me a "look"— our eyes met, and as you know, Anna, I am not a fanciful woman, but I knew I was in the presence of evil.

Your loving mother,

Mum

P.S. In a couple of weeks' time myself and your father are going away to "The Algarve" for a fortnight. It will be nice. Not as nice as the Cipriani in Venice, of course (not that I'd know), but quite nice. While we're gone, Helen will be staying with "Maggie" and "Garv," as you all insist on calling them. This means it will be hard to keep "tabs" on the old woman, but seeing as she gave me such a dirty look, this is probably no harm.

Across the room, the flashing light of the answering machine continued to accuse me. *Go away, go away, why do you torment me so?* I wished I could delete the bloody messages without having listened to them, but the machine wouldn't let me, so I hit play, then legged it to the bathroom, hearing as I went, "Anna, it's Leon. I know this is hard for you, but it's hard for me, too. I need to see you..."

To drown out his voice I ran the taps with such Niagaraesque force that I drenched the front of my dress. I stepped back, counted to twenty-three, then cautiously turned the water toward off, but I heard Leon say "...my pain, too..." and with a lightning-fast flick of my wrist, turned the water back up to torrential, counted to seven and a half, eased it down again, heard "...we can help each other..." and immediately ratcheted the flood up as far as it would go. It was a little like tuning a radio and picking up signals. Radio Leon.

Eventually he finished what he had to say and I tiptoed from the bathroom and hit delete.

"All messages deleted," the machine said.

"Thank you," I replied.

On Saturday night Rachel "invited" me over to her and Luke's—an offer I couldn't refuse. Not unless I wanted a well-meaning lecture.

I had a pleasant-enough time until, a couple of hours in, I was over-taken by a panic that was starting to seem terrifyingly familiar: I had to get away.

Rachel would only permit me to leave after she'd questioned me closely on my plans for Sunday, but I had it all sewn up: Jacqui had ar-ranged for me and her to go to a day spa called Cocoon. She'd said it would be good for me.

And it was. Apart from the aromatherapist telling me I was the tens-est person she'd ever worked with and the pedicurist complaining that she wouldn't be able to paint my toenails until I'd stopped twitching my foot.

Then it was Sunday night; I'd survived another weekend. But instead of being relieved, I was seized with terrible desperation. Something had to happen soon.

28

It finally happened. Aidan finally showed up.

Two and a half weeks after I'd come back from Ireland, I was at work, sitting at my desk, laboring at a quarterly spreadsheet, when he just walked in. The joy at seeing him was like the warmth of the midday sun—I was *thrilled*.

"About time," I exclaimed.

He sat on a corner of the desk and his smile nearly split his face in two. He looked delighted and shy simultaneously. "Happy to see me?" he asked.

"Jesus Christ, Aidan, I'm *so* happy! I can't believe this. I was afraid I'd never see you again." He was wearing the same clothes he'd been wearing the first day we'd met. "But how did you manage it?"

"What do you mean? I just walked in here."

"But, Aidan." Because I'd just remembered. "You're dead."

I woke with a jump. I was on the couch. Lights from the street lit the room with a purplish glow and there was some racket outside: people shouting and the boomy bass line of a bridge-and-tunnel limo, which pulsed below me until the traffic lights changed and it moved on.

I closed my eyes and went straight back into the same dream.

Aidan wasn't smiling any longer, he was upset and confused, and I asked him, "No one told you, you were dead?"

"No."

"That's what I've been afraid of. And where have you been?"

"Hanging around. I saw you in Ireland and everything."

"You did? Why didn't you say anything?"

"You were with your family, I didn't want to butt in."

"But you're family now. You're my family."

The next time I woke it was 5 A.M. The morning beyond the blinds was already citrus bright but the streets were silent. I needed to talk to Rachel. She was the only one who could help me.

"Sorry to wake you."

"I was awake anyway." She was probably lying but there was a chance she wasn't. Sometimes she got up at the crack of dawn to go to an NA (Narcotics Anonymous) meeting before work.

"Are you okay?" She tried hard to stifle a yawn.

"Can you meet me?"

"'Course. Now? Will I come over?"

"No." I was desperate to get out of the apartment.

"How about Jenni's?" It was some twenty-four-hour coffee place. On account of her condition Rachel knew lots of twenty-four-hour coffee places. "See you there in thirty minutes."

I pulled on some clothes and ran out the door; I couldn't wait in the apartment a moment longer. In the taxi I saw him walking along Fourteenth Street, but this time I knew it wasn't him.

I arrived at Jenni's far too early, ordered a latte, and tried to eavesdrop on the intense conversation which was taking place between a foursome of gaunt, good-looking men dressed in black. Unfortunately I only caught the occasional word: "...getting high..."; "...let go with love..."; "...a dash of teriyaki sauce, dude..."

Then Rachel arrived. "It's a while since I've been here," she commented, looking nervously at the boys. "I'm getting introspection flashbacks." She sat down and ordered a green tea. "Anna, are you okay? Has something happened?"

"I dreamed about Aidan last night."

"That's normal, one of the things that's meant to happen. Like seeing him everywhere. So what did you dream?"

"I dreamed that he was dead."

Pause. "That's because he is, Anna."

"I know that."

Another pause. "You're not really acting like you do. Anna, I'm so sorry, but no amount of pretending that everything is the same will change what happened."

"But I don't want him to be dead."

Her eyes filled with tears. "Of course you don't! He was your husband, the man—"

"Rachel, please don't say 'was.' I hate all this past-tense stuff. And it's not about me, it's him I'm worried about. I'm so afraid he'll freak out when he discovers what's happened. He'll be so pissed off and scared and I can't help him. Rachel," I said, and suddenly I couldn't bear it, "Aidan's going to hate being dead."

R achel looked blank. Like she wasn't listening to me, then I realized she was in shock. Was I that bad?

"We had so many plans," I said. "We weren't going to die until we were eighty. And he worried about me; he wanted to take care of me, and if he can't he'll go mental. And, Rachel, he was so strong and healthy, hardly ever sick. How's he going to handle having died?"

"Er...um, let's see." This had never happened before: Rachel always had a theory on emotional ailments. "Anna, this is too big for me. You need professional help, someone who specializes in this. A grief counselor. I've brought you a book about bereavement, which might help, but you really need to see an expert—"

"Rachel, I just want to talk to him. That's all I want. I can't bear to think of him trapped someplace awful and not being able to contact me. I mean, where *is* he? Where did he go?"

Her eyes got bigger and bigger as the dismay on her face worsened. "Anna, I really think—"

The men in black were leaving, and as they passed our table, one of them clocked Rachel and did a double take.

He had a lean face, skin marked from old acne scars, tormented brown eyes, and long dark hair. He wouldn't have looked out of place in the Red Hot Chili Peppers.

"Hey!" he said. "I've met you? The meetings in St. Marks Place?

It's Rachel, right? I'm Angelo. So how're you doing? Still conflicted?"

"No," Rachel said snippily, giving off such strong "this is so inappropriate" vibes you could nearly see them zigzagging through the air.

"So? You gonna marry the guy?"

"Yes." More snippiness. But she couldn't resist sticking out her hand for him to admire her engagement ring.

"Wow. Getting married. Well, congratulations. He is one lucky dude."

Then he looked at me. A look of deep compassion. "Oh, little girl," he said. "It's bad, hey?"

"Were you listening to our conversation?" Rachel's snippiness was back in force.

"No. But it's sorta"—he shrugged—"obvious." To me he said, "Just take it one day at a time."

"She's not an addict. She's my sister."

"No reason for her not to take it one day at a time."

I went to work, thinking, *Aidan is dead. Aidan has died.* I hadn't actually realized it until now. I mean, I knew he'd died but I'd never believed it was permanent.

I moved through the corridor like a ghost, and when Franklin called, "Morning, Anna, how're you doing?" I felt like answering, "Good, except my husband died and we were married less than a year. Yes, I know you know all about it, but I've just realized."

But there was no point saying anything, it was old news for everyone else; they'd long moved on.

We'd been on our way out for dinner, just me and him, and what was unendurable was that this was something we rarely did. Restaurants were for sociable nights out with other people, but when it was just me and him, we were more likely to snuggle on the couch and ring for takeout.

If we'd stayed at home that night, he'd still be alive. In fact, we almost didn't go. He'd booked a table at Tamarind but I'd asked him to cancel it because we'd eaten out just two nights earlier for Valentine's Day. But it seemed to mean so much to him to go that I gave in.

So I was waiting on the street for him to pick me up when, alerted by honks, beeps, and shouted expletives, I saw a yellow cab lurching across three lanes of traffic and heading in my direction. Sure enough, there was Aidan, making a scared face and flashing seven fingers at me. Seven out of ten. Nutter alert. Our personal scoring system for mental cabdrivers.

"Seven?" I mouthed. "Good work."

He laughed and that made me happy. He'd been a bit low for a day or two: a few nights earlier he'd had a call—work—that had wrecked his buzz.

With a shudder, the cab stopped beside me, I hopped in, and before my door was even closed, we screeched back into the heavy traffic. I was flung against Aidan and he managed to kiss me before I was thrown back in the opposite direction. Eagerly, I said, "Seven out of ten? We haven't had one of them in a while. Tell us."

He shook his head in admiration and said in an undertone, "It's good, this one, Anna, it's good stuff. He saw Princess Diana in his local 7-Eleven, buying a bottle of Gatorade and twelve doughnuts."

"What flavor?"

"A mixed box. And last year, he saw the face of Martin Luther King in a tomato. Charged his neighbors five dollars a look until the tomato went moldy."

Without warning, we zigged across Fifty-third Street and were thrown, with force, against the right-hand door. I clutched Aidan. "And, of course," Aidan added, "there's the quality of his driving. Brace yourself for a zag."

Funnily enough the accident wasn't the fault of our seven-out-of-ten driver. In fact, it turned out to be no one's fault at all. Making quite nippy progress through the dense postwork cars, Aidan and I had moved onto a mundane conversation about the state of our apartment and what a pig our landlord was. We were totally unaware of the events playing out on the junction of the cross street—a woman doing an unexpected dash across the road, an Armenian cabdriver swerving to avoid hitting her, and his front wheel connecting with a pool of oil, there from when a car had broken down earlier and spilled its guts onto the road. In blissful ignorance, I was saying "We could try painting the—" when we passed into another dimension. With brutal impact, another cab had plowed into the side of ours and its front bumper was trying to get into our backseat—the sort of thing that only happens in a nightmare. My head was full of grinding and breaking, then we were spinning backward in the road, like we were on an evil merry-go-round.

The shock was—still is—indescribable, and the impact broke Aidan's pelvis and six of his ribs, and mortally injured his liver, kidneys, pancreas, and spleen. I saw it all—in slow motion, of course: the shattered glass filling the air like silver rain, the tearing metal, the short gush of blood from Aidan's mouth, and the look of surprise in his eyes. I didn't know he was dying, I didn't know that in twenty minutes' time he'd be dead, I just thought we should be angry that some asshole, going far, far too fast, had side-rammed us.

Out in the street people were screaming, someone yelled, "Jesus, Jesus *Christ!*," and whirling past me were people's legs and feet. I noticed a pair of red spindly-heeled boots. *Red boots are such a statement,* I thought hazily. I still remembered them so clearly I could have picked them out in an identification lineup. Some details were imprinted on me forever.

I was really lucky, everyone said later. "Lucky" because Aidan took all the impact. By the time the other driver had had his momentum broken by Aidan's body, he was nearly all out of steam, with barely enough force left to break my right arm and dislocate my knee. Obviously there was collateral damage—the metal in our ceiling buckled and tore and gouged a deep furrow in my face, and the tearing metal in the door ripped off two of my nails. But I didn't die.

Our driver hadn't a scratch. When the never-ending backward spinning finally stopped, he got out of the cab and looked in at us through the hole where his window used to be, then backed away and bent over. I wondered what he was doing. Checking his tires? Then, from the sounds he was making, I realized he was throwing up.

"Ambulance is coming, buddy," a man's voice said, and I wondered if I had really heard it or just in my head. For a short time, things were oddly peaceful.

Aidan and I looked at each other in a "can you believe this?" way and he said, "Baby, are you okay?"

"Yes, are you?"

"Yeah." But his voice was weird, kind of gurgly.

On the front of his shirt and tie was a sticky, dark red bloodstain and I was distressed because it was such a nice tie, one of his favorites. "You're not to worry about the tie," I said. "We'll get you another one."

"Does anything hurt?" he asked.

"No." At the time, I felt nothing. Good old shock, the great protector, gets us through the unbearable. "How about you?"

"A little." That was when I knew it was a lot.

From far away, I heard sirens. They got nearer and louder, then they were right up beside us, when abruptly, midshriek, they stopped. *They're for us,* I thought. *I never thought this sort of thing would happen to us.*

Aidan was taken out of the mangled car, then we were in the ambulance and things seemed to speed up. We were in the hospital and on separate gurneys and running through corridors, and from the way everyone paid attention to us, we were the most important people there.

I gave our health-insurance details, which I remembered with crystal-clear, photo recall—even our membership numbers. I hadn't even known that I knew them. I was asked to sign something but I couldn't because of my right arm and hand being destroyed, so they said it was okay.

"What is your relationship to this patient?" I was asked. "His wife? His friend?"

"Both," Aidan answered, in the gurgly voice.

When they rushed him off to the operating room, I still didn't know he was dying. I knew he was hurt, but I had no conception that he couldn't be fixed.

"Make him be okay," I asked the surgeon, a short, tan man.

"I'm sorry," he said. "He's probably not going to make it."

My mouth fell open. Excuse me? Half an hour earlier we'd been on our way to have dinner. And now this suntanned man was telling me that Aidan might not "make it."

And he didn't. He died very quickly, barely ten minutes in.

By then the pain had started in my hand and arm and face. I was in such a fog of agony that I could barely remember my name, so trying to understand that Aidan had just died was like trying to imagine a totally new color. Rachel showed up with Luke; someone must have rung her. But when I saw her I thought they'd also been in an accident—why else would they be at the hospital?—and was confused by the coincidence. Sometime around then, I was given drugs, probably morphine, and it was only at that point that I thought to ask about the other driver, the one who'd rammed us.

His name was Elin. Both his arms had been broken but he was otherwise uninjured. Everyone was adamant that the accident wasn't his fault. There were a million witnesses who insisted he'd had "no choice" but to swerve to avoid hitting the woman, and that it was sheer, unadulterated lousy luck that the patch of oil had been dumped right on that spot of road.

I spent two days in the hospital and all I can remember is a nonstop stream of people. Aidan's parents and Kevin flew in from Boston. Mum, Dad, Helen, and Maggie came from Ireland. Dana and Leon—who cried so much he was given drugs, too—Jacqui, Rachel, Luke, Ornesto, Teenie, Franklin, Marty, people from Aidan's work, and two policemen, who took a statement from me. Even Elin the driver came. Shaking and crying, both of his arms in plaster, he sat next to my bed, apologizing over and over and over again. There was no way I could hate this man—he was going to have nightmares for the rest of his life and he'd probably never get behind the wheel of a car again. But my pity for Elin left me at a bit of a loss: Who *could* I blame for Aidan's death?

Then we were on a plane to Boston, then we were at the funeral, which was like our wedding, but a nightmare version of it. Being pushed up the aisle in a wheelchair, seeing faces I hadn't seen for ages, felt like a dream where a disparate collection of people are inexplicably gathered together.

Then I was on a flight, then I was home in Ireland sleeping in the living room, then I was back in New York, and I'd only just faced what had really happened.

Part 2

30

Extract from *Never Coming Back* by Dorothea K. Lincoln:

About a week after my husband died, I was in my sunroom, flicking through the *National Enquirer*—the only reading matter I was able to concentrate on—when in through the open window flew a butterfly. It was incorrigibly beautiful, intricately patterned in red, blue, and white. As I watched in wonder, it flitted around the room, alighting on the stereo, a pot plant—as if reminding me to water it!— and my husband's old chair. Then it flew to my copy of the *National Enquirer* and landed heavily on it—it seemed to say, "Tut tut, Dorothea!" (Interestingly, my late husband would not permit that particular publication in the house.)

As the World Turns was on the TV, but the butterfly hovered over the remote. It seemed to be telling me something—could it be that it wanted the channel changed? "Well, okay, buddy," I said. "I can try."

I flicked through several channels, and when I got to Fox Sports, the beautiful creature landed on my hand, as if gently telling me to stop. Then it sat on my shoulder and watched half an hour of the U.S. Open; the room was filled with a deep, deep peace. When Ernie Els went to three under par, the butterfly stirred, flitted to the window, hovered on the sill for a moment, as if saying good-bye, and finally flew away into the wide blue yonder. There was no doubt in my mind that this had been a visit from my late husband. He'd been telling me that he was still with me, that he always would be. Several other bereaved persons have reported similar visitations...

I put the book down, sat up, looked around my living room, and thought, *Where's my butterfly?*

It was about four or five weeks since my early-morning conversation at Jenni's with Rachel and not much had changed. I was still working long hours and producing little of value, I was still sleeping on the couch, and Aidan was still dead.

I had a nice, little daily routine going: I'd wake at the crack of dawn, ring Aidan on his cell phone, go to work for at least ten hours, come home, ring Aidan again, construct elaborate fantasies where he hadn't died, cry for a few hours, then doze off, wake up, and do it all again.

Crying had become a great comfort, but it was difficult to arrange times for it because my face took so long to return to normal. It wasn't safe to do it in the mornings because I looked terrible for work. And it wasn't safe at lunchtime for the same reason. But evenings were good. I looked forward to them.

I got through each day and the only thing that kept me going was the hope that tomorrow would be easier. But it wasn't. Every day was exactly the same. Horrific, unbelievable, like having walked through the wrong door of my life, where everything was identical, apart from one big huge difference.

I had hoped that by returning to New York and using normal stuff, like work and friends, the nightmare would disperse. But it hadn't. The work and friends had just become part of the nightmare.

This morning, like every morning, I'd woken horribly early. There was always a split second when I wondered what the terribleness was. Then I'd remember.

I lay down again, a dull persistent ache in my bones, what I'd imagined rheumatism or arthritis would feel like. When the pains had first started, I'd thought that maybe I'd caught a virus, or was suffering side effects of the accident. But my doctor said that what I was feeling was "the physical pain of grief." That this was "normal." Which came as a bit of a shock. I'd known to expect emotional pain but the physical pain was a new one on me.

I looked terrible, too: my nails kept splitting, my hair was dull and broken, and despite access to every exfoliator and moisturizer anyone could need, my skin was flaking off in tiny gray pieces.

I popped a couple of painkillers and switched on the telly, but when I couldn't find anything to catch my interest, I flicked through *Never Coming Back*. Great title, by the way, I thought. Cheery. Bound to perk up the spirits of the recently bereaved.

It was one of a deluge of books—arriving in the post from Claire in London, being left outside my door by Ornesto, handed over in person by Rachel, Teenie, Marty, Nell, even Nell's strange friend—and even though I could barely concentrate long enough to read a paragraph, I'd noticed the butterfly motif was a common one. But no butterflies for me.

Funnily enough, I wasn't that keen on butterflies. It was a hard thing to admit because everyone loves butterflies and not liking them is akin to saying you don't like Michael Palin or dolphins or strawberries. But to me, butterflies were slightly sneaky; all they were were moths in embroidered jackets. And, yes, moths were creepy and their flapping wings made a nasty, papery sound—but at least they were honest; they were brown, they were dull, they were stupid (flying into flames at the drop of a hat). All in all, they hadn't much going for them but they didn't pretend to be anything other than who they were.

And what about that woman and her control-freak husband? Tut tut, indeed. She was well shot of him. And how could I believe a woman who described something as "incorrigibly" beautiful?

Nevertheless, since I'd started reading these books, I'd been looking everywhere for butterflies or doves or strange cats who hadn't been around before. I was desperate for any sign that Aidan was still with me, but so far, I'd seen nothing.

People say it's the finality of death that they can't handle. But what was tearing me apart was that I didn't know where Aidan was. I mean, he had to be *somewhere*.

All his opinions and thoughts and memories and hopes and feelings, all the things that were unique to him, that made him a one-off human being—they couldn't be just *gone*.

I understood that his Aidan-ness was no longer contained in his cremated body, but his personality, or spirit, or whatever you want to call it—it couldn't be just snuffed out. There was too much of him to simply disappear: the way he didn't like *Catcher in the Rye* when everyone else in the whole world did; the slightly goofy way he walked because one leg was a tiny bit longer than the other; the way he sang like the Smurfs when he was shaving. He was so vital and full of—yes, life—that he must be somewhere, it was just a question of finding him.

I still saw him in the street but now I accepted that it wasn't him. I still read his horoscope. I still spoke to him in my head. I still e-mailed him and rang his cell phone, but I understood I wouldn't hear back from him. But some days I'd forget he was dead. I mean, literally just for a moment or two, usually when I had come home from work in the evenings; suddenly I'd find that I was waiting for him to come in the door. Or something funny would happen and I'd think, *Oh, I must tell Aidan that.* And then I'd be overwhelmed with horror—I'd break out in a sweat and black spots would dance before my eyes—the horror that he'd been taken away. Removed from this earth, from this being alive business, and gone to a place where I could never track him down.

Until now, I'd always thought that the worst thing that could happen to anyone was if someone you loved abruptly disappeared.

But this was worse. If he'd been imprisoned or kidnapped or even done a runner, I'd have hope that he might eventually come back.

And my *guilt* was unendurable. His story had been cut off so brutally and prematurely, while I was still here, still alive and well and working and with everything to play for. His body had taken the full impact of the crash, so I felt that he had died in order for me to live and it was the most appalling feeling. Like I'd cheated him out of the rest of his life, and really, I felt it would have been better if I'd died, too, because I was too ashamed to live my life when he was dead.

I fantasized a lot about him still being alive. That somewhere, in a parallel universe, he hadn't died—that the taxi had never crashed into us that day, that our lives had carried on smoothly, and we were blithely living out our allotted forty years or so together, unaware of the lucky escape we'd had, mercifully oblivious to all the pain we were being spared. I went into incredible detail in these fantasies—what we wore, what time we went to work, what we ate for lunch—and at night, when I couldn't sleep, they kept me company.

But what about him? How was he feeling? I hated that he had to go through whatever he was going through, on his own, and I knew that he would be doing all he could to get in contact with me. We had lived in each other's pocket, we had spoken and e-mailed ten times a day, we had spent every second of our spare time together, so that, wherever he was now, he'd be finding the separation terrible, too.

I would have given my life just to know that he was okay.

Where are you?

At the funeral, the priest had said a lot of guff about how Aidan had gone to "a better place," but that was crap. Such crap that, at the time, I'd wanted to shout it out, but I was too bandaged and sedated and hemmed in by family members to manage to.

I hadn't known any dead people before Aidan. The only other ones were my grannies and granddads and you'd expect them to die; they were old, it was right. But Aidan was young and strong and handsome and it was all wrong.

When my grandparents had died I'd been too young or hadn't cared enough to wonder if they'd really gone to heaven (or hell—Granny Maguire was definitely a candidate for down below). Now I was being forced to think about an afterlife and the absence of any certainty was terrifying.

In my teenage years, I'd yearned for a connection with some sort of spiritual being. Not with the Catholic God I'd been brought up with, because that was just way too dull, anyone could have that (if they were Irish). But the vague all-purpose God of dreamcatchers and chakras and fringey skirts had caught my fancy. Especially because you could keep adding to it—Reiki, crystals, guarana; the list, as long as it was "spiritual," was endless. Coincidences and anything remotely spooky thrilled me—anything that would make my life more exciting really. I taught myself to read tarot cards and I wasn't bad at it; I liked to believe that that was because I was quite psychic, but looking back, I knew it was just because I'd read the instruction book and learned what the symbols meant and anyway most people only get their cards read because they want a boyfriend.

I'd knocked off the tarot cards some years back, but I'd never stopped believing in a vague "something." If I didn't get what I wanted—a job, a bus, a pair of jeans in the right size—I used to say that "it wasn't meant to be," as if there was a God, some sort of benign puppet master, with a story line for us all. One who cared about what we wore.

But now that my back was to the wall, now that it really mattered, I found I didn't know what I believed. I didn't believe Aidan was in heaven. I didn't believe in heaven at all. I didn't even believe in God. I didn't not believe in God either. There was nothing to cling on to.

I got ready for work, I rang his cell phone like I did every morning, then in sudden frustration shrieked to the empty air, "Where are you? Where are you? *Where are you?*"

31

To: Magiciansgirl1@yahoo.com
From: Thewalshes1@eircom.net
Subject: Number twos!

Dear Anna,
I hope you are keeping well. Listen, it's gone to hell here altogether, with the old woman and her dog. Since we came back

from the Algarve there hadn't been sign nor sound of her and would you blame us for thinking we had "shaken" her. But by the looks of things she was just "regrouping." She was back with a vengeance this morning. She came early and made her dog do a "number two." Your father stood in it on his way out to buy the paper and as you know he is not a man who is easily stirred to action but this has stirred him. He says we are going to "get to the bottom" of this. This will involve Helen and her "skills." Luckily, she is very annoyed too and says she will do it for free. She says it's one thing to have dog wee at your front gate but dog poo is a different matter entirely.

Your loving mother,

Mum

P.S. What could it be about? As you know, I am not a woman who has enemies. Could it be Helen's fault?

P.P.S. We had the postholiday blues anyway, especially since your father's sunburn became infected, and because of this dog business, we are now very "low." Don't take this up the "wrong" way but I hope you haven't got "closure" yet because there would be little enough point in you coming home, we can hardly cheer ourselves up, never mind the likes of you.

And an e-mail had come from Helen.

To: Magiciansgirl1@yahoo.com
From: Lucky_Star_PI@yahoo.ie
Subject: Burned parent

Mum and Dad back from Algarve. Dad badly sunburned. Looks like Singing Detective. Vay vay funny.

32

My shooting electricity pains woke me up at their usual time—about 5 A.M. Automatically, I popped a couple of painkillers, then lay very still, squeezed my eyes shut, and pretended that I was in bed and Aidan was lying beside me. *All I have to do is stretch out my hand and I'll be able to touch you. You'll be all warm and sleepy and semitumescent and you'll wrap your arms and legs around me without fully waking up.* My fantasy was so detailed and convincing that I could smell him and almost believed I could hear him breathing. So when I opened my eyes and saw that I wasn't in bed and the place where Aidan should be was just empty air, a howl escaped me. I sounded like an animal. Curling into myself, I clutched Dogly to my stomach and tried to rock the pain away. When that didn't work, I turned on the telly. *Dallas.* Two episodes back-to-back. Who knew?

It ended just after seven. Late enough to get ready for work. I tried not to get there before eight most mornings, but some days I just couldn't bear lying awake in the apartment and was at my desk by six-thirty.

Staying busy, working hard, trying to stack up the days, that was the key.

Occasionally I could even lose myself in work, I could go into another place where imagination took over and I stopped being me. For a while.

Having said that, it wasn't all fun and games: there were The Lunches. Even before Aidan had died, I'd dreaded The Lunches. Taking beauty editors out to fancy restaurants was a regular part of my job, I had to do two or three a week and it had always been tricky because of the competitive undereating issue. Sometimes the journalists brought a colleague, so there were even more of us to not eat the one dessert we'd ordered between us. It was like a prizefight: Who would throw the first punch? Who would eat the first forkful? We'd circle one another warily, but as I was the hostess, protocol dictated that it was my job. However, I had to go very easy because if you ate too much, they'd disrespect you.

For the first month of my return I'd been spared The Lunches—not out of any compassion but because my scar was so bad, Ariella didn't want me out and about. However, thanks to vitamin-E capsules and a heavy-duty concealer, it was now a lot more discreet, so lunches were back on the menu.

The only way I coped was by bringing Brooke with me, at least whenever she was available. She was an absolute bloody godsend, she was. Her incredible talent for graciously putting people at ease managed to obscure my jerky, marionette-like attempts at playing the hostess. She'd dazzle the journo with details of her superglam life, without ever sounding like she was boasting, and I'd try to smile and force clods of food down my reluctant throat. Sometimes—and it happened a bit too often for my liking—I'd forget to eat the first forkful of dessert; the chocolate-cream pie, or whatever we'd ordered, would sit throbbing in the center of the table and eventually Brooke would say, "Well, I don't know about you girls, but I'm just going to have to try this delicious-looking thing," thereby letting loose the forks of war.

I forced myself to have a shower, then picked up the phone to ring Aidan's cell phone and that's when it happened. I was curled on the chair, preparing for the balm of his voice—but instead of his message, there was a funny beeping noise. Had I called the wrong number? Already I had a presentiment of doom; my hands were shaking so much I could hardly hit the buttons. Holding my breath, praying for everything to be okay, I waited for his voice but all I got was the funny beeping noise again: his cell phone had been cut off.

Because I hadn't paid the bill.

Until now I'd thought his phone had remained operational as some act of cosmic kindness. But it was simply because he'd paid for his line rental in advance. And now it had been disconnected because I hadn't paid the bill.

With the exception of the rent on the apartment, I hadn't paid any bills. Leon and I were meant to talk about my financial situation but Leon hadn't been able to stop crying long enough for us to do it.

In a breathless panic, I tried Aidan's office number but someone else—someone who wasn't him, naturally—answered, "Andrew Russell's phone." I hung up. Fuck.

Fuck. Fuck. Fuck.

I felt so dizzy that I thought I might faint. "Now how am I meant to get in touch with you?" I asked the room.

I'd depended on that twice-daily chat, on the twice-daily sound of his voice. Obviously, he hadn't chatted back to me. But it had helped. It had made me half believe that we were still in regular contact.

The urge to talk to him was suddenly so huge that my body couldn't contain it. In the space of a second I was drenched in sweat and I had to run to the bathroom to vomit.

Ten, maybe fifteen minutes passed, with me resting my head against the cool porcelain, still too light-headed to get up.

I needed to talk to him. I would have given everything I possessed, I would have been prepared to die myself, just to talk to him for five minutes.

33

I had a second shower, got dressed—in a swirly patterned Pucci dress and jacket from Goodwill—and was so late for work that I called and told Lauryn that I would go straight to my ten-o'clock appointment.

I was sourcing promo items for You Glow Girl! (A highlighter. Nothing more to be said about it. A "soft" launch, i.e., not too much money to spend on it.) With the limited funds available, I was thinking of buying the beauty editors lamps (thereby cleverly picking up on the "glow" theme).

My ten o'clock was with a wholesaler on West Forty-first Street who imported unusual lamps; ones that looked like halos—you clip them onto your mirror and your reflection looks like a saint; wings that go behind your couch, so you look like an angel—if you can position yourself correctly, or red neon ones that say *Select Bar,* if you wished you lived in Williamsburg.

The cab dropped me on the wrong side of the street, and as I was waiting to cross over, I saw a man I knew and automatically nodded hello. Then I realized that I couldn't remember where I knew him from and was afraid I'd Recognized a Famous Person. Rachel had once done that: stopped Susan Sarandon on the street and interrogated her as to where she'd seen her before. Did they go to the same gym? Was she a "friend of Bill's"? Had she seen her at the dermatologist? Then, very faintly, Rachel said, *"Thelma and Louise,"* and backed away, mortified.

But the mystery man was stopping to talk to me.

"Hey, little girl," he said. "How're you doing?"

"Good." I nodded desperately.

"You're Rachel's sister? I'm Angelo. We met one morning in Jenni's."

How could I have forgotten him? He was so unusual-looking, with his gaunt, drawn face, dark deep-set eyes, long hair, and Red Hot Chili Pepper–style magnetism.

"Things any better?" he asked.

"No. I feel very bad. Especially today."

"You wanna go for coffee?"

"I can't. I have a meeting."

"Take my number. Call me if you ever want to talk."

"Thank you, but I'm not an addict."

"That's okay. I won't hold it against you."

He scribbled something on a torn piece of paper. Limply I accepted it and said, "My name is Anna."

"Anna," he repeated. "You take care. *Great* clothes, by the way."

"Bye," I said, and let the scrap of paper fall into the bottom of my bag.

I went to my meeting but I was off form, I couldn't manage to care enough to play hardball on terms with Mr. Fancy Lights, and I left without having agreed on anything.

Back out on the street, I was strolling along, scanning the traffic for a cab, when a guy handed me a leaflet. Normally, I stick them straight in the first bin I see because, in this neck of the woods, they're always flyers for "designer" sales to catch the tourists. But something made me look at this one.

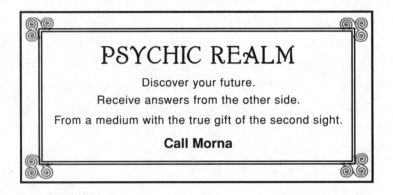

PSYCHIC REALM

Discover your future.
Receive answers from the other side.
From a medium with the true gift of the second sight.

Call Morna

At the bottom was a phone number and suddenly I was seized with excitement close to frenzy. *Receive answers from the other side.* I stopped dead in the middle of the sidewalk, causing a mini pileup. "Asshole," someone said. "Tourist" (a much worse insult), said someone else.

"Sorry," I said. "Sorry, sorry." I moved out of the flow of bodies into the shelter of a doorway, pulled my cell phone out of my bag, and, with fingers that trembled with hope, rang the number. A woman answered.

"Is that Morna?" I asked.

"Yes."

"I'd like to have a reading."

"Can you come now? I have a free appointment."

"Sure! Yes! Absolutely!" Who cared about work!

Morna directed me to an apartment two streets away.

As I went up in the jerky elevator, my blood pounded so hard, I found myself wondering what it would feel like to have a heart attack.

To be given a flyer on Forty-first Street that *didn't* advertise a "designer" sale—what were the chances of that? And to be able to get an appointment with Morna immediately? Surely this was meant to have happened?

For a moment I let myself think my greatest hope: *Aidan, what if she gets through to you? What if we actually make contact? What if I get to speak to you?*

Nearly in tears from excitement, hope, desperation, I found Morna's apartment and rang her bell.

A voice called through the door, "Who is it?"

"My name is Anna. I rang a few minutes ago."

There came the rattle of chains being undone and thunks as keys were turned in heavy locks and finally the door was opened.

In my state of overblown hope, I'd pictured Morna wearing flowy, beaded layers, with badly cut graying hair and heavy kohl around wise old eyes, living in a dimly lit apartment, full of red velvet throws and fringey lamps.

But this was an ordinary woman—probably in her midthirties—in a dark blue tracksuit. Her hair could have done with a wash and I couldn't see how wise and old her eyes looked because she avoided eye contact.

Her apartment was also a disappointment: a TV in the corner blared *Montel,* children's toys were scattered on the floor, and there was a very strong smell of toast.

Morna turned the sound down on *Montel,* directed me to a stool at the breakfast bar, and said, "Fifty dollars for fifteen minutes."

It was a lot but I was so hyped up that I just said, "Okay."

My breath was coming in short, tight gasps and I thought Morna would notice my frantic state and treat me accordingly. But she just clambered onto a stool on the opposite side of the breakfast bar and handed me a pack of tarot cards. "Cut them."

I hesitated. "Instead of a card reading, can you try to contact"—what should I say?—"someone who has died."

"That's extra."

"How much?"

She studied me. "Fifty?"

I hesitated. It wasn't the money, it was the sudden, unpleasant suspicion that I was being had. That this woman wasn't really a medium, but simply a swizzer preying on innocent tourists.

"Forty," she said, confirming my suspicions.

"It's not the money," I said, on the verge of tears. Hope had spilled over into disappointment. "It's just that if you're not a medium, please tell me. This is important."

"Sure, I'm a medium."

"You get in contact with people who have died?" I stressed.

"Yeah. You want to go ahead?"

What was to be lost? I nodded.

"Okay, let's see what we've got." She pressed her fingers to her temples. "You're Irish, right?"

"Right." In a way I wished I'd said I was Uzbeki; I felt uncomfortable giving her any information that she hadn't found out psychically, but I didn't want to do anything to scupper this.

She cast a sharp eye over my clothes and my scars, and came to rest on my wedding ring.

"I have someone here."

My excitement spiked.

"A woman."

My excitement plummeted.

"Your grandma."

"Which grandma?"

"She says her name is . . . Mary?"

I shook my head. No granny called Mary.

"Bridget?"

Another shake of the head.

"Bridie?"

"No," I said apologetically. I hate it when these people get it wrong. I get so embarrassed for them.

"Maggie? Ann? Maeve? Kathleen? Sinéad?"

Morna listed every Irish name she'd ever heard of, from watching *Ryan's Daughter* and buying Sinéad O'Connor CDs, but didn't come up with either of my grannies' names.

"Sorry," I said. I didn't want her getting discouraged and asking me to leave. "Don't worry about the name. Tell me other stuff, what else are you getting?"

"Okay, they don't always give me the correct name, but she's definitely your grandma. I can see her clearly. She's telling me she's very happy to hear from you. She's a little bitty thing, dancing around, in boots and a flowery apron on over a dirndl skirt. She's got gray hair in a bun at the back of her neck and small round eyeglasses."

"I don't think that's my granny," I said. "I think that's the granny from *The Beverly Hillbillies.*"

I didn't mean to be snide; I just had too much desperation and hope swilling around in me and all this time-wasting was doing me in.

And if you'd ever met my granny Maguire, with her black teeth and her pipe and her penchant for setting the dogs on us, or Granny Walsh, with her tendency to growl if you tried to take away her perfume (she drank it whenever they'd found all the other bottles and emptied them down the sink), you'd never confuse them with the granny in Morna's description.

Morna looked at me, alert to my sarcasm. "So who do you want to talk to?"

I opened my mouth, took a big, shuddery breath, which became a sob. "My husband. My husband died." The tears were suddenly sluicing down my face. "I want to talk to him."

I rummaged in my bag for a Kleenex while Morna pressed her fingers to her temples again. "I'm sorry," she said. "I'm getting nothing. But there's a reason for that."

My head jerked up. What?

"You have terrible energy. Someone has put something bad on you, this is why all these bad things are happening to you."

What? "You mean like a curse?"

"A curse is a strong word—I don't want to use that word, but yeah, I guess like a curse."

"Oh, fuck!"

"Don't worry, baby." For the first time, she smiled. "I can take it away."

"You can?"

"Sure, I'm not going to give you bad news like that if I can't help you."

"Thank you, oh my God, thank you." Briefly, I thought I might faint with gratitude.

"Looks like you were meant to come here today."

I nodded, but my blood was running cold. What if I hadn't come to midtown today? What if I hadn't been given the flyer? What if I'd put it straight in the bin?

"So what happens? Can you take it away now?" I could hardly catch my breath.

"Yeah, we can do it now."

"Great! Can we get started?"

"Sure. But you've got to understand that removing a curse as big as the one on you will cost money."

"Oh? How much?"

"A thousand dollars."

A thousand dollars? That jolted me out of the bubble and back to reality. This woman was a chancer. What would she do that could cost a thousand dollars?

"You've got to do this, Anna. Your life will only get worse if you don't deal with this."

"My life will definitely get worse if I throw away a thousand dollars."

"Okay, five hundred," Morna said. "Three? Okay, two hundred dollars and I can remove this curse."

"How come you can do it for two hundred dollars now and it was a thousand dollars a minute ago?"

"Because, baby, I'm afraid for you. You need this removed, like *now*, or something really terrible will happen to you."

For a second she got me again, I was frozen with fear. But what could happen? The worst thing I could ever think of had already happened. But what if there *was* a curse on me? If it was why Aidan had died...?

Suspended between fear and skepticism, my thoughts seesawed back and forth when we were interrupted by the sounds of children banging on a door somewhere in the apartment and calling, "Mom, can we come out yet?"

I snapped back to sanity and couldn't leave that place quick enough. My anger was so immense that on the way down, I kicked the elevator wall. I was raging with Morna and raging with myself for being so stupid and raging with Aidan for dying and putting me in that position. Back on the street, I couldn't stop walking long enough to hail a cab and I powered all the way to Central Park, fueled by hot, sour fury, shouldering into other pedestrians (at least the short ones), not apologizing, and generally giving New York a bad name.

I think I must have been crying because at the Times Square intersection a little girl pointed at me and said, "Look, Mom, a crazy lady." But that might just have been because of my clothes.

By the time I reached the office, I'd calmed down. I understood what had happened: I'd had bad luck. I'd met a charlatan, someone who preyed on vulnerable people—and did it really, really badly because I was as vulnerable as fuck and even I hadn't fallen for her shit.

Somewhere out there is a real psychic who'll put me in touch with you. All I have to do is find them.

34

To: Magiciansgirl1@yahoo.com
From: Thewalshes1@eircom.net
Subject: Baked Alaska

Dear Anna,

I hope you had a "good" weekend. If you see Rachel will you tell her that baked Alaska is a beautiful dessert. The waiters light it with sparklers and turn off the lights and carry it through the room. As you know, I am not a woman who "blubs" easily but when they did it on our last night in Portugal, it looked so beautiful, tears came to my eyes.

Your loving mother,

Mum

I assumed the baked Alaska was wedding related. Rachel wasn't getting married until next March and already she and Mum were sniping at each other. And no way was I getting involved—wedding-menu cross fire could be very messy.

However, I almost brought it up that evening, because Rachel appeared unexpectedly at my apartment, which couldn't have been more inconvenient, as I was just about to start my crying.

"Hello," I said cautiously. I should have expected this: I'd given her the slip all weekend.

"Anna, I'm worried about you, you've got to stop working so hard."

This was a regular gripe of Rachel's. She insisted I was using work as an excuse not to see her—or anyone. And she was right: it actually felt harder, not easier, to be with people. The toughest challenge was my face; maintaining a "normal" expression was utterly exhausting.

And poor Jacqui was so intent on cheering me up that every time we met, she was armed with an arsenal of funny stories from her work and I was knackered from smiling and saying, "God, that's hilarious."

"Working all through the weekend?" Rachel said. "Anna, that's not good."

What could I say? I could hardly tell her the truth, which was that I'd spent most of Saturday and Sunday on the Internet, looking up psychics and asking Aidan for some sort of sign to indicate which one I should use.

"It was an emergency."

"You work with cosmetics, how can it be an emergency?"

"You've obviously never gone out without your lip gloss."

"Oh, I see your...look, anyway! I came to talk to you in person," she said, "because I don't seem to be getting through to you on the phone. And I mean getting through in an emotional sense, by the way, not getting through in a telephonic sense."

Like I'd think anything else. "I know, I know. So tell me, Rachel, how are the wedding plans?" If she badgered me too much, I'd say, "Two words, Rachel. Baked. Alaska."

"Christ," she said. "Wedding plans. Don't ask." Resentfully she exclaimed, "Luke and I just wanted a small wedding. With people we liked. With people we *knew*. Mum wants to invite half of Ireland: several thousand third cousins twice removed and everyone she's ever nodded to on the golf course."

"Maybe they won't come. Maybe it'll be too far."

"Why do you think we're getting married in New York?" She laughed darkly. "Anyway, don't think you'll distract me. I'm here because I'm concerned about you. You can't keep hiding in your work, pretending that nothing has happened. You have to feel things. If you feel things you'll get better. Have you any Diet Coke?"

"I don't know. Look in the fridge. Did you do something to your eyebrows?"

"Got them tinted."

"They're nice."

"Thank you. Practice for the wedding, to see if I'm allergic. Don't want my face puffing up like a puffy puffer fish on the big day." She stopped moving and cocked her ear to listen. "What's that racket?"

In a nearby apartment someone bellowed, "Goooooooooaaaaaald-fin-GAH!" at the top of his voice.

"It's Ornesto. He's practicing."

"Practicing what? Scaring the living bejesus out of people?"

"Singing. He's taking lessons. His teacher says he's got a gift."

"Heeeza maaaan, maaaan wida Midas TORCH!"

"Does he do this a lot?"

"Most nights."

"Doesn't it keep you awake?" Rachel was a bit neurotic about sleep. There was no point telling her I hardly slept anyway.

"BUT HEEZ TOO MARCHHH!"

"Any luck with the Diet Coke?"

"No. There's almost nothing in here. It's a wasteland. Anna, you need to see a therapist."

"To help me buy Diet Coke?"

"Using humor is a classic deflection technique. I know a lovely grief counselor. Very professional. She won't tell me anything that you say, I promise. I won't even ask."

"I'll go," I said.

"You will? Great!"

"I'll go when I'm a bit better."

"Oh, for God's sake. This is exactly what I'm talking about! I see you putting in all those hours at work, trying to forget—"

"No, I'm not trying to forget!" That was an awful thought; the last thing I wanted to happen.

"I'm trying..." How could I put it? "I'm trying to get far enough down the line so that I can remember." I stopped, then continued: "So that I can remember without the pain killing me."

And the days *were* stacking up. And weeks. And months. It was now almost the middle of June and he'd died in February, but I still felt like I'd just woken from a horrible dream, that I was suspended in that stunned, paralyzed state between sleep and reality where I was grasping for, but couldn't get a handle on normality.

"Golden words he will pour in your EA-AH!"

"Oh God, he's off again." Rachel looked anxiously at the ceiling. "I don't know how you cope, I really don't."

I shrugged. I quite liked it. It was a bit of company without me having to actually see him. He kept knocking on my door but I never answered, and when we met in the hallway I told him I was taking a lot of sleeping tablets, which was why I didn't hear him. It was better to lie: he was so easily wounded.

"But his LIES can't DIZ-GUISE what you FEA-AH!"

"There's something I must ask you," Rachel said. "Are you feeling suicidal?"

"No." I studied Rachel's worried face. "Why? Should I be?"

"Well... yes. It's normal to feel like you couldn't be bothered carrying on."

"God, I can't do a thing right."

"Don't be like that. But have you any idea why you don't feel suicidal?"

"Because... because... if I died I don't know where I'd go to. I don't know if it would be the same place that Aidan has gone to. While I'm here I feel close to him. Does that make sense?"

"So you have actually thought about it?"

The idea of not being alive constantly hovered on the verge of my consciousness. Not to the extent that I'd ever made any hard-and-fast plans, but it was definitely there. "Yes, I suppose I have."

"Oh, that's good. That's great to hear." She was visibly relieved. "Thank God for that."

"It's the kissssss of DEATH! From Missss-tah . . . Gold FINGAH!"

"Look, would you like me to give you earplugs?"

"It's okay, thanks."

"This heart is COLD. HELOVESONLYGOLD, HELOVESON-LYGOOOLLLLLDDDDD!"

"God, I'm off. Let's get together for dinner some night this week."

"I'm meeting Leon and Dana on Wednesday night," I said quickly.

"Good girl, very good. I won't be around at the weekend, I'm going on retreat, but let's get together Thursday night? Yes?"

She made me nod yes.

"Good-bye."

I lay on the couch, trying to recover my crying mood. Upstairs, Ornesto continued belting out the tunes and it sparked off a memory: sometimes Aidan and I used to sing. Not serious singing—God, no—but making stuff up, having fun. Like the night we called Balthazar for home delivery and I was in absolute raptures.

"It's amazing," I'd raved. "Balthazar is one of the nicest restaurants in New York—no, scratch that, one of the nicest restaurants in the *world*—and they're not too big for their boots to bring their food to your door."

"This New York is a great place," Aidan said.

"'Tis," I agreed. "You'd never get this in Ireland."

"So why, then, are there so many songs about how sad it is to leave Ireland?"

"*Entre nous, mon ami,* I haven't a clue. I think they're stone mad."

Aidan, belonging to the Boston-Irish diaspora, knew all about the sad emigrant songs and he started singing "'Last night as I lay dreaming, I dreamed of Spancil Hill.'" He might have been quite a good singer, but it was hard to tell because he was doing it in his Smurf's voice, even though he wasn't shaving.

"'I dreamed that I was back there and that thought, it made me ill—'"

"They're not the words."

" '—I met the tailor Quigley, he's as bold as ever still. He used to mend my britches when I lived in Spancil Hill.' "

Abruptly he knocked off the Smurf voice and started really giving it socks.

> " 'But now I don't need my britches mended.
>   When they wear out, I've got a good trick.
>   I buy myself a brand-new pair
>   from Banana Repub-a-lik.' "

"Hurray!" I said, clapping and trying to whistle. "More!"

He stood up for the next verse.

" 'And if Anna tears her britches.' " He extended his arm in dramatic fashion.

> " 'To tailor Quigley she doesn't go.
>   For well-cut britches in cute col-ors,
>   She goes to Club Monaco.
>   They've tops and bags and jewel-ler-ee
>   And lots of other good stuff.
>   I'm told they're very reasonably priced
>   and I'm sorry this doesn't rhyme.' "

"Bravo!" I called. "As Irish people don't say! More!"

"Okay. Final verse. The sad one." He hung his head and sang almost in a whisper.

> " 'The police sir-ens in the morn-ing,
>   They blew both loud and shrill.
>   And I awoke in New York City,
>   Happy I wasn't in Spancil Hill.' "

He bowed low to the floor, then raced toward our bedroom.

"Come back!" I called. "I'm enjoying this."

"You can't sing this stuff without wearing a bad sweater."

He reemerged in the most terrible Aran jumper you've ever seen. It was a wedding present from Auntie Imelda, Mum's most competitive sister. (Mum insisted, "She knew it was horrible.") It made him look like he had a potbelly.

"Will you wear this?" He brandished a tweed cap at me. (Also courtesy of Auntie Imelda.)

"Indeed I will. Now my turn." To the same tune, I sang:

> " 'Back in the county of Claa-are,
>   My one true love waits for me.
>   But I met a far nicer one true love
>   When I came to New York cit-ee.
>   My one true love in County Clare
>   Was actually my first cousin.
>   And if we'd haa-ad a child,
>   His fingers might have numbered a dozen.' "

"Jesus! You're good," Aidan said. "You rock! You rhyme! Freestyle!" Trying to do the funny hand gestures and knee-bendy stuff that rappers do, he said, "I'm a Mick, far from my crib, hanging with my homies, who is wishing they at homie. So you see, I agree, that I'm far across the sea, but I got an U-zi, an SUV, blacked-out windows through which you can't see. I ain't bitchin' that I got no kitchen. Got some dough, got some blow, got my ho, got food from Balthazar ready to go."

We passed the entire evening making up songs about how New York was a much nicer place than Ireland and how we weren't at all sad to be across the foamy sea from it. Usually they didn't rhyme but they were so so funny. At least to us.

O utside Diego's, Leon and Dana were emerging from one cab while I was paying off another. Perfect timing. That used to happen a lot when I was with Aidan and the four of us were meeting up.

There seemed to be some argument with their cabdriver. There usually was.

"Nice driving, buddy," Dana said, very loudly, bending down to the driver's window. "Not!"

Dana was loud and opinionated—she attracted a lot of attention wherever she went—and her favorite phrase was "It's hideous." Said like this: "At's had-i-aaaasss." She said this a lot, because she thought a lot of things were hideous. Especially in her job; she worked in interiors and thought all of her clients had despicable taste.

"Hey, hey, I'll handle this," Leon insisted, not very convincingly.

Standing in the shadows of Dana's height, Leon looked short and plump and anxious. Or maybe he *was* just short and plump and anxious.

"Don't tip him, Leon," Dana ordered. "Leon. Do. Not. Tip. Him. He went totally the wrong way!"

Leon, ignoring her, was fussily counting out notes.

"That's bullshit," Dana exclaimed. "He doesn't deserve that much!" But it was too late, the driver's hand had closed over the money.

"Oh what-*ever!*" Dana spun on her four-inch heel and swished her thick curtain of glossy hair.

Then Leon saw me and his face lit up. "Hey, Anna!"

Leon and Aidan had been friends since childhood, but with Dana and me in the mix, we'd been a perfect fit; the four of us had really clicked. When Dana wasn't shouting about things being hideous and bullshit, she was immensely warm and funny. The four of us used to go away on weekends together and spent a week in the Hamptons last summer and had gone skiing in Utah in January.

We used to see one another for dinner about once a week—Leon was a man who was fond of his food and he got all excited about new restaurants. Our "thing" was to construct elaborate alternative identities for one another—zookeeper, *American Idol* winner, magician's assistant, etc. Then used to come our favorite bit—our fantasies for ourselves. Leon wished he was six-foot-three and in the Special Forces and a Krav Maga master (or whatever the word was). Dana wanted to be a surrendered wife, married to a rich man who was never there, running his home like a CEO. I wanted to be Ariella. But nice. And Aidan's dream life was to be a baseball player, one who hit enough home runs in the World Series to win it for the Boston Red Sox.

For some reason, after I'd come back from Dublin, it had taken me longer to face Leon than anyone else. I was afraid of seeing the full extent of his grief because then I would see my own.

The problem was that Leon had been as desperate to see me as I was desperate not to see him—he was probably thinking of me as an Aidan replacement.

I'd kept ducking him, but I'd caved in a few weeks back and agreed to a meet. "We'll get a table at Clinton's Fresh Foods," he'd declared.

I'd been horrified. Not just at the thought of going *out* out, but at the idea of trying to re-create one of our foursome nights.

"Why don't I just call over to your apartment," I'd said.

"But we always go out for dinner," he'd replied.

And I'd thought *I'd* been in denial.

He'd managed to badger me into going over to their apartment a few more times to hold his hand while he cried and reminisced. Tonight, however, in an attempt to move on, we were going out. Only to Diego's, though. It was a small neighborhood place, our default restaurant, the place we used to go on the (rare) weeks when a new restaurant hadn't opened in Manhattan.

"Whatcha bring me?" Dana looked at the Candy Grrrl bag in my hand.

"Latest stuff." I handed it over.

Dana fingered through the cosmetics and halfheartedly thanked me. The problem with Candy Grrrl was that it wasn't expensive enough for her. "Ya ever get any Visage stuff?" she asked. "I like that."

"Can we go in?" Leon asked. "I'm starved."

"You're always starved."

Diego himself was at the front desk and delighted to see us. "Hey, you guys! Been a while." He made his eyes supersparkly to pretend he hadn't noticed my scar. "Table for four?"

"Four," Leon said, pointing at our usual table. "We always sit there."

Diego started picking up menus.

"Three," Dana and I said together.

"Four," Leon repeated. There was this dreadful pause, then his face buckled. "I guess it's only three."

"Three?" Diego confirmed.

"Three."

At the table all Leon could do was cry. "Sorry, Anna," he kept saying, looking up through hands wet with tears. "I'm so sorry."

Diego approached quietly and respectfully. In subdued tones he asked, "Can I get you guys a drink?"

"A Pepsi." Leon sniffed. "With a twist of lime, not lemon. If there's no lime, don't bring me lemon."

"Glass of Chardonnay," Dana said.

"Me, too."

When Diego came back with the drinks, he murmured, "Would you like me to take the menus away?"

Leon's hand shot out to flatten the menus against the table. "I guess we have to eat."

"Nothing stops him," Dana said.

"Okay." Diego retreated. "Just holler when you're ready."

Leon peered into his drink, took a sip, and said tearfully, "I knew it. This isn't Pepsi. This is Coke."

"Aw, shaddup and drink it," Dana said.

Without replying, Leon picked up his menu and studied it. We could hear him crying behind it.

He managed to pull himself together long enough to order the venison, but broke down as he told Diego, "But hold the capers." Almost wailing, he said, "I caaan't . . . eeeeat . . . caaaapers."

"They give him gas," Dana said.

"Why don'cha tell everyone."

Once the food was ordered, Leon was able to relax and *really* get into the crying.

"He was my best friend, the best buddy a guy could have," he wept.

"She knows," Dana said. "She was married to him, remember?"

"I'm sorry, Anna, I know it's bad for you, too . . ."

"It's okay." I didn't want to get into it with him, the two of us competing to see who could cry the most. I don't know how I managed it, but I didn't let myself think that it was Aidan he was crying about. He was just crying and it was nothing to do with me.

"I'd give everything I have to wind the clock back. Just to see him again, you know?" Leon looked at us questioningly, his face wet with tears. "Just to talk to him?"

That reminded me that I needed a medium. Dana might know of one. In her line of work, she met all kinds of people.

"Hey," I said. "Do either of you know any good mediums? Like, reputable ones?"

Momentarily, the tears paused in their journey down Leon's cheeks.

"A medium? To talk to Aidan? Oh my God, you must miss him so baaad." And he was off again.

"Anna, mediums are *bullshit!*" Dana exclaimed. "Bullshit! They take your money and take advantage. You need to see a grief counselor."

"I see mine three times a week," Leon stopped crying long enough to tell me. "He says I'm doing good."

Then he sobbed for the rest of the meal, pausing only to order bitter-chocolate pie with vanilla ice cream instead of the advertised caramel. "Too many flavors going on," he told Diego with a watery smile.

36

...she channeled my mom, who told me where she'd hidden her wedding ring...

...I got to say a proper good-bye to my brother and finally got closure...

...I was so happy to talk to my husband again, I missed him so bad...

There were pages and pages of these sorts of testimonials on the Internet.

But, I asked Aidan, *how can I trust any of them? The mediums might have written them themselves. They might all be as bad as swizzy Morna. Can't you give me some sort of sign? Can't you get a butterfly to land on the right one, or something?*

Frustratingly, no butterfly appeared to help me out. What I needed was a personal recommendation. But who could I ask? I mean, I didn't want people to think I was bonkers. And they would. Rachel would. She'd be like Dana and go on about therapy. And Jacqui would say I simply needed to get out more and I'd be grand in a little while. Ornesto, on the other hand, was always seeing psychics, but they kept telling him the man of his dreams was just around the corner. They never mentioned that the man of his dreams was already married or had a penchant for hitting him or stealing his good saucepans.

Maybe someone at work might know...? But Teenie wouldn't—instinctively I knew she'd subscribe to the "bullshit" school. And Brooke would be horrified—her WASPy lot don't believe in anything. Anything other than themselves.

The only work people I could think of were the girls at Earth-Source—Koo or Aroon or whatever their names were—but I couldn't risk getting too pally with them in case I ended up being swept along to Alcoholics Anonymous on a wave of misplaced support.

Dispirited, I checked my e-mails. Only one, from Helen.

To: Magiciansgirl1@yahoo.com
From: Lucky_Star_PI@yahoo.ie
Subject: Job!

Anna, I've got a job! Proper job. In crime. Ding-dong! All kicked off yesterday.

In office, nothing to do, feet up on desk, thinking if looked like real PI, something might happen, instead of "case of mystery dog poo." Next thing—as if by magic, like I willed it to happen, maybe have special powers—car pulled up outside, parked on double yellows. Traffic wardens around here ferocious, so looking forward to good fight. Then noticed it looked like crime car, don't know how I knew, but knew. Instinct.

No tinted windows, but backseats had pink ruched curtains, like Austrian blinds but smaller. War crime. I'm thinking <u>Christ</u> when two bozos got out. Ding-dong!

Big, burly, leather jackets, bulges in chest pockets, meant to say <u>guns!</u> but bet were just cheese baguettes. All same, makes difference from upset women arriving in yummy mummy people carriers, saying husbands won't ride them anymore.

In the pair of bozos comes and one says: Are you Helen Walsh?

Me: Too right I am!

Admit I should have said: Who wants to know?

But wasn't going to miss this for anything.

Haven't time at moment to tell you everything—but it's all going on. Criminals, guns, extortion, "muscle," tons of money—and they want ME on board! Am going to write down everything that happened and send it to you. Miles better than poxy screenplay, much more exciting. Stand by for long, thrilling e-mail.

It all sounded more than just a little far-fetched; I went back to Googling random stuff like *Talking to the dead* and *Nonswizzy mediums*, which was when I finally hit gold.

The Church of Spiritualist Communication

I clicked on the site—it seemed to be an actual, legitimate church, which believed you could channel the dead!

I couldn't believe it!

They had a few branches in the New York area. Most were upstate or in the outer boroughs but there was one in Manhattan, on Tenth and Forty-fifth. According to the Web site, there was a service on Sunday at two o'clock.

I looked at my watch: quarter to three; I'd just missed this week's. No, no, no! I would have howled with frustration except that that would have alerted Ornesto that I was in and he'd be down to badger me. Anyway, I told myself, breathing deeply and talking myself down, I'd go there next week.

At the thought of actually speaking to Aidan, I felt giddy with hope. So much so that I thought I could face the world. For the first time since he had died, I actually wanted to see people.

Rachel was away at some Feathery Strokery retreat, so I rang Jacqui. I tried her cell phone because she was always out and about, but it went to voice mail. On the off chance, I tried her apartment and she answered.

"I can't believe you're at home," I said.

"I'm in bed." Her voice sounded choked.

"Are you sick?"

"No. I'm crying."

"Why?"

"I ran into Buzz last night in Bungalow 8. He was with some girl who looked like a model. He tried to introduce me to her but he couldn't remember my name."

"Of course he could," I said. "That's typical Buzz game playing. He was just trying to undermine you."

"Was he?"

"Yes! By pretending that even though he'd been your boyfriend for a year, you're so insignificant he can't even remember your name."

"Whatever. Anyway, it made me feel like shit, so I'm having a duvet day, with my blinds down."

"But it's a beautiful sunny afternoon. You shouldn't be hiding at home."

She laughed. "That's my line."

"Come on, let's go to the park," I said.

"No."

"Please."

"Okay."

"God, you're fabulous. You're so . . . resilient."

"I'm not really. I've just smoked my last cig and I needed to go out anyway. See you in half an hour."

I picked up my keys, and the phone rang. I stood by the door to see who it was.

"Hi, sweetie," a woman's voice said. "It's Dianne."

It was Mrs. Maddox, Aidan's mother. Immediately I felt guilty: I hadn't called her since the funeral. She hadn't called me either. Probably for the same reason: neither of us could face it. While I'd been in Ireland, Mum had rung her a couple of times to keep her up-to-date on my medical progress, but without being told, I gathered the calls were a little rough.

"I called Ireland, they said you were back in the city. Can you call me. We should talk about the . . . ash . . . ash-es." Her voice broke on the word. I heard her try to get herself under control, but squeaking noises kept escaping her. Abruptly she hung up.

Feck, I thought. *I'll have to ring her.* I'd rather have gnawed my own ear off.

• • •

The park was jammers with people. I found a spot on the grass and a few minutes later Jacqui came gangling along. She was in a really short denim dress, her blond hair was in a ponytail, and her red-rimmed eyes were hidden behind massive Gucci shades. She looked great.

"He's a horrible, horrible man," I said by way of hello. "He's got a stupid car and I'm sure he wears mascara."

"But it's more than six months since we broke up. How come I'm so upset? I hadn't even thought about him for ages."

Wearily, she stretched out on the grass, her face toward the sun.

"For your next boyfriend you wouldn't consider a Feathery Stroker, would you?" I asked. "At least they'd never try to make you have a three-some with a prostitute."

"Couldn't. I'd puke."

"But all these non–Feathery Strokers . . . ," I said helplessly. "They're terrible."

Buzz was non–Feathery Strokeryism personified and he was vile.

She shrugged. "I like what I like. Can't help that. D'you think I could risk having a fag without getting stoned by fresh-air fascists? Sure, I'll chance it." She lit a cigarette, inhaled deeply, exhaled even more deeply, then said dreamily, "Anyway, I'll never have another boyfriend."

"Of course you will."

"I don't even want to," she said. "And that's never happened before. I've always been *desperate* for a boyfriend. But now I just couldn't be arsed. They always start out nice, so how do you know they're fuckers? I mean look at Buzz. At the beginning he sent me so many flowers, I could have opened a shop! How could I have guessed that he'd turn out to be the greatest prick of all time."

"But—"

"I'm going to get a dog instead. I saw these really really cute ones called Labradoodles, they're a cross between Labradors and poodles and, Anna, they're the cutest things. They're small like poodles, but shaggy, and they've got Labrador faces. They're the perfect town dog, everyone's getting one."

"Don't get a dog," I said. "It's only one step away from getting forty cats. Don't lose faith. Please."

"Too late. I have. Buzz let me down too often. I don't think I'll ever be able to trust a man again." Putting on an overearnest tone, she said, "He damaged me." She started to laugh. "Listen to me! I sound like Rachel. Ah, fuck it. Let's cheer ourselves up. When I've finished my cig, let's get ice cream."

"Okay."

She never ceased to amaze me. If I could have only a hundredth of her bounce-back ability, I'd be a very different person.

We stayed in the park until the heat of the sun faded, then went back to my place, ordered in Thai food, watched *Moonstruck,* and quoted most of the lines.

It was like old times.

In a way.

To: Magiciansgirl1@yahoo.com
From: Lucky_Star_PI@yahoo.ie
Subject: Job!

So like I said, two burly bozos came into office and one says: Are you Helen Walsh?

Me: Too right I am!

(Anna, at this point, must tell you I will be reporting many conversations. They may not be word-for-word but let me make this clear—I am parrot-phrasing, but NOT EXAGGERATING.)

Bozo Number One: A certain gentleman of our acquain-
tance would like a word. We have instructions to bring you to
him. Get in the car.

Me (laughing head off): I'm not getting in a car with two
men I've never met before—try me again on Saturday night
when I've had sixteen drinks—and I'm certainly not getting in a
car with Austrian blinds. (Remember, I told you there were awful pink ruched yokes on back windows.)

Bozo Number One throws wad of money on table, proper
neatly counted bundle with paper band holding it together, like
they do in the bank, and says: Now will you get in the car?

Me: How much is there?

Him (rolling eyes, because you should be able to tell from
thickness of it): One K.

Me: One K? Do you mean a thousand euro?

Him: Yeah.

Ding fucking dong! Counted it and really was a grand there.

Him: Now will you get in the car?

Me: Depends. Where are we going?

Him: We're going to see Mr. Big.

Me (excited): Mr. Big?! From Sex and the City?

Him (wearily): That bleedin' show has caused trouble for
local crime lords around the world. The name Mr. Big is meant
to inspire dread and terror and instead everyone thinks of this
well-dressed debonair man—

Me (interrupting): Who does phone sex. And owns a vineyard in Napa.

Bozo Number Two (opening mouth for first time): He's selling
it.

Me and Bozo Number One turn to stare.

Bozo Number Two: He's selling the vineyard and moving
back to Manhattan, and buying a place with Carrie.

Looked like he might start clubbing me if I disagreed, so agreed. Anyway, he's right.

Bozo Number One: We've tried out a couple of new names. For a while we tried Mr. Huge, but it never really caught on. And Mr. Ginormous only lasted a day. So we're back to Mr. Big but we have to go through the bleedin' <u>Sex and the City</u> scenario every time we get a new job. Get in the car.

Me: Not until you tell me exactly where we're going. And just because I'm small don't think you can push me around. I can do tae kwon do. [Well, been for one lesson with Mum.]

Him: Oh, do you? Where do you go? Wicklow Street? I teach there, funny I haven't seen you there before. Anyway, we're going to a pool hall in Gardiner Street, where the most powerful man in Dublin crime wants to talk to you.

Well, who could resist an invitation like that?

I stopped reading. Was this for real? It sounded just like Helen's short-lived screenplay. Well, actually, far better. I e-mailed her.

To: Lucky_Star_PI@yahoo.ie
From: Magiciansgirl1@yahoo.com
Subject: Lies?

Helen, this e-mail you've sent me? Is it real? Did any of it actually happen?

She replied immediately.

To: Magiciansgirl1@yahoo.com
From: Lucky_Star_PI@yahoo.ie
Subject: Not lies!

True as God. All of it.

Okay, I thought—still not entirely convinced—and carried on reading.

Sat in front of car beside Bozo Number One. Bozo Number Two had to go in back with shame of Austrian blinds.

Me: Bozo Number One, do you have a name?

Bozo Number One: Colin.

Me: Does Bozo Number Two have a name?

Him: No. Bozo will do.

Me: Whose idea was the Austrian blinds?

Him: Mrs. Big.

Me: There's a Mrs. Big?

Him (hesitating): There mightn't be anymore. That's why the boss wants to see you.

And I'm thinking, Ah bollocks. Thought this might be start of whole new career, instead just looked like sitting in more wet hedges. Only difference is that wet hedges will belong to drug runners and pimps, and that doesn't make it any more exciting. Wet hedge is wet hedge.

Pulled up outside dingy pool hall with war-crime orange lighting. Colin led me down the back to booth with orange stuffing coming out of seat. Why can't crime lords hang out in nice places, like Ice Bar in Four Seasons?

Small neat man sitting in booth, pulling at foam seat stuffing—last thing he was was big. Neatly trimmed bristly mustache.

He looked up, said: Helen Walsh? Sit down. Would you like a drink?

Me: What are you drinking?

Him: Milk.

Me: Cack. I'll have a grasshopper.

Don't even like grasshoppers, hate crème de menthe, as bad as drinking toothpaste, just wanted to be awkward.

Him: Kenneth, get my friend here a grasshopper.

Kenneth (the barman): A glass of what?

Mr. Big: A glass of nothing. A GRASShopper. Right, Miss Walsh, down to business. Anything that's said here goes no further, I'm telling you this in total confidence. Right?

Me: Mmmm.

Because minute I got home was going to tell Mum and now telling you.

Me (indicating Colin): What about him?

Mr. Big: Colin's all right. Me and Colin have no secrets. Right, the thing is...

Next thing, he dipped his head, put hand in front of eyes, like he was going to cry. I flashed excited look at Colin, who looked concerned.

Colin: Boss, are you okay...would you prefer to do this another time?

Mr. Big (sniffing loudly, "pulling himself together"): No, no, I'm all right. Miss Walsh, I want you to know that I'm fond of my wife, Detta. But lately she's being very—how can I put it?—distant, and a little vulture whispered in my ear that she might be spending a bit too much time with Racey O'Grady.

I was finding it hard to concentrate because over my shoulder could hear bar staff in panic...a grasshopper...what the fuck's that?...maybe it's one of those new beers...look down in the cellars, will you Jason...?

Me (calling): Lookit, it's fine, I'll just have a Diet Coke.

Me (turning back to Mr. Big): Sorry, you were saying. Speedy McGreevy.

Him (frowning): Speedy McGreevy? Speedy McGreevy has nothing to do with this. Or does he? (Narrows eyes.) What do you know? Who's been talking?

Me: No one. You said it.

Him: I didn't say Speedy McGreevy, I said Racey O'Grady. Speedy McGreevy's on the run in Argentina.

Me: My mistake. Carry on.

Him: Racey and meself have jogged along nicely together for the last few years. He has his department and I have mine. One of my lines of work is offering protection.

For moment thought he meant bodyguarding, then realized he meant extortion. Strangely, felt a little puky.

Him: Just so you know the kind of man you're dealing with here, Miss Walsh, let me tell you, I'm not some doozy who arrives at the gate of a site, with a couple of lads with iron bars, looking to talk to the foreman. I'm a sophisticated business-man. I have contacts in the planning department, with property lawyers, with banks. I'm *connected.* I know well in advance what's happening, so the deal is all tied up before the first brick is laid. But twice in the last six weeks, I've met with contractors to conclude our usual business and they say they're already covered. Now this is very interesting to me, Miss Walsh, because very few people even know these schemes are going ahead. Most of them haven't even got planning approval yet.

Me: How do you know it's not a leak in the planning office? Or at the contractors?

Him: Because it would need to be several leaks from several sources. Anyway, all the individuals involved have been...(meaningful hesitation)...interviewed. They came back clean.

Me: And you think Racey is the one muscling in on your... er...patch? Why him?

Him: Because they effing told me it was.

Me: So what do you think is going on?

Him: A less paranoid man than me might think Detta is picking my brains, taking her findings to Racey, and the pair of them are creaming me.

Me: And if she is?

Him: None of your concern. All I want you to do is bring

me proof of her and Racey together. I can't tail her and she knows all the lads and the cars. That's why I'm going against a lot of advice and bringing in an outsider.

Me: How did you hear of me?

Thinking I must be legend in Dublin private investigating.

Him: Yellow pages.

Me (disappointed): Oh, right.

Him: Now the thing about Detta is, she has class.

Thought of Austrian blinds in car. Don't think so.

Him: Detta comes from Dublin crime aristocracy. Her father, Chinner Skinner?

Said it like I should have heard of him.

Him: Chinner was the man who opened Ireland's doors to heroin. We all owe him a debt of gratitude. What I'm saying is, Detta's no fool. Have you a gun?

Surprised he said it out like that. Aren't they meant to say, "You carryin'?" And call it shooter, not gun.

Me: No gun.

Him: We'll get you one.

I'm thinking, don't know about this...

Him (insistent): My treat.

Me (thinking better to just play along for while): Okay.

Anna, as you know, I don't believe in fear, just an invention by men so they get all the money and good jobs, but if did believe in fear, this is time when would have felt it.

Me: But why would I need a gun?

Him: Because someone might shoot you.

Me: Like who?

Him: Like my wife. Like her bleedin' boyfriend Racey O'Grady. Like her boyfriend's mother—she's the one to watch out for, Tessie O'Grady, misses nothing.

Colin (speaking unexpectedly): A legend in Dublin crime.

Mr. Big (frowning): If I need your help...

Then Mr. "Big" stood up. Even smaller than I'd expected. Very short legs.

Mr. Big: I've a meeting now. Colin here will drop stuff round to you later. The gun, more money, photos of Detta, Racey, all that. Just one more thing, Miss Walsh. If you fuck this up, I'll be annoyed. And the last time someone annoyed me—when was it, Colin? Last Friday?—I crucified him on that pool table.

Me: You personally? Or one of your assistants?

Him: Me personally. I'd never ask my staff to do something I wouldn't be prepared to do myself.

Me: But that's exactly what happened in that film, <u>Ordinary Decent Criminal</u>. Couldn't you have used your imagination and crucified him to something else? The bar counter, for example. Just to put your personal mark on it, as it were. No one likes a copycat.

He was looking at me funny, and like I say, Anna, it's good job I don't believe in fear because if did, I'd have been cacking myself.

And on that compelling note, it ended. Frantically I keyed down to see if there was any more, but there wasn't. Feck. I'd enjoyed it hugely. No matter how much she insisted every word of it was true, I knew it was wildly exaggerated. But she was so funny and fearless and full of life that a little of it had rubbed off on me.

38

I checked my watch again. Only four minutes since the last time I'd checked. How could that *be*? It felt like at least fifteen minutes.

I was pacing, actually *pacing* with nervy excitement, waiting for it to be time to leave for the spiritualist-church place, for their Sunday service. It was taking every ounce of my restraint not to tell everyone—Rachel, Jacqui, Teenie, Dana. Only the fear that they'd have me institutionalized kept me quiet.

Back and forth I went from the living room to the bedroom, bargaining with a God I no longer believed in. *If Aidan shows up and speaks to me today, I'll... I'll... what? I'll believe in You again. You can't say fairer than that.*

See, I told Aidan. *See what I've promised. See the lengths I'm willing to go to. So you better show up.*

I left home miles too early and got the subway to Forty-second and Seventh and walked across town, passing Seventh, Eighth, Ninth Avenue, my stomach churning with anxiety.

The closer I got to the Hudson, the more bleak and warehousy and seagully the landscape became. This part of town was a world away from Fifth Avenue. The buildings were lower and more cramped, crouching on the sidewalk like they were afraid they were going to be hit. It was always colder here and the air was different, sharper.

The farther west I walked, the more my anxiety burgeoned; there couldn't be a church here. *What should I do?* I asked Aidan. *Keep walking?* I felt even worse when I found the building—it certainly didn't look like a church. It looked like a converted warehouse. Not terribly converted either. I had made some dreadful mistake.

But in the lobby, a sign on the wall listed THE CHURCH OF SPIRITUAL-IST COMMUNICATION as being on the fifth floor.

It *did* exist.

A couple of people passed by me on their way to the elevator, and full of sudden happiness, I ran and squeezed in with them. They were three other women about the same age as me and they looked very normal: one had a bag that I'd have sworn was a Marc Jacobs, then I noticed that another had her nails painted with—I almost gasped—Candy Grrrl Chick-chickachicka (pale yellow). Of all the brands in all the world? What were the chances? I took this as a Sign.

"What floor?" Marc Jacobs bag asked me. She was nearest to the button panel.

"Fifth," I said.

"Same as us." She smiled.

I smiled back.

Obviously talking to the dead on a Sunday afternoon was more commonplace than I had realized.

I followed the trio out of the elevator, down a bare-floored corridor, and into a room, full of several other women. Everyone started saying hi to one another and an exotically attired creature approached me. She had long dark hair, bare shoulders, a long fringey skirt (I had a moment of teenage flashback), and tons of filigree-style gold jewelry, around her neck, around her waist, up her wrists and arms and fingers.

"Hi," she said. "Belly dancing?"

"Excuse me?"

"You're here to learn to belly dance?"

It was only then that I noticed that the other women in the room were also wearing long bell-infested skirts, little belly tops, and spangledy slippers and that my three elevator mates were changing out of their ordinary clothes into jangly fringey things.

"No, I'm here for the Church of Spiritualist Communication."

Now that was a conversation stopper if ever I encountered one. The entire room became one discordant jangle as everyone whipped around to look at me.

"Not here," the chief lady said. "Probably down the hall."

Under the gaze of the filigreed girls, I retreated. Out in the corridor, I checked the number on the door. It was 506; the talking-to-dead-people were in room 514.

I carried on down the corridor, passing rooms on both sides. In one, several elderly women were singing "If I Were a Rich Man"; in another, four people were clustered around what looked like a script; and in yet another, a man with a rich baritone was singing about the Windy City being mighty purty while someone accompanied him on a clapped-out-sounding piano.

The whole place reeked of amateur dramatics.

I *had* to be at the wrong address. How could there be a church here? But I consulted my piece of paper again. It said room 514—and there *was* a room 514. Right at the end of the hallway; it looked nothing like a church; just a bare room with a circle of ten or eleven hard chairs on a dusty, splintery floor.

Uncertainly, I wondered if I should leave. I mean, how mad was this?

But hope intervened. Hope and desperation. In fairness, I *was* early. Extremely early. And I'd come all this way, I might as well see if anyone else showed up.

I sat on a bench in the corridor and passed the time by watching the proceedings in the room across the way.

Eight buff young men—two rows of four—were stamping and clattering across the bare boards, singing that they were going to wash some man right out of their hair, while a sinewy, older man yelled dance cues. "And TURN and SHIMMY and THRUST and TURN, smile, guys, SMILE, for fuck's sake, and TURN and SHIMMY and... okay, stop the music, STOP, STOP!" The piano tinkling petered out.

"Brandon," the older man said peevishly. "Sweetheart? What is going on with your shimmy? I'm looking for..." He leaned forward and gave a beautiful fluid shoulder shake. "And not..." Clumsily he shuddered his upper body like he was trying to shoulder his way through a crowd.

"I'm sorry, Claude." One of the boys—clearly poor Brandon, the bad shimmier—said.

"*This* is what I'm looking for," Claude said imperiously, and launched into a demo: balancing up on his toes, spinning around on the ball of his foot, doing the splits in midair, all the while doing this scary, fake smile. He finished, bowing in pretend humility right down to the floor, his arms in airplane wings up behind him...

"Excuse me," a voice said. "Are you here for the spiritualism?"

I whipped my head around. A young guy, probably early twenties, was looking eagerly at me. I saw him clock my scar but he didn't display any obvious revulsion.

"Yes," I said cautiously.

"Great! It's always great to see a new face. I'm Nicholas."

"Anna."

He extended a hand, and in light of his youth and his pierced eyebrow, I wasn't sure if he was proposing a normal handshake or a funny complicated young person's one, but it turned out to just be a straightforward clasp.

"The other guys should be here soon."

This Nicholas was lean and wiry—his jeans were hanging off him—with dark sticky-up hair, red high-tops, and a T-shirt saying BE UNAFRAID. BE VERY UNAFRAID. Several woven bracelets were twined around his wrist, and he wore at least three chunky silver rings and had a tattoo on his forearm, one I recognized because it was the current hot tattoo: a Sanskrit symbol that meant something like "The word is love" or "Love is the answer."

He looked perfectly normal but that was the thing about New York: lunacy appeared in all shapes and sizes. It specialized in Stealth Nutters. In other places they make it easier—shouting in the street at invisible enemies or going to the chemist to buy Bonjela dressed in your Napoléon costume is usually a dead giveaway.

Nicholas nodded at the *South Pacific* lads being put through their paces. "Fame costs," he said. "And right here's where you start paying."

He *looked* normal. He *sounded* normal. And all of a sudden I asked myself why *shouldn't* he be normal? I was here and I wasn't abnormal, simply bereaved and desperate.

And now that someone had finally turned up, I was avid for answers.

"Nicholas, you've been to . . . this . . . before?"

"Yeah."

"And the person who does the channeling—"

"Leisl."

"—Leisl. Does she really communicate with"—I didn't want to say "the dead"—"the spirit world?"

"Yeah." He sounded surprised. "She really does."

"She gives us messages from people . . . on the other side?"

"Yes, she really has a gift. My dad died two years ago and, via Leisl, I've spoken to him more in the last two years than I did my entire life. We get on a whole lot better now that he's dead."

Out of the blue, I was nearly sick with anticipation.

"My husband died," I splurged. "I really want to talk to him."

"Sure." Nicholas nodded. "But, just so as you know, it's not like Leisl's a telephone operator. If the person doesn't want to be channeled, she can't go after them and hunt them down like a dog."

"I went to another woman." I was talking very quickly. "Someone who said she was a psychic, but she was just a swizzer. She said there was a curse on me and she could take it away for a thousand dollars."

"Oh, man, you've got to be careful." He shook his head ruefully. "There are a lot of hustlers out there who take advantage of vulnerable people. All Leisl asks for is enough money to cover the rent. And here's the lady herself."

Leisl was a short, bowlegged woman, laden with shopping bags, through which I could see a chilled lasagne for one; it had made the inside of the bag wet with little drops of condensation. Her curly hair was lopsided: When Perms Go Bad.

Nicholas introduced me. "This is Anna, her husband bought it."

Leisl immediately put down her bags and gathered me into a tight hug, pulling my face into her neck so that I was breathing into an impenetrable thicket of hair. "You'll be okay, sweetheart."

"Thank you," I mumbled through a mouthful of hair, close to tears from her kindness.

She released me, and said, "And here's Mackenzie."

I turned to see a girl walking down the corridor like she was walking down a catwalk. A Park Avenue Princess, with blown-out hair, a Dior purse, and wedge sandals so high most people would sprain (or strain, whichever is worse) their ankles in them.

"She's coming here?" I asked.

"Comes every week."

By the looks of her, she shouldn't even be in New York. She should be stationed in some colonial-style mansion out in the Hamptons until the start of September. My spirits rose. Mackenzie should be able to afford the best medium money could buy, but she chose to come here. It *must* be good.

Behind Mackenzie lumbered a hulking, eight-foot-nine bloke, in an undertaker's suit and with a green-white face. "That's Undead Fred," Nicholas whispered. "Come on, let's help set up the room."

Leisl had put some spooky-sounding cello music on a tape deck and was lighting candles when people started "flooding" in.

There was a round-faced frumpy girl, who was probably younger than me but looked like she had totally given up, an older gentleman, small and dapper with pomaded hair, and a selection of older women with nervous tics and elastic waistbands. Mind you, one of them had interesting sandals; they looked like they'd been made out of a car tire. The more I looked at them, the more I liked them. Not for me to *wear*, you understand, I got enough of that codology at work, but they were definitely interesting.

When another man walked in, Nicholas grabbed me and said, "Here's Mitch. His wife bought it. You guys must have loads in common. C'mon and meet him."

He shunted me across the room. "Mitch, this is Anna. Her husband died—when? Few months back? She got ripped off by some asshole psychic who told her she'd been cursed. Thought you could help her, tell her about Neris Hemming."

Mitch and I locked eyes and it was like I'd touched an electric fence, there was such a *bzzzzz* of connection. He understood; the only one who did. I saw right through his eyes and all the way down into his bleak abandoned soul and recognized what I saw.

eople were sitting down and holding hands with the people beside them; I managed to slip in between the car-tire-sandals woman and the pomady guy. I was glad I didn't have to hold hands with Undead Fred.

I counted only twelve of us, including Leisl, but with the candles flickering in the dark room and groany cello noises in the background, the mood felt right. Definitely a place where the dead might feel comfortable showing up.

Leisl did a little intro, welcoming me, and saying stuff about deep breaths and centering ourselves and hoping that "Spirit" would deliver what everyone needed. Then we were allowed to stop holding hands.

Silence fell. And continued. And continued. And continued. Frustration burgeoned in me. When would this fucking thing start? I opened one eye and snaked a look around the circle, their faces shadowed in the candlelight.

Mitch was watching me; our looks met and collided in midair. Quickly I closed my eye again.

When Leisl finally spoke, I jumped.

"I have a tall man here." My eyes snapped open and I wanted to put my hand up, like I was at school. It's for me! It's for me!

"A very tall, broad, dark-haired man." My heart sank. Not for me.

"Sounds like my mom," Undead Fred said, in a slow, gargly voice.

Leisl did a quick recalculation. "Fred, I'm sorry; yes, it is your mom."

"Built like a brick shithouse," Fred gargled. "Coulda been a prize-fighter."

"She's telling me to ask you to be careful getting on the subway. She says that you don't pay attention, that you could slip."

After a period of silence, Fred asked, "That it?"

"That's it."

"Thanks, Mom."

"I've got Nicholas's dad now." Leisl faced Nicholas. "He's telling me—I'm sorry, these are his words, not mine—that he's pissed with you."

"So what's new?" Nicholas grinned.

"There's a situation at work that you have issues with?"

Nicholas nodded.

"Your dad says you're blaming the other guy, but you've got to look at where you're responsible for what's happened."

Nicholas stretched out, extended his arms above his head, scratched his chest thoughtfully. "Maybe, yeah, he's probably right. Bummer. Thanks, Dad."

More silence followed, then someone came through for the car-tire-sandals woman—whose name was Barb—and told her to include rape-seed oil in her diet.

"I already do," Barb said tetchily.

"*More* rapeseed oil," Leisl said quickly.

"Okay."

Another older lady got told by her dead husband to "keep doing the next right thing"; the young frumpy girl's mother told her that every-thing was going to work out for the best; Juan, the pomady guy, got told to live in the now; and Mitch's wife said she was happy to see he'd been smiling a bit more this week.

All meaningless, vaguely spiritual-sounding platitudes. Comforting stuff, but obviously not coming from "the other side."

It's all bollocks, I thought bitterly, which was just when Leisl said, "Anna, I'm getting something for you."

Sensation burned through me; I nearly puked, fainted, ran around the room. *Thank you, Aidan, thank you, thank you.*

"It's a woman." *Shite.* "An older woman, she's talking very loudly at me." Leisl looked a little distressed. "Shouting almost. And she's banging a stick on the ground for attention."

Christ! It sounded like Granny Maguire! That was exactly what she used to do when she came to stay with us and needed to go to the bathroom—she'd bang on her bedroom floor with her stick for someone to come up and help her, while downstairs, we'd be drawing straws. I was terrified of her. We all were. Especially if she hadn't done a number two for a while.

Leisl said, "She says it's about your dog."

It took a moment for me to stammer, "I don't have a dog. I have a toy dog but not a real one."

"You're thinking of getting one."

I am? "I'm not."

Mackenzie piped up, quite excited, "I have a dog. This must be for me."

"Okay." Leisl turned to Mackenzie. "Spirit says he needs more exercise, he's getting fat."

"But I walk him every day. Well, I don't, but my walker walks him. I would *never* have a fat dog."

Leisl looked doubtful and cast a glance around the room. Anyone else with a fat dog?

No takers.

This is shit, I thought. *This is so fucking shit.*

Suddenly the door flew open, the light went on, startling us, and four or five plumpish boys ran into the room, singing, " 'Oaakk-la-homa! Where the...!' Whoops! I'm sorry." Strangely, they all looked identical.

The mood was shattered and I, for one, felt a little silly.

"Time's up," Leisl said, then people were putting crumpled dollar bills into a bowl, and getting to their feet and blowing out the candles.

40

In the corridor, I was devastated with disappointment and couldn't hide it.

"Well?" Nicholas asked.

Rigidly, I moved my head from side to side. No.

"No," he admitted sadly, "I guess it didn't really happen for you."

Leisl came racing out and grabbed me. "I'm so sorry, sweetie; I really wanted something good to come through for you, but I've no control over these things."

"What if we tried..." I asked. "I mean, would you be available for an individual reading?" Perhaps if there weren't the dead relatives of all the other people, clamoring in Leisl's ear about rapeseed oil and the like, there would be a chance for Aidan to get through.

But sorrowfully, Leisl shook her head. "One-on-ones don't work for me. I need the energy of the group." For that alone, I respected her. Almost trusted her.

"But sometimes I get messages at unexpected times, like if I'm at home watching *Curb Your Enthusiasm*. If anything comes through for you, I'll be sure to pass it along."

"Thank y—"

I ran out of words because, without warning, her body went rigid and her eyes glazed over. "Oh, wow, I'm getting something for you now. How about that?"

My knees turned to water.

"I'm seeing a little blond boy," she said. "Wearing a hat. He's your son? No, not your son, your... nephew?"

"My nephew, JJ. But he's alive."

"I know, but he's important to you."

Thanks for telling me something I already know.

"He'll become more important to you."

What did that mean? That Maggie was going to die and I was going to have to marry Garv and be a stepmother to JJ and Holly?

"Sorry, sweetie, I don't know what it means, I just pass on the message." And off she went down the corridor, with her lasagne, so bow-legged she looked like she was doing a side-to-side Charlie Chaplin walk.

"What was that?" Nicholas asked.

"My nephew, she said."

"Not your dead husband?"

"No."

"Okay, let's get Mitch over here." Mitch was deep in discussion with Barb, the car-tire-sandals woman—she was really cool considering she was probably well into her sixties; as well as the funky sandals, her tote bag looked like it had been crocheted out of cassette tapes.

"Mitch'll tell you about Neris Hemming," Nicholas promised. "She's often on TV shows and she even helped the cops find a murdered girl. She's so good she spoke in Mitch's wife's voice. Mitch!" he called. "Mitch, c'mere, buddy."

"You go on and talk," Barb said, in a gravelly voice. "I'm going outside for a cigarette. Who'da thought? I marched alongside Dr. King in the civil-rights movement. I fought the good fight in the women's revolution. And look at me now; having to hide in a doorway like a dirtbag just to smoke a cigarette. Where did it all go so wrong?" She laughed a grouchy heh, heh, heh. "See you next week, guys."

Mitch came over.

"Okay," Nicholas told me. "Tell him everything."

I swallowed. "My husband died and I came here today hoping to get in touch with him. I wanted to have a conversation with him. Find out where he is." My throat thickened. "Check if he's okay."

Mitch understood completely, I could see it.

"I told her about you going to Neris Hemming," Nicholas said. "She connected with your wife, she actually started speaking in her voice, didn't she?"

Mitch gave a little smile at Nicholas's enthusiasm. "She didn't speak in her voice, but, yeah, I was really talking to Trish. I've gone to lots of psychics and she's the only one who did it for me."

My heart was beating fast and my mouth was dry. "Do you have a number for her?"

"Sure." He produced an organizer. "But she's very busy. You'll probably have to wait, like, a long time to see her."

"That's okay."

"And it'll cost you. This is going to hurt—two thousand dollars for thirty minutes."

I was shocked: two thousand dollars was an horrific amount. My finances were in a shambles. Aidan hadn't had life insurance—well, neither had I—because neither of us had had any intention of dying and the rent on our apartment was so extortionate that paying Aidan's share as well as my own was eating up nearly every cent of my salary. We'd been saving to buy a place of our own, but that money was tied up in some funny account for another year, so I'd been living on my credit cards and doing a good job of ignoring my mounting debts. However, I was more than happy to go further into debt for this Neris Hemming—I didn't care what it cost.

Mitch was staring at his organizer, looking confused. "It's not here. I could have sworn it was. I keep doing that, like, I keep losing stuff . . ."

So did I. So often I was certain I had things in my handbag, then discovered that I didn't. I felt another jolt of connection with this Mitch.

"I can get the number," he said. "It's got to be somewhere in my apartment. How about I give it to you next week?"

"Can you take my number? Could you call when you find it?"

"Sure." He took my card.

"Can I ask you something?" I said. "Why do you come here after seeing someone so good?"

He stared into the distance, considering. "After talking to Trish via

Neris, I was able to let a lot of stuff go. And I dunno, I like coming here. Leisl is good, in her own way. She doesn't hit gold every week but her averages are pretty high. And the people here understand how it is for me—everyone else in my life, they think I should be over it by now. So coming here, I can be myself." He tucked my card in his wallet. "I'll call you."

"Please do," I said.

Because I wouldn't be coming back.

41

But later on, at home, I wondered if Leisl might have been onto something. The spirit "person," "voice," whatever you want to call it, *had* sounded a bit like Granny Maguire. Then there was the dog connection; I know it had come through a bit garbled, what with talk of my (unfortunately, nonexistent) dog putting on weight. But the thing was, Granny Maguire had kept greyhounds.

Rumor had it that she used to sleep with them. *Sleep* sleep with them, if you know what I mean. Although, now that I think of it, it was Helen who'd told me that and I'd never had it corroborated by a more reliable source.

Whenever we used to visit Granny Maguire, the minute I stepped out of the car, she'd urge, "Go on, Gerry; go on, Martin." (Named after Gerry Adams and Martin McGuinness.) And two blurs of leanness would whip out of the house and pin me to the wall, a paw on either side of my face, barking so hard my eardrums would hurt.

Granny Maguire would be in convulsions. "Don't let on you're a-scared," she'd screech, laughing so much she'd have to thump the ground with her stick. "They can smell the fear. They can smell the fear."

Everyone said that Granny Maguire was a "character," but that was only because she hadn't set the dogs on *them*. They wouldn't have been so quick to say it then.

And what about Leisl mentioning a little blond nephew in a hat? Not everyone had one of those. With a tickle of anxiety, I started to worry about JJ. What if Leisl had been giving me a warning? What if something was wrong with JJ? Fear continued to badger me, until eventually I had no choice but to ring and see if he was okay, even though it was one in the morning in Ireland.

Garv answered the phone.

I whispered, "Did I wake you?"

He whispered back, "Yes."

"I'm very sorry, Garv, but could you do something for me? Could you check that JJ is okay?"

"What sort of okay?"

"Alive. Breathing."

"Okay. Hold on."

Even if Aidan hadn't died, Garv would have humored me. He was nice, that way.

He put the phone down and I heard Maggie whisper, "Who is it?"

"It's Anna, she wants me to check on JJ."

"Why?"

"Just."

Thirty seconds later Garv was back. "He's fine."

"Sorry to have woken you."

"Not at all."

Feeling a little foolish, I disconnected. So much for Leisl.

As soon as I hung up, I was filled with a terrible need to talk to Aidan.

Typing furiously, I looked up Neris Hemming on the Internet. She had her own site, bearing literally hundreds of grateful testimonials. There were also details of her three books—I hadn't known she'd written any, I was going to run out to the nearest Barnes & Noble right now—and information on her forthcoming twenty-seven-city tour: she was playing thousand-seater venues in places like Cleveland, Ohio, and Portland, Oregon, but, to my bitter disappointment, she wasn't coming to New York.

The nearest city was Raleigh, North Carolina. *I'll go,* I thought, with sudden determination. *I'll take a day off work and fly down.* Then I discovered that it was sold out and another wave of wretchedness hit me.

I had to arrange a personal reading with her, but I clicked on every single link until it became clear that there was no way of contacting her via the site. I needed that phone number from Mitch.

42

I was trying to remember if Aidan and I had had rows. I mean, we must have had. I mustn't fall into the trap of turning him into a saint because he had died. It was so important to remember him as he'd really been. But I couldn't remember any major fireworks—no big shouty matches or kitchen implements being flung.

Of course, we'd had our disagreements: I used to get occasional bouts of jealousy about Janie and any mention of Shane made him tight-lipped and surly.

And there was that morning when we were getting ready for work and he was having trouble with his hair.

"It won't go the way I want it to," he complained, trying to push down a stubborn tuft.

"It doesn't matter," I said. "You look cute with it sticking out like that."

Briefly, he lit up, then said, "Oh, you mean Irish cute—like a puppy. Not U.S. cute."

"Cute, like adorable."

"I don't want to be cute or adorable," he griped. "I want to be good-looking. I want to be handsome, like George Clooney."

He put his tube of hair wax back on the shelf with a little more force than was strictly necessary and I got annoyed and accused him of being vain, and he said that wanting to look like George Clooney wasn't vain, it was normal, and I said, "Oh, is it?" And he said, "Yes!" Then we continued our ablutions in huffy silence. But it was early in the morning and we'd had a late night the night before and were tired and had to go to work and we didn't want to, and under the circumstances the whole thing was understandable.

And there were other things—it used to drive him mad when I played with the ingrowing hairs on my shins. I'd be having a great time, squeezing and tweezing—gross, I know, but is there anything more satisfying?—and he'd say, "Anna, please. I hate it when you do that." And I'd say, "Sorry," and pretend to stop, but I'd carry on, hiding behind a cushion or a magazine. After a while he'd say, "I know you're still doing it."

And I'd sort of snap, "I can't help it! It's my . . . thing, my . . . hobby, it helps me unwind."

"Can't you have a glass of wine?" he'd say, and I'd stomp off into the bedroom, where I'd ring someone and gouge away to my heart's content. Sometime later, I'd reemerge in top form and we'd all be friends again.

Then there was that time we went to Vermont in the fall to see the changing of the leaves and I decided that he was taking too many photos. I felt that he was intent on photographing every fecking leaf in the state, and every time he pressed the button and unleashed that whirry noise, I got a funny, angry feeling in my teeth.

But as differences went, that wasn't so bad and even our worst row *ever* had been about something really stupid: we'd been talking about holiday resorts and I said that I wasn't that keen on outdoor showers. He'd asked why and I told him the story of how Claire had been having an outdoor shower in a safari camp in Botswana and had caught a baboon watching her and having a good old wank for himself.

"It wouldn't happen," Aidan said. "She's making it up."

"She's not," I said. "If Claire said it happened, then it happened. She's not like Helen."

(Actually I wasn't at all sure that that was the case. Claire wasn't above embroidering a story.)

"A baboon wouldn't react that way to a human woman," Aidan had insisted. "It would only happen if he was watching a lady baboon."

"A lady baboon wouldn't take a shower."

"You know what I mean."

Then the whole thing deteriorated into a "Are you saying a baboon wouldn't fancy my sister?" sort of thing, but again, we'd had a hard week at work and we were both cranky and would have happily had a scrap about anything.

But, in all honesty, that was as bad as it ever got.

Speaking of sisters, another e-mail arrived from Helen about her new job.

To: Magiciansgirl1@yahoo.com
From: Lucky_Star_PI@yahoo.ie
Subject: Job!

Colin the bozo brought me a gun—heavy, exciting. Imagine, I've a gun!

I'd loads of questions for him. Most importantly...What's Mr. Big's real name? (Again, please remember am parrot-phrasing.)

Colin: Harry Gilliam.

Me: Do you really think something's going on with Mrs. Big and this Racey O'Grady?

Colin: Yeah. Probably. And if it's true, Harry'll be very upset. He's mad about Detta. Detta Big is a lady and Harry's always thought she was too good for him. Anyway, let's get going.

Me: Where?

Him: To a shooting club.

Me: For what?

Him: For you to learn how to shoot.

Me: How hard can it be? I just point the thing and pull the trigger.

Him: (all wearylike): Come on.

Went to funny bunker place in Dublin mountains, full of dirt-smeared, starry-eyed men who looked like they ran their own militia in their back garden.

I wasn't bad. Hit target couple of times. (Pity wasn't *my* target, har har.) My shoulder, though, was killing me. No one said shooting people hurts. Well, obviously hurts person who's shot! (Har har.)

Piss: Don't worry. Know you're all freaked out about death at moment, but promise you (a) Won't get shot (b) Won't shoot anyone.

The talk of guns had been alarming me, so her promise was a relief. Until I saw the final line.

Pissss: Except maybe some bad guys.

All the same it made me laugh. There was probably no point taking her too seriously—God only knew how much of this was embellished. Or downright fantasy.

43

Monday morning. Which meant the Monday Morning Meeting. And here came Franklin, clapping his hands together, rounding up his girls.

Walking to the boardroom, Teenie linked her arm through mine. She looked almost normal today; wearing a silver, Barbarella-style shift dress and long silver-and-gray sneakers that laced right up to her knee. Only the silver-painted skateboarding elbow and knee guards were evidence of proper kookiness.

"Step right up," she said. "Get your humiliation here!"

"Be degraded in front of your peers," I said.

"And undermined by your lessers."

Easy for us to laugh, we were doing okay.

I was getting good newspaper coverage. No great coups, but at the Monday Morning Meetings, I always had a couple of things to show and tell after each weekend. Maybe the beauty editors felt sorry for me with my scarred face and my dead husband. Mind you, I wasn't milking it because something like that could very much count against you: I could be seen as tainting Candy Grrrl with my bad luck and my ruined face. Normally when the MMM is over, there's a feeling that the week can only get better. But not today. Today was day zero for Eye Eye Captain. Today was the day that one hundred and fifty Eye Eye Captain kits would be assembled and packaged, ready to be couriered out to all the magazines and newspapers the following day. The timing was crucial: they couldn't be sent today, they couldn't be sent the day after tomorrow; it had to be tomorrow. Why? Because Lauryn was trying out a new guerrilla-style tactic. Instead of doing what we'd normally do with a launch—giving all the beauty editors plenty of advance notice—we were trying the opposite. She'd carefully calibrated the timing to ensure that Eye Eye Captain would arrive on every important beauty editor's desk *just before* their copy had to go to press. The idea was to dazzle them so completely with something fresh and new, to make them think that they had a jump on a new product, that they'd bump something else and give us the slot instead. Admittedly a high-risk game but one Lauryn insisted that we had to try.

It could work because the concept was novel—a one-stop eye-care kit. Three different products, each of which worked in tandem to enhance the efficacy of the others (or so they said). There was Pack Your Bags (a cooling gel to zap puffiness and undereye bags), Light Up Your Life (a light-deflecting concealer pen to banish dark circles), and Iron Out the Kinks (a whipped-mousse wrinkle killer).

Just one tiny little problem: the trio of products hadn't arrived from the manufacturers in Indianapolis. They were on their way. Oh, they were definitely coming. They'd be with us by eleven. But eleven came and passed. Lauryn made a hysterical phone call and got a guarantee that the driver was in Pennsylvania and would definitely be with us by one. One became two, became three, became four. Apparently the lorry driver had got lost coming into Manhattan.

"Fucking hayseed," Lauryn screamed. "This is fucking crazy." Then she slammed down the phone and looked at me. Somehow this was all my fault. We'd gone to the wire on this because I'd had the temerity to be in a car accident and had missed work for two months.

It was after five by the time the big cardboard boxes were being hefted into the boardroom. No one was meeting anyone else's eyes because we were all thinking the same thing: Who was going to stay late—very late—and do it?

Brooke was going to a benefit, saving something or other: whales, Venice, three-legged elephants. Teenie had school (and it wasn't her job anyway) and there was more chance of Lauryn eating a three-course meal.

It had to be me. Just me.

Everyone was so used to me working late that they didn't even ask if I'd any plans, but as it happened, I was meant to be seeing Rachel. I'd given her the slip over the weekend, citing pressures of work. And now I really *had* to work—the girl who'd cried overtime.

"Does anyone mind if I make a quick call? Just to cancel my sister?"

I sounded so sarcastic that startled looks were exchanged. Now and again unexpected spurts of anger, so red-hot they almost scalded me, were shooting up through me and carrying rage-soaked words out of my mouth.

"Er, no, go right ahead," Lauryn said.

Teenie helped me slit the boxes open and pile the products along the boardroom table, and Brooke, in all fairness to her, had already put a hundred and fifty press releases into a hundred and fifty padded envelopes, even though she'd been out for most of the afternoon because her aunt Genevieve (she wasn't her real aunt, just one of her mother's extremely rich friends) was in town and had hosted a lunch for her in a private dining room at the Pierre.

And then everyone was gone. The building was quiet, nothing but the hum of computers. I took a look at all the stuff on the boardroom table and was stabbed with self-pity.

I bet you're really pissed off with the way they're treating me.

I began by lining the inside of all the padded envelopes with sheets of silver lamé. This took until after eight; I was slower than I'd normally be because of my nails. Then I became a human conveyer belt. At one end of the table I stuck a printed label on the padded envelope, then I moved on to pick a Pack Your Bags from one pile, a Light Up Your Life from the next, an Iron Out the Kinks from the third, let them tumble into the padded envelope, picked up a handful of tiny silver stars, scattered them in on top, sealed the envelope, chucked it in the corner, and returned to the start.

I kind of got a rhythm going. Label, pick-pick-pick, tumble, stars, seal, throw. Label, pick-pick-pick, tumble, stars, seal, throw. Label, pick-pick-pick, tumble, stars, seal, throw. Label, pick-pick-pick, tumble, stars, seal, throw.

It was very soothing and I had been crying for a long time before I noticed. Mind you, I wasn't crying so much as *leaking*. Tears ran down my face without any input from me—no heaving, no gulping, no shoulder shaking; it was very peaceful. I cried the entire way through the job, and although my tears blurred the ink on *Femme*'s address label, no other harm was done.

By the time I finished, it was midnight. But all one hundred and fifty packages were waiting to be couriered in the morning.

My taxi driver home was good and mad. He had a massive mustache and long curly hair, which he went on and on about. He said he was like Samson: he carried his strength in his hair and all his "women" tried to make him cut it off because "they want me to be weak." On the mad-taxi-driver scale, he was easily a seven out of ten, possibly even seven and a half, and I felt he'd been specially sent by Aidan: it was late at night, I'd been working for sixteen hours straight, and he wanted to cheer me up.

Another e-mail arrived from Helen.

To: Magiciansgirl1@yahoo.com
From: Lucky_Star_PI@yahoo.ie
Subject: Job!

First day of surveillance on Detta Big. Stuck in hedge in her back garden in big detached house in Stillorgan, binoculars trained on her bedroom.

She's about fifty, roundy bum, big knockers, leathery cleavage. Shoulder-length blondy curly hair, heated-rollers end product.

Wearing high heels and cream knitted (bouclé?) skirt and jumper. Couldn't see lumps or bumps in her arse area, even with zoom at max. She must wear slip and steel-reinforced girdle. Looks like aging newsreader, maybe.

At ten to ten, she put on coat. We were going out. By-passed car, big silver Beemer (car lacking in personality), and walked to local church. She was going to mass! I sat at back, just grateful not to be in hedge.

Afterward, she went to newsagent, bought *Herald, Take a Break,* twenty Benson & Hedges, and packet of mints (Extra Strong). Then went home again and I resumed vigil in hedge. She put kettle on, made tea, sat in front of telly, smoking and staring into space. One o'clock, she got up, and I thought, Please let's be going out. But she was just making bowl of soup and toast, then went back to sitting in front of telly, smoking and staring into space. About four o'clock, she got up and I thought, Aye, aye, here we go. But she wasn't going out—she was doing the hoovering. Really going for it. Maddest thing you ever heard?

After hoovering frenzy, Detta went back to kitchen, put kettle on, made tea, and sat smoking and staring into space. God, hope tomorrow's going to be bit more exciting.

And an e-mail from Mum.

To: Magiciansgirl11@yahoo.com
From: Thewalshes1@eircom.net
Subject: Organized crime

Dear Anna,
We're in a bad way. Helen no longer cares about our "domestic" issue (i.e., the dog poo). She is too caught up in her new

job. She is "lording" it over us because she is associating with known criminals. If I'd thought, after all we sacrificed for your education, that this is how my youngest daughter would end up, I'd never have sent any of you to school at all. Sharper than a serpent's tooth it is to have a thankless child. She says the one she's surveilling, the wife of the "crime lord," has lovely clothes for an elderly person. Could that be true? And that her house is really clean? And that she does her cleaning herself. Could that really be the case or is Helen just trying to "upset" me?

I tried using her camera but it is a "digital" one and neither myself nor your father could figure it out. How are we to catch the old woman in the act? She was back again on Monday, up to her old tricks. If you are talking to Helen, would you try persuading her to help out. I know you are "bereaved," but she might listen to you.

Your loving mother,

Mum

The flash of red caught me by surprise. Blood. My period. The first one since the accident.

I'd barely noticed it not happening every month; I hadn't worried because in the recesses of my mind, I'd known it was because of the shock and terribleness. I hadn't, for one second, suspected I might be pregnant, but now, with an uprush of grief, I thought: *I'll never have your baby.*

We shouldn't have waited. We should have gone for it straightaway. But how were we to know?

We'd even talked about it. One morning shortly after we'd got married, I was getting dressed and Aidan was lying in bed, bare-chested, his hands behind his head. "Anna," he said, "something weird's happening."

"What? Aliens landing on next door's roof?"

"No, listen. Since I was three years old, the Boston Red Sox have been the love of my life. Now they're not anymore. Now it's you, obviously. I still care about them; I guess I still love them, but I'm not *in love* with them anymore." All this was delivered in bed, in a somber, soul-searching, ceiling-staring kind of way. "In all that time I never wanted to have kids. Now I do. With you. I'd like a miniature version of you."

"And I'd like a miniature version of you. But, Aidan, lest we forget, I have a mad family; a rogue insane gene could pop its head up at any time."

"Good, good, should be fun. And we've got Dogly to think about. Dogly needs a kid around the place." He sat up on his elbow and announced, "I'm serious."

"About Dogly?"

"No, about us having a baby. As soon as possible. What do you think?"

I thought I'd love it. "But not just yet. Soon. Soonish. Like, in a couple of years. When we've someplace proper to live."

To: Magicians.girl1@yahoo.com
From: Thewalshes1@eircom.net
Subject: This can't go on

Dear Anna,
I hope you are keeping well. I don't know if it will make you feel better or worse to know that things are very bad for us here, too. There was more dog number twos parked at our gate this morning. It is like living under siege. Luckily your father didn't stand in it this time, but the milkman did and he was extremely

annoyed and our "relationship" with him is awkward enough
since that time we all "cut out dairy" because of that stupid diet
Helen put us on that lasted five minutes until she realized that
ice cream is dairy. It was hard enough to persuade him to come
back that time.
Your loving mother,
Mum

All week, I was on tenterhooks waiting for the Mitch bloke to call
with Neris Hemming's number, but the days passed and I heard nothing.
So I made a plan: if he hadn't rung by Sunday I'd go back to that place.
That made me feel less panicky and powerless. Then I'd remember that it
was the Fourth of July weekend, what if he'd gone away? And I'd feel
panicky and powerless all over again.

It had been a bad week at work. I'd been ferociously narky, and although
my dislocated knee was officially better, I'd become very clumsy, as though
one side of my body were heavier than the other. I kept bumping into things;
I'd knocked a cup of coffee into Lauryn's desk drawer and I'd made a white-
board topple over at a briefing session and caught Franklin in the goolies. I'd
only grazed them, but he still made a terrible song and dance about it.

But these accidents were nothing compared to the Eye Eye Captain
disaster: because I'd cried all over the *Femme* address label and made it too
blurry to be read, their package had been returned to us by the couriers on
Tuesday afternoon, and we'd missed the print slot. Lauryn was still thin-
lipped with fury. Every morning when I got out of the elevator, I'd barely
set one shoe on the carpet before she shrieked down the corridor, "Do you

know how high the circulation of *Femme* is! Do you know how many women READ it?"

Then Franklin would join in, yelling, "Without his cojones, a man is nothing!"

On Friday evening, when I walked into my local newsagent's to get supplies for my evening of crying, I finally realized why I'd been so narky: I was roasting. The little shop was like an oven.

"It's so hot!" I said to the man.

I wasn't expecting a reply because I didn't think he spoke English, but he said, "Hot! Yes! For many days a heat wave!"

Many days? What did he mean? "What... when did this heat wave start?"

"Hah?"

"When, what day, did it start being hot?"

"Thursday."

"Thursday?" That wasn't so bad.

"Tuesday."

"Tuesday?" Said in high alarm.

"Sunday."

"It wasn't Sunday."

"Some other day. I don't know the name."

Disturbed, I slowly made my way home with my bag of sweets. This heat-wave business was not good. I'd been so locked inside myself that although I'd noticed it, I hadn't noticed it *enough*.

A worry was worming at me: during the week, while I'd been going about my business, wearing the wrong clothes for very hot weather, had I been... *smelly*?

After my regulation-issue three hours' sleep, I woke on Saturday morning with sweat trickling into my hair. Feck. So it was true: we were in the thick of a heat wave and it was summer. Panic seized me.

I don't want it to be summer. Summer is too far away from when you died.

I'd thought I'd wanted enough time to pass so I could think of him without the pain killing me, but now that it was July I wanted it to be February forever.

Time was the great healer, people said. But I didn't want to heal, because if I did I'd be abandoning him.

Flattened by the sweltering heat, I was too hot to move. The air conditioner needed to be set up, but it was a huge big yoke, the size of a telly. Last autumn, Aidan had put it away on a high shelf in the living room.

The horror washed over me. *You're not here to take it down.*

Those odd little gaps where I'd forget, for a split second, that he had died were such a mistake, because then I'd have to remember all over again. The shock always hit with the same force.

When would this get easier? Would it ever get easier? I'd been thinking about other people who'd had horror visited upon them—holocaust survivors, rape victims, people who'd lost entire families. Often they go on to live what looked like normal lives. At some stage they must have stopped feeling like everything was a living nightmare.

Oppressed as I was by heat and grief, the seconds inched by and eventually I said to him, *The grief doesn't seem to be killing me but the heat might.* So I made myself stand up and look for the AC. It was on the highest shelf in the room. Even standing on a chair, I couldn't reach it, and even if I could, it was too heavy for me to move.

Ornesto would have to help me get it down. I knew he was home because for the last ten minutes he'd been singing "Diamonds Are Forever" at the top of his lungs.

He opened the door in gold lamé shorts and flowery Birkenstocks.

"You look lovely," I said.

"Come in," he invited. "Let's sing a song."

I shook my head. "I need a man."

Ornesto opened his eyes wide. "Well, where are we going to find one of them, honey?"

"You'll have to do."

"I dunno," he said doubtfully. "What does this 'man' have to do?"

"Lift my air conditioner down from a high shelf and carry it over to the window."

"You know what? Let's get Bubba from upstairs to help us."

"Bubba?"

"Or something. He's a big guy. With bad clothes. He won't care if he sweats all over them. C'mon." Ornesto led the way upstairs and knocked on number ten's door.

A deep voice called suspiciously, "Who is it?"

Ornesto and I looked at each other and got an unexpected fit of the giggles. "Anna," I called, in a strangled voice. "Anna from number six." I nudged Ornesto.

"And Ornesto from number eight."

"Whaddaya want? To invite me to a garden party?" Pronounced "goo-ah-d'n paw-dee." New York humor, see. That gave us the excuse to laugh.

"No, sir," I said. "I was wondering if you could help me move my air conditioner."

The door moved back and a saggy fiftysomething man in his vest stood there. "You need a bit of muscle?"

"Er, yes."

"Long time since a woman said that to me. Lemme get my keys."

The three of us trooped down the stairs and into my apartment, where I pointed out the AC high up on the shelf.

"Shouldn't be a problem," Bubba said.

"I'll help," Ornesto promised.

"Sure you will, son." But he said it nicely.

Bubba climbed up on the chair, which Ornesto made a big show of holding steady. He also provided a stream of encouraging stuff, like "You got it. Yip, yeah . . . nearly, that's iiiit, just a bit further . . ."

Then the AC was down and was hefted over to the window, plugged in, and—like a miracle—mercifully cold air was blowing into the apartment. The gratitude!

I thanked the man effusively and asked, "Would you like a beer, sir?"

"Eugene." He stuck out his hand.

"Anna."

"A beer would be appreciated."

Luckily I had one. One. Literally. God knows how long it had been there.

As Eugene leaned against the kitchen counter and sucked down his possibly out-of-date beer, he asked, "What happened to the guy who lived here? He move out or something?"

A stricken hiatus followed. Ornesto and I looked at each other.

"No," I said. "He was my husband."

I paused. I couldn't bring myself to say the D-word: it was taboo. Everyone sympathized on my "tragedy" or my "sad loss," but no one would say "death," which often filled me with a terrible compulsion to say loudly, "Actually Aidan *died*. He's *dead*. Dead, dead, dead, dead, dead, dead, dead, dead, dead, dead, dead, dead, dead, dead, DEAD. There now! It's only a word—nothing to be frightened of!"

But I never said anything; it wasn't their fault. We get no lessons in dealing with death, even though it happens to everyone, even though it's the only thing in life we can depend on.

I took a deep breath and flung the D-word into the middle of the floor. "He died."

"Aw, I'm so sorry, kid," Eugene said. "My wife died, too. I've been a widower for nearly five years."

Oh my God. I'd never thought of it like that before. "I'm a widow." I started to laugh.

Strange as it may seem, it was the first time I'd used that word to describe myself. The image I had of "widows" was of ancient, gnarled crones wearing black mantillas. The only thing I had in common with them was the black mantilla, except that mine was pink.

I laughed and laughed until tears ran down my face. But it was the wrong sort of laughter and the boys were clearly aghast.

Eugene gathered me to him, then Ornesto put his arms around the two of us, a strange, well-meaning group hug. "It gets better, you know," Eugene promised me. "It really does get better."

To: Magiciansgirl1@yahoo.com
From: Lucky_Star_PI@yahoo.ie
Subject: Job!

Ashamed to tell you, Anna. Trailing Detta Big, most boring job of all bloody time! You could set watch by routine. Every morning, ten to ten, she leaves house to walk to ten o'clock mass. Every shagging morning. Can't believe it—she's from crime dynasty, up to her neck in extortion and God knows what else and she goes to mass every morning. Then goes to newsagent, buys twenty Benson & Hedges and assorted other stuff. Sometimes bag of cola cubes, sometimes new _Hello!_, once bag of rubber bands. Then she goes home, puts kettle on, makes tea, and sits in front of telly, smoking and staring into space.

One morning after mass, she went to newsagent's AND chemist, where she bought corn plasters. Thought excitement would kill me.

One afternoon, she went out in Beemer and I was praying

she was meeting Racey O'Grady. But only going to the chiropo-
dist, obviously she has trouble with corns, then home, kettle,
tea, smoking, staring into space.

Another afternoon, went for walk on pier. Fast walker, despite corns. When she got to end, sat on bench, smoked cigarette, stared into space, then came back. Nothing sinister. Just
getting exercise. Although some might consider that sinister.

Looks like she'd be good at cards, like she'd fleece you.
Loads of feathery lines around her mouth, from all the fags.
Spends fair amount of time renewing lip liner. Fond of the sun,
she's got that leathery look. But don't get me wrong. Attractive
woman, considering her age and all.

Only have to surveil her in daytime. Harry works nine-to-
five, Monday to Friday. Says no point in being crime lord if you
can't work own hours. Neighbors think he's in rag trade. So
although boredom is war crime, at least got evenings and weekends to myself.

Piss. How are you getting on? Have cheery thought for
you—at least Aidan didn't leave you for other woman. Far
rather someone died than did dirty on me. Mind you, if someone did dirty on me, would kill them, so result would be same.

From anyone else, this would sound unspeakably callous. But this
was Helen. This counted as heartfelt sympathy.

48

Still no word from Mitch by Sunday morning and I bowed to the inevitable and got ready to go to the spiritualist-church place. Once again I got there miles too early and waited while across the hall the *South Pacific* lads did their stuff.

Like the previous week, Nicholas was the first to arrive. Today his T-shirt said DEATH BEFORE DISHONOR. "You came back! This is the best!"

I was so touched that I hadn't the heart to tell him that the second I got the number from Mitch, I was off.

"Does Mitch come every week?" I asked.

"Most weeks. All of us come most weeks."

As I had him on his own, I had to satisfy my curiosity. "Tell me, why does Mackenzie come? Who is she trying to contact?"

"She's looking for a lost will, that would leave this, like *huge* inheritance to her side of the family. Time is running out. She's down to her last ten million dollars."

"I don't believe you."

"Which bit?"

"All of it, I suppose."

"Believe. Try it. It's fun." He grinned. "Look at me, I believe in the craziest stuff and I have a really fun time."

"Like what?"

"Just about everything. Acupressure, aromatherapy, alien abductions—and that's just the As. Government cover-ups, the power of meditation, that Elvis is alive and working in Taco Bell in North Dakota . . . You name it, I believe in it. Try me."

"Um . . . reincarnation?"

"Check."

"JFK was killed by the CIA?"

"Check."

"That the pyramids were built by people from outer space?"

"Check."

Eagerly he watched me, almost bursting out of his skin with the desire to say "Check!" again, when down the corridor came Leisl. She lit up like Times Square when she saw me. "Anna! I'm so happy you came back." She gathered me into her bad perm. "I really hope you'll get a better message this week."

Steffi, the young frumpy girl, was next and she smiled shyly and said she was glad to see me, as did Carmela, one of the older elastic-waist ladies, then dazzling Mackenzie. Even Undead Fred expressed pleasure at my presence.

I felt a huge rush of warmth and gratitude to them . . . but where was Mitch?

Down the corridor they came: Pomady Juan; groovy old Barb; a few more elastic waists—everyone was here except Mitch.

The room was set up and the candles were flickering and we were all taking our places in the circle of chairs and there was still no sign. I was wondering whether I should ask Nicholas if he had a number for Mitch when the door opened.

It was him.

"Just in time," Leisl said.

"Yeah, I'm sorry." He did a quick scan of the circle and his glance landed on me. "Anna, I'm sorry I didn't call. I lost your card. I'm a mess," he said. "But I've got the number here."

He handed me a piece of white paper and I unfolded it and gazed at the number written on it. Ten precious digits that would lead me to Aidan. Right, I could go now!

But I stayed where I was. They'd all been so nice that I felt it would be rude to leave. And now that I was there and the groany cello music was going full blast, I began to hope that something might happen. *I mean, what if today is the day that you decide to "come through" and I'd gone to get a pedicure?*

49

The first message was for Mitch.

"Trish is here," Leisl said, her eyes closed. "She looks like an angel today. So pretty, I wish you could see her. Mitch, she's asking me to tell you that things will get better. She says she'll always be with you, but you've got to start moving on."

Mitch looked as bleak as any person could look. "How?"

"It'll happen, if you're open to it."

"Yeah, well, I'm not open to it," Mitch said. "Trish," he said, and it was shocking hearing him address her directly. "I'm not moving on, because I don't want to leave you behind."

Silence fell and we all shifted a little uncomfortably. After a while, Leisl spoke. "Barb, who's Phoebe?"

"Phoebe?" Barb exclaimed, in her gravelly voice. "Well, who knew? She was one of my lovers, we shared a guy, famous painter, modesty forbids, edcedera, edcedera. She was married to him, I was humping him, then we both got rid of him and took up with each other. For a while. Heh, heh, heh. So what's up, Phoebe, baby?"

"You're not going to like it."

"How do you know?"

"Okay." Leisl sighed. "I'm sorry about this, Barb, but Phoebe wants to tell you that—and I'm quoting here—'he never loved you, you were only sex.'"

"Only sex? Whaddaya mean, 'only' sex? Sex is what it's all about!"

"Let's move on," Leisl said quickly.

This is crazy, I thought. *A beyond-the-grave slanging match. I shouldn't be here. I'm normal and sane, these people are nuts...*

Then Leisl said, "I'm getting a man," and my stomach nearly jumped out of my mouth. It jumped straight back in again when Leisl said, "He's called Frazer. Mean anything to anyone?"

"Me!" Mackenzie said, at the same time as Leisl said, "Mackenzie, it's for you. He says he's your uncle."

"Great-uncle. Cool! So where's the missing will, Great-uncle Frazer?"

Leisl listened for a moment, then said, "He says there is no missing will."

"But there's gotta be a will!"

Leisl shook her head. "He seems totally sure."

"But if there's no will, what am I going to do for money?"

"He says get a job." Pause for Leisl to listen to the voice in her head. "Or marry a rich guy."

"That's outrageous!" Leisl added.

Mackenzie's tanned face was flushed. "Tell him from me he's a drunken asshole who knows nothing. Get me Great-aunt Morag! She'll know."

Leisl sat with her eyes closed.

"Get me Great-aunt Morag!" Mackenzie ordered, as if Leisl was a personal assistant.

I felt very sorry for Leisl—having to pass on stuff that people didn't want to hear, and even though the messages were allegedly coming from somewhere else, she seemed to get the blame.

"He's gone," Leisl said. "And no one else is coming through."

"This is bullshit!" Mackenzie exclaimed. She huffed and puffed for the next little while about how she should be in the Hamptons right now—I knew it!—but that she was coming here to help her family and—

"Shhh," Pomady Juan said. "A little respect."

Mackenzie put her hand to her mouth. "I'm so sorry." Then she dropped her voice to a whisper. "Sorry. Sorry, Leisl."

Leisl was sitting very still. She hadn't opened her eyes in a while.

"Anna," she said slowly. "Someone wants to talk to you."

Instantly my forehead was drenched with sweat.

"It's a man."

I closed my eyes and clenched my fists. *Please God, oh, please God . . .*

"But it's not your husband. He's your grandfather."

Again with the grandparents!

"He says his name is Mick."

My arse! I'd no granddad called Mick. *But hold on a minute,* I thought, *what about Mum's dad, Granny Maguire's wretched spouse? What was his name?* I didn't remember him because . . .

"You never knew him. He died shortly after you were born, he says."

All the little hairs on my arms lifted and a shiver shot down my spine. "That's right. Oh my God. Has he met Aidan? Up there? Like, wherever they are?"

Leisl's brow was furrowed and her fingers were pressed to her temples. "I'm sorry, Anna, someone else is coming through, a woman. I'm losing him."

I wanted to leap from my seat, grab her head, and shriek, "Well, get him back, for God's sake. Find out about Aidan. Please!"

"Sorry, Anna, he's gone. The woman with the stick is back, the angry woman from last week, who was talking about your dog."

Granny Maguire? I was in no mood to talk to that old witch. It was probably her who had scared Granddad Mick away. The words were out of my mouth before I knew I was going to say them. "Tell her to fuck off!"

Leisl flinched, then flinched a second time. "She has a message for you."

"What is it?"

"She says, 'Fuck off yourself.'"

I was speechless.

"Oh boy." Leisl sounded upset.

The mood in the room was extremely uncomfortable.

"I'm so sorry," Leisl said. "Today has been very strange. This is usually a very loving place. A lot of angry energy here today. Should we stop?"

We decided to continue and the remainder of the messages—from Nicholas's dad, Steffi's mother, and Fran's husband—were uncontroversial.

Then the time was up, the *Oklahoma!* boys needed the space, and out in the corridor afterward, I cornered Mitch.

"Thank you so much for this." I indicated the piece of paper. "Do you mind...can I ask you a bit about your reading with Neris? Like, what convinced you she was for real?"

"There was some personal stuff that no one else could have known about. Trish and me, we had special names for each other." He smiled, half embarrassed. "And Neris told me them."

That sounded convincing.

"Did Trish say where she was?" My obsession: Where was Aidan?

"I asked her and she said she couldn't describe it in a way that I'd understand. She said it was less of a question of where she was and more of a question *what* she had become. But that she was always with me.

"I asked her if she was scared, and she said no. She said she was sad for me, but that she was happy where she was. She said she knew it was hard but that I had to try to stop thinking of her as a life interrupted. It was a life completed."

"What happened...to Trish?"

"How did she die? An aneurysm. One Friday night she came home from work, same as usual—she was a teacher, an English teacher. About seven o'clock she said she was feeling dizzy and nauseous, by eight she was in a coma, and by one-thirty A.M. in the ICU, she was dead." He paused. Like Aidan, Trish had died young and suddenly. No wonder I'd felt such a tangible connection with Mitch.

"Nothing anyone could have done. Nothing that would have showed up in any tests. I still can't believe it." He sounded baffled. "It happened so quickly. Too quickly to believe it, you know?"

I knew. "How long ago did it happen?"

"Nearly ten months. It'll be ten months on Tuesday. Anyway." He swung his kit bag on his shoulder. "I'm going to hit the gym."

He looked like he went to the gym a lot. There was a bunched force in his shoulders and upper body, like he lifted weights. Maybe it was his way of coping.

"Best of luck with Neris," he said. "See you next week."

50

I called Neris Hemming's number as soon as I got home, but a recorded message told me that their office hours were Monday to Friday, nine until six. I slammed down the phone far too hard, and in one of those sudden uprisings of acid rage, I shrieked, "Oh, Aidan!"

A storm of tears overtook me and I convulsed with frustration, my powerlessness, and my terrible, terrible need.

A few minutes later, I wiped my face and said humbly, "I'm sorry."

I repeated, "I'm sorry," to every photo of Aidan in the apartment. It wasn't his fault that Neris Hemming's office took Sundays off. And this was a holiday weekend, so they probably wouldn't be in tomorrow either.

I'd ring from work on Tuesday, I decided. I was so terrified of losing the number that I wrote it in several—hopefully unexpected—places, just in case someone ever broke into my apartment and decided to steal all the Neris Hemming numbers. I put it in my organizer, I wrote it on a receipt and hid it in my knickers drawer, I wrote it on the inside cover of

Never Coming Back (never coming back? Oh, we'll see about that, missus), and I indented it in the lid of a very old tub of Ben & Jerry's Chunky Monkey (the pen wouldn't work on the cold, waxy cardboard) and replaced it in the freezer.

Now what?

I braced myself to ring Aidan's parents; Dianne had called while I was out. Somehow—and I'd no idea how it had happened because it was the last thing I wanted—we'd got into a routine where she rang me every weekend. I dialed their number, screwed my eyes up tight, and beseeched, over and over, in my head, *Don't be in, don't be in, oh, please don't be in,* but—damn—Dianne picked up. She sighed. "Oh, Anna."

"How are you, Dianne?"

"I'm pretty bad, Anna. I'm pretty low. I was thinking about Thanksgiving."

"But it's only July."

"I don't want to do it this year. I was thinking of just getting the hell out, going on vacation on my own, to a place where they don't have Thanksgiving. It's a time for family. And I can't bear it."

She began to sob quietly.

"To lose a child, it's the most unbearable pain. You'll meet someone else, Anna, but I'll never get my baby back."

This had happened the few times we'd talked. She engaged in competitive grief: Who has more right to be devastated? A mother or a wife?

"I won't meet someone else," I said.

"But you could, Anna, that's my point, you *could.*"

"How's Mr. Maddox?" I could never think of him as having a first name.

"Coping in his usual way. Buried in his work. I'd get more emotional support from a three-year-old." She laughed, in a scary way. "You know what, I've kind of had it."

I was pretty sure I knew what was coming next for Dianne. It was the old, old story. She'd go on a women's retreat, where they all run around in their pelt, daubed with blue paint, worshiping the female goddess, proud that their knockers reach their belly buttons. When they weren't dancing in a clearing under a full moon, they'd be making big fun of men, so that when she came back to Boston, she'd stop covering the gray in her hair and making dinners for Mr. Maddox. She might even get a Harley and a crew cut and be part of the Dykes on Bikes contingent of Gay Pride.

"I'd better go, Dianne. You take care. We'll talk about the ashes some other time." We still hadn't sorted that out.

"Yeah," she said wearily. "Whatever."

Done for another week! Oh, the relief! Feeling light and free, I rang Mum; I had to check that I had a granddad called Mick. And if I had? Did that make Leisl a real medium? I knew she came through with messages for the others—but she knew all their stories, she knew what they wanted to hear.

However, she knew very little about me. Mind you, how hard would it be to find an Irish family with a man called Mick in it? Lucky guess? But that thing about me never having met him was harder to explain away . . . Another lucky guess?

Mum answered the phone with a gaspy "Hello."

"It's me, Anna."

"Anna, pet! What's happened?"

"Nothing. I'm just calling for a chat."

"A chat?"

"Yes. What's wrong with that?"

"Because everyone knows we watch *Midsomer Murders* at this time on a Sunday night. *No one* rings."

"Sorry, I didn't know. Okay, I'll call back later."

"Ah, sure, go on, stay where you are. We've seen this one already."

"Er, all right. You know Granny Maguire's husband?"

A pause. "Do you mean my father?"

"Yes! Sorry, Mum, yes. What was his name? Was it Michael? Mick?"

Another pause. "Why do you want to know? What are you up to?"

"Nothing. Mick? Yes or no?"

"Yes." Said reluctantly.

My scalp crawled. Oh my God. Leisl must have been onto something.

"And I never knew him? He died when I was born?"

"Two months after."

A wave of tingling flushed right down my body. Surely that was more than just a lucky guess by Leisl. But if she was really talking to the dead, why hadn't Aidan come forward...?

"What's going on?" Mum asked suspiciously.

"Nothing."

"What's going on?" Louder this time.

"NO-thing!"

51

Via a series of cunning lies—I told Rachel I was going to Teenie's, I told Teenie I was spending the day with Jacqui, and I told Jacqui I was hanging out with Rachel—I managed to avoid having to attend any holiday rooftop barbecues and firework displays on Monday and had a pleasant enough time, sitting downwind of my air conditioner and watching reruns of *The Dukes of Hazzard, Quantum Leap,* and *M*A*S*H.*

I liked—loved—being in our apartment. It's where I felt closest to him. God knows we'd gone through hell and back to get it. I know it's a cliché about how hard it is to get a half-decent apartment in Manhattan, but it's only a cliché because it's true. "Large, bright, airy apartment" was the holy grail but you paid through the nose for every inch of floorboard and window. "Poky, gloomy kip, miles from the subway" was what most people ended up settling for.

After Aidan and I got engaged, we'd started looking for a place, but it was impossible. After getting nowhere for weeks, we were walking past a realtor's window one evening when we saw a picture of a "bright and airy loft." In a neighborhood we liked and—much more importantly—at a rent we could afford.

Gripped with a sense that this was our destiny, we set up a viewing for the very next day. This was it, we thought. Finally, we would have a home! So sure were we that we brought along the first two months' rent. Who could blame us for thinking we were pretty savvy?

"We're going to be a normal couple," I said as we got the subway there. "We're going to have a nice apartment and have friends over for dinner and go antiquing at the weekends." (I had only the vaguest idea of what "antiquing" involved but everyone did it.)

However, when we got to the apartment we discovered nine other couples also viewing. The place was so small there was barely room for us all, and as the twenty of us bumped and jostled resentfully, forming queues to peer into closets and examine the shower, the realtor guy watched with an amused smile. Eventually, he clapped his hands together and called for attention. "Everyone had a good look?"

A chorus of yeses.

"You all love it, right?"

Another babel of agreement.

"Okay, here's how it is. You're all great people. I'm going back to my office now and the first couple to reach me with three months in cash gets the apartment."

Everyone froze. Surely the guy couldn't mean...? But he could: the couple who beat off all the other contenders to make it forty-seven blocks uptown in the fastest time got the apartment.

It was like a reality show writ small and already three or four of the guys were wedged in the doorway, trying to get out.

Aidan and I were staring at each other in horror: this was disgusting. And in a split second I saw what was about to happen: Aidan was going to launch himself into the scrum. I knew he didn't want to but he was prepared to do it for me. Before he bolted for the door, I placed a hand on his chest and stopped him.

Barely moving my lips and indicating the scrum with an eye flick, I said, "I'd rather live in the Bronx."

Deep understanding dawned. Just as quietly he replied, "I read you, Lieutenant."

Already the room had emptied. The only people remaining were the realtor and us. The others were already desperately hailing cabs or thundering down the steps of the subways, ready to vault over the ticket machines or running—actually *running*—forty-seven blocks.

"Leave slooowly," I told Aidan.

"Over and out."

The realtor noticed our lazy saunter. Sharply he looked up from whatever he'd been doing with his briefcase. Wanking into it, probably, we later decided. "Hey! You guys better get moving. Don't you want this apartment?"

Aidan held his gaze and said—sadly, like he felt terribly sorry for the man: "Not that badly, buddy."

Down on the street I began to regret our principled stand. It was only then that I understood that we hadn't got the apartment. (In my head, we had already moved in and were living there and had bought a plant.)

Aidan squeezed my hand. "Baby, I know you're choked. But we'll think of something. We'll get a place."

"I know."

I took a strange comfort from knowing that Aidan and I were the same, that we had the same values.

"Neither of us has the killer instinct," I said.

It was like I'd hit him. He recoiled. "I'm sorry, baby," he said.

"No," I said. "No. I hate all that, There's no such thing as second-place stuff. And people with the killer instinct are usually a bit peculiar. They're edgy, they can't relax."

"Yeah, have you noticed they eat too quickly?"

"They get married only when they 'have a window' between racquet-ball matches."

"And they have a compulsive tic to exchange business cards every four minutes."

"And they divorce people by e-mail."

"No. Text message."

"We don't want to be like that, do we?"

Ut we still needed someplace to live.

"We've got to think harder," I said.

"No, we've gotta think smah-tah. I've got a plan."

He explained: the next time that same real-estate firm was having a viewing of a place that we could afford, we'd go prepared: with three months' rent in cash in our pockets and a town car waiting outside. "We'll make sure the guy sees plenty of us, me in particular. And when it looks like it's getting near the time when he assembles everyone, I'll pretend I've got a call on my cell and I'll step outside to take it. Soon as I'm out, I'll run down into the street, get in the car, and go to his office. Let's hope he won't notice I'm not there."

"But when he gets back to his office, you'll be there and I won't have arrived yet," I said. "Don't we have to show up as a couple? Isn't it against the rules not to?"

"They're only his stupid rules, it's not like we can be arrested for breaking them. Okay, I'm thinking, I'm thinking...right, got it!" He snapped his fingers. "When I get to his office, I'll say the reason you're not there is that you're a nurse and you stopped to help a man who was having a cardiac arrest outside Macy's. Yeah." He nodded thoughtfully. "That's what I'll say. We'll guilt the guy into giving us the apartment."

"I hope you're not getting the killer instinct," I said, in alarm.

"Just this once. Let's see if it works."

And, strangely, it did.

Although not exactly in the way we'd hoped. The realtor guy said to

Aidan, "I know you cheated. I know you're lying. But I like your balls. You can have the apartment."

"I felt sullied." Aidan squirmed, afterward. "Dirty, you know? 'I like your balls.' I've been dragged down to his level."

"Yes, yes, that's terrible," I said. "But we've got an apartment! We got somewhere to live! Get over it."

"Neris Hemming's office."

"Oh my God, I can't believe I'm finally through!" I was so over-whelmed I couldn't stop talking. "I'm at work and I've been ringing for *hours* and kept getting your message, then *the very second* the clock hit nine o'clock, I got the engaged tone and it was engaged for, like, *forever,* and I'd got so used to hitting redial and hanging up that when you an-swered, I nearly hung up by accident—"

"Can I have your name, honey?"

"Anna Walsh."

I knew it was crazy but I'd fantasized that when she heard my name she'd go, "Oh yeah, Anna Walsh," then shuffle through some papers on her desk, containing messages from the dead and say, "Yes, there's a mes-sage for you from a guy called Aidan Maddox. He said to say he's sorry he died so unexpectedly like that, but he's hovering around you all the time and can't wait to talk to you."

"A-N-N-A W-A-L-S-H." Keys clicked as she inputted me.

"You're not Neris, are you?"

"No, I'm her assistant, and I'm not even a little bit psychic. Number and e-mail, please."

I called them out, she read them back to me, then she said, "Okay, we'll be in touch." But I didn't want the call to end; I needed *something*.

"You see, my husband died." Tears began to pour down my face and I ducked my head so that Lauryn wouldn't see.

"Sure, honey, I know."

"Do you really think Neris will be able to put me in contact with him?"

"Like I said, honey, we'll be in touch."

"Yes, but—"

"Great talking to you."

She was gone—and here came Franklin, clapping his hands together, rounding up his girls for the Monday Morning Meeting, even though it was Tuesday.

I was still getting pretty good newspaper coverage. So it was a bit of a shock when Ariella said, from the head of the table, "What's going on with you, Anna?"

Shit. I'd thought I was flying beneath the radar: being effective, but not so effective that I'd come to Ariella's attention.

However, all those long hours I'd been putting in paid off and I was able to give a decent answer. "The biggest project I'm working on at the moment is Candy Grrrl going to Super Saturday in the Hamptons."

Super Saturday was a high-profile, celebrity-ridden charity fundraiser. It had started as a sample sale by designers like Donna Karan and had grown over the last decade to one of *the* events in the Hampton calendar. Members of the public (but it was the Hampton public, so it was very select, really) had to pay in—a lot, like several hundred dollars—but once you were in you got to buy designer clothes for next to nothing; there were giveaways, treatments, raffles, and a sensational goody bag when you left.

"Our stand is twice as big as it was last year, we're giving away Candy Grrrl beach bags, and best of all, I've persuaded Candace to actually come and do makeovers. Getting her in person should be a huge draw."

Off the top of her head, Ariella couldn't find anything to criticize in that, so she turned on Wendell. "You're doing Super Saturday, too, yeah? You got a world-famous makeup artist coming along?"

"Dr. De Groot will be attending," Wendell said.

Dr. De Groot was Visage's skin-care scientist. He was the oddest-looking man I'd ever met—he was actually frightening—and he definitely took his work home. We reckoned he practiced chemical peels and Restylane injections on himself. Maybe even the odd bit of surgery in front of the bathroom mirror. He was shiny and stretched and frozen and lopsided. I know I was a fine one to talk with my mutilated face, but really, anyone who met him would never use Visage again.

"The Phantom of the Opera?" Ariella said. "Try to get him to wear a bag over his head."

Wendell nodded efficiently. "Done."

Ariella seemed to sag. There was no one to yell at; we were all too efficient today. "Go on." She nodded at us all. "Beat it, get out of here, I'm busy."

Back at my desk a message was waiting on my computer.

To: Magiciansgirl1@yahoo.com
From: Psychic_Productions@yahoo.com
Subject: Neris Hemming

We have noted your request for a one-to-one reading with Neris Hemming. Due to her busy schedule, Ms. Hemming is fully booked for several months. When a vacancy becomes available her office will contact you to arrange a half-hour phone reading. The cost for Ms. Hemming's time will be $2,500. We accept all major credit cards.

Cripes, it had gone up a lot since Mitch had talked to her. Not that it mattered, I was thrilled that they'd got back to me. If only I could talk to her *now*.

To: Psychic_Productions@yahoo.com
From: Magiciansgirl1@yahoo.com
Subject: Several months?

How long is several months?

I mean, "several months" is far too vague, I need to start planning, I need to start counting down to when I'll be talking to you.

To: Magiciansgirl1@yahoo.com
From: Psychic_Productions@yahoo.com
Subject: Re: Several months?

Between ten and twelve weeks, usually, but this is not a guarantee, simply an estimate. Please note this in any legal action.

What? People *sued* because they didn't get to talk to Neris in the promised time? But I knew how desperate I was, I could understand people losing their head if they were all set to talk to their loved one on a particular date and it fell through.

There was also an attachment full of exemption clauses. It was couched in convoluted legalese, but the gist was that if you didn't get to hear what you wanted from Neris, no way could you hold her responsible, and although she could cancel for any reason she liked, if you weren't there at your appointed slot, you'd forfeit your money.

There was also an e-mail from Helen.

To: Magiciansgirl1@yahoo.com
From: Lucky_Star_PI@yahoo.ie
Subject: Tediarseity

Break in routine! Detta drove to Donnybrook in personality-free Beemer and went to vile dress shop. You know the type—

small boutiques for rich old bats. Have "exotic" names like "Monique's" and "Lucrezia's" and only sixteen things in stock and snobby old assistants who say, "These stinky expensive items are just in from Italy—gooooooooorgeous, aren't they?" And "This yellow would be lovely on you, Annette, really brings out your teeth."

Didn't go in, just hovered outside like homeless person because (a) place was too small and Detta would have spotted me, and (b) once you're through doors of shop like that, if you try to leave without buying anything, they shoot you in the back with sniper's rifle.

Friday, the ninth of July, my birthday; I was thirty-three. To add insult to injury, instead of enjoying a nice peaceful evening at home, crying my eyes out, I was being forced to endure "a great night out."

Rachel wanted to make sure that my first birthday without Aidan was a lovely affair: a lovely restaurant and lovely presents with lovely people who loved me. It would be a bloody nightmare.

I'd begged her to reconsider. I'd reminded her how difficult I found any social event and one that had me at its epicenter would be close to unendurable, but she was immovable.

I was late getting home from work. I had ten minutes before Jacqui came to pick me up and I wasn't remotely ready. I didn't even have a clue where to start. Teeth, I decided. I'd brush my teeth. But when I picked up my toothbrush, a dreadful pain, like a streak of electricity zipping through me, shot up my arm, through my ribs, and down through the marrow of my legs. I still had the arthritis/rheumatism-style aches, but in the last few days they'd been joined by these shooting electric jolts. Once again the doctor said that this was "normal"; all part of the grieving process.

My bell rang. She was early. "Ah, fuck!" I flung my toothbrush hard into the sink.

Jacqui looked me over and said, "Oh, good, you're ready."

Actually, I was still in my work clothes (pink ballerina-style skirt, pink vest, fishnet cutoffs, and ballet slippers embroidered with flowers), but as my work clothes looked more like party clothes than most people's party clothes, I decided I'd do.

As the cab moved through the Friday-night traffic, I thought: *I'm on my way to meet you. You'll be there tonight, you'll have come straight from work to the restaurant. You'll be wearing your blue suit and you'll have taken off your tie, and when Jacqui and I walk in you'll wink at me to show that you know I have to be mannerly and say hello to everyone else first, that you and me can't immediately start slobbering over each other, but the wink will say it all, it'll say, "Just you wait till I get you home..."* "Hmm?"

Jacqui had just asked me something.

"A good sun cream," she repeated. "Factor fifteen at least. Will you steal me one?"

"Sure, yes, whatever you'd like."

Then I tried to climb back inside my head. *We'll politely speak to everyone there but you'll do something small and intimate, something only I'll know about—maybe you'll pass by me and quickly circle your thumb over the palm of my hand or—*

Jacqui had said something else and resentment flared momentarily. I loved being in my own head so much, it was getting harder and harder being with other people. I'd be thinking lovely happy thoughts, then they'd say something and drag me back to their version of reality, the one where Aidan was dead.

"Sorry. What?"

"We're here," she repeated.

"So we are," I said, in surprise.

Flanked by Jacqui, like I was a prisoner on a one-day release, I walked into La Vie en Seine, where a crowd awaited: Rachel, Luke, Joey, Gaz, Shake, Teenie, Leon, Dana, Dana's sister Natalie, Aidan's old roommate Marty, Nell, but not Nell's strange friend, thank Christ. They were standing around, drinking champagne from flutes, and when they saw me they pretended they weren't mortified and a little cheer went up and someone said, overjovially, "Here's the birthday girl." Someone else handed me a flute, which I tried to down in one go, but those yokes are so narrow that I had to tilt my head right back and the glass stuck to my face and left a perfect circle on my cheeks and across my nose.

Everyone was smiling and looking at me—people were always either supercheery or supersolicitous, no one could be normal—and I couldn't think of a single thing to say. This was worse, far worse, than I'd anticipated. I felt I was standing in the middle of the world while everyone and everything retreated farther and farther.

"Let's take our places," Rachel said.

At the table, the insides of my jaws hurting from holding a smile, I picked up another glass of champagne—I wasn't sure it was mine, but I couldn't stop myself—and drank down as much of it as I could without it suctioning onto my face again. Up until now I'd stayed away from heavy drinking because I was afraid I might like it too much. It looked as if I'd been right.

As I wiped sticky champagne dregs from my chin, I realized a waiter was standing patiently beside me, waiting to hand me a menu. "Oh God, sorry, thank you," I murmured, thinking: *Act normal, act normal.*

Jacqui was telling me how hard it was to get hold of a Labradoodle, they were in very short supply and were being sold on the black market, some had even been kidnapped from their owners and sold. I was trying to pay attention but Joey was diagonally opposite her and he was singing

"Uptown Girl," changing the real words for snide ones about Jacqui. "Wannabe girl, she only hangs around with the rich and famous, she wishes she lived in Trump To-wer, so her and Donald co-ould be best buddies..."

He was being very unpleasant—nothing unusual there—but he was really putting an extraordinary amount of work into it. Normally, Joey couldn't ever be coaxed to sing. Then I understood—oh my God...he fancied Jacqui.

When had that started?

Jacqui was adept at ignoring him but my nerve endings were so raw that I had to say, "Joey, could you stop?"

"Wha—? Oh, sorry, man."

I was getting away with a lot: everyone had to be nice to me. There was no telling how long it might last, so I might as well make the most of it.

"It's the voice, yeah?" Joey said. "Tone-deaf, always was. People get asked, what special power they'd like? They always say they'd like to be invisible. Me, I wish I could sing."

At the next table my attention was caught by a young, beautiful woman. She was very New York—sleek and coordinated with shiny, blown-out hair. She was smiling and talking animatedly to the dull-looking man with her, her manicured hands flashing to emphasize what she was saying. I watched her shirtfront rise and fall as she took a breath. And another. And another. And another. And another. And another. And another. And another. And another. And another. And another. Breathing. Staying alive. And one day she wouldn't breathe anymore. One day something would happen and her chest wouldn't rise and fall. She'd be dead. I thought of all that life stuff going on beneath the skin, her heart pumping and her lungs lifting and her blood flowing and what makes it happen and what makes it stop...

Slowly I realized that everyone was staring at me.

"Are you okay, Anna?" Rachel asked.

"Um..."

"It's just that you were staring at that woman."

Oh my God, I was out of control. What should I say? "Yes...wondering if she's had Botox."

Everyone turned to look.

"'Course she has."

Then I felt wretched. Not just because I was sure the woman hadn't had Botox—she was so animated—but because I wasn't fit to be let out.

Gaz squeezed my shoulder. "Have a proper drink." And I decided I would. Something strong.

When my martini arrived, Gaz said encouragingly, "You're okay, there. You're doing great."

"D'you know something, Gaz." I gulped from the glass and heat flooded my system. "I don't think I am. I have this...sensation...that I'm looking at the world through the wrong end of a telescope. Have you ever felt like that? No, don't answer it, because you're so nice, you'll just say that you have. Can I tell you how it feels? A lot of the time, like not just tonight, although it's very bad tonight, it feels like my lens on the world has been interfered with, so that everyone looks much further away, do you know what I mean?" I took another deep gulp of my martini. "The only time I feel half normal is when I'm at work, but that's because it's not the real me, it's because I'm acting a role. Can I tell you what I was thinking when I was looking at that beautiful woman. I was thinking that one day we'll all be dead, Gaz. Her, me, Rachel there, Luke, you, Gaz— yes, you, too. I'm not singling you out, Gaz, please don't think that, you know how fond of you I am, I'm only saying that you'll be dead one day. And it mightn't be in forty years' time or whatever you're counting on. Gaz, you could go like that." I tried to snap my fingers, but couldn't manage it. Could I be drunk already? "I don't mean to be morbid, Gaz, saying you could drop dead any minute, it's the truth. I mean, look at Aidan, he's dead and he was younger than you, Gaz, by a couple of years. If he can die, so can any of us, including you. Not that I mean to be morbid, Gaz."

I have a vague memory of his desperate face as I droned on and on and on. I was watching myself, like I was hovering outside my body, but I couldn't do a thing to stop myself. "I'm thirty-three Gaz, thirty-three today, and my husband is dead and I'll have another martini because if you can't have a martini when your husband is dead when can you have one?"

I continued in this vein for some time. I half noticed a glance being exchanged between Gaz and Rachel but it was only when Rachel got to her feet and said overcheerily, "Anna, I'm coming over to you. I haven't had a proper chat with you all night," that I realized that I was an object of pity and people were almost paying bribes in order not to sit beside me.

"I'm so sorry, Gaz." I grasped his hand. "I can't help it."

"Hey. Nothing to be sorry about." Tenderly he kissed the top of my head, but then he nearly broke into a run. Seconds later he was sitting at the bar, knocking back an amber-colored liquid in one frantic slug. His glass hit the polished wood, he said something urgent to the barman, the glass was being refilled with the amber-colored liquid, then it was down the hatch in another single swallow.

I knew, without having to be told, that the amber-colored liquid was Jack Daniel's.

I woke on Saturday morning with a horrible hangover. I was trembly, tearful, and in terrible pain. The arthritis/rheumatism-style aches were far worse than usual and the shooting zips of electric pain felt like my bones were on fire.

I was also swollen-tongued with thirst.

Old impulses die hard. I wanted to nudge Aidan and say, "If you get up and bring me some Diet Coke I'll be your friend forever."

Images of the previous night flashed through my head—pictures of me getting people into headlocks and doing long slurred monologues on mortality—and I cringed with mortification.

Briefly, my shame mingled with defiance. I had *told* Rachel I couldn't handle people; I'd warned her. But the shame won and I had no one to tell me that I hadn't made a drunken show of myself the night before, that I hadn't been so bad really . . .

He used to be so nice to me whenever I was hungover.

"I wish you were here," I told the empty air. "I really miss you. I really, really, really, really, really, really, really miss you."

In all the time since he had died I had never felt more alone and the memory of what I'd been doing this time last year was almost unbearable. I'd had such a lovely birthday.

A few weeks before it, he'd asked me what I wanted to do and I said, "Let's go away. Surprise me. But it must be someplace that doesn't involve cosmetics. Or antique shops."

"You don't like antique shops?" He sounded really surprised and he was within his rights. I had made him spend at least two Sundays on the upstate "antique route," all of it overrun with couples just like us.

"I tried." I hung my head. "I really tried, but I like new clean modern things, not smelly old yokes riddled with woodworm. One more thing," I'd added. "I don't want to go too far from New York. I can't take the Friday-night gridlock."

"Orders received. Over and out."

A few weeks later, on the night itself, he'd collected me from work in a limo (just a normal one, not a stretch, thank Christ) and was so secretive about our destination that he actually blindfolded me. We drove for *ages* and I thought we must be in New Jersey at least. I had a sudden dreadful fear that he might be taking me to Atlantic City and I began to claw at his arm.

"Nearly there, baby."

But when he took the blindfold off, we were still in New York: about twenty blocks away from our apartment, to be exact. Outside a hot SoHo hotel, with a day spa and a restaurant with a three-month waiting list, unless you were hotel guests, in which case you automatically jumped the queue. I'd done a product launch there about four months previously and had come home *raving* about its beauty. I'd always wanted to stay there, but how could I when I lived five minutes away?

As I climbed out of the car, I nearly got sick with the thrill of it. "This is where I want to be more than anywhere else in the whole world!" I told him. "I didn't even know how badly I wanted it until now."

"Good. Glad to hear it." His tone was mild but he looked like he was going to burst with pride.

We had dinner in the fabulous restaurant then we spent the next two days in bed, only emerging from between our Frette sheets to do a quick foray to Prada. (I'd decided to skip the day spa, just in case they tried to sell me products.) It had been truly magical.

And now look at us . . .

Drunk as I'd been last night, I had picked up on the mood around the table: *She's as bad as she ever was,* they'd all been thinking. *Worse, even. Funny, you'd think that after five months she'd have got it together a bit . . .*

Maybe after five months I *should* have got it together a bit? Leon had improved noticeably. He was a lot cheerier and he could be in my company without crying. Mind you, he had Dana; he hadn't lost everything.

Another image from the previous night popped up: me talking to Shake about the next air-guitar championship heats.

"Play," I'd urged him. "Play your heart out. Play with every fiber of your being, Shake. Because you could be dead tomorrow. Later tonight even."

He and his hair had been nodding eagerly along with me but he'd recoiled speedily when I mentioned the possible imminence of his death.

Rachel had kept moving me along, from person to person, before I wrecked anyone's buzz too much. But I suspected I'd engendered a bit of a panic because after the dinner, as we'd stood outside, deciding where to go next, the Real Men were drunkenly punching the air and hollering that the night was young and that they were going to parteee (play Scrabble) till the sun came up. Even short, neat Leon was tilting his head back and yelling at the sky. They were all in a howling-at-the-moon, grab-life-by-the-balls frenzy.

"I spooked them," I said out loud. "Aidan, I spooked them." And suddenly it seemed funny—and comforting. Me and him were in it together. "We spooked them."

God only knew what they'd got up to: I hadn't stayed around to watch. With my arms filled with gift-wrapped scented candles—everyone bar none had given me one as a birthday present—I'd peeled away quietly, light-headed with gratitude at escaping a big "the bereaved woman is leaving early" scene.

It was too soon to ring anyone to find out what I'd missed, so I went back to sleep—a rare, rare event, I might try these hangovers more often—and when I woke again I felt better. I switched on the computer. Incoming e-mail from Mum.

To: Magiciansgirl1@yahoo.com
From: Thewalshes1@eircom.net
Subject: Many Happy Returns of the Day!

Dear Anna,
I hope you are keeping well and enjoyed your birthday "celebration." I am remembering this time thirty-three years ago. Another girl, we said. We wish you were here. We had a cake in your honor. A chocolate Victoria Sandwich. There was a sale of work for the upkeep of the Protestant church, and although I don't like to encourage them, I cannot deny they are "dab hands" at cake making "et al."
Your loving mother,
Mum

P.S. If you see Rachel will you tell her that my sisters—NONE of them—have heard of sugar-snap peas.

P.P.S. Is it true that Joey fancies Jacqui? A little bird (Luke) tells me there was a bit of a "vrizzon" at your birthday yoke last night. Is it true that Joey stole one of her Scrabble As and put it down his pants and told her that if she wanted it back she knew where to find it? I didn't know if Luke was just "having me on."

P.P.P.S. Was it just in his trousers pants or in his underpants pants, because if it was his underpants pants, I hope he washed it afterward. It is a breeding ground for germs down there. You don't know what you might pick up. Especially from Joey. He gets a lot of "action."

Oh my God. Aidan, what did we miss?

I sat staring at the screen and after a while I rang Rachel.

"Mum's sent me an e-mail."

"Oh yes? If this is to do with sugar-snap peas—"

"No. About Joey and—"

"Christ, he was outrageous! He kept writing words like *sex* and *hot* on the board, then looking meaningfully at Jacqui. Since when did he start fancying her?"

"I don't know. I haven't a clue! It's too weird. Mum says he put one of Jacqui's As down his jocks."

"No, he didn't."

"So why did she think—"

"It was her *J*. Which is worth eight points."

"And what happened?"

"He told her that if she wanted it back, she knew what she had to do, so all credit to her, she rolled up her sleeve, fished around, and got it back out again."

To: Thewalshes1@eircom.net
From: Magiciansgirl1@yahoo.com
Subject: Scrabble down the pants?

No, Joey did not steal one of Jacqui's Scrabble As and put it down his pants and tell her that if she wanted it back, she knew where to find it. He stole her Scrabble J and put it down his pants and told her that if she wanted it back, she knew where to find it.

Love,

Anna

    P.S. It was his underpants pants, not just his trousers pants.

    P.P.S. She did actually retrieve it.

    P.P.P.S. I don't know if she washed it.

To: Magiciansgirl1@yahoo.com
From: Thewalshes1@eircom.net
Subject: Scrabble down the pants?

Your father is upset. He read your last e-mail by mistake, thinking it was for him (although who ever writes to him?). He says he'll never be able to look Jacqui in the eye again. He is not himself, this weather, what with all this dog business.

Your loving mother,

Mum.

    P.S. So she actually delved in and got it back out? She's tougher than she looks, so she is. I'd be able for it, as in "a former life" I was used to handling turkey "giblets," but not everyone would have the stomach for it.

    P.P.S. I have thought of a "pun." Jacqui "scrabbled" around in Joey's jocks.

I reached for the phone. I *had* to talk to Jacqui. This was unbelievable—her and Joey? But her bloody machine picked up. The frustration!

"Where are you? In bed with Joey? Surely to God not? Ring me!"

I left the same message on her cell phone, and paced around, chewing my nails, trying to kill time. Which was when I made a discovery—I had ten nails to chew. Somehow while I hadn't been paying attention, the two missing ones had grown back.

At five past five in the afternoon, Jacqui finally surfaced.

"Where are you!" I asked.

"In bed." She sounded sleepy and sexy.

"Whose bed?"

"Mine."

"Are you alone?"

She laughed, then said, "Yeah."

"Really?"

"Really."

"Have you been alone all night?"

"Yes."

"And all day?"

"Yes."

Casually, I said, "Last night was fun?"

"Yeah."

Then super-*super*-casually I said, "Have you ever thought Joey looks a bit like Jon Bon Jovi?" To which she roared with laughter.

But interestingly, didn't reply.

"I'm coming over to you," she said.

Wearing white cutoffs (Donna Karan) and a tiny white T-shirt (Armani), displaying long, tanned legs and arms, and with an aqua metallic Balenciaga bag which cost approximately a month's rent (gift from a grateful client) slung over her shoulder, she arrived. Her hair was tangled and bed-heady and she seemed to be still wearing last night's makeup, but *not in a bad way*. Her mascara and eye stuff was smudged so that her eyes were dark and come-hither. She looked, if it's possible, like a really sexy ironing board. (Standing upright.)

I told her as much. Yes, even the bit about the ironing board. Because if I didn't say it, she would.

She shrugged off my praise. "I look okay in clothes, but when you see me in my bra and knickers for the first time, you might get a bit of a fright."

"Who's going to be seeing you in your bra and knickers for the first time?"

"No one."

"No one at all?"

"No."

"Okay. Let's go for a pizza."

"Great idea." Little hesitation. "But first I've got to drop by Rachel and Luke's. I left something there last night."

I stared at her steadily. "What? Your sanity?"

"No." She sounded a little annoyed. "My cell phone."

I murmured an apology.

But when we arrived at Rachel and Luke's, lo and behold, who happened to be sprawled on their sofa, moodily kicking the brick wall with his boots, only Joey.

"Did you know he was going to be here?" I asked Jacqui.

"No."

At the sight of Jacqui, Joey sat bolt upright and agitatedly brushed his hair back, trying to smarten himself up. "Hey! Jacqui! You left your cell phone here last night. I called you. Did you get my message? I said I'd swing by with it if you wanted."

I looked at Jacqui. So she *had* known he was here. But she wouldn't look at me.

"Here it is." Joey leaped up and retrieved it from a shelf.

It was quite entertaining, seeing him trying to be nice.

"Thanks." Jacqui took the phone and barely looked at Joey. "Anna and I are going for a pizza. Everyone's welcome to join us."

"And after the pizza," I asked, "will we be playing Scrabble?"

At the word *Scrabble,* something funny happened, as if there had been a power surge in the room. Between Jacqui and Joey there was a vrizzon, a definite vrizzon.

"No Scrabble tonight," Rachel said, dousing the mood. "I need my sleep."

Jacqui and I shared a cab home. We sat in silence. Eventually she said, "Go on. I know you want to say something."

"Can I ask a question? Mum tells me you put your hand down his jocks to get your Scrabble piece back—"

"Jesus H!" She buried her face in her hands. "How does Mammy Walsh know *that*?"

"Luke told her, I think. But it doesn't matter, she seems to know everything anyway. But what I'm wondering is, was it nice?"

She thought about it for a while. "Quite nice."

"Quite nice? Just quite nice?"

"Just quite nice."

"And was he soft or ... er ... you know?"

"Softish when I started. Hard when I finished. It took me a while to find the piece."

She flashed me a sudden minxy smile.

"Something you might like to think about," I said.

"What's that?"

"Your beef with other men is that they're always nice to begin with, keeping the fact that they're bastards well under wraps. At least with Joey, you know where you are. He's a narky prick and he's never pretended to be anything else."

Jacqui was thoughtful, then she spoke. "You know, Anna, that's not really a recommendation."

55

Aidan? The spiritual place? Should I go today?"

No voice answered. Nothing happened. He just continued to smile from the photo frame, frozen in a long-ago moment.

"Okay," I said. "Let's do a deal." I tore out a page from a magazine and scrunched it up. "I'll throw this ball of paper at the bin over there, and if I miss, I'll stay at home. If I get it in, I'll go."

I closed my eyes and threw, then opened them to see the scrunched-up page lying in the bottom of the bin.

"Right," I said. "Looks like you want me to go."

First, I had to make excuses to Rachel, but because the weather was still boiling, she wanted to go to the beach. I told her I was going to spend the day at a spa, which she seemed happy enough about. "But next time, tell me or Jacqui and one of us will come with you."

"Grand, grand," I said, relieved to be off the hook.

Nicholas was already waiting in the corridor. This week his T-shirt said DOG IS MY COPILOT. He was reading a book called *The Sirius Mystery* and I made the mistake of asking him what it was about.

"Five thousand years ago, amphibious aliens came to earth and taught the Dogon tribesmen of West Africa the secrets of the universe, including the existence of a companion star to Sirius, a star so dense that it's actually invisible—"

"Thanks! Enough! Okay, do you believe Princess Diana is working at a truck stop in New Mexico?"

"Check. And I also believe the royal family murdered her. That's how good at believing I am. I am a true believer."

"Roosevelt knew in advance about Pearl Harbor and let it happen because he wanted America in the war?"

"Check."

"They faked the moon landing?"

"Check."

Along lumbered Undead Fred—while everyone else was sweltering, he was in his black suit and barely breaking a sweat. Next to arrive was Barb.

"What about this heat?" she asked.

She dropped down beside me on the bench, her thighs apart, lifted the hem of her skirt, and flapped vigorously. "That'll get a bit of air up there." She added, "Not a day to be wearing underpants."

Oh God. Had she just told me she wasn't wearing knickers? My head went spinny: this was what Aidan's death had reduced me to, hanging around with these oddballs.

But were they oddballs? (Apart from Undead Fred, who *was* as odd as they come.) Were they not just broken people? Or broke people, as Mackenzie thought herself.

"Don't tell the guys." Barb winked and indicated the hem of her dress. "Drive 'em wild if they knew I was bushing."

As "the guys" consisted of Nicholas and Undead Fred, I wasn't so sure but said nothing.

Her dress was a button-down and it gaped at the hips. I didn't want to look, I did everything I could think of to stop myself, but it was like Luke and his crotch, the draw was simply too powerful. Entirely against my will, I caught a glimpse of her pubes.

"Barb," I said, a little high-pitched, as I fastened my eyes firmly on her face, "what brings you here every Sunday?"

"Because all the interesting people I know are dead. Drug overdoses, suicides, murders, awww, I tell ya!" She made it sound as if people didn't know how to die properly nowadays. "And I can't afford even two seconds of Neris Hemming's time."

"You'd like to talk to her?"

"Oh yeah. She's the real deal." My heart lifted. If Barb, with her gravelly voice and her grouchiness, said Neris Hemming was the real deal, then she really must be. "If anyone can channel your husband for you, it's Neris Hemming."

"You talked to her?" Mitch had arrived.

"To her office. They said I'd get to speak to her in eight to ten weeks."

"Wow. That's great."

Everyone agreed it was fantastic. Their wishes were so warm and their excitement so genuine that I forgot that what we were celebrating was actually very unusual.

We all went into the room and Leisl started. Great-aunt Morag came through for Mackenzie and reiterated that there wasn't a will. Nicholas's dad advised him on his job—he seemed like such a nice man, he really did. So concerned. Pomady Juan's wife told him to eat properly. Carmela's husband said she should think about replacing the stove, that it was dangerous.

Then Leisl said, "Barb, someone wants to talk to you. Could it be... it sounds like . . ." She seemed a little confused. "Wolfman?"

"Wolfman? Oh, Wolfgang! My husband. Well, one of them. What's he want? On the scrounge again?"

"He says... does this make sense? Don't sell the painting yet. It will rocket in value."

"He's been telling me that for years," Barb groused. "I've gotta live, you know."

By the end of the hour, no one had come through for me, but still on a high from my Neris Hemming contact, I didn't mind.

I said good-bye to everyone and went toward the elevator, joining forces with some of the belly-dancing posse, then behind me someone called my name. I turned around: it was Mitch.

"Hey, Anna, do you have to be someplace now?"

I shook my head.

"Want to do something?"

"Like what?"

"I dunno. Get a coffee?"

"I don't want to get a coffee," I said. It had started to make me feel nauseous. I feared I was going to have to start drinking herbal teas (pronounced "horrible teas" by me and Aidan) and run the risk of turning into those aggressively calm people who drank peppermint-and-chamomile infusions.

Mitch's face didn't change. At the best of times his eyes were those of a man who had lost everything. Someone refusing to go for coffee with him didn't even touch the sides.

"Let's go to the zoo." I had no idea why I'd said this.

"The zoo?"

"Yes."

"The place with animals?"

"Yes. There's one in Central Park."

"Okay."

The zoo was busy, with loved-up couples twined around each other and straggling family groups with strollers and toddlers and ice creams. Me and Mitch, the walking wounded, didn't stand out; only if you got up really close to us would you see that we were different.

We started with the Rain Forest, which was mostly monkeys, or apes or whatever their technical name is. There were quite a selection— swinging from trees and scratching themselves and staring grumpily at nothing—too many to be interesting and the only ones who caught my attention were the ones with bright red bottoms which they wiggled at the crowd. "They look like they've shaved their butts," Mitch said.

"Or," I said, "had a back-to-front Brazilian." I looked at him to see if I needed to explain what a Brazilian was, but he seemed to get it.

As we watched, one of the red-bums fell off a branch and two more red-bums came along to taunt and make high-pitched laughing sounds, which pleased the crowd enormously. They surged forward with their cameras and I got separated from Mitch. It was only when I was looking around for him that I discovered I didn't really know what he looked like.

"I'm over here," I heard him say, and I turned and found myself looking into those wells of bleakness. I tried to file a couple of other details about him for future reference: he had very short hair and a dark blue T-shirt—mind you, he mightn't wear that all the time—and he was a bit older than me, late thirties probably.

"Shall we move on?" he asked.

Suited me. I didn't have the concentration span to linger on anything. We found ourselves in the Polar Circle.

"Trish loved polar bears," he said. "Even though I kept telling her they were vicious guys." He stared at them. "Cute-looking, though. What's your favorite animal?"

He caught me on the hop; I wasn't sure I even had a favorite animal.

"Penguins," I said. They'd do. "I mean, they try so hard. It must be tough being a penguin; you can't fly, you can barely walk."

"But you can swim."

"Oh yes. You know, I'd forgotten that."

"What was Aidan's favorite animal?"

"Elephants. But there are no elephants here. You have to go to the Bronx Zoo for that."

We arrived at the sea lions' pool just as feeding time was about to begin. A large crowd of people, mostly family groups, were waiting, the air electric with anticipation.

When three men in Wellingtons and red overalls appeared with buckets of fish, the atmosphere became almost hysterical. "Here they come, here they come!" Bodies pushed toward the barrier, the air filled with the clicks of a hundred cameras, and children were lifted up in the air for a better look.

"There's one, there's one!" An enormous shiny gray-black force erupted out of the water, stretching up for his fish, then belly flopped back into the water, sending a huge wash across the pool. The crowd breathed "Wow" and children were shrieking and cameras were flashing and ignored ice creams were melting, and in the middle of it all, Mitch and I watched impassively, like we were cardboard cutouts of ourselves.

"Here's another one, here's another one! Mommy, look, it's another one!"

The second sea lion was even bigger than the first and the splash he made on his return to the water resulted in half the crowd getting spattered. Not that anyone cared. It was all part of it.

We waited until the fourth sea lion had eaten a fish, then Mitch looked at me. "Keep moving?"

"Sure."

We walked away from the people who were still starry-eyed and in thrall.

"What's next?" he asked.

I consulted our map. Feck. It was penguins. I'd have to pretend that I was thrilled to see them, what with them being my favorite animals and everything.

I enthused as best I could, then Mitch suggested we walk on. We'd spoken very little. I wasn't uncomfortable with it, but I knew next to nothing about him, except that his wife had died.

"Do you have a job?" I asked. It came out a bit bald.

"Yeah," he said.

We kept walking. He said nothing further. After a period of silence, he suddenly stopped. He even laughed. "Oh my God! I should have told you what it is. That's why you asked. You weren't wondering if I was on welfare."

"Well, no, no," I blustered. "Not if you don't want—"

"Sure, I want. It's a regular question. It's what people ask. Jeez, it's no surprise I don't get invited to dinner parties any longer. I'm a mess."

"Not at all," I said. "I'm the one who forgot penguins could swim."

"I design and install home-entertainment systems. I can tell you more if you want to hear it, as much as you like. It's kinda technical."

"No, it's okay, thank you, but I couldn't pay attention long enough to understand. Hey, we've missed the Temperate Territory—snow monkeys, red pandas, butterflies, ducks."

"Ducks?"

"Yes, ducks. We can't possibly miss them. Come on."

We retraced our steps, halfheartedly admired the Temperate Territory animals, and took an executive decision to skip the kiddie zoo, and suddenly things started to look familiar; we were back where we started. We had walked in one big circle.

"Is that it?" Mitch asked. "Are we done?" Like it was a chore.

"Looks like it."

"Okay, I'm going to hit the gym." He shouldered his kit bag and made for the exit. "See you next Sunday?"

"Okay."

I waited until he was good and gone. Even though I'd spent the last couple of hours with him I was suffering from fear of the "false good-bye syndrome": when you don't know someone that well, and you've just said a lovely warm farewell to them, maybe even kissed them, and then you unexpectedly bump into them a few minutes later, at the bus stop or the subway station or on the same stretch of street, trying to hail a cab. I don't know why but it's always mortifying and the nice, easy conversation that you'd been having only a few minutes earlier has dissipated entirely and the mood is tense and strained and you're looking at the tracks and praying, *Come on, train, for fuck's sake, come on.*

Then when the train or taxi or bus comes, you say good-bye once more and you try to make a laugh of it by saying gaily "Good-bye, *again*," but it's nothing like as nice as the previous time and you're wondering if you should kiss them again, and if you do, it feels fake, and if you don't, you feel as if you've ended on a bad note. Like a soufflé, a successful good-bye can really only be done once. A good-bye can't be reheated.

While I waited until it was supersafe to leave, I watched the normal people still flooding into the zoo and I wondered about Mitch: What had he been like before? Or what would he be like in the future? I knew I wasn't seeing the real him; at the moment all he was was his bereavement. Like me. I wasn't the real Anna right now.

A thought struck me: maybe I wouldn't ever be again. Because the only thing that would snap things back to the way they were would be if Aidan hadn't died, and that could never happen. Would I be holding my breath forever, waiting for the world to right itself?

I looked at my watch. Mitch had been gone ten minutes. I made myself count to sixty, then felt I could chance it. On the street, I did a few furtive look-arounds and there was no sign of him anywhere. I hailed a cab, and when I reached my apartment I was feeling quite good. That was most of Sunday taken care of.

56

Before hitting my desk, I did a quick dash into the ladies' room and found someone bent over one of the basins, sobbing her eyes out. Because it was Monday morning, it wasn't unusual for someone to be crying, in fact the cubicles were probably packed to capacity with girls throwing up because they hadn't enough coverage to bring to the Monday Morning Meeting. But I was surprised to see that the crying someone was Brooke Edison. (Wearing some elegant taupe linen getup while I was in a cerise suit from the fifties with a boatnecked jacket and a pencil skirt, worn with rose-patterned ankle socks, pink patent peep-toe sling-backs, and a handbag shaped like a two-story house.)

"Brooke! What's happened?"

I couldn't believe she was crying. I had thought it was practically illegal for WASPs to show emotion.

"Oh, Anna... ," she wept. "I had a little spat with my dad."

Oh my God! Brooke Edison had spats with her father? I admit it: I found it a little thrilling. It was a comfort to know that other people had problems. And maybe Brooke was more normal than I'd realized.

"There's this Givenchy gown," she said.

"Couture or off the peg?"

"Ohhh." She sounded like she didn't understand the question. "Couture, I guess. And... and..."

"And he won't buy it for you," I prompted, finding a packet of tissues in my house-shaped handbag. They were patterned with shoes, which sort of shocked me. This kookiness thing really had me in its grip.

"No," she said, her eyes widening. "Oh no. It's because Dad wants to give it to me as a present and I said I already have enough fabulous gowns in my closet."

I just looked at her, aware of a sinking feeling.

"I said that there's so much poverty in the world and I really didn't need another gown. But he said he couldn't see what was wrong with wanting his little girl to look beautiful." A fresh crop of tears sprang from her eyes.

"My dad is my best friend, you know?"

Not really, but I nodded anyway.

"So it's horrible when we don't get along."

"Well, I better get going," I said. "Keep the tissues."

The rich really are different, I thought: *they're fucking freaks.*

I hurried toward the office, keen to share my insight with Teenie.

That night I got an e-mail from Helen.

To: Magiciansgirl1@yahoo.com
From: Lucky_Star_PI@yahoo.ie
Subject: Tediarseity

Another break in routine! Detta had lunch in restaurant with "the girls": three other women, all about same age as her, maybe also married to crime lords? Chanel handbags, really war-crime quilted ones with gold chain handles. Rotten. Again had to hang around in street like homeless person, watching through window, and this time someone tried to buy methadone from me. No sign of Racey O'Grady, though. Just to be sure, went in on pretense of using loo (mind you, not pretense, in this job, you make wees every chance you get) and the four of them were sitting in cloud of gagzo perfume, scuttered drunk, and cackling about husbands. On way in, one of them—sunken-eyed, dark-haired, nails like Freddie Kruger's—screeched: He couldn't find his arse in the dark.

On way out, another one, face like satsuma (squat, orange,

pores big as manholes) was saying: So I said to him, you're welcome to ride me, but I'm going to sleep!

Banshee shrieks of laughing, but not from Detta. Not smoking, but only 'cos illegal. She looked like she would if could.
Smiling absently and sort of staring into space. Took couple of
pics on mobile, in case they're of any interest to Harry Big—
but how could they be? This is so fucking boring, but I'll tell you
something, Anna, am getting paid bloody fortune.

Then one from Mum.

To: Magiciansgirl1@yahoo.com
From: Thewalshes1@eircom.net
Subject: Latest update

There is none. No blasted update. Helen is spending all her
time in Mr. Big's hedge. We are still being scourged with the
dog poo, twice this week. I am going to Knock on Saturday, it's
been a while since I did a pilgrimage, and I feel I need one because I am upset by so much "venom" being directed on me. I
will dedicate the Sorrowful mystery to you, Anna, that our
good Lord will bring you peace and acceptance over your circumstances.
Your loving mother,
Mum
P.S. Has Jacqui said the Bon Von Jodi line yet?
P.P.S. Will you tell Rachel that if she wants to wear cream,
then she should wear cream. It's her wedding. It's just that I
think that cream always looks a bit "dirty" on a wedding dress.
But that's just "me."

"Hey, Anna." Some man had left me a message. "It's Kevin. I'm in
town on business."

It was Aidan's brother. My heart sank.

Poor Kevin, I was fond of him, but I just couldn't face him. I didn't even know him that well. What would we say to each other? "I'm sorry your brother died." "Thanks, well, I'm sorry your husband died"?

It was hard enough speaking to Mrs. Maddox on the phone every weekend, never mind spending an entire night in the company of Kevin.

"I'm here until the weekend and I'm staying at the W," he went on. "We could maybe get some dinner or something. Give me a call."

I looked helplessly at the answering machine. *Sorry, Aidan, I know he's your brother, but I'm just going to have to be rude and ignore him.*

To: Magiciansgirl1@yahoo.com
From: Lucky_Star_PI@yahoo.ie
Subject: Update

Colin drove me in Austrian-blinds mobile for meet with Harry Big today.

Told Harry: I've been trailing Detta for weeks and she hasn't seen Racey O'Grady at all.

Him: So?

Me: So, I want to put a tap on her phones, I'll need your help with her mobile, and I need copies of her mobile bills.

Him (uncomfortable): It doesn't seem right. It's an invasion of her privacy.

Me (thinking, what a gobshite): You're paying me to trail her, day in day out and report every time she lights a cigarette—

Him (all alert now): What? She's smoking again?

Me: Smoking? She never stops.

Him: But she said she has. She has to for her blood pressure. How much is she smoking?

Me: At least twenty a day. She buys twenty after mass every morning, but she might have more stashed in the house.

Him (going into visible slump): You see, she's lying to me. But leave her phones alone. Keep on watching her.

Jesus, Anna, the boredom is killing me.

I had a sudden thought . . .

To: Lucky_Star_PI@yahoo.ie
From: Magiciansgirl1@yahoo.com
Subject: Colin

Helen, what does Colin look like?

To: Magiciansgirl1@yahoo.com
From: Lucky_Star_PI@yahoo.ie
Subject: Colin

Big, burly, dark-haired, sexy. Not bad. Like him best when he puts gun in waistband of his jeans. View of sexy stomach and space to slip hand in. And down, of course . . .

You see, that was the difference between Helen and me. I'd just be afraid that with his gun stuck in his waistband, he might accidentally shoot himself in the flute.

Your next question will be, Do I fancy him? Yes. But sometimes he talks about giving up crime and going straight and then I think he's gobshite. Sexy beast or deluded gobshite? Can't decide.

57

"achel, you *have* to go to the beach," I said. "Because if you don't get your fix of sunlight, you might get depressed and 'go pure mental on the drugs again,' as Helen so sensitively puts it."

"Yes, but...," Rachel sounded helpless.

"And I can't go because of my scar," I said, brooking no argument.

"I'm so sorry," Rachel said guiltily.

"It's okay, it's okay, it's fine."

And it was. I wanted to go to the spiritualist-church place. Very quickly, it had become part of my Sunday routine. I liked the people who went; they were very kind, and to them, I wasn't Anna with her Catastrophe—well, maybe I was—but they'd all had catastrophes, too. I was no different.

But I told no one—especially not Rachel or Jacqui; they wouldn't understand. They might even try to stop me. Luckily, Rachel was off my case because the hot weather was continuing and Jacqui worked such irregular hours that I was often in the clear with her as well. As for Leon and Dana, they only ever wanted to see me in the evenings when we could go somewhere fancy for dinner.

ll the gang was there, sitting in a line on the benches in the corridor.

Nicholas saw me. "Cool! Here's Miss Annie." Today his T-shirt said FREE KATIE. Mitch was slouched back against the wall and he shifted forward to get a look at me.

"Hey, peanut." He stretched out his leg to touch me with his foot. "How was your week?"

"Oh, you know," I said. "How was yours?"

"'Bout the same."

We took our places in the circle of chairs, the cello groaning started up, and several people got messages, but nothing for me.

Then Leisl slowly said, "Anna . . . I'm seeing the little blond boy again. I'm getting the initial *J*."

"Because his name is JJ."

"He really wants to talk to you."

"But he's alive! He can talk to me anytime he wants!"

Afterward I cornered Leisl. "Why would I be getting messages from my nephew who's still alive? Or my horrible granny? And not from Aidan?"

"I can't answer that, Anna." Her eyes, underneath her frizzy fringe, were so kind.

"There isn't some sort of waiting period after someone has died before they start being channeled, is there?"

"Not that I know of," she said.

"Have you tried EVP?" Barb growled. "Electronic voice phenomenon?"

"What's that?"

"Recording the voices of the dead."

"If this is a joke . . ."

"Not a joke!" All the others knew about EVP. A flurry of voices said, "That's a good idea, Anna. You should try it."

Defensively, I asked, "How do you do it?"

"Just on a regular tape recorder," Barb said. "Use a new tape. Set it to record, leave the room, come back one hour later, and pick up your messages!"

"You need a quiet room," Leisl said.

"Hard to find in New York City," Nicholas said.

"And a positive, cheerful, loving attitude." Leisl again.

"That's hard, too."

"It's got to be done after sunset on the night of a full moon," Mackenzie said.

"Preferably during a thunderstorm," said Nicholas. "Because of the gravitational effect."

"Nicholas, I'm really in no mood for any of your bonkers beliefs."

"No." Several voices insisted, "It's not one of his bonkers beliefs!"

"What's a bonkers belief?" I heard Carmela ask.

"There's actually a scientific basis for this," Nicholas said. "The dead live in etheric wavelengths which operate at much higher frequencies than ours. So we can hear them on tape when we can't hear them talking directly to us."

I asked, "Have you done it?"

"Oh, sure."

"And your dad spoke to you."

"Oh, sure. It was kinda hard to hear him, though. You might have to speed the tape up or down a lot when you're listening back."

"Yeah, sometimes they speak really fast," Barb said. "And sometimes they speak sloooow. You've got to listen real careful."

"I'll e-mail you all the instructions," Nicholas said.

I asked Mitch, "Have you tried it?"

"No, but only because I spoke to Trish via Neris Hemming."

"When's the next full moon?" Mackenzie asked.

"Just missed it," Nicholas said.

"Aw, too bad!" was the general consensus. "But there's another in less than four weeks. You can do it then."

"Okay. Thanks. See you all next week."

I started walking away, wondering if Mitch would follow.

He caught me up before I reached the lift. "Hey, Anna, do you have to be someplace now?"

"No."

"Wanna do something?"

"Like what?" I was interested to see what he came up with.

"How about MoMa?"

Why not? I'd lived in New York for three years and I'd never been there.

· · ·

Being with Mitch had many of the advantages of being alone—like not having to keep smiling in case he felt uncomfortable with my real face—but without the actual aloneness. Speedily, we moved from painting to painting and we barely spoke. At times we were even in different rooms, but were linked by an invisible thread.

When we'd seen everything, Mitch checked his watch.

"Look at that!" He sounded pleased and almost smiled. "That took two hours. The day is nearly done. Have a good week, Anna. See you next Sunday."

Anna, pick up the phone. I know you're in there. I'm outside and I need to talk to you."

It was Jacqui. I grabbed the phone. "What's up?"

"Let me in."

I buzzed the door and heard her pounding up the stairs. Seconds later she burst in, a tangle of limbs, her face distraught.

"Has someone died?" That was always my worry now.

That stopped her in her tracks. "Um, no." Her face changed. "No, this is just . . . ordinary . . . stuff."

Suddenly she resented me. Whatever was going on, it was huge for her and I'd reduced it to something shallow because my husband had died and no one could top that.

"Sorry, Jacqui, sorry, come and sit—"

"No, I'm sorry, scaring you like that—"

"All right, we're both sorry, so tell me what's up."

She sat on the couch, leaning forward, her forearms on her thighs, her knees neatly together. She looked exactly like the Pixar lamp. If she'd started bunny-hopping around the room, even her mother would have been hard-pressed to tell them apart.

She stared into the middle distance, locked into silence for quite some time.

Eventually she spoke. One word. "Joey."

Well, at least now I could tell Mum.

"Or as I call him," she said, "Narky Joey." She sighed heavily. "I was over in his apartment just now."

"What were you doing?!"

"Playing Scrabble."

Sunday-afternoon Scrabble playing! I felt a slight sting at my exclusion. But who could blame them? They were blue in the face from inviting me and getting turned down.

"I wasn't even looking at him, but out of the corner of my eye, I suddenly thought he looked like...looked like..." She paused, took a shuddery, tearful breath, and burst out, "Jon Bon Jovi!"

In shame, she buried her face in her hands.

"You're okay," I said gently. "Carry on. Jon Bon Jovi."

"I know what it means," she said. "I've seen it happen with other women. One minute they say they think he looks a bit like Jon Bon Jovi, that they'd never noticed it before, the next thing they fancy him. And I don't want to fancy him, I think he's a fool. And not even nice, you know? Narky."

"You don't have to fancy him. Just decide not to."

"Is it that simple?"

"Yes!"

Well, maybe.

"Mum?"

"Which one of you is that?"

"Anna."

A gasp. "Any news on Jacqui and Joey?"

"Yes, actually! That's why I'm ringing."

"Go on! Tell us!"

"She thinks he looks like Jon Bon Jovi."

"That's it, then. Game over."

"Not at all. Jacqui is made of sterner stuff."

"He gives love a bad name."

"I suppose he does."

"It's a *song*," she hissed. "A Real Men song. By Guns and Leopards, or whatever they're called. I was making a joke."

"Sorry," I said. "Sorry."

"Did she get that dog yet? That Labradoodle dandy?"

"No." Buying a nuclear warhead would be easier, she'd said. And how did Mum know about the dog?

"Just as well, the poor creature wouldn't be getting much attention from her now that she fancies Joey."

"She doesn't."

"She does, she just doesn't know it yet."

A couple of nights later, by accident—but an accident that was obviously meant to happen, especially since I spent more and more time watching the spiritual channel—I saw Neris Hemming on telly! This wasn't just a televising of one of her shows, it was a profile, a half-hour special. On cable, but so what?

Probably in her late thirties, with shoulder-length bubble curls and wearing a blue pinafore dress, she was curled in an armchair, talking to an invisible interviewer.

"I was always able to see and hear 'other' people," she said in a soft voice. "I always had friends that no one else could see. And I knew that stuff was going to happen before it did, you know? My mom used to get so mad with me."

"But something happened to change your mom's mind," the invisible interviewer prompted. "Can you tell us about it?"

Neris closed her eyes in order to remember. "It was an ordinary morning. I'd just gotten out of the shower and was drying myself off with my towel when . . . it's kinda hard to describe, but everything went sort of misty and I wasn't in my bathroom anymore. I was in a different place. I was in the open air, on a highway. I could see and feel the hot tar under my feet. About thirty feet away from me, a huge truck was on fire and the heat was intense. I could smell gasoline, and something else, something really bad. Lots of cars were on fire, too, and the worst bit was that bodies were scattered on the highway. I didn't know what kind of shape they were in. It was horrible. And suddenly I was back in my bathroom again, still holding my towel.

"I didn't know what was happening to me. I thought I was losing my mind. I was so scared. I called up my mom and told her what I'd experienced and she was real worried."

"She didn't believe you?"

"No way! She thought I was cracking up. She wanted to get me to the hospital. I didn't go to work that day. I felt sick to my stomach and went back to bed. Later, that evening, I turned on the TV. CNN had a report on a horrible accident that had just happened on the interstate and it was totally what I'd seen. A big truck carrying chemicals had exploded, other cars had caught on fire, a bunch of people were dead . . . I couldn't believe it. I really did wonder if I'd gone crazy."

"But you hadn't?"

Neris shook her head. "No. Next thing the phone rings. It was my mom, and she said, 'Neris, we've got to talk.'"

I knew all of this, I'd read it in her books, but it was fascinating to hear it from her own mouth.

I also knew what happened next. Her mom decided to stop telling her she was a nut job and instead started booking gigs for her. All her family worked for her now. Her dad was her driver, her little sister was in the booking office, and although her ex-husband didn't work for her, he was suing her for millions, so that was nearly as good.

"People tell me that they'd love to be psychic," Neris said. "But, you know what, it's a tough road. I call it a blessed curse."

Then the screen cut to coverage of one of her live shows. Neris was standing on a huge stage, just her, looking very little. "I have a . . . I'm getting something for . . . do we have someone here tonight called Vanessa?"

A camera panned over rows and rows of audience, and somewhere near the back, a heavyset lady put her hand up and got to her feet. She mouthed something and Neris said, "Wait a minute, honey, until the mike gets to you."

A runner was pushing her way between the seats. When the heavyset woman was holding the mike, Neris said, "Can you tell us your name? You're Vanessa?"

"I'm Vanessa."

"Vanessa, Scottie just wants to say hi to you. Does that mean anything?"

Tears started to pour down Vanessa's face and she mumbled something.

"Say again, honey."

"He was my son."

"That's right, honey, and he wants you to know he didn't suffer." Neris put her hand to her ear and said, "He's telling me to tell you you were right about the bike. Mean anything?"

"Yeah." Vanessa's head was bowed. "I told him he drove that thing too fast."

"Well, he knows that now. He's telling me to say, 'Mom, you were right.' So, Mom, you get the last word here."

Somehow Vanessa was smiling through her tears.

"Okay, honey?" Neris asked.

"Yes, thank you, thank you." Vanessa sat back down.

"No, thank *you* for sharing your story. If you could just give the mike back to the—"

Vanessa was still holding on to the microphone with a clawlike grip. She relinquished it with reluctance.

Back to Neris on the armchair, who was saying, "The people who come to my shows, nearly all of them are looking to hear from their loved ones who have passed over. These folks are in bad pyschic pain and I have a responsibility to them. But sometimes," and she gave a little laugh here, "if lots of spirit voices are all trying to get through at the same time, I have to say, 'Calm down, guys, take a ticket, get in line!'"

I was mesmerized. She made it all sound so ordinary, so possible. And I was touched by her humility. If anyone could put me in contact with Aidan, it was this woman.

The camera cut back to another of Neris's live shows. She was wearing a different dress, so it must have been a different event. From the stage she asked, "I've got a message here for a man called Ray."

She scanned the theater. "We got a Ray? Come on, Ray, we know you're here."

A large man got to his feet. He was wearing an enormous plaid shirt and had a big redneck quiff held in place with shiny pomade; he looked mortified.

"You're Ray?"

He nodded, and gingerly accepted the mike from the runner.

"Ray," and Neris was laughing. "I'm being told here that you don't believe in any of this psychic BS. Is that so?"

Ray said something that we didn't hear.

"Speak into the mike, honey."

Ray leaned over and enunciated into the microphone, like he was under oath at a murder trial, "No, ma'am, I do not."

"You didn't want to come here tonight, did you?"

"No, ma'am, I did not."

"But you came along because someone else asked you to, right?"

"Yes, ma'am. Leeanne, my wife."

The camera moved to the woman beside him, a shrunken little thing with a mushroom of teased blond hair, like cotton candy. Leeanne, presumably.

"You know who's telling me all this?" Neris asked.

"No, ma'am."

"It's your mama."

Ray said nothing, but his face kind of shut down—the sign of a hard-man redneck trying to fight back emotion.

"She didn't die easy, did she?" Neris said gently.

"No, ma'am. She had the cancer. The pain was real bad."

"But she's not in pain now. Where she is is 'better than any morphine,' she's telling me. She wants me to tell you that she loves you, that you're a good boy, Ray."

Tears were pouring down Ray's ruddy cheeks and we were shown shots of several other people who were also crying.

"Thank you, ma'am," Ray said hoarsely, and sat back down, receiving claps on the back and handclasps from the people around him.

The next scene was of people streaming out of the theater into the lobby, saying stuff like "I don't mind telling you I had no faith in this woman. I'm not too proud to tell you that I was wrong."

A brisk, loud, New York type cut in. "Unbelievable. I mean, *unbe-lievable.*"

Someone else said "Awesome," and someone else said, "I got a message from my husband. I'm so happy he's okay. Thank you, Neris Hemming."

This cranked up my excitement to fever pitch. I'd have her all to myself for an entire half hour. *Half an hour* to talk to Aidan.

To: Magiciansgirl1@yahoo.com
From: Lucky_Star_PI@yahoo.ie
Subject: Week from hell

God, Anna. Disastrous week. Mum went to the shrine at Knock last Saturday and brought back holy water in Evian bottle and left it in kitchen. Sunday morning when I'd bit of a thirst on me 'cos of amount drank night before, guzzled it down before realizing it tasted disgusting and there were funny things floating in it.

Two hours later, thrun down, roaring for a bucket. Puking rings around myself. Dying. Dry heaves, bile, the whole lot. Worse than any hangover. Lying on bathroom floor, holding stomach, begging to be put out of misery.

Monday morning, still puking at full throttle. No way could sit in Detta's hedge for ten hours. Doc came, said I was badly poisoned and I'd be out of action for four/five days. Rang Colin, told him sorry story. He laughed and said, I'll tell Harry, but he's not going to like it.

Two seconds later, Harry rang, shouting his head off, going on about "more than generous retainer" (it is) he has me on, and what if today is the day that Detta checks into hotel room with Racey O'Grady and I'm not there to record it and that would really annoy him and I know what happens to people who annoy him. (Get nailed to pool table, just in case you forgot.) So I said, Hold on minute. Went and puked, then came back and said, I'll sort something out.

What could I do? Had to send Mum. She'd been dying to see Detta's clothes and house anyway. Off she goes with binoculars and sandwiches and cardboard cup in case she was caught short and as luck would shagging well have it, on Thursday Detta publicly met Racey O'Grady. (Maybe was wrong to think that Harry Big is delusional paranoid.) They met in restaurant in Ballsbridge—can't get more high-profile than that. Even had decency to sit in window.

Mum shot off load of photos on phone and came home and we got them on computer, which was when discovered that Mum doesn't know how to work phone camera. She'd taken the pictures using wrong side of phone and we had load of lovely close-ups of her skirt, up her sleeve, and half of her face.

Low moment. Really thought it was crucifixion time. Thought about skipping country, then thought, Ah, what the hell, how bad can crucifixion be? So rang Colin, who took me to Harry, who took it surprisingly well. Just sort of sighed and looked into his glass of milk for a long time, then said, These things happen even in the best run of organizations. Carry on with the surveillance.

But, to be honest, Anna, I've had enough. Job too boring, apart from times when afraid am going to be nailed to pool table. Only thing that's interesting about it is Colin.

So said to Harry: From Mum's description, Detta was definitely with Racey. Can't you just confront Detta?

Him: Are ya mad? Have you a clue? No one goes into any situation making half-baked allegations. Nothing happens until I've proof.

Later Colin told me that Harry is in denial. No amount of proof will ever be enough. In other words, will be doing this fucking job until end of time.

Mum demanded cash for the week's work. Also had to promise to lie in wait for woman with dog and take photos.

An e-mail from Mum arrived, too.

To: Magiciansgirl1@yahoo.com
From: Thewalshes1@eircom.net
Subject: Crucifixion

Dear Anna,

I hope you are keeping well. I had a terrible week. Helen drank my Knock holy water, and I had it promised to Nuala Freeman, who seemed quite annoyed when I told her what happened. Can you blame her, she has been very good to me, bringing me back a "bootleg" DVD of <u>The Passion of the Christ</u> that time she went to Medjagory (or however it's spelled). (Just out of curiosity, do you know why are there so many *thes* in <u>THE Passion of THE Christ</u>?)

Anyway, Helen was as "sick" as a "dog." I offered to ring in sick for her, but she went mad and said that when you work for a crime lord, you can't ring in sick. She said I'd have to "cover" for her. Oh, when she's stuck, she comes to me all right. I had her "over" a "barrel," and I said I'd surveil Detta Big if she promised to take photos of the old woman and her dog when she was better. Mind you, she is not above going back on her word, that one.

I had thought Detta Big would be a brassy "moll" and her house would be a "kip." But her home was very tasteful and her clothes cost a fortune, you could tell just by looking at them. I don't like admitting it, but the "green-eyed monster" was at me. Then I took the photographs of Racey O'Grady with the wrong side of the phone camera and Helen went mad again, saying that Mr. Big would crucify her and that she'd have to "skip" the country. Then she calmed down and said that eff it (and she didn't say "eff," she said the full word), she'd take her medicine. Her father said she was very brave and he was proud of her. I said I thought she should be locked up in the mental hospital, that crucifixion is no joke, our Lord himself dreaded it, and I rang Claire to see if she could provide a "safe house" in London. But Claire said no, that Helen would keep trying to "get off" with Adam.

Anyway, Helen went to see Mr. Big and he didn't crucify her and I suppose all is well that ends well. But between that fiasco and the old woman and the Knock holy water, I am not myself. Even though I made a hames of the photos, Helen gave me some "blood money" and I am trying some "retail therapy" to see if I could get a bit of a lift.

Your loving mother,

Mum

P.S. Any more on Joey and Jacqui? I would not have thought they'd make a likely couple, but the strangest people "hook up" together.

Mitch and I stood patiently in line while I eyed the girl on the gate taking the money. She was wearing a ballerina outfit, motorcycle boots, and pointy fifties-style glasses with diamante on the wings. I shuddered at her getup; it made me think of work.

Mitch and I seemed to be taking turns to suggest some kind of an outing every Sunday. This week was my go and I'd come up with something a little special: a quiz in Washington Square, my local park. It was for charity, to raise money for a ventilator or a wheelchair or something (I found it so hard to focus on specifics) for some poor guy whose insurance wouldn't pay for any more.

Today's session had been particularly low-key. Mitch hadn't heard from Trish, I hadn't heard from anyone, not even Granny Maguire, and Mackenzie hadn't shown up at all. Maybe she'd decided to call it a day and gone out to the Hamptons where she belonged, to find that rich husband whom her great-uncle Frazer had recommended she get herself.

"Next!" Diamante Glasses Girl said.

Mitch and I stepped forward.

"Okay." She slapped stickers on our fronts and handed me a form. "You're team eighteen. Where are your partners?"

Our partners? Mitch and I turned to each other. What should we say?

"The other two?" she pressed. "The two who should be with you?"

"I . . . um—" I tilted my head at Mitch and he looked openmouthed at me.

The girl, confused by our reaction, said impatiently, "Four in a team. I'm only seeing two of you."

"Oh. Oh! Christ! Right, of course! It's just us two."

"It's still twenty dollars. It's for charity."

"Sure." I gave her the note.

"You have a better chance of winning if there's four of you."

"Ain't that the truth," Mitch said.

We picked our way through the happy, chatting groups of people sitting on the grass in the sunshine until we found a place to sit. Then I looked at Mitch. "I nearly said they were dead."

"Me, too."

"Could you imagine? 'Where are your partners?' 'They're dead!'"

"They're dead!" I repeated, and a great ball of mirth rolled up from my stomach. "'Where are your partners?' 'They're dead!'"

I laughed so much I had to lie down. I laughed and laughed and laughed and laughed until I heard some concerned stranger say, "Is she, like, okay?"

Then I tried very hard to get ahold of myself. "Mitch, I'm so sorry," I said, finally righting myself and mopping tears of laughter off my temples. "I'm really sorry. I know it's not a bit funny, it's just . . ."

"It's okay." He patted my back and my face settled into its usual expression, but periodically I'd think, *They're dead,* and my shoulders would start shaking again.

Mitch looked at his watch. "Should be starting soon." Just like me, I noticed: he couldn't handle any stretch of time that wasn't structured and filled with stuff.

Right on cue, a man appeared, wearing a sparkly lounge suit and carrying a microphone and a sheet of what looked like questions; everyone perked up.

"Looks like we're ready to get going," Mitch said.

I was just about to say "good" when a yell was carried to me on the warm air. "Hey, it's Anna!"

Jesus H. Christ! I looked around. It was Ornesto, with two other Jolly Boys whom I recognized from going up and down the stairs to his apartment, and nice Eugene who had moved my air conditioner.

Eugene, in a massive, unironed shirt, looked meaningfully at Mitch, and gave me a thumbs-up and several encouraging nods. Oh no! He thought Mitch and I...

Ornesto had clambered to his feet. He was on his way over. Aghast, I watched him. How stupid was I? I should have considered that I might know some of the people here. Not that there was anything to hide. There was nothing between Mitch and me, but people might not understand...

"Ladies and gentlemen," Sparkly Suit's voice boomed through a microphone. "Are you ready to raaaaah-ck?" He twirled his microphone stand.

"Ornesto, come back," the Jolly Boys called. "We're starting. You can talk to her later."

Go back, I thought. *Go back.*

Momentarily, he froze, suspended by invisible strings of indecision, then to my enormous relief, he returned to his pals.

"Who's he?" Mitch asked.

"Upstairs neighbor."

"First question!" Sparkly Suit said. "Who said, 'Whenever I hear the word *culture,* I reach for my revolver'?"

"Do you know?" I asked Mitch.

"No. Do you?"

"No."

We sat, looking helplessly at each other, while all around us, groups of four consulted energetically.

"Göring," I muttered to Mitch. "Hermann Göring."

"How . . . how do you know?"

"Heard them say it." I flicked my eyes at the group next to us.

"Awesome. Write it down."

"Next question! Who directed *Breakfast at Tiffany's?*"

"Do you know?" I asked Mitch.

"No. Do you?"

"No." Annoyed, I said, "These questions are very hard."

"The girl on the gate was right," Mitch said sadly. "You do have a better chance if there's four of you."

We sat in silence, the only people in the park not talking. But there was nothing to say. If I didn't know it and Mitch didn't know it, what could we discuss? Shamelessly we eavesdropped on the groups around us. "Blake Edwards," Mitch said quietly. "Who knew?"

A girl from the next team turned around and gave us a sharp look. She'd heard Mitch. She said something to her teammates and they all checked us out, then drew into a tighter huddle, audibly dropping their voices. Mitch and I looked abashed.

"That's a little unsporting of them," he said.

"I *know.* I mean, it's for charity."

Being unable to hear the other teams' answers was a serious handicap, but occasionally we knew the answer.

"What is a patella?"

"A kitchen thing?" Mitch asked. "For scraping out cake mix?"

"You're thinking of a spatula. A patella is a kneecap," I said with glee. "When you've dislocated one, it's easy to remember what it's called."

"What's the capital of Bhutan?"

Everyone else was muttering disgruntledly; they didn't even know where Bhutan was, let alone its capital, but Mitch was thrilled. "Thimphu."

"Really?"

"Yeah."

"How do you know that?"

"Trish and I went there on our honeymoon."

Neither of us knew the answer to the following six questions, then Sparkly Suit asked, "Babe Ruth was sold by the owner of the Boston Red Sox to finance a Broadway musical. What was the name of that musical?"

Mitch lifted and dropped his shoulders helplessly. "I'm a Yankees fan."

"It's okay," I whispered, in excitement. "I know. It's *No, No, Nanette.*"

"How?"

"Aidan's a Red Sox fan."

No. I'd said something wrong there. Aidan *was* a Red Sox fan. The shock lifted me out of my body. I felt almost as if I was looking down on myself, sitting in the park, like I'd parachuted into the wrong life. What was I doing there? Who was the man I was with?

While the scores were added up, the raffle was held. All the prizes had been donated by local businesses. I won a bag of nails (assorted sizes) and a twenty-foot length of rope donated by Hector's Hardware. Mitch won a free piercing (body part of his choice) from Tattoos and Screws, the bodyart salon on Eleventh and Third.

Then the quiz scores were read out. Team Eighteen (Mitch and me) did quite badly; we were about fifth from bottom, but we didn't care. It had disposed of most of Sunday afternoon, that was all that really mattered.

"Okay." Mitch got to his feet, slinging his ever-present kit bag over his shoulder. "Thanks for that. I'll hit the gym. See you next week."

"Yes, see you then." I was glad to say good-bye. I wanted him out of the park before Ornesto appeared.

And not a second too soon. Ornesto came springing over, full of the joys and with good reason: his team had come in fourth and in the raffle he had won free dry cleaning for a year.

"Aw, he's gone! Hey, Anna, who was that maaaaan you were with? Who was that hunka burnin' lurve?"

"He's nobody."

"Oh, he ain't nobody, he's definitely somebody."

"He's not. He's a widower. He's like Eugene."

"Oh, baby cakes, he is *nothing* like Eugene. I saw those shoulders. He works out?"

Reluctantly I shrugged, yes. "Please, Ornesto." I really didn't want Rachel or Jacqui or anyone hearing about Mitch; they might think it was some sort of romance, which was so far from the truth. "He lost his wife. We're just—"

"—comforting each other. I know." The way he said it sounded so sleazy.

The only comfort I got from Mitch was that he understood how I felt. Fury surged up my throat, almost burning my tongue. I shrieked at Ornesto, but in a kind of whisper because we were in public, "How dare you!"

My face was on fire and my eyes were bulging. He took a big, alarmed step back.

"I love Aidan," I whisper-shrieked. "I'm devastated without him. I couldn't even *think* of being with another man. Ever."

andy Grrrl's new range of cleansers was called Clean and Serene and I had an inspired idea for a press release—I'd do it in the form of the 12 steps. But I only knew the first one:

1. We admitted we were powerless over alcohol; that our lives had become unmanageable.

I changed it to:

1. We admitted we were powerless over our oily T-zone; that our skin had become unmanageable.

I was pretty pleased, but to get any further, I needed all 12 steps. I tried Rachel and couldn't get her, so reluctantly I asked Koo/Aroon at EarthSource. She opened her desk drawer and handed over a little booklet. "They're right here on the front page!"

"I only need them for a press release," I said hastily.

"Sure," she said. But the minute I'd gone, she went over to one of her colleagues and their excited whispers and hopeful glances alarmed me. Shite. That had been a stupid thing to do. Really stupid. I'd opened up that whole can of worms again where they thought I was going to admit I was an alcoholic.

Then Rachel rang back, and when I told her why I'd called, she said, "You're way out of line to use the 12 steps to publicize makeup."

"Makeup *remover*," I said.

"Whatever."

She hung up. Back to the drawing board.

Impulsively I rang Jacqui. "How's the Narky Joey situation?" I asked.

"Oh, fine, fine. I can look at him, acknowledge that he does bear a resemblance to Jon Bon Jovi, but it doesn't matter. I don't fancy him in the slightest."

"Thank God!" Suddenly I got a mad rush of fondness and really wanted to see her. "Would you like to do something later?" I asked. "Watch a video or something?"

"Oh, I can't tonight."

I waited for her to tell me why she couldn't. When she didn't I said, "What are you doing?"

"Playing poker."

"Poker?"

"Yeah."

"Where?"

"Gaz's apartment."

"Gaz's apartment? You mean Gaz *and Joey's* apartment?"

Grudgingly she conceded that yes, she supposed Joey did share an apartment with Gaz.

"Well, can I come?" I asked.

I mean, I thought she'd be delighted. She'd been badgering me for months to get out more.

The thing was, though, that Gaz wasn't there. Only Joey was in and he didn't look one bit happy to see me. I mean, he never did. But this was a different sort of displeasure.

"Where's Gaz?" I asked.

"Out."

I looked at Jacqui but she wouldn't meet my eyes.

"The place looks lovely," I said. "Beautiful candles. Ylang-ylang, I see, *very* sensual. And what are those flowers called?"

"Birds of paradise," Joey mumbled.

"Gorgeous. Can I have one of these strawberries?"

Narky pause. "Go ahead."

"Delicious! Ripe and juicy. Try one, Jacqui. Come here, let me feed one to you. What's this scarf for, Joey? Is it a *blindfold*?"

He made some angry "I haven't a clue" gesture.

"Lookit, I'm off," I said.

"Stay," Jacqui said. She looked at Joey. "We're only playing poker."

"Yeah, stay," Joey said, about as halfheartedly as anyone could.

"Please stay," Jacqui said. "Really, Anna, it's great to see you out and about."

"But . . . are you sure?"

"Yes."

"Maybe I should. Like, can you even *play* poker with just two people?"

"Well, there's three of us now," Joey said sourly.

"True for you. Although do you mind if we don't play poker?" I asked. "I just don't get it. You can't really do it properly if you don't smoke, it's all in the squinting. Let's play a proper game. Let's play rummy."

After a long silence, Joey said, "Rummy it is."

We sat at the table and Joey flung seven cards at each of us. I bowed my head and stared hard. Then I asked, "Would it be okay if we turned on a light? It's just I can't see my cards."

With short, jerky movements, Joey leaped up, hit a switch with venom, and threw himself back into his chair.

"Thank you," I murmured. In the bright of the overhead light, all the flowers and candles and strawberries and chocolates suddenly looked a little shamefaced.

"I suppose you want the music off, too, so you can concentrate," he said.

"No. I *like* Ravel's *Boléro*, actually."

I was sorry to be ruining the seduction scene but I hadn't realized I'd be intruding. Jacqui had more or less said that Gaz would be there. And both her and Joey had insisted that I stay, even though neither of them had meant it.

I looked up from my—admittedly excellent—hand of cards and caught Joey openly watching Jacqui. He was like a cat with a fluff ball, he was mesmerized. She was harder to read; she wasn't staring at him the way he was at her, but she wasn't her usual outgoing self. And her mind certainly wasn't on her cards because I kept winning. "Rummy!" I said gleefully, the first couple of times. Then it got embarrassing, then a little boring.

As an evening, it was not a success and it drew to an early close.

"At least poor Gaz can come home from wherever Joey banished him to," I said as Jacqui and I waited for the elevator.

"We're just friends," she said defensively.

To: Magiciansgirl1@yahoo.com
From: Lucky_Star_PI@yahoo.ie
Subject: Great news

Two weeks off from Detta Big, thanks be to jaysus. She's going to Marbella with "the girls" (collective age three thousand and seven if that crowd I saw her having lunch with are anything to go by). When Harry told me he said: And you needn't think you'll be going along with her for an all-expenses-paid fortnight in the sun.

Me: Like I'd want to go to that kippy kip.

Him (wounded): Why? What's wrong with it?

Me: Full of knackery crims, wearing too much gold, bought with their ill-gotten gains. Costa del War Crime.

Him: I didn't know the middle class thought that about Marbella. We thought yiz were jealous. Detta loves it.

Go figure. (Didn't say it tho'.)

Him: But you needn't think you're off the hook. Keep an eye on Racey O'Grady. Make sure he stays in the country.

To: Magiciansgirl1@yahoo.com
From: Thewalshes1@eircom.net
Subject: Photos!

Dear Anna,

I hope you are keeping well and sorry about "bellyaching" in my last e-mail. Well, finally we have photos of the woman and Zoe the dog! Helen is a good girl and hid in the hedge and "fired off a roll." She wanted to shout, "We're onto you, missus," but I told her not to. Stealth will be to our advantage. I will be taking the best pictures to mass next Sunday and will ask people if they recognize either the woman or Zoe. God help poor Zoe, it's not her fault, dogs have no sense of right and wrong. Human beings have a conscience, that's what separates us from the animals. Although Helen says the difference is that animals can't wear high heels. Either way, I must admit the whole business has me baffled. Obviously the old woman has some sort of "grudge" against us.
Your loving mother,
Mum

To: Magiciansgirl1@yahoo.com
From: Lucky_Star_PI@yahoo.ie
Subject: Racey O'Grady

Racey O'Grady lives in Dalkey, respectable neigborhood. Surprised. Thought all crime lords would live near one another so they could pop in and out of one another's houses all day, borrowing cups of bullets and saying they had to nip down to shops for a minute, so would other person keep an eye on their hostage, and so on. Racey—vay keen on privacy—big house, own grounds, electronic gates, high walls, spikes on top.

I parked down road and not one person went in or out all day. Not even postman. Tediousity of it. Seriously worried that Racey might have gone to Marbella and that I'd have to go, too. Then at five o'clock the gates opened and out comes Racey. Looks well in flesh. Tanned, bright blue eyes, pep in step. Sadly, wearing very bad mushroom-colored shoes, open-necked shirt, and gold chain. Looked like football manager, but far, far better than Mr. Big.

He was carrying kit bag. I was convinced it was full of saws, pliers, and other torture tools, but he was just going to gym. Followed him (on foot) to Killiney Castle health club, where they wouldn't let me in because I wasn't member, so I said, was thinking of becoming member and would they give me tour? Okay, they said, and when they showed me the gym there was Racey, his blue veiny legs going hell for leather on the StairMaster. Innocence itself. Ages later he left, I followed him back, sat in car for another hour, then thought, fuck this for a game of skittles, he's obviously not going to Marbella this evening, I'm going home.

On the train, Mitch and I rocked shoulder to shoulder in silence. We were returning from Coney Island amusement park, where we'd partaken of the rides a little too grimly. But that was fine. We weren't there to enjoy ourselves, simply to pass the time.

The train rounded a particularly sharp corner and we both nearly fell out of the seat. When we'd straightened up again, I suddenly asked, "What were you like before?"

"Before...?"

"Yes, what kind of person were you?"

"What am I like now?"

"Very quiet. You don't say much."

"I guess I talked more." He thought about it. "Yeah, conversations, I had opinions, I liked to talk. A lot." He sounded surprised. "Issues of the day, movies, whatever."

"Did you smile?"

"I don't smile now? Okay. Yeah, I smiled. And laughed. What were you like?"

"I don't know. Happier. Sunnier. Hopeful. Not terrified. I liked being around people..."

We sighed and lapsed back into silence.

Eventually I spoke. "Do you think we'll ever go back to being who we were?"

He thought about it. "I don't want to. It would be like Trish had never happened."

"I know what you mean, but, Mitch, are we going to be like this forever?"

"Like what?"

"Like...*ghosts*? Like we died, too, but someone forgot to tell us."

"We'll get better." After a pause he added, "We'll be better but different."

"How do you know?"

He smiled. "Because I know."

"Okay."

"Did you notice I smiled just there?"

"Did you? Do it again."

He arranged his face in an ultrabright smile. "How's that?"

"A bit game-show host. *Wheel of Fortune.*"

"Practice. That's all I need."

To: Magiciansgirl1@yahoo.com
From: Thewalshes1@eircom.net
Subject: Latest update

No one at mass recognized the old woman in the photo. I am going to bring it to golf and bridge and if I still don't get a "result" I am going to ring RTE and see if I can get it on <u>Crimewatch</u>. Or <u>Crimeline</u>. Or <u>Crimetime</u>. Or whatever they're calling it these days. <u>Crimewhine,</u> there's another one. Can you think of any more? Helen calls it *Grass Up Your Neighbors*. Mrs. Big is back from Marbella and Helen will be resuming sitting in the hedge from tomorrow morning.
Your loving mother,
Mum

A "ll set for tonight?" Nicholas asked. "The full moon?"

"Yes," I said quietly, bringing the phone very close to my face. I was at work, and although it was unlikely that anyone would guess that I was discussing recording my dead husband's voice, I wasn't taking any chances.

"You got your tape recorder?"

"Yep." Specially purchased.

"And you know not to start until after sunset?"

"Yes. I know everything." Nicholas had e-mailed me a vast quantity of information on electronic voice phenomenon. To my surprise some scientific studies seemed to take it seriously.

"Well, take this to the bank!"

"What?"

"Weather Channel says there's an eighty percent chance of thunderstorms this afternoon. That's going to totally up the chances of Aidan talking to you."

"Really?" My insides clenched with almost unendurable excitement.

"Yes, really. Good luck. Call me."

I was agitated and fidgety. I couldn't work, all I could do was pace and stare out the window. Late afternoon, the sky abruptly became purple and swollen and the air hot and still.

Teenie looked up from her desk. "Looks like we're going to have a thunderstorm."

I was so overwhelmed, I had to sit down.

The sky got darker and darker and I willed it on, and when the first rumble of thunder rolled over Manhattan, I let out a sigh of relief. Seconds later the sky cracked with lightning and the heavens opened.

Listening to the hiss of torrential rain drenching the city, I was trembling with anticipation; even my lips were. When my phone rang, I could barely talk. "Candy Grrrl publicity. Anna Walsh speaking."

It was Nicholas again. "Can you believe it?" he exclaimed.

"A full moon *and* a thunderstorm," I said numbly. "What are the chances of the two happening together?"

"Actually higher than you might think," he said. "You know how the full moon affects the tides . . ."

"Stop, stop! You're killing it for me."

"Sorry."

The next phone call was from Mitch. "Good luck tonight."

"Can you believe the two happening together?" I asked.

"No. It's got to be a sign. Call me later if you want to talk."

• • •

Every cab and car service in Manhattan had been commandeered and I got drenched running from the subway to my apartment; my bag on my head provided no protection whatsoever. Not that I cared; I was elated. I paced the floor, drying my hair with a towel and wondering what time could be officially considered "after sunset."

When the storm had started, day had turned to night, but I worried that just because it looked dark out there, it didn't necessarily mean it was "after sunset." The sun might have been scared off by the thunder and lightning but mightn't have actually *set*.

I wasn't sure how much sense that made but the instructions Nicholas had sent were very specific—the recording must not start until "after sunset"—and I couldn't afford to cut any corners because it would be another four weeks until the next full moon.

Waiting to talk to Aidan was killing me but I forced myself to hold out until after ten; under normal nonstormy circumstances, the sun would have definitely set by then.

I put the tape recorder up in the bedroom because it was far quieter than the front room, which faced onto the street. The rumbles of thunder had stopped but the rain was still tumbling from the sky.

To make sure everything was working fine, I said "testing, one, two" a couple of times. I felt like a roadie but it had to be done, and at least I didn't say it in a stupid roadie way ("Dezdin, wan, jew"), then I took a deep breath and spoke into the mike. "Aidan, please talk to me. I'm . . . um . . . going to leave for a while, and when I come back, I'm really hoping to hear a message from you."

Then I tiptoed out and sat in the front room, jiggling my foot, watching the clock. I'd give it an hour.

When the time was up, I tiptoed back in; the tape had come to an end. I rewound it, then hit play, all the time praying, *Please Aidan, please Aidan, please have left a message, please Aidan, please.*

I jumped when I heard my own voice at the start, but after that came nothing. My ears were straining to hear anything, anything at all. But all there was, was the hiss of silence.

Suddenly a high-pitched shriek came from the tape; faint but definitely audible. I recoiled with fright. Oh my God, oh my God, was that Aidan? Why had he screamed?

My heart was thumping as fast as an express train. I put my ear close to the speaker; there were other sounds, too. A muzzy jumble, but undeniably the sound of a voice. I caught a word that might have been *men* then a ghostly *oooooooh*.

I couldn't believe it. It was happening, it was really happening, and was I ready for it? Blood was pounding in my ears, my palms were drenched, and the follicles of my scalp were tingling. Aidan had contacted me. All I had to do was listen hard enough to hear what he had to say. *Thank you, sweetheart, oh, thank you, thank you, thank you.* The voice sounded more high-pitched than Aidan's; I'd been told that this could happen and that I should slow the tape down in order to hear better. However, that made it harder to pick out anything meaningful, so I put it back to normal speed, every one of my muscles tensed, desperate to hear something that made sense. I was still only getting a sound or a word here and there, when out of nowhere I caught an entire sentence. There was no doubt as to what it was. I heard each word with crystal clarity.

It was, "Ab-so-lut-lee soooaaak-ing WET!"

It was Ornesto. Upstairs. Singing "It's Raining Men."

As soon as I knew what it was, all the other muzzy indistinct sounds instantly fell into place.

"Hall-ell-ooooooooooooooooh-ya! It's raining men! La la la la la LA."

For a moment I felt nothing. Nothing at all. I'd never been in such a situation before and there was no precedent.

I sat in the dark room for I couldn't tell you how long, then I went through to the living room and automatically switched on the telly.

64

To: Psychic_Productions@yahoo.com
From: Magiciansgirl1@yahoo.com
Subject: Neris Hemming

I contacted you on July 6 so that I could speak to my husband, Aidan, who died. You confirmed that I would have an appointment with Neris Hemming in ten to twelve weeks. It has been over five weeks and I was wondering if it would be possible to have my appointment moved to an earlier date? Or even if you could tell me what date it'll be on, it would probably make things a little easier to bear.
Thank you in advance for your help,
Anna Walsh

Impulsively I dashed off a P.S.

I am sorry to badger you, I know Neris is very very busy but I'm in agony here.

A day later I received this reply.

To: Magiciansgirl1@yahoo.com
From: Psychic_Productions@yahoo.com
Subject: Re: Neris Hemming

It is not possible to move your appointment to an earlier date. At the moment it is not possible to confirm your appointment

date. You will be contacted approximately two weeks before
the date. Thank you for your interest in Neris Hemming.

Mute with frustration, I stared at the screen. I wanted to scream but it
wouldn't do any good.

Let's do something on Saturday night," Jacqui suggested.

"What? No two-personed poker matches lined up?"

"Stop." She giggled.

"You just giggled."

"No, I didn't."

"Jacqui, you did."

She thought about it. "Shit. Anyway, let's do something on Saturday
night."

"Can't. I'm doing Super Saturday in the Hamptons."

"Oh! You lucky, lucky bitch."

That's what everyone said when they heard I was going.

"The dirt-cheap designer clothes!" Jacqui said. "The freebies! The
parties afterward!"

But I was working at it. *Working.* And it was very different when you
were working.

65

In the Friday-afternoon haze, Teenie and I sat on the Long Island Expressway in bumper-to-bumper traffic. The car was crammed with boxes and boxes of product—in the trunk, on the floor, on our laps. We had to bring it all ourselves because if we trusted it to couriers there was a very real chance that it wouldn't arrive on time. (Or if we sent it the day before, there was a very real chance it would get nicked.) But we weren't complaining: at least we hadn't been made to go on the jitney like last year.

Mind you, breathing in the exhaust fumes of a million cars wasn't pleasant; one of the windows had to be open because the three massive Candy Grrrl backdrops were too long to fit inside the car.

"We'll have contracted lung cancer by the time we get there," Teenie remarked. "Ya ever seen a smoker's lungs?"

"No."

"Oh, great!" With relish she launched into a gory description, until the driver—a large gentleman with the yellow fingers of a cigarette lover—said, "Can you please shut up. I'm not feeling too good."

It was after nine by the time we got to the Harbor Inn. First we had to check Candace and George's suite, to ensure that it was sufficiently fabulous and that champagne, a fruit basket, exotic flowers, and handmade chocolates were awaiting their arrival. We tweaked a few cushions, smoothed the comforter on the bed—leaving nothing to chance—then Teenie and I had a late dinner and retired to our single cots for a few hours' sleep.

The following morning we were at the exhibition center by seven. The doors opened to the public at nine and we needed to have a mini–Candy Grrrl store assembled by then.

Shortly after seven-thirty Brooke arrived; she'd been in the neighborhood since Wednesday, staying with her parents in their mansion.

"Hey, you guys!" she said. "How can I help?"

Funnily enough, she meant it. Within seconds she was balanced on a stepladder, suspending the six-foot-by-ten-foot backdrops from the ceiling. Then she figured out how to click together the separate pieces of the black lacquer display table. Say what you like about rich people with a sense of entitlement, but Brooke was extraordinarily practical and obliging.

Meanwhile, Teenie and I were unpacking box after box of product. We were promoting Protection Racket, our new sun-cream range. It came in (fake) glass bottles, with (fake) cut-glass stoppers, like old-fashioned perfume bottles, and the creams were an array from the pink spectrum; the highest protection factor, thirty, was a deep burgundy color and the range went through several, progressively lighter pinks, down to the lowest factor—four—in baby pink. They were gorgeous.

We also had hundreds of Candy Grrrl T-shirts and beach bags to give away, countless goody bags of trial sizes, plus every item of cosmetics we carried, for Candace to do her makeovers.

Just as we'd got the last lip gloss slotted into place on the display table, Lauryn arrived.

"Hey," she said, her poppy eyes moving in a restless quest to find something to criticize. Disappointed, she could find nothing wrong, so she turned her attention to the crowds, scanning like a hungry hunter.

"I'm just going to . . ."

"Yeah," Teenie muttered, when she'd gone. "You just go find some famous butt to suck."

This made Brooke squeal with laughter. "You guys are so funny!"

By ten o'clock, the place was thronged. There was a lot of interest in Protection Racket but the question everyone asked was "Will it make my skin look pink?"

"Oh no," we said, again and again and again, "The color disappears on the skin."

"The color disappears on the skin."

"The color disappears on the skin."

"The color disappears on the skin."

Every now and then you'd hear a surprised posh voice say, "Oh, hello, Brooke! You're working, how adorable! How's your mother?"

Trade was brisk in the giveaway beach bags (not so brisk in the T-shirts, but never mind) and all three of us conducted dozens of miniconsultations: skin type, favorite colors, etc., before pressing a load of suitable trial sizes on the woman in question.

We were smiling, smiling, smiling, and I was getting a horrible crampy feeling in my mouth, at the hinge of my gums.

"Buildup of lactic acid," Teenie said. "Happens when a muscle is overworked."

I didn't feel the time passing until Teenie said, "Shit! It's nearly twelve. Where's the line of women crazy to meet Candace?"

Candace was due at noon. We had advertised in the local press and it had been announced every fifteen minutes on the P.A. system, but so far no one had shown.

"We gotta start badgering people," Teenie said. She loved the word *badger*. "If we don't have a long line, our ass is grass."

"Okay, let's badger—" The words died in my mouth as over the chatter of the crowd came a sudden shriek. It sounded like it came from a small child.

The three of us looked at one another. What was that?

"I think Dr. De Groot has just arrived," Teenie said.

66

Lauryn reappeared.

"To pretend to Candace and George she's been here all morning," Teenie said quietly.

"So what's happening?" Lauryn asked, roaming restlessly. She picked up a bottle of Protection Racket, then asked as if it was the first time she'd ever seen it, "But won't it make people look pink?"

In unison, Brooke, Teenie, and I chanted, "The color disappears on the skin."

"Jeez," she said, affronted. "No need to yell at me. Omigod!" She'd just noticed the lack of queue. "Where are all the people?"

"We're just rounding them up."

"It's okay. Here they come."

I looked. Four women were approaching the stand. But instinctively I knew they hadn't come for a Candy Grrrl makeover. They all had excellent cheekbones and jaw-length bobs, and were dressed in sun-bleached shades of stone and sand. They looked like they'd stepped straight out of a Ralph Lauren ad and turned out to be Brooke's mother, Brooke's two older sisters, and Brooke's sister-in-law.

Then through the crowds I saw someone I knew, but for a moment I couldn't remember who she was or where I knew her from. Then it clicked: it was Mackenzie! Wearing clean-faded blue jeans and a man's white shirt, quite different from the glam rig-outs she'd worn to the spiritualist place every Sunday, but definitely her. I hadn't seen her for three or four weeks now.

"Anna!" she said. "You look adorable! All that pink!"

It was strange, I barely knew her, but she felt like my long-lost sister. I flung myself into her arms and we hugged tightly.

Naturally, being posh, Mackenzie knew all the Edisons, so there was a flurry of kisses and inquiries after parents and uncles.

"How do you two guys know each other?" Lauryn asked, her eyes bulging suspiciously from me to Mackenzie.

Mackenzie's eyes flashed a desperate signal. *Don't tell them, please don't tell them.*

Don't worry, I flashed back. *I'm saying nothing.*

We were saved from a mortifying "How do we know each other Anna?" "I don't know, Mackenzie, how *do* we know each other?" shtick by the arrival of Queen Candace and King George.

Candace—dressed in downbeat black—thought the Edison women and Mackenzie were the crowd waiting to be made over by her.

"Well, hey." She almost smiled. "Better get started." She picked the obvious alpha female and extended her hand. "Candace Biggly."

"Martha Edison."

"Well, Martha, would you care to take a seat for your makeover?" Candace indicated the silver-and-pink vinyl stool. "You other ladies will just have to wait."

"Makeover?" Mrs. Edison sounded aghast. "But I only use soap and water on my skin."

Confused, Candace looked at an Edison sister, then at another one, then at the sister-in-law, and seemed to notice that they were all clones of Martha.

"Soap and water," they parroted, shrinking away. "Yes, soap and water. Bye, Brooke, see you at the Save the Moose picnic."

"Mackenzie," I said brightly. "How about you?"

"Hey, why not?" Obligingly she got up on the stool and introduced herself to Candace as "Mackenzie McIntyre Hamilton."

George said to Candace, "Okay, babes, seeing as you're all set, I'll just take a stroll."

Teenie and I made steady eye contact, silently saying, "He's off to suck Donna Karan's butt." Brooke intercepted the look and got a massive fit of the giggles. "You guys!"

"Shaddup," Lauryn hissed. "And start rounding up a crowd."

But it proved impossible: a high proportion of passersby were planning to attend the Save the Moose picnic and didn't want to look overly made up for it. They were happy to accept a Candy Grrrl beach bag and free samples but not to "take the chair."

Candace strung out Mackenzie's makeover for as long as possible, but finally Mackenzie descended from the stool and I cornered her.

"Will I see you soon?" I asked, without actually moving my lips.

She shook her head. "I don't think so," she said very, very quietly. "I'm trying something different."

"The rich husband route?"

"Yeah. But I miss you guys. How's Nicholas?"

"Um, good."

"What did his T-shirt say last week?"

" 'Jimmy Carter for President.' "

She laughed out loud. "Vintage. God, he's just adorable. A little cutie. Is it just me or is he kinda...*hot?*"

"I'm not really the person to ask."

"Sure. Sorry." She sighed, quite sadly. "Well, tell Nicholas I said hey. Tell everyone I said hey."

She left and I resumed my badgering of the crowd. Still no takers, which was bad enough, but then someone said, "I totally broke out when I tried Candy Grrrl's day cream," and—horror of horrors—Candace heard.

She dashed down her pony-skin blusher brush and said, "I've got better fucking things to do with my time than try the hard sell on these assholes. I've got an annual turnover of thirty-four million dollars."

I feared client meltdown. Anxiously, I looked around for George, but he was off sucking up to any half-famous fool he could find. Lauryn, naturally, had also disappeared.

"I want ice cream," Candace said petulantly.

"Er...okay. I'll go and get you some. Teenie and Brooke will stay with you."

"I'm sorry but I have to leave now," Brooke said. "I've pledged to sell raffle tickets at the moose benefit."

"Okay. Well, thanks, Brooke, you've been a total star today. See you Monday."

"Wednesday," she reminded me. "I'm not back until then."

"Right, Wednesday." I dived into the throng, desperately seeking ice cream.

Fifteen frustrating minutes later I returned, triumphantly bearing an Eskimo Pie, a Dove Bar, and three other assorted ice creams. Covering all bases.

Grumpily Candace accepted the Eskimo Pie and sat slumped on the high stool, her chin on her chest, tucking in. She looked like an orangutan who'd been left out in the rain.

This was the moment, of course, that Ariella, visiting friends in East Hampton for the weekend, did a drop-by. It didn't look good. Mercifully, Ariella couldn't linger. She was on her way to the Save the Caribou cookout.

"Is that different from the Save the Moose picnic?" Teenie asked.

"Totally," she snapped.

Then they were all gone and it was just me and Teenie.

"So what's up with the moose anyway?" Teenie asked. "I didn't even know it *was* endangered. Or the caribou."

I shrugged. "Dunno. Maybe they've just run out of stuff to save."

Anna, it's me, your mother, it's urgent—"

I grabbed the phone. Something was wrong with someone. Dad? JJ?

"What?" I asked. "What's urgent?"

"What's the story with Jacqui and Joey?"

I had to wait for my racing heart to slow down. "That's why you're ringing? Because of Jacqui and Joey?"

"Yes. What's going on?"

"You know. He fancies her. And she fancies him."

"No! She's slept with him. Over the weekend, while you were in those Hamptons."

She hadn't told me. In a little voice I said, "I didn't know."

Fake cheerily, Mum said hastily, "Sure it's only Monday morning, she'll tell you soon. And, God knows, who *hasn't* slept with Joey?"

"I haven't."

"And neither"—she sighed heavily—"have I. But just about everyone else has. Was it a one-night stand?"

"How the hell do I know?"

"No, it's a joke. A whole night? Does Joey do that kind of commitment?" Mum said.

"Good one." Then I said, "Well, I can't help you. I don't know what's going on. Ask Rachel."

"I can't. We're not talking."

"What now?"

"The invitations. I want nice silver italics on nice white paper."

"And what does she want?"

"Twigs and twine and shells and woven papyrus stuff. Would you have a word with her?"

"No."

A startled silence came from Mum's end, then I explained, "I'm the daughter who's been recently bereaved, remember?"

"Sorry, pet. Sorry. I was mixing you up with Claire for a minute."

It was only after she hung up that I wondered how she knew about Jacqui. Luke, I presumed.

Straightaway, I rang Jacqui, but she wasn't picking up either of her phones. I left messages for her to call me immediately, then went to work, bursting with curiosity.

She didn't call all morning. I tried her again at lunchtime but still no reply. Midafternoon, I was just about to ring her once more when a shadow fell over my desk. It was Franklin. Very quietly, he said, "Ariella wants to see you."

"Why?"

"Let's go."

"Where?"

"Her office."

Oh God, I was sacked. I was so sacked.

Ah, well.

Franklin walked me in and I was hugely surprised to discover several people already there: Wendell from Visage, Mary Jane, coordinator of the other seven brands, and Lois, one of Mary Jane's "girls." Lois worked on Essence, one of our more worthy, touchy-feely brands, although nothing like as bad as EarthSource.

Was this going to be a job-lot sacking?

Five chairs were set in a semicircle around Ariella's desk.

"Siddown," she Don Corleoned. "Okay, the good news is that you're not fired. Yet."

We all laughed far too loud and long.

"Settle down, kids, it wasn't that funny. First thing you've got to know is, this is superconfidential. What you hear here today, you do not discuss outside this room, with anyone, anywhere, anytime, anyhow, got it?"

Got it. But I was intrigued. Especially because we were such an unlikely combination of people. What did we have in common that made us privy to some huge secret?

"Formula Twelve." Ariella asked. "Heard of it?"

I nodded. I knew a bit. It had been formulated by some discoverer man who had been down in the Amazon Basin badgering the locals, trying to record their lifestyle, that sort of thing. When the local lads got wounded, an ointmenty thing would be made up of ground roots and plants and other stuff you'd expect; the explorer had noticed how quickly the wounds healed and how residual scarring was minimal.

The discoverer bloke tried to make the ointment himself, but didn't get it right until the twelfth go, hence the title.

It had been regarded as medicinal and he'd been trying to get approval from the FDA, which was a long time coming.

Ariella took up the story. "So while he's waiting and waiting for FDA appro, Professor Redfern—that's the guy's name—had an idea: skin care. Using the same formula, in a diluted form, he's created a day cream." She handed out an inch-thick pile of documents to each of the five of us. "And the trials have been phenomenal. Like, off the scale. It's all there."

The funny thing about Ariella is that when she had to talk for any length of time, she stopped the Don Corleone carry-on. Clearly it was just an affectation to scare people. Mind you, it worked.

"It's been bought by Devereaux." Devereaux was a massive corporation; they owned dozens of cosmetic lines. Including Candy Grrrl, actually. "Devereaux is going huge on it. It's going to be the hottest brand on the planet." She half smiled, moving eye contact from one of us to the next. "You're wondering where do we come in? Okay, take this to the bank: McArthur on the Park . . . is pitching for their publicity."

She took a moment to let us say wow and how fabulous that was.

"And I want each of you three"—she pointed at me, Wendell, and Lois, in turn—"to come up with a pitch. A separate pitch."

Another momentous pause. In fairness, that *was* fabulous. A pitch of my own. For a totally new brand.

"If they're good enough, we pitch all three to them. If they go with your pitch, maybe you get to head up the account."

Oh. Now, that *would* be amazing. A promotion. Although what would a Formula Twelve girl have to wear? Stuff inspired by the Amazon Basin? Even Warpo would be better than that.

"How much time do we have?" Wendell asked.

"Two weeks today, you three pitch to me."

Two weeks. Not long.

"That gives us time to nix any glitches before the real thing. Not that I want any glitches." Ariella was suddenly low and menacing. "Another thing, you do all of this in your own time. Coming in here every day, you carry on like normal, giving one thousand percent to your current brands. But you can forget about having a life of your own for the next couple weeks."

I was in luck. I had no life of my own anyway.

"And like I said, *no one must know.*"

Suddenly she switched to regal mode. "Anna, Lois, Wendell, you don't need me to tell you what an honor this is. Do you?" Energetically we shook our heads. No, indeed, we did not. "Do you know how many people I have working for me?" No, we didn't, but plenty, for sure. "I spent a lot of time with Franklin and Mary Jane assessing every single one of my girls, and out of all of them, I picked you three."

"Thank you, Ariella," we murmured.

"I am putting my trust in you." Ariella smiled, for the first time, with real warmth. "Don't fuck it up."

As Franklin walked me back to my desk, he said low and urgent, right into my ear, "You heard her. Don't fuck it up."

Dread took ahold of me.

Lauryn looked up with eager interest. "Did you get fired?"

"No."

"Oh. So what did she want to see you for?"

"Nothing."

"What's in the file?"

"Nothing."

God, I was doing a great job at stealth. *Tonight you sleep in the unemployment line.*

Already I was sorry to be one of the chosen ones.

I opened the Formula Twelve file and tried reading the information. Lots of it was scientific data about the biological qualities of the plants and the properties they contained and why they worked the way they did. It was highly technical, and much as I would have loved to just skim over it, I couldn't, because if we got the account, it would be my job to reduce all this information to understandable, bite-size pieces for beauty editors' consumption.

One of the sad things about my job was that I no longer believed any antiaging promises or miracle claims. Why would I? I wrote them.

The file contained a photo of Professor Redfern, who looked nice and explorery. Suntanned and wrinkled around the eyes and wearing a hat and one of those sleeveless khaki gilets that seem to be mandatory for explorer blokes. Beardy? But of course. Not unattractive, if you like that sort. Promotable? Possibly. Maybe we could present him as an Indiana Jones du jour.

Finally, there was a little jar of the magic cream itself. It was a nastyish mustard yellow with dark-colored flecks—a bit like "real" vanilla ice cream. Most face creams were either white or palest pink, but the mustard yellow wasn't necessarily a bad thing; it might make it seem more "authentic."

I rubbed a thin layer over my face and a few minutes later my scar started to tingle. I rushed to the mirror and almost expected to see the puckered skin bubbling and expanding, like something in a scientific experiment gone very very wrong. But, no, nothing unusual was happening, my face looked the same as it always did.

B efore I went to bed, I tried Jacqui one more time. I'd got used to her not answering, so I was very surprised when she did.

"Hay-lllloooo." She sounded all breathy and gaspy.

"It's me. What's up with you and Narky Joey?"

"We've been in bed since Friday night. He's just left."

"So do you fancy him?"

"Anna, I'm mad about him."

68

She insisted on regaling me with stories about how great the sex was. *Sex,* I thought, saying the word in my head. *Having sex.* Impossible to imagine. I was so dead, so numb.

The funny thing was that even though my libido was entirely kaput, one of my regrets was that Aidan and I hadn't had more sex. I mean, we'd had plenty—well, a normal amount. Whatever that is. It's hard to know exactly because most people are so paranoid that everyone else is at it morning, noon, and night that they lie about how often they do it, inflating the numbers, and obviously the people they lie to *also* feel the need to lie, so it's very hard to get at the truth.

Anyway, Aidan and I used to have sex about twice or three times a week. In the beginning, though, it was more like twice or three times a day. I know that you can't carry on like that indefinitely, ripping each other's clothes off and having showers together and doing it in public places and generally going for it round the clock. You'd be knackered and you'd have no buttons left on your clothes and you might get arrested.

To my sorrow, we'd never done anything terribly adventurous; it had all been pretty vanilla. But maybe the kinky stuff doesn't happen straightaway. Maybe you have to work your way through all the straightforward sex first and perhaps in ten years' time we'd have moved out to the suburbs and been in the thick of a riotous, swinging, husband-swapping scene.

What was killing me were all the opportunities I had wasted—almost every morning of my life with him. Getting ready for work, he'd be parading around naked, his skin still damp from the shower, his mickey jiggling, and I'd be scooting past, looking for a deodorant or a hairbrush or something, and I'd half notice his tiny bottom and the hollow down the side of his thighs, and I'd think, *God, he's magnificent.* But straightaway I'd think something like *I still haven't had my boots heeled, I'll have to wear different shoes and that throws all my calculations out.*

Mornings were a race against the clock; it didn't stop Aidan grabbing at me as I zipped past, half dressed, but I nearly always batted him off and said, "Away, away, we haven't time."

Mostly he was a good sport about it, but one morning, shortly before he died, he said, quite sadly, "We never do it in the mornings anymore."

"No one does," I said. "Only weirdos, like company CEOs with trophy wives or mistresses. And the women only submit because the CEO gives them expensive jewelry. And the CEO only does it because he was born with too much testosterone, and if he doesn't have sex, he'll have to invade a country or something."

"Yes, but..."

"Come on now," I chivvied him. "We're not living in a *Joy of Sex* video."

"What happens in a *Joy of Sex* video?"

"*You* know. Spontaneity." I whizzed up the zip on my skirt. "You'd be ready for work, like you are now, and I'd be having a bubble bath."

"We don't even have a bath."

"Never mind. I'd be pointing my toes in the air and soaping my shins all luxuriously and you'd lean over the side to kiss me good-bye..."

"...oh, I get it. You'd pull me by the tie..."

"...exactly! Into the bath..."

"...wow. Wild..."

"Not wild. You'd go apeshit. You'd shout, 'For God's sake, this is my Hugo Boss suit. What in the name of fuck am I going to wear to work now?'" As I spoke, I was rummaging furiously through a drawer looking for a bra. I found it.

"Look." Aidan pointed down at his crotch. He seemed to be indicating activity in that region. I ignored it and continued. "You'd say, 'We'd better get all this water mopped up before Mr. Downstairs comes up to humble us for destroying his bathroom ceiling.'"

Aidan was still looking at his crotch. I followed his eyes to the tent-pole shape in his trousers. He made a "shucks, honey," gesture and I said, "We've got to go to work."

"No." He unsnapped the bra I'd just put on.

"No!" I tried to put the bra back on.

"But you're beautiful." Gently he bit the back of my neck, "And I want you so baaaad. Feel." He took my hand, and through the cloth I felt his erection, bent and springy and striving to be upright. Under my touch it noticeably thickened and straightened.

Suddenly this was starting to seem like quite a nice idea but I made a last attempt to put him off. "I'm wearing my tangerine knickers."

They were like boy's jocks. I loved them; Aidan didn't.

"I don't care," he said. "Just get them off. Like now." He wrestled me onto the bed, hiked up my skirt, hooked his index fingers into the waistband of my tangerine jocks, whizzed them right down to my ankles, and unhooked them over my feet.

Leaning over me, he pulled his tie undone, unzipped his fly, and whispered, "I'm gonna fuck you." He tugged down his Calvins and his fully erect penis sprang out. I pushed him back on the bed, the bottom buttons of his shirt undone, his pants down to his knees, his skin pale against the navy of the suit and his shock of dark pubic hair.

His erection curved upward and he reached for me.

I slid myself down onto him, suddenly very turned on and, holding on to the headboard, began rocking up and down. My button was rubbing against the shaft and my breasts were swinging in his face. He nipped my nipples between sharp teeth, his hands tight on my hips, moving me up and down his shaft, faster and faster.

The headboard was squeaking in time with his noises. "Ah! Ah! Ah! Ah!" Then: "Oh, fuck, no!" With a final "AHHH!" and a shiver, he reared up into me, pulling me down to him. He gasped and shuddered and bucked, and when he could speak again, he said, "Sorry, baby."

I shrugged. "You know what to do."

He rolled me over, slid a pillow under my bum, pushed my thighs apart, and I rose to meet him.

I swear to God, I thought I could see an improvement in my scar the very next morning. I couldn't be sure, but I took a photo of it just to be on the safe side. If Formula Twelve could effect a visible improvement after one go, what would it be like after fourteen? It might come in very handy for my pitch.

I couldn't decide which way to go with it, but obviously I didn't want to overlap with Wendell or Lois.

I could guess what Wendell would propose because I knew her style: Wendell threw money at things. Every beauty editor in New York would be off to Brazil on a private plane if Wendell had anything to do with it.

Lois was a lesser-known quantity. Because the brand she currently worked on was a bit of a Feathery Stroker one, she might stay with that approach and go on about the natural ingredients and that sort of thing.

So, if the Brazilianness and the Naturalness aspects of Formula Twelve were already annexed, where did that leave me?

Nothing was coming. No starbursts of inspiration. It was all I thought about; it filled my head right up and left very little room for me to think about anything else. But something would come. Something would have to.

What do you think? I asked Aidan. *Any ideas? Divine inspiration? Now that you're dead, any chance it could come in handy?*

But no voice answered in my head. I stared at the little yellow jar and wondered.

To: Magiciansgirl1@yahoo.com
From: Lucky_Star_PI@yahoo.ie
Subject: Result!

After fuck knows how many weeks since started tailing her, finally got picture of Detta Big at Racey O'Grady's house. Took loads of shots of Detta talking into gate intercom, driving in, parking, getting out of the car, ringing front doorbell, going inside...

Printed them off at high speed! Then rang Colin and told him to collect me. I never meet Harry anywhere except Corky's, but am not allowed to make own way there. Have to suffer mortification of Austrian-blindsmobile and local kids mocking.

As usual Harry down the back drinking milk. I put envelope of photos in front of him.

Me: There's your proof. Now give me my money and let me off this boring job.

Harry opened envelope, shuffled through pics, then said: You're still on the job.

Me: Why?

Him: I like having you around the place.

Me: Do you?

Could have sworn he hated me.

Him (wearily): No. I don't know why I said that.

Me: I'm sick of this job. I want out.

Him: Well, you can't. I want you in.

Me: And I want out.

Him: You're very fond of your mother, aren't you?

Me (surprised): No, I'm not.

Where did he get that mad idea from?

Me: Are you threatening me?

Him: Yes.

Me: Well, you'll have to try a bit harder than threatening my mother.

Him: So who are you fond of?

Me: No one.

Him: You've got to be fond of someone.

Me: I'm not, I'm telling you. My sister Rachel says there's something wrong with me, like I've a bit missing.

Him: And she's the shrink, is she?

Me: Yes. (I know she's not proper shrink, just acts like one.)

Him: Well, she'd know. Fuck.

Harry put head in hands. Sign that he was thinking. He looked up: I need better proof than this. I need proof of them together, if you get me?

Me: Do you mean them riding each other?

Him (wincing): In my day women used to have some decorum. I'll double what I'm paying you. How does that sound?

Me (desperate): It's not about the money. Look, Harry, this job has got to get more exciting. I'm losing the will to live.

Him: Stop calling me Harry. Show a little respect.

Me: Actually, Harry, I was thinking about the whole Mr. Big thing. I've been trying lateral thinking. Instead of focusing on size, we could try other things.

Him: Like what?

Me: How does Mr. Fear grab you?

Him (nodding slowly): I like it.

Me: Will we try it for a while, see if it catches on?

Him: Okay.

He tells Colin: D'you get that? We're going to run with Mr. Fear for a while. Put the word out to the lads.

Because I want to get off this job, I said: Harry, you have photographic proof of your wife with another crime lord. Why would they be meeting if they weren't up to something dodgy?

Him: Lots of reasons. Racey's mammy, Tessie O'Grady, was great friends with Detta's da, Chinner Skinner. Detta could just be being friendly, like.

Me: So Detta and Racey are old friends! Why am I surveilling old friends?

I'm thinking, he's cracked. Cracked and mad. And insane, to boot.

Him: No, *they're* not old friends. Their ma and da were old friends.

Me: But still a perfectly innocent reason for them to meet up.

Him (shaking head): No. Because then there was a bit of bad blood over an arms shipment from the Middle East and Chinner Skinner got rubbed out.

Colin: Along with most of the crème de la crème of Dublin crime.

Harry (looked at Colin really meanly): If I want your input, I'll ask for it.

He turned back to me: Yeh, most of Dublin's brightest stars—Bennie the Blade. Rasher McRazor. The Boneman. Ironing-board Jim—all taken out in the space of a fortnight.

He sighed: The best of the best. But the biggest shock was Chinner Skinner. No one fucked with the Chinner but word was that Tessie O'Grady took him out. No one's ever been able to prove it like, but only Tessie O'Grady would have the balls to do it.

Me: How long ago was this?

Him: Donkeys. Twelve. Fifteen?

He looked at Colin.

Colin: Fourteen years this summer.

Me: So Detta and Racey are old friends who became enemies who might be friends again?

Fuck's sake.

Piss: Didn't entirely mean it when said I wasn't fond of anyone. Quite fond of you.

Pissssss: Not just saying that because your husband died.

I couldn't come up with a pitch for Formula Twelve. For the first time
ever, all my inspiration had deserted me.

Franklin asked how it was coming along.

"Good," I said.

"So tell me."

"I'd rather not," I said. "If that's okay. It's not fully there yet and I
don't want you to see it half-assed."

With sudden anger, he said, "Are you fucking with me?"

"No, Franklin, I swear. Trust me, I won't let you down."

"Because I took a risk on you with Ariella."

"I know. I appreciate it. I'm good for this."

But I wasn't.

By Sunday I'd still drawn a blank, so at Leisl's I jokingly asked the
gang for help.

"If anyone comes through for any of you today, will you ask them
what I should do for my pitch."

"What've you done so far?" Nicholas asked.

"Nothing. I've come up with nothing."

"Isn't that telling you something?" Nicholas asked.

"Telling me what?"

"To do nothing."

"And get sacked? I don't think so."

"How do you get the goose out of the bottle?"

"*What* goose?"

"It's a Buddhist thing. There's a goose trapped in a bottle—how do you get it out?"

"How did it get in, in the first place?" Mitch asked.

Nicholas laughed. "That doesn't matter. So how do you get it out?"

"Break the bottle," Mitch said.

Nicholas shrugged. "That's one way." He looked at me. "Any other suggestions?"

"Smoke him out," Barb said. "Heh, heh, heh."

"I give up," I said. "Tell me."

"This isn't a riddle. There isn't a straight answer."

"What? So the goose stays in the bottle?"

"Not necessarily. If you wait. Wait long enough and the goose will be thin enough to slip out of the bottle. Or if he gets fed, he'll grow and break the bottle himself. But all you have to do is nothing."

"Little one, you are wise beyond your years," Barb said.

"I don't know," I said. "I was hoping for more practical advice."

To: Magiciansgirl1@yahoo.com
From: Thewalshes1@aircom.net
Subject: "Result!"

Dear Anna,

I hope you are keeping well. Well, we have finally "nailed" the old woman. I brought the photos to golf and no one knew her but we "hit pay dirt" at bridge. Dodie McDevitt identified her. Funnily enough it was Zoe the dog she recognized first. She said, "That's Zoe O'Shea, as sure as eggs." When she said "Zoe" I thought I might topple off my chair. "Yes!" I said. "Zoe, Zoe! Who owns her?" "Nan O'Shea," says she.

Dodie was even able to give me her address—Springhill

Drive, which is not that far away, although it is a long way to make a small dog walk every day. I am not sure what to do now. I might have to "beard" her in her "den." "Front" her "up." But whatever happens I will keep you "in the loop."

Your loving mother,

Mum

The Formula Twelve pitch was all I could think about but I hadn't come up with a single idea. I had never experienced a block like it. I knew that if it came to it, I could do a pitch similar to Wendell's—private plane to Rio, fancy hotels, half-day trip to the favelas—but my heart wouldn't be in it. I *had* to come up with something. In the past I had always managed to pull the rabbit out of the hat. But, to my horror, still nothing came and I only had six days left . . .

   . . . five days . . .

   . . . four days . . .

   . . . three days . . .

   . . . two days . . .

   . . . one day . . .

   . . . no days . . .

The morning of the pitch to Ariella, I wore my only sober suit, the one I'd worn the first time I'd met Aidan, when he'd spilled coffee on me. It might help me be taken seriously. I almost died of shock when I saw the usually überchic Wendell.

She was wearing a yellow suit. *Yellow.* With feathers. She looked like Big Bird. She must be pitching some carnival-type theme. Quickly I looked over at Lois, who was wearing a sleeveless khaki gilet with loads of pockets, just like Professor Redfern's. Her pitch must be going the explorer route.

At five to ten, Franklin gave us the nod and led Wendell and me to the boardroom. Coming from the opposite direction were Mary Jane and Lois. Wendell and Lois had storyboards tucked under their arms. I had none.

All five of us met at the door, where Franklin and Mary Jane fronted each other in a hostile face-off. Out on the floor, everyone craned their necks and stared; this highly confidential pitch was one of the worst-kept secrets of all time.

"Please enter," said Shannon, Ariella's PA. "Ariella is waiting inside. I will be guarding the door." To keep us in, rather than anyone else out, I thought.

"Siddown, siddown," Ariella said from the head of the table. "Now, *amaze* me."

Wendell went first and what she proposed was no great surprise. She wanted to showcase the Brazilianness of Formula Twelve by flying twelve superselected beauty editors to Rio for Mardi Gras. "They'll have a blast. We'll fly them down in a private plane." *I knew it! Private plane! I knew it!*

She revealed her first storyboard, which was a photograph of a small executive jet.

"This is similar to the plane we would fly them in," she said. "Then we're gonna put each editor in a suite in a five-star hotel in Rio—so many to choose from."

Here she unveiled her second card—a photograph of the Rio Hilton. Her third card was a picture of a large hotel room. And so was her fourth. "This is an example of the type of hotel they would stay in. Then we'll get them fitted out in fabulous carnival costumes."

More cards were produced. Pictures of lithe tanned women in skimpy yellow bikinis and massive spangly, feathered headdresses.

"Let me guess," Ariella said. "These are the type of costumes they'll be wearing."

Wendell's smile never wavered. "Absolutely! This will be a trip they will never forget. The coverage will be *beyond*."

I smiled encouragingly and felt it would be mean-spirited to mention that Rio was thousands of miles from the Amazon Basin and that there wouldn't be a Mardi Gras for at least another six months.

Lois was next, and as I'd suspected, her pitch was a little po-faced. She proposed to take the beauty editors—twelve of them, just like

Wendell—with Professor Redfern, to meet the indigenous people who invented Formula Twelve. "We fly to Rio, where we take a light aircraft to the jungle." She unveiled her first visual: a photo of a plane. It looked very similar to Wendell's plane. It was probably exactly the same; they probably downloaded them from the same executive jet site.

"After landing in the jungle"—a photo of thick jungle was thrust before us—"we will then trek for half a day. The editors can see the actual plants that are used to make up the product." A picture of a plant was produced for our inspection.

"Trekking in a jungle?" Ariella said. "I'm so not loving the sound of that. What if they get bitten by an anaconda and we have a freaking lawsuit on our hands?"

"Leeches, I've got a thing about leeches," Franklin said, almost to himself. "And bats. They get stuck in your hair." He shuddered.

"We'll have guides," Lois said, speedily producing a picture of a half-naked, smiling, black-toothed man.

"Nice," Franklin murmured.

"Everyone will be given appropriate clothing. Like this." Lois pointed to her gilet. "It'll be totally safe. This will be great, something very different. Those girls are so spoiled with glamour and luxury that they're blasé about everything."

I agreed with that.

"They'll feel proud that they survived the jungle—we'll make a big deal of it, we'll tell them afterward that we weren't sure they were tough enough—and they'll appreciate having connected with another culture."

It was good. Better in a way than Wendell's, although Wendell's was safer.

And then it was my turn. I took a deep breath and held up the little jar between my thumb and index finger.

"Formula Twelve." I swiveled so that everyone could see the jar. "The most revolutionary advance in skin care since Crème de la Mer. How best to promote it? Well, I'll tell you." I stopped talking, looked each person in the eye, and announced. "We do . . . nothing."

That got their attention: I'd lost it. Clearly, I'd totally lost it. Horror sat on Franklin's face: he'd allowed me to keep my pitch secret until now. Ariella would kill him. Of course, Wendell and Lois were thrilled—half of the opposition dispatched without them having to do a thing. Just before Ariella got off her chair and bitch-slapped me, I opened my mouth again.

"Well, not *quite* nothing." I twinkled. At least I tried; I'd been out of twinkling practice for a while.

"I'm thinking: a whispering campaign. Every time I have lunch with an editor, I drop hints that there's a new skin-care product coming. Something off the map. But if they ask me questions, I clam up instantly, say that it's top secret, beg them to say nothing about it to anyone . . . but that when they get it, they'll be amazed."

Everyone was watching me very carefully.

"These plants and roots that make up Formula Twelve are very rare and can't be synthesized. Therefore the product will be rare. I plan to give one jar—one tiny jar—to, say, the beauty editor at *Harper's*. The *only* beauty editor in the United States to get it. Literally. And I don't mail it. I don't even messenger it. I bring it, in person, to her. Not to her office but to some neutral venue. Almost like we're doing something illegal." Now I had them. "She gets it if she promises me a full page. And if she can't do it, I go to someone else. *Vogue,* probably. And the jar should be made out of a semiprecious stone, like amber or tourmaline. I'm thinking this tiny, heavy thing that fits in the palm of my hand. Weighty, you know? Like a little bomb of superpowered stuff."

Still no one spoke, but Ariella inclined her head in a tiny gesture of approval.

"And there's more," I said. "Read my lips. No. Celebrity. Endorsement."

Franklin blanched. Celebrity endorsement was his life.

"Nobody gets this stuff for free. If Madonna wants it, Madonna pays for it—"

"Hey, not Madonna," Franklin objected.

"Even Madonna."

"This is crazy," he muttered.

"And no advertising," I said. "Formula Twelve should be a word-of-mouth phenomenon, so that people feel they're in on a big secret. The buzz should build slowly so that by the time it finally goes on sale—in one outlet in the United States—Barneys? Bergdorf?—the waiting list is already full. There's a waiting list to go on the waiting list. Women will be waiting outside the store before it's even opened. Jars of Formula Twelve will be changing hands on the black market. Women will be frenzied, it'll be like new-season Chloé bags, to the power of ten. The most elite thing in New York. Which means the most elite thing in the world. Money can't buy it. Contacts can't swing it. You just have to wait your turn—and people will wait because it's worth waiting for."

On the other hand, everyone might just decide, fuck that, I couldn't be arsed, give me my usual order of La Prairie. It was a risk. There was no guarantee that New Yorkers would get whipped into a frenzy. If they felt they were being manipulated they would turn against the whole idea. However, now was not the time to mention this.

"Nine months later we do it all again with the serum, and six months after that the base. Then we've got the eye cream, the lip balm, the body repair, the body wash, and the exfoliator all to come."

Ariella gave another of those almost invisible nods. This was the equivalent to her jumping on her desk, shrieking, "Go, Anna!!!"

"But that's not all," I said, striving for a wry tone.

Oh yes?

"I've got an added extra." I paused, made them wait, then pointed to my scar. "As you may have noticed, I am the lucky owner of a badly scarred face."

I let them have their embarrassed little chuckle.

"In the two short weeks since I've started using Formula Twelve, there's been a huge improvement. I took a photo of my scar just before I started using Formula Twelve." It was actually after the first night, but never mind. "The difference is already visible. I believe in this product. I genuinely do." Well, I'd give it a go. "When I pitch to beauty editors, I will be visible proof that Formula Twelve is amazing."

"Yes!" Ariella was hugely impressed with this proposal. "And if the results aren't dramatic enough, we can always send you for a little plastic surgery."

To: Magiciansgirl1@yahoo.com
From: Lucky_Star_PI@yahoo.ie
Subject: Bitten arse!

Last night, got call from Colin. Said he had info that Detta Fear was in Racey's posh Dalkey pad! Delighted. Fucking delighted. Might finally nail this shagging job. Drove over there fast! But Racey's house still had electronic gate, high walls, spikes on top. How do other private investigators get in anywhere? Maybe they have handy little device to disable gate. Or they'd be mountaineers in spare time, so could loop rope around one of spikes on top of wall and they'd be in garden before you could say "into the void."

All I have going for me is am brazen. Pressed gate intercom, waited. After while, woman's voice, all crackly, says Hello?

I tried to sound desperate: Missus, I'm very sorry to trouble you, but I'm supposed to be meeting my friend at the Druid's Chair and I'm lost and desperate to go to the loo and I've tried two other houses along this road and they wouldn't let me in and I was wondering if you'd do an act of Christian charity and let me use your bathroom. I can hardly drive the car I'm so bad...

I shut up—gate was opening! Walked up drive, like entering heaven. Front door opened, shining out rectangle of light. Inside all looked warm, inviting, and hopefully full of Detta and Racey in incriminating poses. Tiny woman at front door—approx three foot six, extremely old, easily hundred and seven. Curly white hair, glasses, shapeless tweed skirt, and lopsided chunky cardigan she must have knitted herself. Racey O'Grady's housekeeper?

Her: Come in, you poor pet.

Me (with real gratitude): Oh, thank you, missus.

Her: The facility is this way.

Pointed me toward downstairs cloakroom but I wanted to be upstairs where might catch Detta and Racey in the act.

Me: Missus, I'm sorry to sound so ungrateful, but I have a "condition."

She stepped back.

Me: No, not like that, it's not contagious. It's a kind of obsessive-compulsive disorder and I can only use toilets that no one else uses.

Her (looking doubtful): Well, there's an en suite in one of the spare bedrooms that doesn't get used much. Would that do? Come on, I'll show you.

Me: There's no need for you to come upstairs on your aged legs. I'm putting you to enough trouble. Just point me in the right direction.

Her: Okay, top of the stairs, go right, second door.

Then she called after me: And don't confuse the wardrobe with the bathroom like Racey did one night when he had a few jars on him.

I went to bathroom, decided might as well make wees, seeing as was there. Then crept around and opened doors of other four bedrooms, camera at ready. Nobody in any of them. Where the hell were Racey and Detta?

The old woman was waiting at bottom of stairs: All done?

Me: All done.

Her: It's a scourge, isn't it? An unreliable bladder.

Me: It certainly is.

Her: But the incontinence pants are great. Would you like a biscuit?

Into kitchen, proper kitchen, blue Aga, rough wooden table, dried flowers hanging upside down. Top-class biscuits. Belgian. All fully chocolate coated (not just on one side), some even wrapped in goldy paper.

Me: These are top-notch biscuits.

Her: Sure, you have to have a little bit of luxury in your life, don't you? What's your name, pet?

Me: Helen.

Her: Helen what?

Me: Helen…er.

Had been just about to say "Walsh" when occurred it mightn't be smartest idea.

Me: Keller.

It was first thing that came to mind: Helen Keller.

Her: Helen Keller? That has a kind of familiar ring to it. Have we met before?

Me: I don't know.

Her: And I'm Tessie O'Grady.

Holy Jesus! Nearly choked. This was the famed Tessie O'Grady, the most dangerous woman in Dublin crime? And does that mean that Racey O'Grady lives with his mammy?

Quickly recovered meself. Doesn't do to show your weakness.

Me: Thank you for letting me use your jacks, Tessie. You're a Christian woman.

(The aged like if you call them Christian.)

Me: You're like Saint Paul on the road to Damascus, helping

our Lord put out the burning bush before it had the whole Bible burned down.

Her: No bother at all. Take a biccie for the drive.

She consulted biscuit guide: Do you like orange creams?

Me: No. No one does.

Her: Mint creams?

Me: Fine.

She put two mint creams in my pocket and patted them, narrowly missing gun, then followed me down hall. As we passed half-open door, saw Racey and Detta! Sitting close together on couch in overbright sitting room drinking tea, eating biscuits (same high quality as ones in kitchen, from brief glance I got) and watching <u>Some Mothers Do 'Ave 'Em</u>. War crime. (UK Gold does reruns.)

At door, thanked Tessie again, and as walked toward gate, she called after me, in surprisingly loud voice: Mind how you go, now. Suddenly got that feeling again. The one where if I was able to feel fear, fear would have been what I'd felt.

I looked back. Tessie was still standing in lit hall and something about way porch light glinted on her glasses made me think of Josef Mengele.

At bottom of drive, I went outside and gates began to close behind me. Waited until very last second, then slipped back in, threw down rucksack in spot where the two gates would close, to break electronic beam and keep gate open for my escape. Cunning.

Cut back across grass toward sitting room. Curtains drawn but didn't meet fully in middle—lazy—so had good gawk in. Detta and Racey sitting shoulder to shoulder, still drinking tea and still watching <u>Some Mothers Do 'Ave 'Em</u>. People have oddest tastes.

Took good few photos, then heard something behind me: growling.

I turned around. Dogs. Two. Stinky, big, black yokes with red eyes and war-crime breath. Like Claire with hangover. Tessie must have whistled them off when she let me in, but now I was "gone," they were back patrolling garden. Hate everyone and everything in life, but hate dogs more than most.

They growled softly and quick as flash, I growled back. There! Weren't expecting that, stupid, smelly yokes.

You are dogs, I said, But I have a gun. Look.

Slowly took gun out of shoulder holster to give them closer look. A gun, I said. Very dangerous. You might have seen them on telly. I've had training in a bunker with funny militia men. I will shoot you and I will kill you. Understand? Now I'm going to back away slowly, with my gun trained on you and you will stay where you are, confused but obedient.

They did. I kept circling gun on them, and repeating: Gun. To kill you with. Gun. Highly dangerous.

Kept backing away, across endless fucking lawn, finally almost at gate. That's when made my mistake: Started to run. So did dogs. Hey! They were thinking. So she was scared, after all. Let's get her.

Barking heads off, they raced across grass and were nearly on me when I found that the fucking gate had closed on rucksack, slicing everything inside in two: eyeliners, lip glosses (discovered this later). I was tugging at gate, hoping fecky thing wasn't fully closed because then was trapped with these...beasts.

But too late, one of them got me. Had half my bottom between teeth. Gate gave slightly—poor sliced rucksack had kept lock from fully closing—got myself through, pulled gate behind me, clanged it shut.

Through the bars the dogs kept barking.

I yelled: Which one of you bit me, you fuckers?

Neither fessed up, so decided to shoot them both, but in

enough trouble and thought better skedaddle because O'Gradys would hear barking and be straight out to investigate. (If they could tear themselves away from <u>Some Mothers Do 'Ave 'Em</u>.)

Arse killing me, could hardly sit down to drive, but had to. Drove to Dalkey, parked outside chipper, rang Colin.

I gave short account. Said: There's nothing to connect me to Harry Fear, but the O'Gradys will be suspicious. Also the dogs bit me in the bum. I think I need stitches. Do you know where the nearest hospital is?

Him: St. Vincent's in Booterstown. I'll come to keep you company.

By time he arrived I'd been examined.

Me: I've to get stitches and a tetanus injection.

Seeing as I couldn't sit down, he also stood. Solidarity.

Me: If I get lockjaw, Harry Fear will pay.

Him: You'll never get lockjaw.

He smiled and suddenly I thought, Cor! Really fancy him. Ding-dong!

After I'd got my arse patched back together (eight stitches; apparently if dog destroyed in fire, you could use imprint on my bum as dental records to identify him), we went back to Colin's flat. We-hay!

I stared at the screen: this wasn't funny. Helen messing around with guns and getting bitten by guard dogs was no joke—assuming it was true; and if she'd had to get stitches, I presumed it was. Fretfully, I wondered what to do; the problem was that Helen was so contrary that if I asked her to be careful, she might do the opposite. Maybe I should talk to Mum? But the way Mum was treating the whole business—offering to ring in sick for Helen, etc.—made me think she wasn't taking it terribly seriously either.

Because I couldn't fix on the best course of action, I decided to do nothing, at least for the moment. But I remained riddled with anxiety; I didn't want anything bad to happen to anyone else I loved.

• • •

G reat news!" Franklin was giddy with triumph. "Ariella picked your pitch! We're going to use Wendell's, too, for insurance, but she liked yours the best." He chuckled. "I have to say . . . at the start . . . I'm like, oh my *God,* she's wacko, what have I done! But your pitch is great. Totally great. Mommy is very happy."

H ey, Nicholas," I called down the corridor. "Thanks for your funny Buddhist goose advice. It got me the gig."

I got close enough to see him coloring with pride. "You really did nothing?"

"Not exactly. But I made a big thing of doing *almost* nothing."

"Oh, wow. That's so cool. So tell me."

"Okay." But I was distracted by his T-shirt. Today's said THE GEEK SHALL INHERIT THE EARTH.

"Nicholas, I've never seen you with the same T-shirt twice. How do you do it? Do you wear a different T-shirt with a different message every day of your life or just on Sundays?"

He grinned. "Hey, you'll just have to meet me during the week to find out!"

The mood turned suddenly awkward, his grin faded to nothing, and a blush inched its way up his face.

"Oh, wow; sorry, Anna." He bowed his tomato-colored head. "Flirting with you. Totally inappropriate."

"Were you? Look, don't worry . . ."

"I mean, you and Mitch..."

"What! Mitch? Oh my God, no, Nicholas. It's not like that with Mitch. Not at all!"

*D*o you mind me spending so much time with Mitch? I mean, you know it's just as friends, don't you? You know we're just helping each other?

I'd been so thrown by Nicholas's comment that, after the channeling, I told Mitch I couldn't go on today's outing. I felt filthy with guilt and I couldn't escape fast enough; I set off walking in the direction of home. Though I'd have preferred not to face it, I saw how easy it would be to get the wrong idea about him and me. Why else had I been so mortified when Ornesto saw us together at the quiz? And why hadn't I told Rachel or Jacqui about him? I mean, *I* knew the truth and Mitch knew the truth—but did Aidan?

Aidan, if you mind, just show me and I'll never see him again. Give me some sort of sign. Anything at all. Okay, I'll make it easy for you—I'm going to keep walking down this street, and if you're angry about Mitch, how about...how about...making a flowerpot fall from a window ledge right into my path. I'd prefer if it didn't actually land on me, but if that's what you need to do...

I walked and walked and nothing happened and I wondered if I'd been too specific. Maybe I shouldn't have said "flowerpot." Maybe I should have just said "something." Make "something" fall into my path.

Okay. Anything at all. Not just a flowerpot.

But nothing landed on or near me and I was hot and tired and eventually I hailed a cab. The driver, a young Indian man, was on his mobile. I gave my address and slumped back into the seat and suddenly I heard, "You're a filthy, dirty man and I'm going to punish you."

It was the driver, talking into his phone. I sat up straight, keen to eavesdrop.

"Pull down your pants, you bad, bad man. I am going to punish you!"

"Excuse me, sir, who are you talking to?"

He turned around quickly, raised a finger to his lips, leaving a grand total of none on the steering wheel, then he went back to his conversation. "I am going to beat you for being so bad. Yes, beat you, you bad, bad man. Beat you on the butt with the cane. On the butt with the cane. Because you're bad, bad, dirty and bad!"

Oh, Aidan, you have *sent me a sign. A nine-out-of-ten taxi driver! So you don't mind about Mitch!*

"Hard, hard is how I will beat you. Bend over and I will count the strokes. Swish, one! Swish, two! Swish, three! Swish, four! Swish, five! Swish, SIX!"

Swish six seemed to bring things to a head: a cry came from inside the phone, then all went quiet for a while, until the driver said, "Thank you, sir. It is my pleasure, sir. Please call again."

He hung up, and bursting with curiosity, I asked, "What was that all about?"

"I am a sex worker." He said this quite proudly.

"You are?"

"Yes. Men pay me to abuse them. But I must also drive the cab. I have a large family back in Punjab. I send—" The chirp of his phone interrupted; he checked the caller and slightly wearily answered, "Good day, young master Thomas. What have you been doing? Have you been bad? How bad?"

To: Magiciansgirl1@yahoo.com
From: Thewalshes1@eircom.net
Subject: The woman and her dog

Dear Anna,
She has "upped the auntie." (I've never understood that phrase. Is it meant to be vulgar? Let me know as I will not say it at bridge if it's vulgar. I will simply say she has "raised her game.") More number twos.

Helen stood in it on her way home, all "loved up" (disgusting phrase) from sleeping with that Colin fellow, and she went mentalist. Effing and blinding out by the gate. "Come on," sez she. "We're going to see the old boot."

There and then we drove over. I rang the bell and Zoe started to bark, then suddenly Zoe stopped barking. The old woman must have seen us through some spy hole and decided to pretend she wasn't in. It's Zoe I feel for. Locked away wearing a gag. A sock, or maybe a "bandanna." She could suffocate that way. Helen shouted through the letter box, "We'll be back, you mad old boot. I'm one of Ireland's premeer private investigators, you know."

Ireland's, no less! I said nothing, but the night with Colin had obviously gone to her head.

Your loving mother,

Mum

73

J oey in love was compelling viewing. A dinner had been organized for no other reason than everyone wanted to see the unlikely combination of Jacqui and Joey together.

It wasn't just for the usual suspects of Rachel, Luke, me, Shake, etc., but a whole swath of second-tier Real Men who held Joey in high regard. Not to mention Leon and Dana, Nell and Nell's strange friend, and some people from Jacqui's work. Even some people from *my* work asked to come: Teenie (who had slept with Joey ages ago) and Brooke—Brooke *Edison.*

In all, twenty-three of us came along to Haiku on the Lower East Side one Thursday night. (We'd had to keep ringing the restaurant to increase the table size.)

Joey and Jacqui were twined around each other in the center of a long booth and there was a bit of unseemly jostling from the rest of us to get the seats nearest to them. The places with the highest premium were the ones directly opposite the lovers.

"Check out Joey's 'in love' face," Teenie whispered.

It was strange: Joey hadn't started smiling or anything—he still looked narky—but when he was tracing the curve of Jacqui's face with his finger, or staring into her eyes, his narkiness looked quite nice. Quite sexy, actually. Intense, Heathcliffy, although his hair wasn't dark enough. It might be if he stopped using Sun-In (he denied it vigorously but we all knew), but he was very attached to his goldeny-brown lowlights.

"This is going to be good," Teenie said with glee.

And it was. All through the dinner, Joey and Jacqui were constantly at each other, whispering and giggling and feeding each other.

The only person who wasn't mesmerized was Gaz and that was presumably because, night after night, he got a ringside seat in his own apartment. He wandered among us, bearing a sinister-looking little leather pouch; I knew what was in there.

"Anna," he said, "I can help with your grief. I'm learning acupuncture!" He whipped open the pouch to display a load of needles inside. "I know which acupoints will give you relief."

"That's lovely. Thank you."

"You mean you'll let me do it?!"

"What? Now? Oh God, no, Gaz, not now. We're in a public place. I can't be sitting in a restaurant with needles sticking out of me. Even if we are on the Lower East Side."

"Oh. I thought you meant... Well, some other time? Sometime soon?"

"Mmm." I'd heard what had happened to Luke. He'd been feeling fine until Gaz had offered to "increase his endorphins." The next thing, Luke was curled in a fetal position on the bathroom floor, unable to decide whether he was going to puke or to faint.

"I also do cupping," Gaz said. "Another Chinese remedy. I heat up little cups and suction them to your back. It draws out all kinds of toxins."

Yes, I knew about that, too. I also knew about how he'd put his flaming cups too close to Rachel and Luke's window and managed to set their curtains on fire.

"Thanks, Gaz, but—" I indicated Jacqui and Joey. "I can't concentrate on anything else at the moment."

Actually, they looked as if they were planning to leave.

They were! They were standing up and Joey was throwing down a couple of twenties and they were "excuse me, excuse me"ing their way out.

"Going home early to have sex, without caring how rude it looks." Brooke Edison sighed dreamily. "Not even leaving enough money to cover their share of the bill because they're so in love, they assume the rest of the world is happy to cover them. Which we totally are."

"It's nice of them to leave early," Teenie said, "Because now we can talk about them. So what's everybody's take?"

Reactions were mixed. You could tell the second-tier Real Men were confused because Jacqui had no breasts. But at least she was blond.

Almost everyone else, however, was charmed.

"It's adorable." Brooke clasped her hands, her eyes ashine. "True love can happen with anyone. Like, who says he has to work on Wall Street! He could be, like, just a plumber, or like a construction worker." Her gaze fastened on Shake, on his tight, tight jeans and his grand head of hair, and took on a sudden, acquisitive gleam.

74

The arrival of fantastic news!!!

To: Magiciansgirl1@yahoo.com
From: Psychic_Productions@yahoo.com
Re: Neris Hemming

Your phone interview with Neris Hemming is scheduled for 8:30 A.M. on Wednesday sixth of October. The number to call will be sent to you closer to the date. The cost for Ms. Hemming's time is $2,500. Please forward your credit-card details. Also note that you must not call the number until 8:30 A.M. and that you must finish exactly at nine.

I rang Mitch to tell him. I was so excited. In just over two weeks' time I'd be talking to Aidan.

I couldn't wait. I couldn't wait. I couldn't wait.

75

Franklin leaned over my desk, flicked a furtive look at Lauryn, and said, "Anna, we've finally got a confirmation date from Devereaux for the Formula Twelve pitch."

He smiled happily and suddenly, with a cold trickle down my spine, I knew what was going to happen. Even before he spoke the words, I knew exactly what he was going to say. "Wednesday of next week. October sixth. Nine A.M."

Electric pains shot up and down my legs. Wednesday the sixth of October was the morning of my conversation with Neris Hemming. This was like a cosmic joke.

I couldn't be at the pitch. I had to tell him. But I was afraid. *Say it, go on, say it.*

"I'm sorry, Franklin." My voice sounded shaky. "It won't be possible for me to be there. I have an appointment."

His eyes turned to chips of ice. What kind of appointment did I have that could be more important than this?

"It's, um, medical."

"So reschedule." Franklin acted as if the matter was now closed.

I cleared my throat. "It's urgent."

He frowned, almost in curiosity. First her husband dies, now she needs urgent medical attention. How much bad luck does this loser attract?

"We need you at this pitch," Franklin said.

"I can be here by nine-thirty."

"We need you at this pitch," Franklin repeated.

"Maybe even nine-fifteen if the traffic is good." Not a chance.

"I don't think you're hearing me. We need you at this pitch." Then he turned his back on me and walked away.

I couldn't concentrate on work, so, with trembling hands, I checked my e-mails to see if there was anything nice. Helen had received a death threat.

To: Magiciansgirl1@yahoo.com
From: Lucky_Star_PI@yahoo.ie
Subject: Death threat

Oh God, loads has happened. This morning, Colin came to my office to bring me to Harry Fear to give him photos of Detta and Racey snuggled up together on couch drinking tea and eating top-notch biscuits.

Next thing, an almighty bang! Gunshot! Eardrum still twanging from it. My window fell in on my desk, glass everyplace. Someone had just tried to shoot me! Bloody nerve!

Colin yelled: Get down. Then legged it out to see what was going on.

But I could hear tires screeching away and he was back in a second.

Him: They're gone. Looked like some of Racey's lads.

He knelt down on floor, in the splinters, cradled me to him, and said: It's okay, baby.

Me (pulling self away. Morto): What the eff are you at?

Him: Comforting you.

Me: Get off. I don't like that sort of stuff. At all. I don't need comforting.

Him: Cup of tea, even?

Me: No. No. Nothing.

Jaysus!

Through space where window used to be saw deputation of angry mothers, in leggings and anoraks and ring of fag smoke like that planet, heading down from the flats. Quick off the mark round here.

Chief mother, name of Josetta, said: Ah, Helen, this is a respectable neighborhood.

Me: No, it's not.

Her: Okay, it's not. But guns being fired at ten-thirty in the morning? That's not on.

Me: Sorry. The next time someone tries to kill me I'll ask them to wait until after lunch.

Her: Do that. Good girl.

They went away.

Me: Janey, I've just had an attempt on my life.

Him: Nah. Just a warning shot across the bows.

Me: Well, the next time they'll kill me.

Him: That's not how it works. They'll do something, like, say, kill your dog. There's a strict protocol to be followed here.

Me: But I don't have a dog. I hate all living creatures.

Him: Well, maybe they'll burn out your car—you like your car, don't you?

Me (nodding): So it'll be a while before they really try to kill me.

Him: Yeah, you've loads of time.

This had gone too far. I rattled off a reply to Helen.

To: Lucky_Star_PI@yahoo.ie
From: Magiciansgirl1@yahoo.com
Subject: Death threat

Helen, this isn't funny anymore. If someone really tried to shoot you—and I can't imagine even you lying about something as serious as that—you've got to stop all this. Right now!
Anna

With shaking fingers, I sent it off, then e-mailed Neris Hemming's people to see if my interview with Neris could be rejigged to the following day. Or the previous day. Or earlier that same day. Or later. Anytime other than 8:30 A.M. on October 6. But nothing doing. A speedy reply told me that if I missed this window, I'd have to go to the back of the queue and wait the mandatory ten to twelve weeks before the next appointment became available.

And I couldn't! I just couldn't! I was so desperate to talk to Aidan and I'd waited so long, been so patient.

But if I didn't make the pitch, I'd be sacked. There was no doubt about it. But couldn't I always get another job? Maybe not, actually. Especially if potential employers found out why I'd been sacked—not showing up for the most important pitch the company had ever done? And my job was pivotal to me. I needed it; it kept me going. It gave me a reason to get up in the morning and it took my mind off things.

Not to mention that I got paid for it, which was vital, as I was up to my eyes in debt. I'd moved two and a half grand into a separate account as soon as I'd heard from Neris Hemming's people, so at least that was safe. Other than that, I was just making the minimum card payments every month. I'd done a very good job of shutting out the fear but the idea of being unemployed brought it all rushing in. I'd read somewhere that the average New Yorker was just two paychecks away from the street. For as long as I was earning money I could keep the show on the road, but even a couple of wageless weeks could mean everything collapsing. I'd probably have to give up the apartment, I might even have to go back to Ireland. And I couldn't do that, I had to be in New York to be near Aidan. I *had* to do this pitch.

Then I got indignant: What if I really was seriously sick? What if I had cancer and was due my first session of lifesaving radiation treatment the morning of the pitch to Devereaux? Wasn't Franklin being a little inhumane? Hadn't this whole work ethic thing gone too far?

I tried to think of other ways around the dilemma: I could call Neris on my cell phone from a coffee shop near work, then be at work just after nine. Indeed, I could even try to make the call from my desk. Except I couldn't; I wouldn't be able to properly savor my conversation with Aidan.

Things clicked into place; I'd made my decision. Not that there had ever really been any doubt. I would talk to Neris and blow off the pitch.

I made my way to Franklin's desk.

"Can I have a word?"

Coldly, he nodded.

"Franklin, I can't be at the pitch. But someone else could do mine. Lauryn could."

Exasperated, he said, "We need *you*, you're the one with the scar. Lauryn hasn't got a scar." He was silent for a moment, and I'm sure he was considering if he *could* scar Lauryn. He must have decided that, darn, he couldn't because he asked, "What's got you so sick?"

"It's, um, gynecological." I thought it would be safe saying that to him, what with him being a man. It had always worked in other jobs— telling a man boss I had period pains, when I just wanted the afternoon off to go shopping. Usually they couldn't get rid of me quick enough— you could see the terror written all over them: *Just don't say the word* menstruating. Instead Franklin leaped up from behind his desk, grabbed me, and wove speedily through the desks.

"Where are we going?"

"To see Mommy."

Shite, shite, shite, shite, shite.

"She says she can't make the pitch," Franklin said, very loudly. "She says she's got a medical appointment. She says it's gynecological."

"Gynecological?" Ariella said. "She's having an abortion?" She looked at me in powder-blue shoulder-padded fury. "You're missing my pitch to Formula Twelve for a lousy abortion?"

"No. Oh my God, no, not at all." I was terrified at what I'd got myself into, terrified by her rage, terrified by my lies, terrified at what I'd unleashed.

And I'd have to come up with more lies. And quickly.

"It's um, my, cervix."

"Is it cancer?" She tilted her head inquiringly and held my look for a long, long moment. "Do you have cancer?" The message was clear: if I had cancer, she'd allow me to miss the pitch. Nothing less would do. But I couldn't bring myself to say it.

"Precancerous," I choked out, dying with shame at what I was saying.

Jacqui had had a precancerous situation in her cervix a couple of years back. At the time we'd all cried, convinced she was going to die, but after the tiniest little operation that didn't even involve a *local* anesthetic, she was fully restored to health.

Suddenly Ariella went very calm. Scary calm. Her voice dropped to her sore-throat whisper.

"Anna, have I not been good to you?"

I felt sick. "Of course, Arie—"

But there was no stopping her. I'd have to sit through the whole speech.

"Have I not taken care of you? Put clothes on your back? When we were representing Fabrice & Vivien before the ungrateful fucks went elsewhere? Do I not put makeup on your face? Food in your mouth in the finest restaurants in town? Did I not keep your job open for you when your husband bought the farm? Took you back although you have a scar on your face that would scare even Dr. De Groot?"

As she said the final, damning line, I said it, too, in my head.

And this is how you repay me?

To: Magiciansgirl1@yahoo.com
From: Lucky_Star_PI@yahoo.ie
Subject: Off the case!

All right, all right, keep your pants on! Just 'cos Aidan died doesn't mean rest of us will. Anyway, showed Harry the photos of Detta drinking tea with Racey and he said: Ah, there's no sexual chemistry there at all. Nothing going on there, nothing. No, the leak must be coming from somewhere else. Colin, back to the drawing board. Miss Walsh, I'm happy to say you can go now.

Me: Thanks be to Christ. Antipathy is mutual. (Liked saying that.) Bye, Colin, nice working with you, stay in touch.

Gave him little smile, he looked quite bereft.

So there you are, all over, not shot, nothing to worry about, you big wussy wuss-girl.

It was a relief to know that she wasn't putting herself in danger any longer. (If she ever had been.) Funnily enough, now that it was over, I had to admit that I was slightly curious—had Detta *really* been giving Harry's secrets to Racey? It was strange because it felt more like a soap opera than real life, but unlike a soap opera, it had come to an abrupt end.

Over the next two weeks, Wendell and I were put through myriad run-throughs of the pitch so that we were letter-perfect. Ariella and Franklin cross-examined us, pretending to be the Devereaux executives. They flung queries on costings, timings, customer profile, competitors—every conceivable question we might be asked. Then some of the other senior girls were brought in to see if any questions had been left unasked, so there would be no surprises on the big day.

I went along with it even though I knew I wouldn't be there.

But I'd co-opted Teenie; we'd gone for lunch and I'd sworn her to secrecy.

"The pitch on Wednesday? I can't make it."

"Wha—?"

"You do my pitch. Cover yourself in glory."

"But, oh my God! I mean, like, you can't be... Ariella will go *crazy*."

"Yes, and then she'll need someone to do my pitch. Make sure it's you. Do not let Lauryn muscle in on this."

To: Magiciansgirl1@yahoo.com
From: Thewalshes1@eircom.net
Subject: All is revealed

Dear Anna,
You'll never guess who Nan O'Shea is. Go on, have a go. You'll never get it. I'll give you a hint. It is all your father's fault. Something I should have known all along. Go on, guess. I'm not going to tell you yet. I want you to have a good long guess at it. Wait'll you hear, though—you'll never believe it!
Your loving mother,
Mum

On the eve of the pitch, Wendell and I were put through our paces one final time. At about six-thirty, Ariella called it a day.

"Okay, that's enough," she said. "Let's keep it fresh."

"See you tomorrow, Anna," Franklin said meaningfully.

"Bright and early," I said.

I hadn't decided if I would come in after the phone call with Neris, or if I would simply never come back.

Just in case, I took my framed photo of Aidan off my desk, put it in my bag, and said good-bye to Teenie and Brooke.

It felt like the night before the most important day of my life. I couldn't settle to anything. I was excited, but also anxious.

Aidan, what if you don't come through? How will I cope? Where can I go from there?

When the phone rang I jumped. It was Kevin; I let the machine pick up. "Anna," he said. "I gotta talk to you, this is urgent, urgent, urgent. Call me."

I barely registered it.

Sometime later—I had no idea how long—my buzzer went. I ignored it but it rang again. On the third go, I answered. Whoever was out there wanted to talk to me pretty badly.

It was Jacqui. "You'll never guess," she said.

"So tell me."

"I'm pregnant."

I stared at her and she stared back at me. "What?" she said.

"What what?"

"You looked weird."

I'd felt weird. My womb had sort of twanged.

"Are you jealous?" she asked. Just like that.

"Yes," I said. Just like that.

"I'm sorry. And I don't even want to be effing pregnant. Isn't life shit?"

"Yes. And isn't this a bit fast? You're only barely in love."

"Do you know when it happened? The first night. The first effing night! When you were in the Hamptons. Can you believe it? Condom burst, I meant to get the morning-after, but we spent the next three days in bed and I forgot about it and then it was too late. I'm only six weeks' pregnant but they count from your last period, so I'm officially eight weeks."

"Does Narky Joey know?"

She shook her head. "No, and when I tell him, he'll break up with me."

"But he's mad about you."

She shook her head. "Dopamine. Teenie explained it to me at your birthday—she knows a lot, that girl—when men think they're in love, it's only because their brain is producing too much dopamine. It usually goes away after the first year, which explains a lot. But if I tell him I'm pregnant, I bet it'll go away immediately."

"Why would it?"

"Narky Joey doesn't want responsibility."

"But..."

"It's too soon. We barely know each other. Maybe if it had happened in six months' time we might have been secure enough to take it, but it's too soon."

"Talk to him about it, it might all be okay."

"Maybe."

I made myself say it, but curiously I didn't want to. "You do have other options."

"I know. I've been thinking." Pause. "Being pregnant isn't the horrible disaster it would have been five years ago, or even three years. Back then, I'd no security, I hadn't a bean, and I'd definitely have had a termination. But now...I have an apartment, I have a well-paid job—it's not *their* fault that I can't live within my means—and I sort of like the idea of having a baby round the place."

"Um...Jacqui, having a baby is a huge life-changing event. It's not like getting a Labradoodle. You mightn't even be able to *do* your well-paid job. Are you sure you've really thought this through?"

"Oh yeah! It'll cry a lot, I'll be skint." She paused, "Skint*er;* I'll look like a hag, my nanny will steal from me, but it'll be fun! Let's hope I get a girl baby, their clothes are much nicer."

Then she burst into tears.

"Thank God," I said. "That's the first normal thing you've done."

After she left, I tried but never got properly to sleep. I just skimmed the surface and was fully awake again by 5 A.M. I was also in worse pain than usual—something to do with my heightened emotional state? I watched the clock count down to eight-thirty, when I would finally get to talk to Aidan. My stomach churned and I felt tingly and sick. To pass the time, I got my e-mails.

To: Magiciansgirl1@yahoo.com
From: Lucky_Star_PI@yahoo.ie
Subject: Full frontals

You're not going to believe what's happened. This morning in post, got A-4 envelope, full of photos of Racey and Detta riding the arse off each other. Nothing left to imagination—mickeys and full frontals and the whole war-crime business. You'd need strong stomach.

So they were at it all along! Harry was right, I was wrong. But why is someone sending me pictures of them, especially now I'm off case?

Rang Colin. Asked him what should I do?

Let's discuss it, he says. In bed.

Oo-er, don't mind if I do, missus!

To: Magiciansgirl1@yahoo.com
From: Thewalshes1@eircom.net
Subject: All is revealed

Dear Anna,

I know you have a fair bit on your mind at the minute but I must admit I am slightly hurt that you haven't seen fit to reply to me with your guesses. I know that our little "drama" here isn't anything as exciting as the things that go on in New York city but I thought you might humor us a bit. So go on, guess who Nan O'Shea is. Go on, try! You'll never guess!
Your loving mother,
Mum

P.S. If you don't "guess," I will be very annoyed.

To get her off my back, I dashed off an absentminded reply.

To: Thewalshes1@eircom.net
From: Magiciansgirl1@yahoo.com
Subject: Re: All is revealed

I don't know. I give up. Is she an old girlfriend of Dad's?

I'd waited so long to talk to Aidan that I'd started to believe that eight-thirty would never come. But it did. Light-headed, I looked at the two hands on the clock; they were in the magic formation, the time had finally arrived. I picked up the phone and punched the numbers.

It rang four times, then a woman's voice said hello and I was shaking so much I could hardly speak to say, "Hello, is that Neris?"

"Yeees?" Said cautiously.

"Hello, it's me, Anna Walsh, I'm calling from New York for my reading."

"Um." She sounded perplexed. "Do you have an appointment?"

"Yes! Yes! Of course I do! I've paid and everything. I can give you the name of the person who set this up."

"Oh, I'm sorry, honey, I've got construction workers in here, running all over the place. I told the office. No way can I concentrate on a reading."

Shock robbed me of speech. This couldn't be happening. My call waiting started clicking. I ignored it.

"You mean you're not going to channel for me?"

"Not right now, honey."

"But we have an appointment. I've been desperate for this day to come—"

"I know, honey. Call the office. Let's reschedule."

"But I had to wait three months for this appointment and—"

"I'll tell them to prioritize you."

"There's no chance we could do something quick just now, is there?"

"No, there sure is not." Her breezy tone stayed breezy but with a steely addition. "Call the office. Y'all take care now."

And she was gone.

78

I stared at the phone, then a tangle of outrage, disappointment, and thwarted hope erupted together. Unlike the occasional surges of terrible anger, which usually departed after one snarky sentence, I was overwhelmed by an entire reservoir of white-hot fury—not with Neris but with Aidan.

"Why won't you talk to me?" I screeched. "Why are you blocking me at every fucking turn? I've given you every fucking opportunity." I was pulling at my hair. "And why did you have to die? You should have tried harder, you lazy, useless BASTARD. If you'd loved me enough, you'd have stayed alive, you'd have held on to your life. You fucking useless PRICK, just giving in like that."

I hit redial and got the engaged tone and that just made me worse. This was no accident.

"Why won't you talk to me?" I shrieked. "You're too fucking CHICKEN, that's why! You had a CHOICE, you could have STAYED, but you didn't care about me enough, you didn't love me enough, you were more concerned with YOURSELF."

Eventually I ran out of words, and over and over again, I shrieked into my hands, tearing my throat raw as I tried to get the rage out of me.

I couldn't stay in the apartment; it was too small to contain my feelings. In a haze of red, I made for the door. Passing the computer, I saw that a new e-mail had arrived. I didn't know what I was hoping for—a new appointment time with Neris, maybe?—but it was only from Helen.

To: Magiciansgirl1@yahoo.com
From: Lucky_Star_PI@yahoo.ie
Subject: Full frontals

Showed photos to Harry. Colin said he had right to know. Harry was broken man. Vay funny. Then he said to Colin: I'm going out to Dalkey to kill Racey O'Grady. I'll be back in a couple of hours, depending on traffic. You hold the fort.

I ran out of the apartment and stood on the street and found I had nowhere to go except work. I didn't give a damn about the pitch, but, as is the way with these things, I got a cab immediately, there was almost no traffic, and every light was green. I'd never got to work so quickly in my life.

I took my time ambling from the lift to my desk, where Franklin, Teenie, and Lauryn were in a head-to-head.

"...flaky bitch," Lauryn was saying. "We should never have let her come back after her husband..."

Franklin was the color of chalk. Then he turned and saw me and I almost laughed when I saw his expression. He was too relieved to be angry. "You're here."

"Yeah. Teenie, I'm so sorry to mess you around like this."

"No way," she said. "It's your pitch, it's your baby." She gave me a little kiss. "Way to go."

79

They're not here yet," Franklin said breathlessly, taking me by the arm and hurrying me to the boardroom.

"Here she is!" Triumphantly, he displayed me to Ariella, who said, "Cutting it a little fine, no?"

"I told you, I had an appointment."

Glances were exchanged: What was going on with me? But then word came that the Devereaux people were on their way up and everyone stapled on their happy faces.

Wendell—in her yellow Big Bird rig-out—went first and gave a pretty dazzling display. Then it was my turn. I watched myself do my pitch, almost as if I was standing outside of my body; I was full of adrenaline, my voice was louder than usual, and I laughed a little too bitterly when I pointed out my scar, but nothing else untoward happened.

I answered their tricky questions with perfect ease—I was letter-perfect after the countless hours of practice. Then it was all over and hands were being shook and they were gone.

As soon as the elevator doors closed behind them, I walked out of the boardroom, leaving Ariella and Franklin staring after me in bewilderment.

Back at my desk, Teenie said, "How'dit go?"

"She couldn't do it. She had the contractors in."

"Excuse me?"

"Oh, the pitch. Fine, fine."

"Are you okay?"

"Fine."

"Right. Messages for you. Jacqui rang. She's breaking the news to Narky Joey tonight. Does she have chlamydia?"

"No. I'll tell you when Narky Joey knows."

"'Kay. Then Kevin rang. You know Kevin, Aidan's brother?"

I nodded wearily.

"You've gotta call him, like, now. He said it was way urgent."

"What kind of urgent?"

"It's okay. No one's dead. I asked him. So just regular urgent, I guess."

That had probably been Kevin on my call waiting this morning. With sudden curiosity, I switched on my cell phone; there were two messages from Kevin.

Why did he want me to call him? Why was it urgent? And all at once, I knew why. Kevin wanted to talk to me for the very same reason that Aidan wouldn't.

Uneasiness, which had existed, wraithlike, at the back of my mind for months, abruptly moved to the forefront.

I'd hoped this would never happen. I'd even managed to convince myself that it wouldn't. But whatever this was, it was coming to a head; I was powerless to stop it.

I had to talk to Leon.

I called him at work. "Leon, can I see you?"

"Great! How's Friday sound? There's a Sri Lankan restau—"

"No, Leon. I need to see you now."

"But it's ten-thirty. I'm at work."

"Fake something. A meeting. A sore tooth. You're important. Just for an hour, Leon. Please."

"And what about Dana?"

"It's not that kind of meeting, Leon. Can you be in Dom's Diner in twenty?"

"Okay."

I announced to the desks around me, "I'm going out in ten minutes, I'm taking an early lunch."

Lauryn didn't even answer. She didn't care. I'd messed up so badly by almost missing the pitch that I was probably going to be sacked anyway.

To: Magiciansgirl1@yahoo.com
From: Thewalshes1@eircom.net
Subject: All is revealed

Dear Anna,

How in God's name did you know?! Was it a lucky guess? Do you have a sixth sense? Or did Helen tell you? Yes, Nan O'Shea is the woman your father "dumped" for me. She has carried a grudge all these years. Isn't it a gas? Who would have thought that someone would feel so strongly about your father?

It all came out when I made your father come over with me to her house to "front her out." We rang the bell and the front door was opened very "forcefully," then your woman spots your father and "fell to pieces."

She said, "Jack?" And he said, "Nan?" And I said, "You know this woman?"

Your father said, "What's going on, Nan?" And she said, "I'm sorry, Jack."

I said, "You'd bloody well want to be, you raving lunatic," and your father said, "Sshh, sshh, she's upset."

She brought us in for a cup of tea and your father was all

chat, sitting down and accepting Hobnobs but I remained "standoffish." I am slower to forgive.

Anyway, it all "came out." She had been heartbroken when your father "kicked her to the curb" and had never forgotten him. As Rachel would say, she has "never moved on." (A flogging offense, to hear Rachel talk about it, it is nice that the child has had an education but sometimes...anyway, don't mind me getting on my "hobbyhorse.")

I asked your father why he hadn't recognized the name and he said he didn't know. Then I asked Nan O'Shea why she had started pestering us only recently and warned her not to say that she didn't know either. She said she had lived "away" for many years. Up close she has the look of an off-duty nun, like she might have joined the missions, badgering those misfortunate Africans, but it turned out that she has been living in Cork, working for the ESB, since 1962. She has recently "retired" and moved back to Dublin. (I was quite shocked as I had thought she was much older than me.)

Your father was all palsy-walsy, and when we were leaving Nan O'Shea said. "Maybe you'll drop in for a cup of tea once in a while, Jack."

"No," I said. "He certainly won't. Come on, Jack, home."

So that's the end of that. How are things with you? Anything strange at all?
Your loving mother,
Mum

80

Leon was already there. I slid into the brown vinyl booth opposite him and said, "Leon, I know this is hard for you, and if you have to cry, feel free. I'm going to ask you some questions and I'm begging you to be honest with me. Even if you think you're going to hurt me."

He nodded anxiously. But that was no indication. He did everything anxiously.

"The night that Aidan died, he was about to tell me something. Something important."

"What was it?"

"I don't know. He died, remember?"

"Sorry, I thought you meant . . . So how do you know he was going to tell you big stuff?"

"He'd booked a table for us at Tamarind."

"What's funny about that? Tamarind is an 'exquisite spot for Brahmins and their bankers.' Direct quote from *Zagat*."

"Leon, it's funny because Aidan and I hardly ever went for dinner, just the two of us. We had takeout at home, or went out with you and Dana, or Rachel and Luke, or whoever. And we'd already been for a fancy romantic dinner, two nights before, because it was Valentine's night, remember?"

"Okay."

"And looking back, something had upset him. He'd had a call on his cell—he said it was work, but I don't think it was because he was very subdued after it, like he'd had the stuffing knocked out of him."

"Work stuff can do that to a guy."

"I don't know, Leon, it seemed bigger than that, and he stayed subdued and sort of ... distant. I mean, he tried his best, especially on Valentine's night, but those things are so cheesy and stilted anyway ... Anyway, the next thing is he'd booked a table at Tamarind, and I said I didn't understand why we were going out for dinner again so soon, but he said please, so I said okay."

"Jeez, I wish Dana was more like you."

"I'm not. I wasn't usually like that, but I remember thinking that if it was important to him that we go out to talk—because obviously we weren't just going for the food"—I stopped Leon before he got going—"*no matter how nice it is*—then I would do it."

"But you never got there."

"No. And I sort of forgot about it. I mean, not really. Not always. But ... there was too much other stuff going on. Leon, you were his best friend. Did Aidan love me?"

"He would have taken a bullet for you." Stricken silence. "Sorry, wrong thing to say. He was crazy about you. Me and Dana, we knew him and Janie together, but you and him were different. The real thing."

"Okay, here comes the tough question. Are you ready?"

Fearful nod.

"At the time that he died, was Aidan cheating on me?"

Leon looked appalled. "No way!"

"But how do you know? Would he have told you?"

"Absolutely. He had that guilt thing, always felt the need to confess."

Now, that was true. He'd probably have confessed to *me*, never mind Leon.

"And I'd have guessed it anyhow," Leon said. "We were tight, you know. He was my best buddy." His voice broke. "The best buddy a guy could have."

Automatically, I reached into my bag and passed him a tissue.

Leon spread the tissue over his face and choked into it while I asked myself if I believed him. Yes, I decided. I believed him. So what was going on?

· · ·

But when I got back to the office, there was a series of frantic messages from Kevin on my voice mail, the last one saying, "I'm coming to see you in New York tomorrow morning. I can't get there before then. Anna, this is big stuff. If anyone calls you, any woman you don't know, don't talk to her, Anna, don't talk to her until I get there."

Oh my God. My knees were trembly and I sank onto my chair. Leon was wrong and I'd been right. This was what I'd been waiting for.

I felt sick. But calm. It was out of my hands now.

I could have rung Kevin and found out everything, but I didn't want to. I knew anyway. And I needed a little longer to remember my life with Aidan the way I'd thought it had been.

Anna. Anna!" I was brought back to the present by Franklin. Looking at me oddly.

"Ariella's office, right now."

"O-kay." I trailed along slowly. I didn't give a shite.

"Close the door," Ariella said.

"O-kay."

I sat down without Ariella telling me to. She flashed another of those "what the fuck?" looks at Franklin, who was standing behind me.

Go on then, sack me. Get on with it.

"Yeah." Ariella cleared her throat. "Anna, we have some news for you."

"I don't doubt it."

Another perplexed exchange.

"Devereaux is going with our pitch."

"Hey, that's just great," I said superperkily. "Wendell's or mine?"

"Yours."

"But you want to fire me. So fire me."

"We can't fire you. They loved you. The head guy, Leonard Daly, thought you were, I quote, 'a great kid, very courageous' and a natural to do a whispering campaign. He said you had believability."

"That's too bad."

"Why? You're not quitting!"

I thought about it. "Not if you don't want me to. Do you?"

Go on, say it.

"No."

"No what?"

"No, we don't want you to quit."

"Ten grand more, two assistants, and charcoal suits. Take it or leave it."

Ariella swallowed. "Okay to the money, okay to the assistants, but I can't green-light charcoal suits. Formula Twelve is Brazilian, we need carnival colors."

"Charcoal suits or I'm gone."

"Orange."

"Charcoal."

"Orange."

"Charcoal."

"Okay, charcoal."

It was an interesting lesson in power. The only time you truly have it is when you genuinely don't care whether you have it or not.

"Right," I said. "I'm giving myself the rest of the day off."

• • •

It was only when I got home that I remembed about Helen. In her last e-mail her situation had sounded a little hairy but I hadn't really taken it in at the time.

To: Lucky_Star_PI@yahoo.ie
From: Magiciansgirl1@yahoo.com
Subject: Are you okay?

What's happening?

A short time later, I got a reply.

To: Magiciansgirl1@yahoo.com
From: Lucky_Star_PI@yahoo.ie
Subject: Denooming!

Back at my office a note had been shoved under door. It said, "Do you want to know who sent the nudie pictures of Detta and Racey? Do you want to know what's really going on?"
'Course bloody well did!

It said to show up tonight, 10 P.M., at address on docks. Looked it up on map: it was a warehouse. Was prepared to bet was a *deserted* warehouse. Why can't denooming ever take place in nice comfortable bar?

Turned on radio. Made the news! (Sort of.) Shooting incident in Dalkey was main story. A man in his fifties (Harry Big) had "shot several times at another man" (Racey). Target had escaped injury, and although police quickly arrived on scene, gunman had "evaded capture." Police warning people "not to approach him."

This was utterly ridiculous. She was out of her mind to be involved in all of this; she could end up getting killed.

To: Lucky_Star_PI@yahoo.ie
From: Magiciansgirl1@yahoo.com
Subject: Denooming!

Helen, do NOT go to that warehouse place. You are way out of your depth. I want you to promise me you won't go. You have to do whatever I ask because my husband died.
Anna

To: Magiciansgirl1@yahoo.com
From: Lucky_Star_PI@yahoo.ie
Subject: Denooming!

Ah, feck.
    I promise.

To: Lucky_Star_PI@yahoo.ie
From: Magiciansgirl1@yahoo.com
Subject: Denooming!

Good!

82

I settled down to wait. In a way, it felt like a rerun of the previous night, but back then I'd been full of hope and now I was weighed down with foreboding.

Kevin rang and once again I didn't pick up; I just couldn't face it. He said he'd be arriving on the 7 A.M. shuttle from Boston. I'd see him tomorrow. Tomorrow I would know everything.

Then Jacqui showed up: she'd broken the news to Narky Joey. The fact that she was here did not bode well.

She shook her head. "Dopamine wipeout."

"Oh no!"

"Yeah, he doesn't want to know."

"For God's sake! Like he didn't have anything to do with it! Was he horrible?"

"Not horrible. Just the old nondopamine Narky Joey."

"Horrible, then."

"Yes, I suppose. I mean, I knew he wasn't going to go for it, but I was hoping, you know . . ."

I nodded. I knew. She sank onto the couch and had a good old sob while I murmured what a fuckhead he was. After a while she began to laugh even though she was still crying. "I mean, Narky Joey," she said, wiping her cheeks with the heel of her hand. "What was I thinking of, falling in love with him? Talk about asking for trouble. And you know something, Anna, you'll have to be my birthing partner. We'll have to go to the prenatal classes together and all the other man-and-woman couples will think we're a pair of Jolly Girls." She even went to the trouble of doing an Indian accent when she said "Jolly Girls."

"You're a trouper," I said.

"I'm a gobshite, and I can't even drown my sorrows. Stick on *Dirty Dancing* there, would you? That's the only comfort available to me for the next eight months. I can't drink, smoke, eat too much sugar, buy lovely clothes, or have sex; the only men who'll want to sleep with me are those weirdos who are into pregnant women. Sappy movies are all that's left. Who's the message from?"

I was on the floor, searching for the DVD. "What?"

"Your message light, it's flashing."

"Oh, it's Kevin, he's coming to town tomorrow." It was amazing how normal I sounded. I couldn't tell Jacqui what was going on; she had enough on her plate.

After she left, I went to bed, went to sleep—sort of—then got up around 7:30, feeling like I was going to be executed.

I washed and got dressed as usual. My mouth was as dry as cotton wool, so I had a glass of water, but it came right back up again, and when I tried to brush my teeth the pressure of the toothbrush against my tongue made me gag.

I didn't know what to do. Until Kevin arrived, everything was on hold. I made a bargain with myself: if I could find an episode of *Starsky & Hutch* on the telly, I'd watch that. And if I couldn't? Well, then I'd go to work.

Strange as it sounds, not one single episode of *Starsky & Hutch* was on. Plenty of other stuff—*The Streets of San Francisco, Hill Street Blues, Cagney & Lacey*—but a bargain was a bargain. I'd go along to work and see if anything was happening. Maybe they might have changed their minds and decided to sack me after all, which would certainly provide distraction.

I forced myself toward the door and slowly descended the stairs. The mailman was just leaving. It was the first time this year that it felt like autumn; leaves were skittering past outside and there was a chill and a hint of wood smoke in the air.

I wasn't going to bother opening my mailbox. What did I care if I'd got post? But something told me to unlock the box. Then right off, something else told me to walk away.

But it was too late. I was unlocking it, and there, waiting in my mailbox, was one letter, addressed to me. Like a little bomb.

There was no return address on the envelope, which was a little weird. Already I was slightly uneasy. Even more so when I saw my name and address: it had been printed neatly—by hand. Who sends handwritten letters these days?

The sensible woman would not open this. The sensible woman would throw it in the bin and walk away. But apart from a short period between the ages of twenty-nine and thirty, when had I ever been sensible?

So I opened it.

It was a card, a watercolor of a bowl of droopy-looking flowers. And flimsy enough that I could feel something inside. *Money,* I thought? *A check?* But I was just being sarcastic, even though there was no one there to hear me, and anyway, I was only saying it in my own head.

And indeed, there was something inside: a photograph. A photograph of Aidan. Why was I being sent this? I already had loads of similar ones. Then I saw that I was wrong. It wasn't him at all. And suddenly I understood everything.

Part 3

84

I woke up in the wrong room. In the wrong bed. With the wrong man.

Apart from one small lamp, the room was in darkness. I listened to the sound of his breathing but I couldn't look at him.

I had to get out of there. Stealthily I slid from between the sheets, determined not to wake him.

"Hey," he said. He hadn't been asleep. He sat up on his elbow. "Where are you going?"

"Home. Why aren't you asleep?"

"I'm watching you."

I actually shuddered.

"Not like that," he said. "Watching you to see that you're okay."

With my back to him, I foraged on the floor for my clothes, trying to hide my nakedness.

"Anna, stay until the morning."

"I want to go home."

"What difference can a few hours make?"

"I'm going home." I couldn't find my bra.

He got out of bed and I recoiled; I didn't want him to touch me. "Just going out front," he said. "Giving you some privacy."

He left the bedroom. I could look only at his legs, and even then just from the knees down.

When he came back I was dressed. He handed me a cup of coffee and said, "Let me call you a car."

"Okay." I still couldn't look at him. The previous day was coming back to me, in all its horribleness. I remembered tearing off my clothes and shrieking at him, "Fuck me, fuck me. What's it to you? You're a man. You don't have to be emotionally involved. Just fuck me."

I had lain, naked, on his bed and screeched, "Come on!" I wanted him to drive out my rage, my loss, my despair. I wanted him to drive out my dead husband so I wouldn't feel the pain anymore.

"Car's here."

The sun was coming up and everything was early-morning quiet as I went home. Even though I hadn't touched a drop the day before, I felt like I had the worst hangover of my life.

I let myself into my silent apartment, snapped on a light, and once again got the envelope out of my bag and looked at the photograph of the little boy who was the image of Aidan but who wasn't Aidan.

The previous day, as I'd stood on my front step, examining the picture of the toddler in the Red Sox cap, it was the scar through the eyebrow that had given the game away. Aidan had got his the day he was born; a tiny nick in his just-new skin that had never healed. This boy in the picture had two perfect eyebrows, no scar. Then I'd seen the date on the photo. I'd stared at it, my head thinking, *This can't be right,* but my gut knowing it was: this little boy had been born only eighteen months ago.

A letter had come with the photo: the flimsy card opened out to become a big sheet of writing paper. But I wasn't interested in reading what she had to say, all I wanted to know was who she was. I scanned for the name at the end and—surprise, surprise—who was it, but Janie.

The red mist had descended and I felt like I was going crazy. She had had him for all those years. Now she had a son by him. And I had nothing.

Immediately I'd known what I was going to do.

My fingers trembling in the chilly morning, I rang Mitch. But some-one who wasn't Mitch said, "Mitch's phone."

"Can I speak to Mitch, please?"

"Not right now." The person chuckled. "He's suspended from a twenty-foot ceiling, doing microelectronics."

I couldn't think of anything to say. I was too angry. Well, get him the fuck down!

"Tell him it's Anna. Tell him it's urgent. Really, really urgent."

But the phone answerer wouldn't even yell up to Mitch. He said to me, "Mitch is way under pressure up there. Minute he's finished, I'll get him to call you."

I cut the call and agitatedly kicked the front step, thinking, *Who, who who?* It couldn't be any of the Real Men. The only one who was single was Gaz and he might try to "heal" me by setting me on fire.

Then I got it. It wasn't meant to be Mitch. It was meant to be Nicholas.

Cute little Nicholas. He'd do.

I called him at work: got his voice mail. I called him on his cell: got his voice mail. That meant he had to be at home. I called him at home and got his voice mail.

I couldn't believe it. I simply could not believe it. I needed this. Why were all these obstacles being put in my way?

In the middle of the rage I remembered something. Hands shaking, I grabbed my handbag and tipped the contents all over the step, going through the mountains of shite, searching for that little bit of paper. I didn't really believe I'd find it. Although I had to.

And there it was. A small curling strip of paper. My lifesaver: Ange-lo's number. Angelo whom I'd met with Rachel in Jenni's one morning.

It wasn't meant to be Nicholas. It was meant to be Angelo.

But I got a no-show on Angelo's number, too. "I'm not here right now. You know what to do."

"Angelo, my name is Anna, I'm Rachel's sister, we met one morning in Jenni's, then again on West Forty-first Street. Can you call me."

I left my cell-phone number, hung up, scooped everything back into my bag, and sat down on the step. I couldn't think of anyone else. There was no one. Maybe I should just go to work.

Then, like salvation, the phone rang. One of them ringing back! Which one? "Hello?"

But it was Kevin, who sounded like a maniac. "Anna, I'm here, at LaGuardia. I'm in the city. We've got to talk."

"It's okay, Kevin. I know all about it."

"Shit. I wanted to tell you gently! But don't worry about it. We'll fight for custody and we'll get it! We'll bring him up, you and me, Anna. Where do you want to meet?"

"Where are you staying?"

"The Benjamin."

"Go straight to your hotel. I'll see you there."

So it wasn't meant to be Mitch, Nicholas, or Angelo. It was meant to be Kevin. Well, who knew?

I hailed a cab and climbed in. "Benjamin Hotel. East Fiftieth." Then I got the envelope out again and studied the photo, which had been taken only four days earlier, and tried to figure out the sequence of events. When had I first met Aidan? When did we go exclusive? What age exactly was this child? He looked like he was eighteen months but he could be big for his age, or small. If he was only, say, sixteen months, what implications did that have? Would it be worse if he was nineteen or twenty months? What if he'd been a preemie? But my head was too mental and I couldn't nail the time line. I'd nearly have it hooked and then it would all slide away again.

When my cell phone rang, I almost didn't hear it because it was buried deep in my handbag.

"Hi," a voice said. "This is Angelo. You called me?"

"Angelo! Yes. I'm Anna, Rachel's sister, we met—"

"Sure, I remember you. How you doing?"

"Very, very badly."

"Would you like to meet for a coffee?"

"Where are you right now?"

"At my apartment. Sixteenth, between Third and Fourth."

I looked out the window, managed to focus on street numbers long enough to see that we were on Fourteenth.

"I'm in a cab, two blocks away," I said. "Can I drop by?"

It wasn't meant to be Kevin. It was meant to be Angelo.

My buzzer jolted me awake—every cell in my body got such a fright I thought I was going to have a seizure. I'd lain down, with the photograph of the little boy on my chest, and I must have dozed off.

On shaky legs, I got to my feet and the buzzer went again. Christ Almighty! What time was it? Just gone 8 A.M. This early in the morning, it could only be one person: Rachel.

Angelo had called her the day before, when it became clear that he had a total lunatic on his hands. She had showed up with Luke, and I'd given a garbled account of the photo and letter, which they insisted on seeing. Then they tried to take me home but I refused to leave and eventually they went away again. But I guessed that Angelo had kept Rachel up-to-date with my movements, letting her know that I'd gone home.

It *was* Rachel. "Hi," she said.

"Hi."

"How are you?"

"As good as can be expected considering that my dead husband was unfaithful to me."

"He wasn't unfaithful."

"I hate him."

"He wasn't unfaithful. Read the letter. Where is it? In your bag? Get it out."

Under her watchful gaze, I reluctantly unfolded the letter and tried to read it, but the words were jumping all over the place. With a sharp rustle, I thrust it at her. "You read it."

"Okay. And listen carefully."

Dear Anna,

I don't even know how to start this letter. Start at the beginning, I guess. This is from Janie, Janie Wichs (née Sorenson), Aidan's ex-girlfriend. We met briefly at Aidan's funeral, but I'm not sure if you remember me, there were so many people there.

I don't know how much you know of what's been going on, so I'll just tell it all. It's hard to write this without drawing a bad picture of myself, but here goes. After Aidan left Boston to work in New York, he came home a lot on the weekends, but the in-between bits were not good, and after, I guess, about fifteen, sixteen months, I met someone else (Howie, the man I'm married to now). I didn't tell Aidan about Howie (or Howie about Aidan) but I said to Aidan that he and I should take time off and date nonexclusively, just to see.

So for a while I was dating (and sleeping with) both Howie and Aidan—whenever he was home from New York.

Then I found out I was pregnant. (I used contraception, I'm not a candidate for Jerry Springer, but I guess I was that one person in ten thousand or whatever the stats are.) The problem was I didn't know if the father was Aidan or Howie. (Take it from me, I know how trashy that sounds.)

I wanted to talk to Aidan about it, but the next time he came home to Boston, it was to break up with me. He'd met someone else (you), he was crazy about you and wanted to marry you, he was sorry to break up with me like this, we'd always be friends, you can imagine the script. So I had a choice to make: Do I tell him I'm pregnant and completely f**k things up for him and you? Or do I take a chance and hope that the child is Howie's? So I took that chance and Howie and I got married and I had little Jack and we're all crazy about him. He didn't look much like Howie when he was born, but he didn't look much like Aidan either, so I decided to act like there was no problem.

But when Jack got a little older, he started to look lots like Aidan. I swear to God, it was like every day, his features became more and more Aidan's. It was all I could think about and I was just sick with worry. Then my mom noticed and called me on it. I admitted the truth to her and she made me see I had a moral obligation to tell Aidan he had a son and the Maddoxes that they had a grandson. (Totally honestly? I so didn't want to tell them. Being selfish, I was worried about Howie and my marriage.)

Anyway, first I told Howie. It was really horrible, especially for him. He moved out for a while but now he's back and we're trying to work things out. Then I called Aidan, and like anyone being hit with that sort of news, he went into a total tailspin. His worry was all about you, he was freaked out that you might think he'd cheated on you. But just to make it way clear: this happened before he and you were exclusive. (Like, at least eight weeks before.)

Anyway, I e-mailed him some photos of Jack so as he could see the similarity for himself. But, a day or so later, Aidan got in the accident and I don't know if he ever got to tell you about Jack. If all this comes out of the clear blue sky, I am truly, truly sorry.

I was ready to tell the Maddoxes about Jack when I heard about the accident and then I didn't know what to do and my mom said Dianne and Fielding ["Fielding? Is that Mr. Maddox's first name?" Rachel asked. "Funny, I never thought of him as having one."] were not doing so good, that the news might be too big a shock for them and I ought to wait until they were improved.

But Dianne and Fielding are still not so good and the right time to tell them still hadn't come along.

Lots of times I wanted to call you and check to see if you knew about Jack and also just to let you know that I miss Aidan, too. He was a great guy, the best. But I sorta felt I couldn't talk to you about

Jack until I'd told Fielding and Dianne and I felt it would be wrong to just talk to you about Aidan and not tell you about Jack. Does that make any sense?

Anyway, I was just waiting for a good time to tell everyone, but, as you probably know, Kevin has fast-tracked it. On Tuesday I bumped into him at Pottery Barn (isn't that the most unlikely thing ever? Kevin Maddox at Pottery Barn?). I hadn't seen him in the longest time and I was really happy to see him. But then Kevin looked in the stroller and he was staring at Jack like he was looking at a ghost.

Right there in Pottery Barn, Kevin started yelling, "This is Aidan's son! Aidan had a son! Mom has a grandson! Who knows? Does Anna know? How come no one told me?" Then he burst out crying and I was trying to explain but security came over and asked us to leave.

I said, "Kevin, let's go get a coffee and I'll tell you everything," but you know Kevin. A bit of a hothead. He took off, yelling that he was going to apply for custody and he was going to call you right away and tell you everything. So I guess you've had at least one manic phone call from Kevin.

I wanted to call you, too, but I thought it would be better if I wrote it all down. Least that way there's no room for confusion.

This might be way, way too soon, but would you like to meet Jack? Whenever is good for you. I could bring him to New York if you didn't want to come to Boston.

Once again I apologize for any distress I might have caused by telling you this. I felt you have a right to know and that seeing a part of Aidan living on might make your loss a little easier to bear.

Yours sincerely,
Janie

"So you see," Rachel said. "He didn't cheat on you, he wasn't unfaithful."

"I don't care," I said. "I still hate him."

86

Rachel brought me up to speed on everything that had been happening in my life while I'd been absent without leave.

"You still have a job. I spoke to that Franklin guy. I told him you weren't well."

"Oh God." The Devereaux execs and Professor Redfern himself were keen to meet with me to get the Formula Twelve campaign up and running. This was a terrible time for me to be "not well." "Did he start hyperventilating?"

"Yeah, a bit. But then he took a Xanax. Actually we had quite a grown-up chat. He suggested that you take the rest of the week and all of next week off. Try to get it together, he said."

"The milk of human kindness. Thank you, Rachel, thank you very much for dealing with it. For taking care of me." My gratitude was immense. If she hadn't spoken to Franklin, I'd probably never have dared to reappear at work; at least now I had the option if I wanted to. Then I thought of something else. "Christ! Kevin!" Was he still in his hotel, waiting for me to show up?

"It's all taken care of. I spoke to him, told him the story. He's gone back to Boston."

"God, thank you, you're so good to me."

"Give him a ring."

"What time is it?" I looked at the clock. "Twenty past eight. Is that too early?"

"No. I think he's keen to hear from you. He was very worried."

I winced with shame and picked up the phone.

A sleepy voice answered, "Kevin here."

"Kevin, it's me, Anna. I'm so, so sorry. I'm really so sorry to abandon you like that. I went bonkers."

"It's okay," he said. "I went crazy, too, when I found out. I got thrown out of Pottery Barn. Can you believe it? *Pottery* Barn? I said to the guys, 'I've been thrown out of better places than this.' "

I waited for him to start yelping about what a bitch Janie was and how he and I could apply for custody of "little Jack," but he didn't. Apparently the situation with Janie had changed; overnight it had become very civilized and everyone was pals now.

"We went to see little Jack last night, me, Mom, and Dad, and he is such a cute little guy. Loves the Red Sox already. We're going to see him again today. Why don't you come?"

"No."

"But—"

"No."

"How about this weekend?"

"No."

"Oh. Okay, Anna, you take your time. Take all the time you need. But he really is the cutest. And funny, you know? I said to Janie, 'I'll take a beer,' and he said, 'I'll take a beer' in *exactly* the same voice. Coulda been me! And he has this bear—"

"Sorry, Kevin, I've got to go. Bye."

I hung up and Rachel said, "You might want to apologize to Angelo."

Angelo! "Oh Christ." I put my head in my hands. "I was mental, pure mental. He wouldn't have sex with me."

"Of course he wouldn't. What kind of man did you take him for?"

"Just a man man. Speaking of which, has Joey gone back to Jacqui yet?"

"No. I don't think he's going to."

"What!" I'd thought that he'd take a day or two to process the pregnancy news and then he'd be round at Jacqui's begging her to take him back.

"Fuckhead," I hissed.

87

All I can remember from that time was that my bones ached, every single one of them, worse than ever. Even my hands and feet hurt. I was silent and brooding, like a female Joey but without the stupid rocker clothes. I removed every photo of Aidan—the ones hanging on the walls, standing on frames on top of the telly, even the one in my wallet—and dispatched them to the dusty Siberia of Under the Bed. I wanted no reminders of him.

The only person I wanted to be with was Jacqui, who couldn't stop crying.

"It's just hormones," she kept saying, between bouts of sobbing. "It's not Joey. I'm absolutely fine about him. It's just the hormones."

When I wasn't with Jacqui, I went shopping and spent money aggressively. I'd just been paid and I spent it all, including my rent money. I didn't care. I shelled out a fortune on two charcoal suits, black high-heeled shoes, sheer hose, and a Chloé handbag. Way, way too much. Every time I signed for another purchase I thought of the two and a half grand that I'd paid Neris Hemming and I flinched. I should pursue her, try to get the money back—although there was bound to be something in the small print that said I couldn't—but I didn't want to have anything to do with her. I wanted to forget I'd ever heard of her. And there was no way I wanted to reschedule; I knew it was all nonsense. Talking to the dead? Don't be so silly.

In the evenings, for some strange masochistic reason, I watched baseball on the telly. The World Series was on: the Red Sox playing the St. Louis Cardinals. The Red Sox hadn't won since 1919—since the curse of Babe Ruth—but I knew with a cold unwavering certainty that this year they were going to end their losing streak. They were going to win because that asshole had been stupid enough to die and miss it.

The pundits, the newspapers, and the Red Sox fans were in an ecstasy of anxiety; they were so close but what if they didn't win?

I never doubted that they would, and just as I had predicted, they did and I was the only person in the world who wasn't surprised.

The jubilation of the fans was indescribable. All of those who had kept the faith during those barren decades were finally rewarded. I watched grown men weeping and I wept along with them. But that, I decided, would be the last time I cried.

"You stupid fucker," I told him. "If you hadn't died, you could have seen this."

And that, I decided, would be the last time I spoke to Aidan.

The day I'd got Janie's letter a massive e-mail had arrived from Helen. She had lied when she'd promised me that she wouldn't go to the warehouse for the denooming. Why was I even surprised? Her e-mail brought me up to date with her crime story, but once I knew she was alive, I wasn't interested in the details and I didn't read it until almost two weeks after it had arrived.

To: Magiciansgirl1@yahoo.com
From: Lucky_Star_PI@yahoo.ie
Subject: Lucky to be alive

Sorry I lied to you. But curiosity too great.

Will now tell everything that happened but cannot remember every word with exact recall, so, as usual, will be parrot-phrasing. But not exaggerating, as I am always being accused of!

Here we go. At 10 P.M., went along to address on docks—as expected, was deserted warehouse. Stinky smell. Uneven floors. Mice. Went up stairs. No one on first, second, or third floor. But on fourth floor woman's voice said: Come on in.

Thought it must be Tessie O'Grady. Especially as she'd have access to Racey's bedroom to take those nudie photos.

But wasn't. It was Detta! In tailored trousers, silky blouse, and gun! Ah, here!

She said: Sit down.

Pointed at a chair. Well, *the* chair, really. Lone wooden one under bare lightbulb with bloodstained flex wire coiled around legs.

Me: No. Look, I'm sorry I showed those photos to Harry.

Her (shaking head, like she couldn't believe how thick I was): I sent you those photos.

Me: Why?

Her: Because nothing short of pictures of me in bed with Racey would make Harry believe I was being unfaithful and giving away his secrets. Meeting Racey for lunch wasn't enough—talk about denial! Mind you, your mammy made a right hames of that. There we were, sitting in the best seat in the house, and it turns out she can't use her phone camera.

Me: You wanted to be photographed?

Her: Yessss (like snake). How many chances did me and Racey give you?

Me: Not that shagging many, actually. I spent about three centuries sitting in that hedge in your back garden. And why did you want me to show the photos to Harry?

Her: In the hope that he might kill himself. Or kill Racey and end up behind bars.

Me: But Racey's your boyfriend!

Her (more you-thick-fool head-shaking): Racey's not my boyfriend.

Me: Well, your colleague, then.

Her (shaking head again): It was all a setup. You thought you were being such a great little investigator but we picked you because we knew you'd never figure out what was really going on. The laugh we had at you sitting in the hedge with your binoculars and your bags of sweets. Was it boring enough for you? Did you enjoy mass every morning? And did you really think Tessie O'Grady would just open her gate to a stranger looking to use her loo? Do you know how many attempts have been made on that woman's life?

Said nothing. Was mortifed. And confused. But think she was saying that I'd been given the job because I'm crap investigator. And who was "we"? As in "we picked you"? Obviously not Harry Big, but someone in Secret Cahoots with Detta, who'd recommended me to Harry?

On floor below a rat, or something equally stinky, scuttled.

Me (after while): So if Racey isn't your boyfriend or your colleague, what is he?

All haughty, Detta said: Racey O'Grady is nothing to me. Now will you sit down.

Me: No.

Her: Why not?

Me: Because I've stitches in my arse. Also you might shoot me.

Her: That's right, now—

Her mouth fell open. She was looking at top of stairs. I looked, too. Tessie O'Grady had just appeared, all smiles, in her cardigan and slippers. And gun.

Tessie (exclaiming happily): Girls! I haven't been here in ages. Not since we wiped out the Foley family, one by one.

She looked around fondly: Ahhh, happy times.

She focused on the chair: Don't tell me it's the same chair! Ah, it is! Isn't that lovely?

Detta (frozen-faced): How did you know where to find me?

Tessie: Where else would you come? You've no imagination. Never had. Carry on, Detta. I believe you were telling Miss Weeny Bladder here that Racey O'Grady is nothing to you.

Detta: No, I just meant—

Tessie: I'll tell you what you meant. You set him up. I'm quite cross with you, Detta. You wanted to send poor Harry bananas with jealousy and you used Racey. Harry could have killed Racey today.

Detta: Racey is fine. No harm came to him. I made sure it wouldn't.

Tessie: And he's quite upset. He thought when you two had relations, that it meant something.

Detta: Yeah, well, you killed my dad.

Tessie (tutting): Talk about holding a grudge.

Detta: Look, just go away and let me kill girlie here.

Me: Why do you want to kill me?

Detta: Because of Colin.

Me: Colin? What the—? Oh my God, is Colin your son?

Detta: Colin's not my son. Colin is my boyfriend.

Me: Your BOYFRIEND? But he had sex with me!

Detta: That's why I'm going to kill you.

I was thinking she must be badly deluded—Colin being her boyfriend? I don't feckin' think so!—when Tessie starts talking.

Detta, she said, I'm quite cross with you about something else, too. I've a friend in the bank, a lovely man, a lovely, lovely man, a member of Opus Dei and very good at making scale models of opera houses out of ice-pop sticks—extraordinary talent!—and he tells me that this afternoon, you emptied several of your accounts and moved the funds to a bank in Marbella. You're off, aren't you?

Detta (hanging head): Yes; sorry, Tessie, I am. I've lost interest, Tessie. I never thought I'd hear myself say it but this whole business...I don't know...I've lost heart.

Tessie (helpfully): Well, you don't have to work protection. You could try guns for a while. Or girls! You'd run a lovely establishment, you've good taste, you always had. You like the dear stuff.

Detta: Ah, it's not just the work, Tessie. I can't take the winters here anymore. I like the sun. And Colin wants to go straight. We're thinking of opening a bar. Maybe one with a U2 theme, like with U2 memorabilia, guitars, playlists—

Tessie (going all Josef Mengele glinty): I know what a theme bar is, Detta, but where does that leave our arrangement?

Me: What arrangement?

Detta: Don't tell her!

Tessie: Why not?

Detta: Because this isn't some American film where everything is explained before the end.

Me: Tell me.

Tessie: I'm telling her, Detta.

Detta: You're only doing it to spite me.

Tessie: Spite you! You nearly got my son killed this afternoon! All right, Weeny Bladder. Detta promised me and Racey that Harry would soon be out of the picture—mind you, she never told us she was going to nearly get Racey killed in the process—and that she was setting up with Colin. The O'Grady family were going to show our support for the new setup, in return for a little renegotiation of boundaries in our favor. Now she's shafting us.

Detta (annoyed): But what do you care? You must have more money than God!

Tessie: It wasn't just the money. It was...(wistful pause)...it was a bit of fun. There hasn't been any proper bloodletting in ages...recarving up Dublin, the thrill of the turf wars...I was looking forward to it...

Me: Will you be my mentor?

Tessie (studying me): You show a small amount of promise. If you'd shot the dogs that time they bit you, I'd be interested.

Me: I nearly did. I was going to. But I was trying to get the job done.

Tessie (making regretful face): I see your point. But the true psychopath wouldn't care about the job.

Then came sound of footsteps belting up stairs.

Detta: Fuck!

She shot at me and missed by a mile.

Tessie: Behave yourself, Detta.

Then Tessie shot at her.

Took advantage of confusion, ran for stairs, legged it down a flight, and bumped into person coming other way. Colin. Come on, he said, all urgent like. Quickly. Get out!

Starts shoving me in front of him down stairs while hear at least two more shots upstairs.

Me (galloping down stairs): Detta's trying to kill me.

Him (galloping after me): I know. She gets very jealous since she started the change. It was her who shot out your window.

Me: How did you know where to come tonight?

Him: This is where Detta always takes people to deal with them.

We burst out door, onto deserted street; Austrian-blinds mobile was idling curbside, Bozo behind wheel. Colin shoved me in back and said urgently to Bozo: Take her home.

Me (surprised): Aren't you coming with me?

Him: No.

Me (even more surprised): Why not?

Him: Ahhhh, you see…I'm leaving.

Me (bad feeling in gut): Going where?

Him: Marbella.

Me: Are you going with Detta?

Him: Yeah, I'm going straight, we're going to open a bar—

Me: Yes, yes, with a U2 theme, I heard. So do you love her?

Him: Ah, I do. She's a great woman. A real lady.

Me: Oh. But you and me…?

Him: You and me, Helen, we'll always have St. Vincent's Hospital.

Then Bozo drives away.

So what do you think, Anna? Am mortified. Feel right fool. Thought Colin was mad about me but he was in Secret Cahoots with Detta—probably him who took the nudie photos. Thought I was proper private investigator doing stuff like talking way into O'Gradys' pad, when all along they were making it easy for me. Low moments. War crime.

"See?" I told the screen. "They're all bastards."

89

Wearing the more expensive of my two charcoal suits, I returned to work.

"I'm good to go," I told Franklin.

He wanted to say, "You better be," but he couldn't; right now I was too valuable to upset.

He hustled me straight in to Ariella, who brought me up to speed on

Formula Twelve: the Devereaux execs wanted a day-by-day schedule of my whispering campaign—when could they expect the brand to break; the jeweler needed to speak to me about my vision for the amber pot; the marketing team wanted my input on label design . . .

"You've got a lot of work ahead of you."

"I'll set up meetings right away."

"There's just one thing . . . ," Ariella said.

I turned and fixed her with an inquiring look, one that bordered on impatience.

"Your clothes," she said.

"We agreed charcoal," I said. "Charcoal or I walk."

"Not that. Your plan is a whispering campaign, right? Rumors of an amazing new product but no details yet, right? Which means you've got to be a Candy Grrrl girl until Formula Twelve breaks. Which means Candy Grrrl clothes."

Openly I glared at her; she was right.

She shrugged happily. "Hey, it was your freaking idea."

"For how long?" I asked.

"It's your campaign. How long until you build a buzz? Coupla months anyway."

"No hats," I said. "I'm not wearing hats."

"Yes, hats. You gotta do this the right way. Those beauty editors gotta think you're still a Candy Grrrl. They find out they're being set up? It's all over."

"If you want hats, you pay me ten grand more. Another ten grand. Making twenty."

We locked looks: a standoff. Neither of us moved, then she said, "I'll think about it."

I swiveled on my heel; the money was mine.

I would rather have chopped my hand off than made the call. But for as long as I didn't apologize to Angelo, the shame would be with me.

"Angelo, it's Anna, Rachel's sis—"

"Hey, little girl, how're you doing?"

"I'm sorry."

"Forget it."

"No, Angelo, I'm so sorry, it was a terrible way to treat you. I'm so embarrassed, I could die."

"Hey, you were in shock, I've been there. There is nothing that you could ever do that I haven't done. And worse. I swear to you."

"What? You've really called around to a total stranger's place, demanding sex."

"Sure I have. But anyway, I wasn't a total stranger to you."

"Thank you for not . . . you know, taking me up on my offer."

"Aw, come on! I'd have been a pretty poor excuse for a man if I had."

"Thank you for not saying that if things were different that you would have . . . you know . . . taken me up on my offer."

"Bummer."

"What?"

"'Cause that's just what I was thinking."

At work, I began living a double life. To most people I was still a Candy Grrrl, wearing my goofy clothes and purveying my goofy products. But I was also an undercover Formula Twelve girl, who had intense meetings with Devereaux, thrashing out publicity plans and fine-tuning packaging.

Any leftover time I had, I spent with Jacqui, reading baby books and saying what a prick Joey was.

I never cried and I never got tired: a pilot light of bitterness fueled me.

I didn't reschedule with Neris Hemming, and abruptly, I stopped going to Leisl's.

The first Sunday, Mitch rang. "We missed you today, peanut."

"I think I'm going to give it a miss for a while."

"How'd it go with Neris Hemming?"

"Bad, and I don't want to talk about it."

Silence. "They say anger is good. Another phase in the grieving process."

"I'm not angry." Well, I was, but not for the reasons he thought. It
had nothing to do with any grieving process.

"So when am I going to see you?"

"I've got a lot on at work right now . . ."

"Sure! I totally understand. But let's stay in touch."

"Yes," I lied. "Let's."

Then Nicholas called and we had a similar conversation, and for
months afterward, they both rang regularly, but I never spoke to them
and never returned their calls. I didn't want any reminder of what an idiot
I'd been, trying to talk to my dead husband. Eventually they stopped
ringing and I was relieved; that part of my life was over.

I'd closed up like a flower at night, a bitter little bud, sealed tight.

But I was far from being unprofessional—on the contrary, I was probably more professional than I'd ever been before. People actually seemed
slightly unnerved by me. And it appeared to be paying off because just
before Thanksgiving, the first tantalizing reference to Formula Twelve
appeared in the press: described as a "Quantum Leap in skin care."

90

Anna, it's a miracle," Mrs. Maddox gushed. "I was dead. I was walking around, dead. And this little boy . . . I know he's not Aidan, I know
Aidan will never be back, but he's like a part of Aidan."

Dianne had completely abandoned her Thanksgiving plans to take
off on a women's retreat and dance in her pelt and paint herself blue

beneath a full moon. Instead it was business as usual—turkey, best crystal, etc.—because "little Jack" was coming to visit.

"He's beautiful, just beautiful. Please say you'll come and meet him."

"No."

"But—"

"No."

"You used to be such a sweet girl."

"That was before I found out my dead husband had fathered a child with someone else."

"But it was before he met you! He didn't cheat on you!"

"Dianne, I have to go now."

R achel and Luke are doing Thanksgiving," I told Jacqui. "You're invited too. But—"

"Yes, I know, Joey will be there. So obviously I won't be going."

I offered to boycott it also. "We can spend it together, just the two of us."

"No need. I've had another invitation."

"Where?"

"Um...Bermuda."

"Bermuda? Don't tell me it's Jessie Cheadle's place!"

Jessie Cheadle was one of her clients; he owned a record company.

"None other."

"How're you getting there? Don't tell me—he's sending a plane?"

She nodded, roaring with laughter at my jealousy. "And there'll be staff to unpack my LV wheelie case and a butler to run rose-petal baths. And when I leave, they'll repack my case and put tissue paper between every layer. *Scented* tissue paper. D'you mind me going?"

"I'm delighted for you. You're not crying so much now, had you noticed?"

"Yeah. It was just hormones." Then she added, "But he's still a prick. Look!" She pointed at herself. "What's wrong with this picture?"

"Nothing." She looked fantastic, all aglow and sporting a neat little bump. Then I noticed. "You've got a chest!"

"Yes! For the first time ever. It's *great* having knockers."

Luke opened the door. He had a needle sticking out of his forehead, like he was a unicorn. "Gaz," he explained. "Gaz and his acupuncture. Happy Thanksgiving. Come on in."

Sitting around the dinner table were Gaz, Joey, and Rachel's friends Judy and Fergal. Shake wasn't present. He'd gone to Newport to spend Thanksgiving with Brooke Edison's family. Apparently, Shake and Brooke were having amazing sex; he'd told Luke she was "filthy."

Everyone had acupuncture needles sticking out of their foreheads; they were straight out of *Star Trek*, like an alien council of war. Gaz jumped up when he saw me, his needle at the ready. "To stimulate your endorphins."

"Okay," I said. "Go on. But I remember the days when we used to wear paper hats at this sort of thing."

Gaz inserted the needle and I took my place. Dinner was just about to be served; I'd chosen my time carefully: I hadn't wanted to be late but I didn't want to do any of that sitting-around predinner-chatting stuff either.

Rachel emerged from the kitchen with a massive nut roast and plonked it on the table.

Immediately Gaz lunged at it.

"Oi," Rachel said. "Wait a minute. We've to say grace."

"Oh yeah, sorry."

Rachel bowed her head (chinging her needle against a Kombucha bottle) and said a little piece about how lucky they all were, not just to be getting a yummy dinner, but for all the excellent things in their lives.

Everyone nodded in agreement, their needles flashing in the candle-light.

"It's also timely," Rachel said, "to remember those who are no longer with us." She picked up her glass of sparkling apple juice and said, "To absent friends." She paused, like she was fighting back tears, and said, "To Aidan."

"To Aidan." Everyone raised their glasses. Everyone but me. I sat back in my chair and folded my arms.

"Anna, it's a toast to Aidan." Gaz was scandalized.

"I know. I don't care. He had a child with someone else."

"But..."

"She's angry with him for dying," Rachel explained.

"Aidan couldn't help that," Gaz said.

"Her anger is illogical, but not invalid."

At that point I *really* felt like I was in an episode of *Star Trek*.

"Aidan couldn't help dying," Gaz repeated.

"And Anna can't help how she feels."

"Oh, would the pair of you just shut up," I said. "Anyway, I don't hate Aidan for dying."

"So why do you hate him?" Rachel said.

"I just do. Come on, Gaz. Set the curtains on fire, or something."

Later on, Joey cornered me. "Hey, Anna."

"Hey," I muttered, looking at the floor. These days I did my best never to speak to him.

"How's Jacqui doing?"

I looked up and stared in cold astonishment. I would have curled my lip if I'd been able, but when I try lifting one side of my mouth, both sides go up, so it looks like I'm being examined for gingivitis. *"How's Jacqui doing? If you want to know how Jacqui is doing, why don't you pick up the phone and ask her yourself?"*

He glared at me, a long, long one, but he was the first to look away; no one could outstare me these days. "Fine, then," he said angrily, "I will."

He got his cell phone out of his pocket and started punching buttons like they'd personally offended him.

"I hope you're not trying her home phone because she's in Bermuda, on Jessie Cheadle's estate."

He stopped punching numbers. "Jessie Cheadle's estate?"

"Yes. Why? You thought she'd be spending Thanksgiving sitting alone in her apartment? Just her and her fatherless fetus?"

"What's her cell number?"

I closed my mouth. I didn't want to tell him.

"It's okay," he said. "I've got it at home. You can tell me now or I can get it myself later."

Defeated, I rattled it off.

Another series of button punching, possibly less aggressive this time, and he said, like he was Alexander Graham Bell making the first-ever phone call, "It's ringing! It's ringing!" Then his entire body slumped with anticlimax. "Voice mail."

"Leave a message, you moron. That's what it's there for."

"Nah." He snapped the phone shut. "She probably wouldn't want to speak to me anyway." He gave me a coy look but I made my face stay expressionless. I didn't know if she would want to speak to him (she probably would, I feared) and I didn't know just how much he'd had to drink—if this sudden interest in Jacqui's welfare would disappear just as soon as Thanksgiving was over and his hangover had kicked in.

The minute Jacqui got home I reported the entire episode verbatim and she put it down to the goodwill and overindulgence of the season. Her exact words were, "Pissed fool."

Anna, this new 'quantum leap' skin care? What do you know about it? I coulda sworn you said something last time we had lunch."

My phone was ringing off the hook: beauty journos, their curiosity piqued.

"What have you heard about it?" I asked.

"That it's like nothing we've ever seen before."

"Yes, I heard that, too."

All through December the buzz around Formula Twelve built. Amid the craziness of Christmas drinks and parties and shopping, the whispers intensified. *"I heard it was from the Brazilian rain forest." "Is it true that Devereaux is doing it?" "They say it's a supercream, like Crème de la Mer, to the power of ten."*

The time had almost arrived. I'd decided that *Harper's* was the magazine we were going for and I set up a lunch with their beauty editor, Blythe Crisp, for early in the new year. "A very special lunch," I promised her.

"End of January," I told Devereaux. "That's when we break it."

The nurse moved the scanner over Jacqui's gel-covered bump, paused, and said, "Looks like you're having a little girl."

"Cool!" Jacqui punched the air from her prone position, nearly braining the woman. "A girl! Much better clothes. What'll we call her, Anna?"

"Joella? Jodi? Joanne? Jo?"

In a sappy voice Jacqui said, "So Narky Joey will know how much I stiiilll love him. Or better still! How about Nark-Ann? Or Narketta? Or Narkella?"

"Narkella!" The thought of calling the little girl Narkella struck us as so funny that we collapsed into convulsions; the more we laughed, the funnier it became, until we were clutching each other and apologizing weakly to the nurse for our unseemly behavior. Every time we thought we'd stopped, one of us would say, "Narkella, tidy your room," or "Narkella, eat up your carrots," and we'd explode again. I couldn't remember the last time I'd had a belly laugh like it and it felt great, like two ten-pound weights had been lifted from my shoulders.

In the cab home, I said, "What if Rachel and Luke ask about the scan?"

"What do you—oh, you mean, they might tell Joey?"

"Mmm."

She thought about it, then said, almost impatiently, "I suppose he'll have to know at some stage that he's having a girl. Yeah." She was becoming defiant now. "I don't care what he knows. Tell them what you like. Tell them *all* about Narkella."

"Grand. Fine. I just didn't want to do the wrong thing..." I let a little time elapse, then said, "In all fairness, though, Jacqui, no stupid names."

"How d'you mean?"

"Foofoo, Pom-pom, Jiggy, that sort of thing. Call your baby something normal."

"Like what?"

"I dunno. Normal. Jacqui. Rachel. Brigit. No Honey, Sugar, Treacle—"

"Treacle! That's so cute. We could spell it with a *K*. And an *il*. Treakil. Ikkil Treakil."

"Jacqui, no, that's terrible, please..."

92

Where's that invitation?" Mum shrieked. "Where's that fecking invitation?"

In the dining room, over the remains of our Christmas dinner, I exchanged perplexed looks with Rachel, Helen, and Dad. A moment ago Mum had been on the phone to Auntie Imelda, and now she was screeching and flinging things about in the kitchen.

She flung open the dining-room door and paused at the threshold, breathing heavily, like a rhinoceros. In her hand she held the twig-and-papyrus wedding invitation. Her eyes sought Rachel's.

"You're not getting married in a church," she said thickly.

"No," Rachel said calmly. "Like it says on the invitation, Luke and I are having a blessing in a Quaker hall."

"You made me think it was a church and I have to find out from my own sister—who incidentally got a Lexus for her Christmas box; I get a trousers press, she gets a Lexus—that you're not getting married in a church."

"I never said it was a church. You simply chose to assume it."

"And who'll be carrying out this so-called"—she almost spat the word—"*blessing*? Any chance it might be a Catholic priest?"

"It's a friend of mine, a minister."

"What kind of minister?"

"A freelance one."

"And this would be one of your 'recovery' friends?" Mum sneered. "Well, I've heard it all now. Between that and the sugar-snap peas, no one at all belonging to me will come. Not that I want them to be there."

Mum's fury set the tone for what remained of the Christmas period.

What made her even more angry was that she didn't have the option of bending Rachel's will to hers by threatening to withdraw funding, because Luke and Rachel were paying most of the costs themselves.

"It's a joke," she raged impotently. "It's not a wedding, it's a travesty. A 'blessing' no less! Well, she can count me out. And there was me worried about the color of her dress. If she's not getting married in a church, she can wear any color she shagging well likes."

But not everyone was upset by Rachel's not-getting-married-in-a-church news. Dad was secretly thrilled because he thought that if it wasn't a "proper" wedding he wouldn't have to make a speech. Rachel, too, was serene and unflappable.

"Aren't you upset?" I asked. "Do you mind getting married without Mum and Dad being there?"

"She'll be there. Do you honestly think she'd miss it? It would kill her."

I hunkered down and hid in soppy films and chocolate Kimberley biscuits and counted the days until I got back to New York. I'd never been that keen on Christmas, it always seemed to involve more fights than usual, but I was finding this one particularly tough.

Janie had sent me a Christmas card, which was a photo of "little Jack" in a Santa hat—she *kept* writing and sending photos and saying we could meet whenever I wanted. The Maddoxes were also badgering me to meet "little Jack" and I was still stonewalling them. I would never meet him.

93

Chopper's taken off," the man with the walkie-talkie said. "Blythe Crisp on board. ETA twenty-seven after twelve."

To create the necessary air of drama around Formula Twelve, I was having Blythe Crisp helicoptered from the roof of the *Harper's* building to a hundred-and-twenty-foot yacht, moored in New York Harbor. (Hired for only four hours, unfortunately, and four very expensive hours at that.)

Even though the weather was freezing—it was January 4—and the water was choppy, I thought the yacht was a nice touch; it smacked a little of drug smuggling.

I got up and paced the cabin—just because I could. I had never before been on a yacht that was big enough to pace in. In fact, I don't think I'd ever been on a yacht at all.

After some good, enjoyable pacing, I thought I could hear a helicopter. "Is that it?" I strained to listen.

Walkie-talkie man checked his big, black, waterproof, nuclear-bomb-proof watch. "Right on time."

"Stations, everyone," I said. "Don't let her get wet," I called after him. "Don't do anything to annoy her."

Inside a minute, a bone-dry Blythe was *click-clicking* down the parquet hallway in high leather boots, to where I was waiting in the main salon, champagne already poured. "Anna, my God, what's all this about? The chopper, this . . . boat?"

"Confidentiality. I couldn't risk our conversation being overheard."

"Why? What's going on?"

"Sit down, Blythe. Champagne? Gummi Bears?" I'd done my research; she loved Gummi Bears. "Okay, I've got something for you but I want it in the March issue." The March issue was due to come out at the end of January.

She shook her head. "Oh, Anna, you know I can't. It's too late, we've put March to bed. It's about to go to the printers."

"Let me show you what this is about." I clapped my hands (I really enjoyed that bit, I felt like a baddie in a James Bond movie) and a white-gloved waiter brought in a small heavy box on a tray and presented it to her. (We'd rehearsed it several times earlier.)

Wide-eyed, Blythe took it, opened it up, stared into it for a long moment, and whispered, "Oh my God, this is it. The supercream of super-creams. It's *real*."

All right, so it wasn't a cure for cancer, so it was only face cream, but it was still a proud moment.

"I'll just go wake March up," she said.

After the chopper had whisked her back uptown, I rang Leonard Daly at Devereaux. "It's a go."

"Take the rest of the day off." A joke, of course. I had tons to do and now that Formula Twelve was about to officially exist, I had to set up our office. I wanted to locate the Formula Twelve camp of desks as far away from Lauryn as possible; she was not happy, not at all happy that I'd landed another job. She was even less happy that I was taking Teenie with me. My other assistant was a bright young spark called Hannah—I'd stolen her from Warpo and saved her from a life of terrible clothes. Her gratitude would guarantee loyalty.

On January 29, the March issue of *Harper's* hit the stands and imme-diately work went *mental*. I emerged, a beautiful Formula Twelve butter-fly from my Candy Grrrl chrysalis, and paraded around in my charcoal suits for all to see.

94

Check them out. They're Jolly Girls for sure," Jacqui muttered.

"Just because they've got short hair. You can't judge."

"But they've got quiffs, matching ones!"

It was our first night at Perfect Birth class, and of the eight couples, only five were male-female. But Jacqui was worried that she was the only woman there who had been deserted by her baby's father.

Mind you, Joey had been ringing her from time to time. Well, at Christmas, New Year's Eve, and on his birthday, to be precise—times, as she so rightly said, when he was drunk and mawkish—and left rambling, apologetic messages on her machine. Jacqui never picked up and never rang back, but she denied that she was being strong.

"If he rang me in the cold light of day with nothing in his system other than Gatorade, I might talk to him," she said. "But I'm not making an arse of myself by believing declarations of love made when he's jarred out of his jocks. Could you imagine it if I took him at his drunken word and rang him back?"

Sometimes we acted it out: I'd be Joey, leaving slurred messages on Jacqui's machine, while Jacqui pretended to be a sappier version of herself, dabbing her eyes and saying, "Oh, he *does* love me after all! I am so heppy, the heppiest girl alive. I shall ring him soonest."

Back to me, pretending to be Joey, waking up with a hangover and looking nervously at his phone as Jacqui said, "Ring ring, ring ring."

"Hello," I'd say narkily, answering the imaginary phone.

"Joey!" Jacqui squealed. "It's me. I got your message. I knew you'd come round. How soon shall we be merrhied?" For some reason in these scenarios she always pronounced *married* as "merrhied" like we were in a period drama.

I'd throw down the invisible phone and break into a run and shout, "I want to join the witness protection program," then we'd both shriek with laughter.

But at the Perfect Birth class, Jacqui wasn't laughing. She looked highly uncomfortable, and not just because the whole thing was *acutely* Feathery Strokery. The facilitator was so good at yoga, she could put the sole of her foot behind her ear. Her name was Quand-adora. "Which means Spinner of Light," she said. But she didn't say in which language.

"Her own makey-uppy Feathery Strokery language," Jacqui said later. "Spinner of Shite, more like."

Spinner of Light invited us all to sit cross-legged in a circle, sip ginger tea, and introduce ourselves.

"I'm Dolores, Celia's birthing partner. I'm also Celia's sister."

"I'm Celia."

"I'm Ashley, this is my first baby."

"I'm Jurg, Ashley's husband and birthing partner."

When we got to the suspected Jolly Girls, Jacqui paid particular interest.

"I'm Ingrid," the pregnant one said, then the woman beside her said, "And I'm Krista, Ingrid's birthing partner, and lover."

Jacqui nudged me with her pointy elbow.

"I'm Jacqui," Jacqui said. "My boyfriend broke up with me when he found out I was pregnant."

"And I'm Anna, I'm Jacqui's birthing partner. But not her lover. Um, not that it would matter if I was."

"I'm sorry," Celia interrupted, looking anxious. "I didn't realize we would be sharing so much information. Should I have said that I used a sperm donor?"

"Hey, so did we," Krista said. "It's no biggie."

"Share as much or as little as you feel comfortable sharing," Quand-adora said, the way her type do. "Today we're going to focus on pain relief. How many of you plan to give birth in a birthing pool?"

Lots of hands went up. Cripes! Seven of them were. Jacqui was the only one who wasn't.

"Gas and air are available in the birthing pools," Quand-adora said. "But over the next six weeks, I'm going to share with you some wonderful techniques, so you won't need them. Jacqui, did you have any thoughts on pain relief?"

"Um, yeah, the thing, you know, the epidural."

As Jacqui said later, it wasn't that they looked disapproving; it was more that they looked sad for her.

"Oo-kaay," Quand-adora said. "How about you don't make your mind up right now? How about staying open to whatever energy comes your way?"

"Ah . . . sure."

"The first thing you must remember is that the pain is your friend. The pain is bringing your baby to you, without the pain there would be no baby. So everybody close your eyes, find your center, and begin to visualize the pain as a friendly force, as 'a great golden ball of energy.'"

I hadn't known I had a center, but I did my best, and after we'd visualized for a good twenty minutes or so, I learned how to massage Jacqui's lower back to provide pain relief, just in case the visualization wasn't working, then we were shown a technique to slow the labor down. We had to get on all fours, our bottoms in the air, panting like dogs on a hot day. Everyone had to do it, even the nonpregnant people. It was quite fun, actually, especially the panting. Although having my face right up against another woman's—Celia's, as I remember—nether regions was rather disconcerting.

Jacqui and I were panting goodo, then we exchanged looks and stuck our tongues out and panted a little harder.

"Do you know something?" she whispered. "That bastard doesn't know what he's missing."

95

As soon as January clicked over into February, the anniversary of Aidan's death began to loom, like a big shadow. As the days passed, the shadow darkened. My stomach churned and I had moments of real panic, a genuine expectation that something terrible might happen.

On the sixteenth of February I went to work as normal, but with su- perreal recall, I relived every second of the same day the previous year. No one at work knew what day it was; they'd long forgotten, and I didn't bother to tell them.

But by midafternoon I'd had enough. I invented an interview, left work, went home, and commenced a vigil, counting down the minutes and seconds to the exact time of Aidan's death.

I'd wondered if, at the moment of impact from the other cab, I'd feel it again; a kind of psychic action replay. But the time came and went and nothing happened and that didn't feel right. I'd expected *something*. It was too huge, too massive, too terrible, to just feel nothing.

The seconds ticked away and I remembered us waiting in the wrecked car, the arrival of the ambulance, the race to the hospital, Aidan being rushed into the operating room . . .

Closer and closer I got to the time he died and I have to admit that I was desperately—crazily—hoping, that when the clock reached the exact second he'd left his body, a portal would open between his world and mine and that he might appear to me, maybe even speak. But nothing happened. No burst of energy in the room, no sudden heat, no rushing wind. Nothing.

Straight-backed, I sat staring at nothing and wondered: *Now what happens?*

The phone rang, that's what. People who'd remembered what day it was, checking that I was okay.

Mum rang from Ireland and made sympathetic noises. "How are you sleeping these days?" she asked.

"Not so good. I never get more than a couple of unbroken hours."

"God love you. Well, I've good news. Me, your father, and Helen are coming to New York on the first of March."

"So soon? That's more than two weeks before the wedding." *Oh God.*

"We thought we'd have a little holiday while we were at it."

Mum and Dad *loved* New York. Dad was still mourning the end of *Sex and the City;* he said it was "a marvelous show," and Mum's favorite joke of all time was "Can you tell me the way to Forty-second Street or should I just go fuck myself?"

"Where are you staying?" I asked.

"We'll farm ourselves out. We'll spend the first week with you, then we'll see if we've made any new friends who'll put us up."

"With me! But my apartment is tiny."

"It's not that small."

That wasn't what she'd said the first time she'd seen it. She'd said it was like Floor 7 1/2 in *Being John Malkovich.*

"And we'll hardly be there. We'll be out all day shopping." In Daffy's and Conway's and all the other manky discount stores that Jacqui and I wouldn't go to if you put a gun to our heads.

"But where will you all sleep?" I asked.

"Me and Dad will sleep in your bed. And Helen can sleep on the couch."

"But what about me? Where will I sleep?"

"Aren't you just after telling me that you hardly sleep at all? So it doesn't matter, does it? Have you an armchair or something?"

"Yes. But—"

"Ha-ha, I'm only having you on! As if we'd stay in your place; there isn't room to swing a mouse, never mind a cat. It's like that Floor Seven and a Half in *Seeing Joe Mankivick*. We're staying in the Gramercy Lodge."

"The Gramercy Lodge? But didn't Dad get food poisoning the last time you stayed there?"

"He did, I suppose. But they know us there. And it's handy."

"Handy for what? Catching food poisoning?"

"You don't *catch* food poisoning."

"Fine, fine, whatever." Old dogs, new tricks.

A couple of days later I woke up and felt . . . different.

I didn't know what it was. I lay under my duvet and wondered. The light outside had altered: pale lemon, springlike, after the gray drear of winter. Was that it? I wasn't sure. Then I noticed that I wasn't in pain; for the first morning in over a year I hadn't been woken by aches in my bones. But it wasn't that either and suddenly I knew what the difference was: today was the day that I'd completed the long journey from my head to my heart—finally I understood that Aidan wouldn't be coming back.

I'd heard the old wives' tale that we need a year and a day to know, really *know*, at our core, that someone has died. We need to live through an entire year without the person, to experience every part of our lives without them—my birthday, his birthday, our wedding anniversary, the anniversary of his death—and it's only when that's done and we're still alive that we begin to understand.

For so long I'd kept telling myself and trying to make myself believe that he would come back, that somehow he'd manage it because he loved me so much. Even when I was so angry over little Jack that I'd stopped talking to him, I'd still held out hope. Now I knew, really knew, like the last part of a jigsaw locking into place: Aidan wouldn't be coming back.

For the first time in a long time I cried. After months of being frozen to my very center, warm tears began to flow.

Slowly I got ready for work, taking much longer than I usually did, and as I pulled the door behind me to leave, Aidan's voice said, in my head, *Put some hurtin' on them L'Oréal girls.*

I'd completely forgotten how every morning he used to say something similar, a rousing "go team" form of encouragment. And now I'd remembered.

The bags containing our dinner had arrived. Rachel plonked a stack of mismatched plates onto the middle of the table and began dishing it up.

"Helen, you're lasagne." She handed her a plate. "Dad, pork chop. Mum, lasagne."

She slid Mum's plate in front of her, but instead of thanking her, Mum stuck out her bottom lip.

"What?" Rachel asked.

Mum said something into her chest.

"What?" Rachel asked again.

"I don't like my plate," Mum said, this time a lot louder.

"You haven't tried it yet."

"Not the food. The plate."

"What's wrong with it?" Rachel was frozen in position with her serving spoon.

"I want one with flowers on it. *She* got one." Mum indicated Helen with a savage twist of her head.

"But your plate is nice, too."

"It's not. It's horrible. It's brown glass. I want white china with blue flowers, like *she* got."

"But..." Rachel was perplexed. "Helen, I don't suppose...?"

"Not a chance."

Rachel was at a loss. This was only Mum, Dad, and Helen's first night in New York. There were another two weeks to get through and already they were acting up. "There aren't any of the blue-flowers ones left. Dad has the only other one."

"She can have mine," Dad offered. "But I don't want the horrible brown glass one either."

"Will a plain white one do?"

"It'll have to."

Dad's pork chop was moved onto a white plate, and the swap-over of Mum's dinner was effected.

"Everyone happy now?" Rachel asked sarcastically.

We settled down to our food.

"Anna, how's your new brand going?" Luke asked politely.

"Great, thanks. Just today, the *Boston Globe* did a comparison of five supercreams: Sisley's Global Anti-Ride, Crème de la Mer, Clé de Peau, La Prairie, and Formula Twelve. And Formula Twelve got the highest. They said—"

"Yes, but your new crowd don't do lipsticks or anything, do they?" Mum clearly thought my new position was a demotion. With that, the subject was closed, but not before I'd had a flashback of how Aidan used to celebrate all my coverage and the dingbats of my rivals. How many times had he come home waving a newspaper and saying something like "Rocking good news. *USA Today* didn't like the new Chanel cream. Girl said it clogged her pores. Whooh! High five!" *Clap.* "Low five." *Clap.* "Behind-the-back five." *Clap.* Lifting his leg, he'd go, "Under-the-knee five!" *Clap.* "And through-the-legs-and-out-the-back five!" *Clap.*

I was distracted from this unexpectedly happy memory by someone shouting, "Get out!"

It was Helen: Dad had walked in on her in the bathroom.

"You'd want to get a lock on that door," Mum said.

"Why?" Rachel asked. "You don't have one on your bathroom door."

"That's not our fault. We'd like one."

"Why don't you have one?" Luke asked.

"Because Helen filled the keyhole with cement."

We all fell silent as we remembered that day. Helen had got the cement from the builders who were converting next door's garage into a granny flat, and when she'd finished filling the keyhole, she went on to cement around the bathroom door, trapping Claire, who was in the bath, doing a home-spa day. Dad had to spend hours on his knees, in a chiseling frenzy, before she was finally freed, by which time the stairs and landing had filled with concerned neighbors and builders doing a vigil. The granny of the granny flat who was the cause of all the trouble had even suggested saying the rosary.

To: Magiciansgirl1@yahoo.com
From: Psychic_Productions@yahoo.com
Subject: Neris Hemming

Your rescheduled appointment with Neris Hemming will take place on March 22 at 2:30 P.M. Thank you for your interest in Neris Hemming.

"I'm not interested," I told the screen. "Neris Hemming can go and fuck herself."

Two seconds later, I put the date and time in my organizer. I hated myself for it, but I couldn't help it.

Anna! Hey, Anna."

I was hurrying along Fifty-fifth Street, on my way to a lunch with the beauty editor of *Ladies' Lounge*, when I heard my name being called. I turned around. Someone was running toward me: a man. As he got closer, I thought I recognized him but I couldn't be sure. I was pretty sure I knew him . . . Then I saw that it was Nicholas! He was wearing a big winter coat, so I couldn't see what his T-shirt said, but his hair was still sticky-up and cute.

Before I knew what was happening, he'd scooped me up and we were hugging each other. I was surprised by how warmly I felt toward him.

He put me down and we smiled into each other's face.

"Wow, Anna, you look great," he said. "Sorta sexy and scary. I like your shoes."

"Thanks. Look, Nicholas, I'm sorry I never called you back. I was going through a really bad time."

"That's okay, I understand. Truly."

I felt a little embarrassed asking, "Do you still go to Leisl's?"

He shook his head. "Last time I was there was about four months ago. None of the old gang go anymore."

In a strange way I felt sad. "Nobody? Not even Barb? Or Undead Fred?"

"No."

"Wow."

After a little lapse into silence, we both started talking at the same time. "No, you go ahead," he said.

"Okay." This was something I had to ask. "Nicholas, you know when Leisl used to channel your dad? Do you think she really did? Do you really think you were talking to him?"

He thought about it, fiddling with his funny string bracelet. "Yeah. Maybe. I don't know. But I guess that at the time, I needed to go and hear what I heard. It got me through. What do you think?"

"I don't know. Probably not, actually. But like you said, it did what it needed to do at the time."

He nodded. He'd changed since I'd last seen him. He looked older and bulkier, more like a grown-up. "It's good to see you," I blurted.

He smiled. "And it's good to see you. Why don't you call me sometime? We could do something."

"We could investigate conspiracy theories."

"Conspiracy theories?" he asked.

"Yes, don't tell me you're not interested anymore!"

"Oh, sure, I am, it's just—"

"Got any good new ones?"

"Um, yeah, I guess."

"Well, tell me!"

"Okay. Um, like, haven't you noticed how many people are dying by skiing into trees? One of the Kennedys, Sonny of Sonny and Cher—lotsa people. So what I'm asking is, is it a conspiracy? Is someone interfering with the direction-ness of their skis? And instead of 'tonight he sleeps with the fishes,' the new Mafia catchphrase could be 'tonight he skis with the trees.'"

"'Tonight he skis with the trees,'" I repeated. "You're lovely. You're absolutely hysterical."

"Or maybe we could just catch a movie," he said.

Which one of you stole my Multiple Orgasm?" Mum opened her bedroom door and shrieked down the hotel corridor. "Claire, Helen, give me my Multiple Orgasm!"

A middle-aged couple, wearing practical sightseeing clothes, was just leaving their bedroom. Mum saw them and, without missing a beat, did her "polite greeting"—a strange chin-raising gesture—and said, "Lovely morning."

They looked scandalized and hurried toward the lifts; as soon as they'd disappeared around the corner, Mum yelled, "You let me have nothing!"

"Calm down," I said from inside the room.

"Calm down? My daughter's getting married today even if it isn't in a church and one of you five bitches has stolen my Multiple Orgasm. It's like the time you stole all my combs"—this was an often-repeated resentment—"and I was going to mass because it was a holy day of obligation and I had to comb my hair with a fork. Reduced to combing my hair with a fork! What's your father doing in the bathroom, he's been in there for days. Go down to Claire's room and see did she steal my lipstick."

Claire and family and Maggie and family were also staying in the Gramercy Lodge. Everyone was on the same floor.

"Go on," Mum urged. "Get me a lipstick."

Out in the corridor, JJ was kicking a fire extinguisher. He was wearing a wide-brimmed yellow hat, what Helen might call a "lady hat"—part of Maggie's wedding ensemble, I deduced. I watched his spirited assault on the fire extinguisher and wondered about what Leisl had said; why was JJ so important to me? Why would he become "more important"? Then it hit me: maybe Leisl hadn't been talking about JJ at all. She'd said "a blond-haired little boy in a hat" and "the initial *J*"; little Jack fitted that description just as much as JJ did. Maybe Aidan—through Leisl—had been trying to tell me about him? A shiver shot down my spine and I was suddenly covered in goose bumps.

So had Leisl really been channeling Aidan? I didn't know. And I supposed I would never know. And what did it matter now anyway?

"What have you done with my good hat?" Maggie had rushed out onto the corridor; she was wearing a sober navy suit. "Give it to me and stop kicking that thing."

From Maggie's room came the sound of baby Holly singing her head off.

Then Claire appeared. "This place is a kip," she said. "Mum said it was lovely."

"The radiators don't work," Maggie said.

"And nor does the lift."

"It's handy, Mum said."

"But handy for what? Kate, don't kick that, it might explode."

Claire and Kate, her twelve-year-old daughter, were wearing very similar clothes: knicker-skimmingly short skirts, tottery high heels, and a lot of glitter.

By contrast, Claire's six-year-old daughter, Francesca, wore old-fashioned buckle shoes and a puff-sleeved smock, trimmed with *broderie anglaise*. She was like a china doll.

"You're gorgeous," I told her.

"Thank you," she said. "They tried to make me wear all that shiny stuff but this is my look."

"Has anyone an iron?" Maggie asked. "I need to iron Garv's shirt."

"Give it to me," Claire said. "Adam will do it."

"He's more like an indentured houseboy than a man!" Helen's voice shouted from a nearby bedroom. "How can you respect him, even if he does have a larger-than-average mickey?"

Outside the Quaker hall everyone was milling about, looking their shiny best; clear-skinned 12-steppers, elderly, red-faced Irish people, mostly aunts and uncles, and big-haired Real Men, so many they looked like they'd been bussed in from Central Casting. Through the throng I spotted Angelo, all in black. I'd known he was going to be there; he and Rachel had become quite pally since the terrible day I'd showed up at his apartment. I gave him a polite smile—not unlike Mum's chin-raising gesture—and positioned myself ever more in the thick of my sisters and nieces. I didn't want to talk to him. I wouldn't know what to say.

"I'm opening a book on how late they're going to be." Helen was circulating and gathering money.

"Rachel won't be late," Mum said. "She doesn't believe in it. She says it's disrespectful. Put me down for right on time."

"That'll be ten dollars."

"Ten! Oh, cripes, here's Mr. and Mrs. Luke! Marjorie! Brian!" Mum grabbed Dad by the sleeve and sailed forward to greet them. "Lovely day for it!"

They'd met a few times in the past but they didn't know one another well. Mum had never seen any point in getting to know the Costellos until their son had done the "decent thing" by her daughter. Wreathed in bright, brittle smiles, both sets of parents circled one another warily—like dogs sniffing one anothers' bums—trying to ascertain who had the most double glazing.

Someone called out in alarm, "Don't tell me this is the happy couple!" Everyone turned to see a champagne-colored vintage car heading our way. "It is! It is the happy couple. Right on time!"

"What? Already?" startled voices asked. "Come on, better get in." A ministampede ensued as everyone stormed the door and crowded, with unseemly haste, into seats. The hall was festooned with spring flowers—daffodils, yellow roses, tulips, hyacinths—and their scent filled the air.

Moments later, Luke marched up the aisle to the front of the hall. His collar-skimming hair was glossy and neat, and although he was wearing a suit, his trousers seemed tighter than necessary.

"Do you think he gets them taken in specially?" Mum whispered. "Or does he just buy them that way?"

"Dunno."

She gave me a sharp look. "Are you all right?"

"Yes."

This was the first wedding I'd been at since Aidan had died. I'd never admitted it but I'd been dreading this. However, now that it was happening, it seemed to be okay.

Up the aisle came Dad and Rachel. Rachel was wearing a pale yellow sheath dress—it sounds horrible but it was simple and stylish—and carrying a small posy of flowers. A thousand camera flashes lit her way.

"Your father's tie is fecking crooked," Mum hissed at me.

Dad delivered Rachel to Luke, then shoved his way into our row and the service began: someone read a poem about loyalty, someone else sang a song about forgiveness, then the freelance minister spoke about how he'd first met Rachel and Luke and how suited they were to each other.

"For the vows," the minister said, "Rachel and Luke have written their own."

"They would." Mum elbowed me to share the joke, but I was remembering my own vows. "For richer, for poorer, for better or worse, in sickness and in health." I thought I was going to choke when I remembered "All the days of our lives." It felt like a hand around my throat. *I miss you,* I thought. *Aidan Maddox, I miss you so much. But I wouldn't have forgone my time with you. The pain is worth it.*

I pawed around in my little handbag for a tissue; Helen pressed one into my hand. My eyes filled with tears and I mouthed, "Thanks." "'S'okay," she mouthed back, her own eyes brimming over.

Up on the little dais, Luke and Rachel held hands and Rachel said, "I am responsible for my own happiness, but I surrender it to you; it is my gift to you."

"Before I met you," Luke said, "been a long time, been a long time, been a long lonely, lonely, lonely, lonely, lonely time."

"...as we strive for self-actualization, together we will be more than our respective parts..."

"...all that glitters is gold and you are my stairway to heaven..."

"...I pledge to you my loyalty, my trust, my faith, and no passive-aggressive acting-out..."

"...if there's a bustle in your hedgerow, don't be alarmed now..."

Dad's forehead was furrowed. He was baffled. "Is it not all a bit...what's that word you say?"

"Feathery Strokery," Jacqui whispered loudly from the row behind us.

"That's right, Feathery Strokery." Then he realized it was Jacqui who'd spoken, and mortified, he stared at the floor. He still wasn't over the Scrabble e-mail.

I can't believe a drug addict owns a hotel," Mum said. "Even if it is a small one." She gazed around the beautifully decorated room, at all the

ribbons and flowers. "Would you look at the way Narky Joey keeps staring over at Jacqui?"

Everyone snapped their heads around. Joey was at a table crammed
with Real Men. (*One* of the tables, there were actually three in all, each
housing eight Real Men. Several second-tier Real Men and possibly even
some third tier.) Undeniably, he was staring at Jacqui, who was at the
"Single People and Gobshites" table.

"Mind you," Mum admitted reluctantly, "she's looking very well for
an unmarried woman who's nearly eight months pregnant."

Seated among our peculiar cousins, including the oddball priest who
was visiting from Nigeria, Jacqui positively glowed. Most pregnant
women I knew got eczema and varicose veins; Jacqui looked better than
she ever had before.

"Cripes!" Mum yelped as something hit her in the chest. A yellow
hat. Maggie's.

Claire's son, Luka, and JJ were playing Frisbee with it.

"Best thing for it," Mum said. "It's rotten. She looks more like the
mother of the bride than I do. And I *am* the mother of the bride." She
twirled the hat back to Luka, then looked down at her plate. "What the hell
are these yokes? Oh, these must be the famed sugar-snap peas. Well, I
won't be touching them." She shoved them onto her side plate. "Look," she
said. "Joey's still staring at her."

"At her bazoomas." This from twelve-year-old Kate.

Mum looked at her sourly. "You're your mother's daughter and no
mistake. Go back to the children's table. Go on! Your poor auntie Margaret is over there trying to control the lot of you."

"I'm going to tell her what you said about her hat."

"Don't bother your barney. I'll tell her myself."

Kate sloped off.

"That put that little madam in her place," Mum said, with grim satis-
faction.

"Where's Dad?" I asked.

"Powdering his nose."

"Again? What's up with him?"

"His stomach is sick. He's nervous about his speech."

"He's got food poisoning!" Helen declared. "Hasn't he?"

"No, he has not!"

"Yes, he has."

"No, he has not!"

"Yes, he has."

"Anna, there's some man, over there, who keeps sneaking looks at you," Claire said.

"The one who looks like he's out of the Red Hot Chili Peppers?" Mum said. "I've noticed him, too."

"How do *you* know about the Red Hot Chili Peppers?" several voices asked.

"I don't know." Mum looked confused. In fact, she looked quite upset.

"Givvus a look," Helen said. "The one in black? With the long hair?" She drawled, "He looks like a bad, bad man."

"Funny, that," I said. "Because he's a very good one."

"How's everyone here?" Gaz asked. "Any headaches? Sinus problems?"

"Go away," Mum said.

Rachel had warned Gaz not to acupuncture anyone and he had said he wouldn't unless it was an emergency. But despite his best efforts to drum them up, no emergencies had happened.

"Go on, be off, yourself and your needles! Don't be badgering people. The dancing is about to start."

"Okay, Mammy Walsh." Forlornly, Gaz wandered off, with his pouch of accoutrements, almost tripping over a posse of little girls who had been liberated from the children's table.

Francesca collared me. "Auntie Anna, I'll dance with you because your husband died and you've no one to dance with." She took my hand. "And Kate will dance with Jacqui because she's having a baby and she doesn't have a boyfriend."

"Um, thank you."

"Hold on," Mum said. "I'm coming for a bop, too."

"Don't say 'bop'!" Helen said, in anguish. "That's a terrible word, you sound like Tony Blair."

"Dad?" I asked. "Will you dance?"

Carefully he shook his head, his face as white as the tablecloth.

"Maybe we should get him a doctor," I said quietly. "Food poisoning can be dangerous."

"He's not poisoned, it's just nerves! Hit the floor."

We merged forces with Jacqui and Kate, all of us holding hands. Helen joined us, then Claire, then Maggie and baby Holly, then Rachel. We were a girl circle, our party dresses swinging, everyone happy and smiling and laughing and beautiful. Someone handed me baby Holly and we twirled together, my sisters' hands helping to spin me. Swirling, whirling past their radiant faces, I remembered something I hadn't known I'd forgotten: Aidan wasn't the only person I loved; I loved other people, too. I loved my sisters, I loved my mother, I loved my dad, I loved my nieces, I loved my nephews, I loved Jacqui. At that moment I loved everybody.

Later, the music abruptly changed from Kylie to Led Zeppelin and the Real Men thundered onto the dance floor. There were an awful lot of them and suddenly great swaths of hair were whipping around in a blur and air guitars were being played with verve. Eventually a circle cleared around Shake; they were giving the master space to do his thing. Shake played and played, sinking to his knees, leaning right back, his head almost on the floor, his face a picture of ecstasy as he twiddled his fingers on his crotch.

"Doesn't it look like he's . . . *at* . . . himself?" Mum murmured.

"Hmm?"

"*Playing* with himself. You know."

"You're obsessed," Helen said. "You're worse than the rest of us put together."

"Neris Hemming here."

"Hello, it's Anna Walsh. I'm calling for my reading." I was curious. Curious but not hopeful.

Okay, maybe a bit hopeful.

Silence whistled on the line. Was she going to tell me to shag off again? More builders?

Then she spoke. "Anna, I'm getting . . . I'm picking up . . . yes, I've got a man here with me. A young man. Someone who was taken before his time."

Well, top marks for not trying to fob me off with a dead grandparent, but when I'd originally made the booking, I'd told the reservations person that my husband had died. Who was to say that she hadn't passed that information to Neris?

"You loved him very much, didn't you, honey?"

Why else would I be trying to contact him? But my eyes welled up.

"Didn't you, honey?" she repeated, when I remained silent.

"Yes," I choked, ashamed of crying when I was being so crudely manipulated.

"He's telling me he loved you very much, too."

"Okay."

"He was your husband, right?"

"Yes." Damn. I shouldn't have told her.

"And he passed on after an . . . illness?"

"An accident."

"Yes, an accident, in which he became very ill, which caused him to pass on." Said firmly.

"How do I know it's really him?"

"Because he says so."

"Yes, but—"

"He's remembering a vacation you took by the ocean?"

I thought of our time in Mexico. But who hasn't had a vacation by the ocean with their husband? Even if it's just in a trailer in Tramore.

"I'm getting a picture of a blue, blue sea, a blue sky, barely a cloud in it, a white beach. Trees. Probably palm trees. Fresh fish, a little rum." She chuckled. "Sounds about right?"

"Yes." I mean, what was the point? Tequila, rum, they were both holiday drinks.

"And, oh! He's interrupting me. He has a message for you."

"Hit me."

"He says, don't mourn him any longer. He's gone to a better place. He didn't want to leave you, but he had to, and now that he's where he is, he is happy there. And even though you can't see him, he's always around you, he's always with you."

"Okay," I said dully.

"Have you any questions?"

I decided to test her. "Yes, actually. There was something he wanted to tell me. What was it?"

"Don't mourn him any longer, he is gone to a better place..."

"No, it was something he wanted to tell me *before* he died."

"That was what he wanted to tell you." Her voice was "don't fuck with me" steely.

"How could he have wanted to tell me, before he died, that he was gone to a better place?"

"He had a premonition."

"No, he didn't."

"Hey, if you don't like—"

"—you're not talking to him at all. You're just saying stuff that could apply to anyone."

She blurted out, "He used to make you breakfast." She sounded— what? Surprised?

I was surprised, too—because it was true! I'd once remarked that I loved porridge and Aidan had asked, "Is porridge the same as oatmeal?" I'd said, "I think it is," and the following morning I found him standing at our barely used stove, stirring something in a saucepan. "Porridge," he'd said. "Or oatmeal, if you prefer. Because you can't eat at the lunches with those scary beauty ladies in case they judge you. So have something now."

"I'm right, yeah? He made you breakfast every morning?"

"Yes." I was meek.

"He really loved you, honey."

He did. I remembered what I'd forgotten: he used to tell me sixty times a day how much he loved me. He'd hide love notes in my handbags. He'd even tried to persuade me to go to self-defense classes because, as he said, "I can't be with you every second of every day, and if anything happened to you, I'd shoot myself."

"Didn't he, honey?" Neris prompted.

"What did he used to make me for breakfast?" If she could answer that, I'd believe in her.

Confidently she said, "Eggs."

"No."

Pause. "Granola?"

"No."

"Toasted muffin?"

"No, forget it. Here's an easier one. What was his name?"

After a silence she said, "I'm getting the letter *L*."

"Nope."

"*R?*"

"Nope."

"*M?*"

"Nope."

"*B?*"

"Nope."

"*A?*"

"Okay. Yes."

"Adam?"

"That's my sister's boyfriend's name."

"Yes, of course, it is! He's here with me and is telling me—"

"He's not dead. He's alive, in London, probably ironing something."

"Oh. Okay. Aaron?"

"Nope."

"Andrew?"

"No. You'll never get it."

"Tell me."

"No."

"It's driving me crazy!"

"Good." Then I hung up.

Mitch looked like a different person. Literally, like a different person. He actually appeared taller and so sure of himself he was almost cocky. Even his face was a different color. Six, seven, eight months ago, I hadn't known that he looked gray and rigid. It was only now that he'd lost that terrible stiffness and had become animated and face-colored that I noticed.

He spotted me and broke into a massive smile. A real dazzler, the likes of which I'd never seen him do before. "Anna. Hey, you look great!" His voice was louder than it used to be.

"Thank you."

"Yeah. You don't look so much like a stunned seal."

"Did I look like a stunned seal?" I hadn't known.

He laughed. "I wasn't too good either, right? Dead man walking."

I'd called him after my reading with Neris Hemming; there were a couple of questions I wanted answers to. He'd professed himself delighted to hear from me and suggested we meet for dinner.

"Right this way." He led me into the restaurant.

"For two?" the desk girl asked.

Mitch smiled and said, "We'd prefer a booth."

"So does everybody."

"I guess they do," he acknowledged, with a laugh. "But see what you can do."

"I'll go see," the girl said grudgingly. "But you might have to wait."

"That's okay."

He smiled again. He was flirting with her. And it was working. I thought, *I've never met this person before.*

I noticed something else. "You don't have your kit bag! This is the first time I've seen you without it."

"Really?" He barely seemed to remember. "Oh yeah," he said slowly. "That's right. Back then, I just about lived in the gym. Wow, that seems so long ago."

"And you've spoken more in the last five minutes than in all the months I knew you."

"I didn't talk?"

"No."

"But I love to talk."

The girl was back. "Gotcha a booth."

"For real? Thank you," Mitch said sincerely. "Thank you so much."

She colored. "My pleasure."

So the real Mitch was a charmer. Who knew? My speedy reassessment of him continued apace.

After we'd ordered I said, "I have to ask you a question."

"So ask it."

"When you spoke to Neris Hemming did you really believe she was channeling Trish?"

"Yeah." He hesitated. He seemed embarrassed. "You know..." He gave a short laugh. "Look. At the time, I was out of my mind. Looking back, I can see I was actually crazy. I needed to believe." He shrugged. "Maybe she channeled Trish, maybe she didn't. All I know is, it worked for me at the time, probably stopped me from going totally over the edge."

"Do you remember you told me that she guessed your nicknames? Yours and Trish's for each other. What were they?"

Another hesitation, another embarrassed little laugh. "Mitchie and Trixie."

Mitchie and Trixie? "I could have guessed that for free."

"Yeah. Well, like I said, it did what it needed to do at the time."

"How do you feel now about everything?"

He thought about it, staring into the distance. "Some days it's as bad as it ever was, sometimes it feels like day one all over again. But other days I feel good. That it's true that her life wasn't interrupted, but completed. And when I think that, I think I can have a life again someday, without the guilt killing me."

"Do you still try to, you know, *contact* Trish?"

He shook his head. "I still talk to her and have pictures of her everywhere but I know she's gone, and for whatever reason, I'm still here. Same goes for you. I don't know if you'll ever contact Aidan, but the way I see it is, you're alive. You've got a life to live."

"Maybe. Anyway, I'm not going to any more psychics," I said. "That was just a phase."

"Glad to hear it. Hey, are you free Sunday afternoon? I've got a billion great places for us to go to. How about the Immigrants in the Garment Industry Museum—that's got some niche appeal. Or the Planetarium, they do simulated spacecraft rides. Or bingo, we could go to bingo."

Bingo. I liked the sound of that.

"Take a look!" Jacqui hiked up her skirt and pulled down her knickers.

I averted my eyes.

"No, look, look!" she said. "You'll love it. I've had a Brazilian and something a little bit special. Can you see?"

She angled herself so that I could see beneath her massive bump; she'd had a dinky diamanté rose appliquéd to her naked pubic bone. "So we'll have something pretty to look at while I'm in labor."

Every time she said the word *labor* I felt dizzy. Please, God, don't let it be too terrible. She was due on April 23, less than two weeks away, and I was staying with her, in case it all kicked off in the middle of the night.

"And let's face it, it's bound to," she said. "No one ever seems to go into labor at a nice convenient time, like a quarter to eleven on a Saturday morning. It's always some godforsaken hour in the dead of the night."

Her beloved LV wheelie bag stood by the door, packed with a Lulu Guinness wash bag, two Jo Malone scented candles, an iPod, several Marimekko nightdresses, a camera, a lavender eye mask, Ipo nail polish in case her mani-pedi got chipped "while I'm pushing," a teeth-whitening treatment to fill the time because "I could be doing a lot of hanging around," three Versace baby outfits, and her most recent scan.

The other scans were stuck up on the wall. And that reminded me of something...

Before the accident, I used to be a right hypochondriac. Not that I faked being sick, but when it happened, I was very *interested* in it and tried to involve Aidan in the drama. If I had, say, a toothache, I'd give him regular bulletins on my symptoms. "It's a different kind of pain

now," I'd say. "Remember when I said it was a kind of hummy ache—
well, it's changed. More darty." Aidan was used to me and my drama,
and he'd say, "Darty, hey? That's new."

I'd even broken a bone about a year and a half ago; I'd been rummaging through cupboards looking for something and I turned around too
quickly, cracked my finger against a drawer, and started bellyaching,
"Ooh, Christ, oh God. Oh, my finger, that's awful."

"Sit down," Aidan said. "Show me. Which one?"

He took my finger and—I know this sounds a little weird—he held it
in his mouth. His mom used to do it for him and Kevin when they were
little and now he did it for me whenever I injured a body part. (I seemed
to have a very accident-prone crotch.) I shut my eyes and waited for the
heat of his mouth to effect the merciful ebbing away of pain.

"Better?"

"Actually, no." Surprising—it usually worked.

"That's bad, it'll have to come off." Before our eyes, my finger swelled
and fattened, like a speeded-up video of bread rising. At the same time
the color changed from red to gray to almost black.

"Christ," Aidan said, "that *is* bad, maybe it *will* have to come off. Better get you to the ER." We jumped in a taxi, my hand laid across our laps,
like a sick little rabbit. At the hospital they took me off for an X-ray and I
was thrilled—yes, I admit it, thrilled—when the doc clipped an X-ray to
a light box and said, "Yep, there we are, hairline fracture across the second knuckle."

Even though I didn't get put in proper plaster, just a splinty-type
thing, it felt nice not to be dismissed as a malingerer. I had "a Fracture."
Not just a bruise, not even a strain (or sprain, I'm never sure if they're
the same thing, and if they're not, which is more impressive) but a
Fracture.

In the following days, when everyone looked at my splint and asked,
"What happened?" Aidan always answered on my behalf. "Downhill
skiing slalom, she clipped one of the poles." Or "Mountaineering, small
rockfall, hit her hand."

"Well," as he said to me, "it's got to be better than saying 'looking for my blue shoes.' "

The hospital had given me my two X-rays to bring home, and hypochondriac that I am, I used to study them; I held them up against the light and marveled at how long and slender my fingers really were beneath all that pesky muscle and skin and stuff, while Aidan watched indulgently.

"See that tiny line on my knuckle," I said, holding an X-ray right up close to my face. "It just looks like a hair, but it causes so much pain."

Suddenly anxious, I said, "Don't tell anyone I do this."

A few days later, he was home from work before me—an unusual occurrence—and there was an air of suppressed excitement about him. "Notice anything?" he asked.

"You combed your hair?"

Then I saw it. Them. My X-rays. Hanging on the wall. In frames. Beautiful distressed-gold frames, like they were holding old masters instead of ghostly black-and-whites of my spindly fingers.

My arms wrapped themselves across my stomach and I sank onto the couch. I hadn't even the strength to stand. It was so funny that for ages I couldn't even laugh. Finally the noise fought its way up through my convulsed stomach and heaving chest and emerged as a ceiling-ward shriek. I looked at Aidan, who was clutching the wall; tears of laughter were leaking from the sides of his eyes.

"You mad bastard," I finally managed.

"But there's more," he gasped. "Anna, Anna, there's more. Watch; no, wait, watch."

He doubled over again with hilarity, then straightened up, wiped his face, and said, "Look!"

He pressed a switch and suddenly my two X-rays lit up, blazing into glory, just like they were on a hospital light box.

"I got lights," Aidan sobbed. "The guy in the frame place said I could get lights, so . . . so . . . so . . . *I got lights.*"

He turned them off, then on again. "See? Lights."

"Stop," I begged, wondering if it was possible to actually die from laughing. "Oh, please, stop."

When I was able, I said, "Do the lights again."

He flicked them on and off several times, while further waves of mirth seized me, and when we were eventually exhausted from laughing, and curled up on the couch, Aidan asked, "You like?"

"I love. It's the best present I ever got."

J acqui? Jacqui?"

"I'm down here," she called.

"Where?"

"In the kitchen."

I followed her voice and found her on her hands and knees with a basin of soapy water. "What on earth...?"

"I'm scrubbing the kitchen floor." With the bathroom cleaner, I noticed.

"But you're forty weeks' pregnant, you're due to have a baby any minute. *And* you have a cleaning lady."

"I just got the urge," she said brightly.

I watched her doubtfully. They hadn't said anything about scrubbing the kitchen floor in the Perfect Birth classes.

"Other than the fact that you seem to have lost your mind, how are you?" I asked.

"Funny you should ask, I've been having twinges all day."

"Twinges?"

"Pains, I suppose you could call them," she said, almost sheepishly. "In my back and up my jacksie."

"Braxton Hicks," I said firmly.

"Not Braxton Hicks," she said. "Braxton Hicks go away when you do something physical."

"I bet they're Braxton Hicks," I insisted.

"And I bet they're not. And I'm the one who's getting them, I've a better chance of knowing."

It was her hand that I noticed first: it began to close in on itself, until it was clenched so tightly that the skin over the bones went white. Then I saw that her face was contorted and her body was arching and twisting.

In horror, I ran to her. "Twinges like that?"

"No." She shook her head, her face bright red. "Nothing like as bad as this."

She looked like she was dying. I was about to call 911 when the spasm started to ease.

"Oh my God," she gasped, lying on the floor. "I think I've just had a contraction."

"How do you know? Describe it."

"It hurt!"

I grabbed one of the helpful leaflets we'd been given and read. "Did it 'begin in the back and move forward in a wavelike motion'?"

"Yes!"

"Oh shit, that sounds like a contraction all right." Suddenly I was terrified. "You're going to have a baby!"

Something caught my eye: a pool of water was spreading across the clean kitchen floor. Had she knocked over the basin of soapy water?

"Anna," Jacqui whispered. "Did my waters just break?"

I thought I was going to faint. The water was coming from under Jacqui's skirt. In a burst of agitation, I accused, "What were you thinking of, washing that bloody floor? Now look at what's happened."

"But this is meant to happen," she said. "My waters have to break."

She was right. Oh my God, her waters had broken, she really *was* going to have a baby. All the preparation we'd done suddenly counted for nothing.

I focused enough to ring the hospital. "I'm Jacqui Staniforth's birthing partner, although we're not Jolly Girls; her waters have just broken and she's in labor."

"How far apart are the contractions?"

"I don't know. She's only had one. But it was terrible."

From the other end of the phone I heard something that sounded suspiciously like a snigger. "Time the contractions, and when they're five minutes apart, come in."

I hung up. "We've to time them. The stopwatch! Where's the stopwatch?"

"With all the other labor stuff."

I wished we didn't have to keep saying the word *labor*. I found the stopwatch, rejoined her on the kitchen floor, and said, "Right. Anytime you like. Go on, give us a contraction."

We collapsed into nervous giggles.

"At least I didn't have a comedy waters-breaking moment," she said.

"How d'you mean?"

"You know in films how the waters always break on someone's really expensive rug or new suede shoes. Hugh Grant is usually in them. Oh gosh! Oh, I say! Gosh! You know the sort of thing. Just out of curiosity, is there any particular reason we're sitting on the wet floor?"

"No, I suppose not."

We got up and Jacqui changed her clothes and had two more contractions. Ten minutes apart, we established. I rang the hospital back. "They're ten minutes apart."

"Keep timing them and come in when they're five minutes apart."

"But what should we do until then? She's in terrible pain!"

"Rub her back, use your TENS machine, have her take a hot bath, walk around." I'd known all that already, it was just in the panic of the labor actually starting that I'd forgotten.

So I rubbed Jacqui's back and we watched *Moonstruck* and said all the words and paused it during every contraction so that Jacqui wouldn't miss anything.

"Visualize," I urged each time her body spasmed and she ground the bones of my hands to smithereens. "The pain is your friend. It's a great big golden ball of energy. Come on, Jacqui. Great big golden ball of energy. Say it with me."

"'Say it with me'? What are we, in *Dora the Explorer?*"

"Come on," I urged, and we yelled it together. "Great big golden ball of energy. Great big golden ball of energy."

After *Moonstruck* finished we watched *Gone With the Wind*, and when Melanie went into labor—that word again—Jacqui asked, "Why do people always boil water and tear up sheets when they're birthing babies?"

"I don't know. Maybe to take their mind off things, before they had DVDs. We could try it ourselves if you liked? No? Okay. Oh God, here we go again. Great big golden ball of energy! Great big golden ball of energy!"

By 1 A.M., the contractions were seven minutes apart.

"I'm getting in the bath," Jacqui said. "It might help with the pain."

I sat in the bathroom with her and put on some relaxing music.

"Turn off that whale racket," Jacqui said. "Sing us a song instead."

"What kind of song?"

"About what a dickhead Joey is."

I thought about it. "So long as you don't mind that it doesn't rhyme."

"Not at all."

"Joey, Joey is a knob," I sang. "His face is narky and his boots are stupid. Like that, do you mean?"

"Lovely, yes. More."

"When everyone else is ha-a-appy, Jo-oe-ey is na-a-arky. He wouldn't kno-ow happiness, if it jumped up and bit him on the lad. Chorus, all together now. Joey, Joey is a knob."

Jacqui joined in and we sang together. "His face is narky and his boots are stupid!"

"Joey doesn't know how to smile, at the chance of happiness he will run a mile—that one even rhymed," I said happily. "Okay, chorus. JOEY, JOEY IS A KNOB. HIS FACE IS NARKY AND HIS BOOTS ARE STUPID."

We got a good forty-five minutes out of that: I'd sing a verse and Jacqui would join in with the chorus. Then Jacqui made up some verses of her own. It was tremendous fun, marred only by Jacqui's contractions, which were still seven minutes apart. Would we ever reach the magic figure of five minutes?

"I think you need to do some walking," I said. "Spinner of Shite said we should use gravity. It might speed things up."

"You mean go outside? Okay, let me just do my face. Neaggg!" She raised a palm and cut off my objections.

"But..."

"Hurpp! Nee-eddge! I refuse to compromise on standards just because I'm having a baby. Start as you mean to go on."

The dark streets were quiet. With our arms linked, we walked. "Tell me things," Jacqui said. "Tell me lovely things."

"Like what?"

"Tell me about when you fell in love with Aidan."

Instantly I was pierced by feelings, so mixed up I couldn't put names on them. Sadness was there and maybe some bitterness, although not as much as used to be. And there was something else, something nicer.

"Please," Jacqui said. "I'm in labor and I've no boyfriend."

Reluctantly, I said, "Okay. In the beginning I used to say it out loud. I used to say, 'I love Aidan Maddox and Aidan Maddox loves me.' I had to hear myself say it because it was so fabulous that I couldn't believe it."

"How many times a day did he tell you he loved you?"

"Sixty."

"No, seriously."

"Yes, seriously. Sixty."

"How did you know? Did you keep count?"

"No, but he did. He said he couldn't sleep easy until I'd been told sixty times."

"Why sixty?"

"Any more and he said I'd get bigheaded."

"Wow. Hold on." She grabbed tight on to some railings and moaned and gasped her way through another contraction. Then she straightened up and said, "Tell me five lovely things about him.

"Go on," she urged, when it looked like I was about to refuse. "Remember, I'm in labor and I've no fella."

Grudgingly, I said, "He always gave a dollar to bums."

"Tell me a more interesting one."

"I can't remember."

"Yes, you can."

Well, yes, I could, but this was harder to talk about. My throat felt tight and achy. "You know how I get cold sores? Well, there was one night and we were in bed and the light was off and we were just going to sleep when the tingling started. If I didn't put my special ointment on it immediately I'd look like a leper by the morning, and I had a lunch with the *Marie Claire* girls the following day. But I hadn't filled my prescription. So he got up and got dressed and went out to find a twenty-four-hour drugstore. And it was December and snowing and so cold and he was so kind and he wouldn't let me come with him because he didn't want me getting cold, too..." All of a sudden I was in convulsions, crying. So bad I had to lean over some railings, just like Jacqui had in the throes of a contraction. I sobbed and sobbed and sobbed as I remembered him going out in the cold. I sobbed so much I started to choke.

Jacqui rubbed my back, and when the storm of crying passed, she patted my hand and murmured, "Good girl, three more."

Feck. I'd thought because I'd got so upset, she'd let me off the hook. "He used to come shopping for clothes with me, even though he was mortified in girls' shops."

"Yes. True."

"He did excellent Humphrey Bogart impersonations."

"That's right, he did! It wasn't just the voice; he was able to do something brilliant with his upper lip so he actually looked like him."

"Yes, he sort of made it stick to his upper teeth! It was great."

"Okay, I've got one," Jacqui said. "Do you remember when you moved in with him, and as consolation, he helped me to move to my new place? He hired a van and drove it and lifted all my boxes and stuff. He even helped me clean the new place and you got me by the throat and said, 'If you say he's a Feathery Stroker for this, I'll hate you." And I was so confused because even though it *looked* like Feathery Strokery behavior, it just made him seem more macho and sexy, and I said to you, 'That guy hasn't a Feathery Strokery bone in his body. He must really love you.'"

"I remember."

She sighed and we walked in silence, then she said, "You were so lucky."

"Yes," I said, "I was." It didn't kill me to say it. I didn't feel any rush of bitterness; I just thought, *Yes, I was so lucky.*

"Incoming contraction!" Jacqui crouched down on the front steps of a brownstone as the spasm gripped her. "Oh God, oh God, oh God."

"Breathe," I instructed. "Visualize. Oh Christ, come back!" Jacqui had toppled off the step and rolled onto the sidewalk. She mewled with pain and I crouched over her, letting her squeeze the bejayzus out of my ankle. From the corner of my eye I noticed that we'd attracted the attention of a cruising black-and-white. It pulled in—shite—and two cops, walkie-talkies crackling, got out and walked over. One looked like he lived on Krispy Kreme doughnuts but the other one was tall and handsome.

"What's going on?" Doughnut Boy demanded.

"She's in labor."

Both men watched Jacqui as she writhed about on the sidewalk.

"Shouldn't she be in the hospital?" the handsome one asked, looking deeply distressed and even more handsome.

"Not until her contractions are five minutes apart," I said. "Can you believe it? It's barbaric."

"Does it hurt?" Doughnut Boy asked anxiously.

"She's in freaking labor!" Handsome said. "Sure it hurts!"

"How would you know?" Jacqui shouted up. "You . . . you . . . *man*."

"Jacqui?" Handsome said in surprise. "Is that you?"

"Karl?" Jacqui rolled onto her back and smiled graciously up at him. "Good to see you again. How've you been?"

"Good. Good. And you?"

"Five minutes!" I said, staring at my stopwatch. "They're five minutes apart. Come on."

102

Jacqui changed into an elegant Von Furstenberg–style wrap dress. With her LV wheelie, she looked like she was going on vacation to St. Bart's.

"Gimme that." I grabbed the case. "Come on."

Down on the street we hailed a taxi. "Don't panic," I told the driver. "But she's in labor. Drive carefully."

I turned to Jacqui. "How do you know your man? Officer Karl?"

"We worked together on one of Bill Clinton's visits." She huffed and puffed as another contraction got under way. "He was doing security."

"Good-looking, isn't he?"

"Feathery Stroker."

"In what way?"

"Too nice."

By the time we got to the labor and delivery suite at the hospital, the contractions were four minutes apart. I helped Jacqui out of her lovely dress and into a horrible gown, then a nurse appeared.

"Oh, thank God," Jacqui said. "Quick, quick, the epidural!"

The nurse inspected Jacqui's down-theres and shook her head. "Too soon. You're not dilated enough."

"But I must be! I've been in labor for hours. I'm in agony."

The nurse gave a patronizing smile that said, *Millions of woman do this every day,* then she left the suite.

"If she was a man, I bet you'd give it to her," I called after her.

"Here we go again," Jacqui whimpered. "Oh God, oh God, oh God. I want an epi-DUR-al. I want an epi-DUR-al. It's my RIGHT!"

This brought the nurse hurrying back. "You're distressing the women in the birthing pools. It's too soon for an epidural. It will slow down the labor."

"When can I have it? When?"

"Soon. The midwife is on her way."

"Don't fob me off, she can't give me an epidural, only the man can."

The nurse left and the contraction faded away.

"Is anything happening down there?" Jacqui asked.

She got a little compact from her bag, then held the mirror between her legs, but couldn't see over her bump.

"Feck." Then she looked at her face. "Look at the cut of me, I'm all red and shiny."

She combed her hair, refreshed her lipstick, and powdered her red cheeks. "Who knew labor was so unflattering?"

"Get out of bed and squat," I said. In the Perfect Birth classes we'd been taught that squatting would speed up dilation. "Gravity is your friend," I reminded her. "Use it."

"Thank you, O Spinner of Shite."

Time passed nightmarishly slowly. When the contractions were two and a half minutes apart, she said, "I thought the pain was unbearable before, but it's much worse now. Get the bitch nurse, will you, Anna?"

Almost in tears, I hurried off down the corridor, relieved to be doing something useful. Racing toward me was a heavily pregnant woman; she was naked and drenched and wild-eyed. A bearded man was slapping along in her wake; he was also naked (and revolting. Orangey pubes). "Ramona, come back to the birthing pool," he ordered.

"Fuck the birthing pool," Ramona shrieked. "Fuck that fucking pool. No one told me it would hurt this bad. I'm having an epidural."

"No drugs," Orangey Pubes said. "We agreed no drugs! We want a beautiful natural experience."

"You can have the beautiful natural experience, I'm having drugs."

I found the same nurse as last time; she copped another feel of Jacqui's cervix. "Still not dilated enough."

"That's bollocks. I *am* dilated enough. It's just because you don't want to get the anesthetist out of bed. You fancy him, don't you. Go on, admit it."

The nurse blushed and Jacqui yelled, "Ha-ha! Gotcha!"

But it did Jacqui no good. The epidural was still not forthcoming and the nurse joined Orangey Pubes in hot pursuit of Ramona, who was still refusing to return to the birthing pool. The sounds of the three of them slipping and scuffling outside in the corridor provided entertainment for a good while. At some stage I noticed it was ten in the morning, so I rang work and left a message with Teenie, telling her what was happening.

Then the midwife appeared and had a good long fiddle up Jacqui's "canal."

"God, there's no dignity in this at all," Jacqui complained.

"You should be ready to start pushing," the midwife said.

"I'm pushing nothing until I get my epidural. Oh, holy Jaysus," she screeched. "It's happening all the time now. It's one long fucking contraction."

"Push," the midwife urged.

Jacqui huffed and puffed frantically, when the curtains swished aside dramatically and who was standing there, only Narky Joey.

"What's he doing here?" Jacqui yelled.

"I love you."

"Close the curtains, asshole!"

"Yeah, sorry." He pulled the curtains closed behind him. "I love you, Jacqui. I'm sorry, sorrier than I've ever been about anything."

"I don't care! Get out. I'm in agony and this is all your fucking fault."

"Jacqui, push!"

"Jacqui, I love you."

"Shut up, Joey, I'm TRYING to push. And it makes no difference if you love me because I'm never having sex again."

Joey came nearer. "I love you."

"Get away from me," Jacqui screeched. "Get away from me with your man's thing!"

The nurse reappeared. "What's happening now?"

"Please, oh please, lovely nurse, can I have my epidural now?" Jacqui begged.

The nurse had a quick feel, then shook her head. "It's too late."

"*What?* How can that be? Last time it was too soon, this time it's too late! You were never going to give it to me."

"Give her the goddamned epidural," Joey said.

"You shut up." From Jacqui.

"Keep pushing," the midwife said.

"Yeah, push, Jacqui," Joey said. "Push, push."

"Would someone tell him to shut *up*."

"Jacqui." I was staring between her legs, in high alarm. "Something's happening!"

"What?"

"It's the head," the midwife said.

Oh yes, the head. Of course. For a minute I'd thought Jacqui's insides were coming out.

More and more of the head appeared. Oh my God, it was a human being, an actual new human being! It happens every day, millions of times, but when you see it happening with your own two eyes, it's nothing short of miraculous.

And then its face appeared.

"It's a baby," I yelped. "It's a baby!"

"What were you expecting?" Jacqui gasped. "A Miu Miu handbag?"

Then the shoulders had appeared, and with a gentle tug, the baby slithered out. The midwife counted ten fingers, ten toes, then said, "Congratulations, Jacqui, you've got a beautiful baby girl."

Narky Joey was in floods. It was hilarious.

The midwife swaddled the baby in a blanket, then handed her to Jacqui, who cooed, "Welcome to the world, Treakil Pom-pom Vuitton Staniforth."

It was a beautiful moment.

"Can I see her?" Joey asked.

"Not yet. Give her to Anna," Jacqui ordered. "Let Anna have a go of her."

Into my arms was placed a tiny scrunched-faced mewing bundle, a new person. A new life. Her doll-size shrimp fingers stretched up at me, and in my heart, the last shard of bitterness toward Aidan melted and I recognized the feeling I hadn't been able to name earlier. It was love.

I handed Treakil to Joey.

"I'll leave you three to get to know each other," I said.

"Why? Where are you going?"

"Boston."

103

When we touched down at Logan Airport I was the first off the plane. Dry-mouthed with anticipation, I followed the signs for arrivals. As fast as I was going, fast enough to make me breathless, the walk still seemed to take forever. I *clip-clopped* along the linoleum floors, breathing hard, sweat patches under my arms.

My grown-up ladies' handbag bounced against my side. The only thing to mar my sophisticated image was Dogly, whose head was sticking out of my bag. His ears were swinging enthusiastically and he looked like he was checking out everything we passed. He seemed to approve. Dogly was going back to his Boston roots. I'd miss him but it was the right thing to do.

Then I was passing through the automatic glass doors and I looked beyond the barrier, searching for a blond-haired two-year-old. And there he was, a sturdy little boy, in a gray sweatshirt, blue jeans, and a Red Sox cap, holding hands with the dark-haired woman beside him. I felt, rather than saw, her smile.

Then Jack looked up and saw me, and even though he couldn't have known who I was, he smiled, too, showing his little white milk teeth.

I recognized him immediately. How could I not? He looked exactly like his daddy.

Epilogue

Mackenzie married some dissipated heir of a hundred-million-dollar canned-goods fortune. He owns seventy-five vintage cars, has a conviction for drunk driving, and is the subject of regular paternity suits. The wedding cost half a million dollars and was in all the society pages. In the photos, despite the fact that she seemed to be holding the groom up, Mackenzie looked very happy.

Jacqui and Joey and Treakil are a modern-day family unit—Joey babysits Treakil when Jacqui goes out with Handsome Karl, the cop. She's reconsidering her ban on Feathery Strokery men, especially as Handsome Karl—who really is *very* handsome—is as besotted with Treakil as he is with Jacqui. However, there's no denying there's still a vrizzon between herself and Narky Joey, so who knows...

Rachel and Luke are the same as ever; a pair of happy, Feathery Strokery licks.

At work, all is well except that Koo/Aroon and the other EarthSource alcos are on my case again. I went to a charity ball with Angelo—just as friends—in aid of some 12-step recovery center and I bumped into a couple of them at the fizzy-water reception.

"Anna! What are you doing here?"

"I'm Angelo's date."

"Angelo! How do you know Angelo?"

"Just...from around."

Oh yeah, their eyes said. *Just from around? You're one of us, why don't you just admit it?*

Gaz is learning Reiki. I shudder to think.

Shake and Brooke Edison broke up. There is speculation that Mr. Edison paid him off, although Shake denies it. He puts the split down to "pressures of work." He had the air-guitar finals coming up again, and between the hours of practice and his hair being so work-intensive, they didn't see each other enough, he says.

Ornesto had a lovely boyfriend, an Australian called Pat. It seemed to be going very well, especially as Pat didn't hit Ornesto or steal his saucepans, but then Ornesto got his phone bill and it was over a thousand dollars and it turned out that Pat had been making daily phone calls to his ex-boyfriend in Coober Pedy. Ornesto was devastated—again—but found solace in his singing. He now has a reg-ular gig at the Duplex, where he sings "Killing Me Softly" and wears ladies' clothing.

Eugene from upstairs has met a "special" friend called Irene. She is warm and kind and sometimes they go to hear Ornesto singing.

Helen is working on a new case, it's all very exciting. Nothing has been heard from Colin and Detta since they left for Marbella. Harry Big, however, was never arrested for trying to shoot Racey O'Grady and Racey didn't finger him. Apparently, they're both running their respec-tive empires, just like they've always done, and it's business as usual in Dublin crime.

Almost every Sunday I go to bingo with Mitch. It's great fun, espe-cially as the new Mitch—or is it the old Mitch?—has turned out to be highly competitive. He dances when he wins and sulks when he doesn't and it's very funny, especially the sulking.

Leon and Dana are expecting a baby. Dana complains that every symptom of pregnancy is "had-i-aaaasss," and Leon is thrilled because he has more things than ever to worry about.

Supply has finally caught up with demand in the Labradoodle mar-ket, but all the fashionable people have moved on. The dog of the moment is a cocker spalsatian, a cross between a cocker spaniel and an Alsatian; you can't get one for love or money.

There was a thing in the paper a few weeks ago about, of all people, Barb! She'd put the painting by Wolfgang, her husband (well, one of them), on the market and it caused a big fuss in the art world. Apparently, the painting was an exemplar of a short-lived but influential movement in the sixties called the "Asshole School." The reason it was so short-lived was that all the protagonists killed themselves, or fell off balconies, or shot each other in drunken rows over women. Barb had been their muse, and the main reason for the suicides and drunken shootings. She says she had nothing to do with anyone falling off any balconies, however. She is currently being feted by the media and showered with money; interviewers are desperate to know how many people she was sleeping with at any given time, but all Barb wants to talk about is how disgraceful it is that no one can smoke anywhere anymore.

Mum and Dad are well. There has been no recurrence of the dog-poo situation. Dad got very excited when *Desperate Housewives* started, but quickly lapsed into disappointment. He says that Teri Hatcher is no Kim Cattrall.

Nell's strange friend got put on different medication and is now not half as strange. In a dim light, she could pass for normal.

I meet Nicholas regularly. I brought him to Treakil's "welcome to the world, baby girl" party and he worked the room, conversing on subjects as diverse as Fassbinder movies (Nicholas a movie buff? Who knew?) to the rumors that coded messages were being given to Al Qaeda via the shopping channel. Everyone declared that he was "adorable!" and the Real Men seem to have adopted him as a mascot.

The other day I came home after doing Pilates. It was a warm afternoon and I curled up on a corner of the couch, which was in a pool of sunshine. I started to feel sleepy, to drift, and the membrane between being awake and asleep was so barely there that when I passed into a dream I dreamed that I was awake. I dreamed I was on the couch, in my front room, just like I really was.

It was no surprise to suddenly find Aidan there beside me. It was such a great, great comfort to see him and to feel his presence.

He took my hands and I looked into his face, so familiar, so beloved.

"How are you?" he asked.

"Okay, better than I was. I met little Jack."

"What did you think of him?"

"He's a cutie, a total sweetheart. That's what you were going to tell me, isn't it? The day you died?"

"Yeah. Janie told me a few days before. I was so worried about you, how you were going to feel."

"Well, I feel okay now. I really like Janie—and Howie, actually. And I see a lot of Kevin and your parents. I go to Boston to see them, or they come here."

"It's weird how stuff turns out, isn't it?"

"Yes."

We sat in silence and I couldn't think of anything more important to say than "I love you."

"I love you, Anna, I'll always love you."

"I'll always love you, too, baby."

"I know. But it's okay to love other people, too. And when you do I'll be happy for you."

"You won't be jealous?"

"No. And you won't have lost me. I'll still be with you. But not in a creepy way."

"Will you visit me again?"

"Not like this. But look for the signs."

"What signs?"

"You'll see them if you look for them."

"I can't imagine loving anyone except you."

"But you will."

"How do you know?"

"Because I'm privy to that sort of info now."

"Oh. So do you know who it is?"

He hesitated. "I shouldn't really . . ."

"Oh, go on," I cajoled. "What's the point of you visiting from the dead if you don't give me some juice?"

"I can't give you his exact identity—"

"Meaner."

"But I can tell you, you know him already."

He kissed me on the lips, placed his hand on my head, like a benediction, and left. Then I woke up, and moving from sleeping to waking seemed like nothing at all. Deep, joy-filled calm sat inside me and around me and I could still feel the weight and warmth of his hand on my head.

He'd really been here. I was certain of it.

I sat without moving, my blood flowing as slow as molasses, and felt the miracle of my breath, moving in and out, in and out, in the circle of life.

And then I saw it: a butterfly.

Just like in all the bereavement books I'd read.

Look for the signs, Aidan had said.

This one was beautiful; blue and yellow and white, decked out in lacy patterns, and I took it all back about butterflies only being moths in expensive embroidered jackets.

It flitted around the room, landing on our wedding photo (I'd restored all pictures of Aidan to their rightful places), my framed X-rays, the Red Sox banner, everything that had meaning for Aidan and me. Cocooned on the couch, mesmerized as a stoned person, I watched the show.

It touched down on the remote control and fluttered its wings very fast so that it looked like it was guffawing. Then, with a touch I could barely feel, it landed on my face; on my eyebrows; my cheeks; beside my mouth. It was kissing me.

Eventually it moved to the window and sat on the glass, waiting. Time to go. For now.

I opened the window and the noise rushed in; there was a great, big world out there. For five or six seconds, the butterfly hovered on the sill and then off it flew, small and brave and living its life.